P9-CDS-359

"The paranormal genre has met its next star—
Colleen Gleason."
—Kathryn Smith, author of *Let the Night Begin*

Praise for
the Gardella Vampire Chronicles

The Bleeding Dusk
"The latest addition to Colleen Gleason's addictively readable Gardella Vampire Chronicles is the perfect mix of delectably acerbic writing and a captivating plot seasoned with just the right dash of danger and sexy romance."   —*Chicago Tribune*

"Gleason is really on a roll."   —*Publishers Weekly*

"Complex and filled with depth. . . . Fans of Colleen Gleason's Gardella Vampire Chronicles will want to sink their teeth into this complex entertaining chapter of the saga."
—*Midwest Book Review*

"The undead rise to great heights through Gleason's phenomenal storytelling. She creates a chilling world with the perfect atmosphere of fear and sexual tension. The sophistication and intelligence of her storytelling are evident on each page of the Gardella Vampire Chronicles." —*Romantic Times*

"Gripping action will chill your blood, and the detail of the prose is so vivid that you will believe it is all happening right here and now around you. . . . If you love a good story, particularly a good vampire one, get this whole series."
—Huntress Book Reviews

"It's kind of Stoker meets Emily Brontë meets Mrs. Pollifax with a little of the Van Van Helsing anime series thrown in for kicks. . . . Victoria is an ass-kicking, take-no-prisoners, prim, and fairly proper cozy mystery heroine, sometimes just slightly too delicate in the sensibilities but with an admirable ability to make quick decisions and impromptu plans."
—*The Romance Reader*

"Fans of Colleen's first two books in the *Gardella Vampire Chronicles* will not be disappointed. . . . I loved the setting for this book. It was dark with a hint of melancholy and mystery throughout . . . heart pounding."
—Stuff As Dreams Are Made On

continued . . .

"Colleen Gleason has done something cool here: She's created a real, full-blooded (sorry) heroine and given her an entertaining and intriguing cast of secondary characters with whom to interact.... The author really hits her stride with this one. If you're looking for an intelligent new spin on the vampire genre, *Rises the Night* fits the bill perfectly."   —All About Romance

The Rest Falls Away

"Sophisticated, sexy, surprising! With its vampire lore and Regency graces, this book grabs you and holds you tight to the very last page!"
  —J. R. Ward, *USA Today* bestselling author of *Lover Revealed*

"So what would Buffy as a debutante death dealer, Buffy in a bonnet, have been like? ... You can see the result in *The Rest Falls Away*, Gleason's publishing debut that turns vampire stories—and romances—on their ear with a decidedly dark, decidedly unsentimental Regency heroine who stakes the undead with the best of them."   —*Detroit Free Press*

"A promising, enthusiastic beginning to a new paranormal historical series.... Gleason quickly establishes an alluring world all her own. Her Buffyesque lead is similarly afflicted, but the change of setting makes an intriguing, witty, and addictive twist."   .—*Publishers Weekly*

"A paranormal for smart girls who like historicals. Buffy in a bonnet takes on the forces of darkness in Regency-era London." —Janet Mullany, award-winning author of *Dedication*

"Lush and dark and powerful—deliciously sexy, utterly compelling."   —Jackie Kessler, author of *Hell's Belles*

"Buffy goes Regency with this terrific vampire slayer historical romantic fantasy that will have readers craving more Gardella adventures."   —*Midwest Book Review*

"An entertaining ride of suspense, British wit, and romance.... If you like Buffy the Vampire Slayer, you'll like *The Rest Falls Away*."   —Romance Reviews Today

**The Gardella Vampire Chronicles
by Colleen Gleason**

The Rest Falls Away

Rises the Night

The Bleeding Dusk

When Twilight Burns

AS SHADOWS FADE

The Gardella Vampire Chronicles

Colleen Gleason

A SIGNET ECLIPSE BOOK

SIGNET ECLIPSE
Published by New American Library, a division of
Penguin Group (USA) Inc., 375 Hudson Street,
New York, New York 10014, USA
Penguin Group (Canada), 90 Eglinton Avenue East, Suite 700, Toronto,
Ontario M4P 2Y3, Canada (a division of Pearson Penguin Canada Inc.)
Penguin Books Ltd., 80 Strand, London WC2R 0RL, England
Penguin Ireland, 25 St. Stephen's Green, Dublin 2,
Ireland (a division of Penguin Books Ltd.)
Penguin Group (Australia), 250 Camberwell Road, Camberwell, Victoria 3124,
Australia (a division of Pearson Australia Group Pty. Ltd.)
Penguin Books India Pvt. Ltd., 11 Community Centre, Panchsheel Park,
New Delhi - 110 017, India
Penguin Group (NZ), 67 Apollo Drive, Rosedale, North Shore 0632,
New Zealand (a division of Pearson New Zealand Ltd.)
Penguin Books (South Africa) (Pty.) Ltd., 24 Sturdee Avenue,
Rosebank, Johannesburg 2196, South Africa

Penguin Books Ltd., Registered Offices:
80 Strand, London WC2R 0RL, England

First published by Signet Eclipse, an imprint of New American Library,
a division of Penguin Group (USA) Inc.

First Printing, March 2009
10   9   8   7   6   5   4   3   2   1

This one is for Claire.

Acknowledgments

With every book, my list of people to thank grows and grows. This time, I owe special thanks to Lisa Szajnecki for meeting me for lunch on the spur of the moment to tell me about her trip to Prague.

Also, I'm greatly indebted to the bloggers, readers and fans who e-mail me and support the series in a variety of ways. . . . It's hard to believe that this is the last Victoria book, and I know many of you feel as bittersweetly about it as I do. Thanks in particular to Carl V, Nancy Bookfool, Cheya, Michelle Buonfiglio, Kati, the DIK ladies, AAR, Kristin, Shay, Danita & Jen, Paperback Outlet and everyone who's blogged about the series, or joined one of the "teams."

I also give a big thank-you and many hugs to the Brighton Borders and the fabulous baristas there, who keep me sane while I'm on deadline.

I simply couldn't do it without Tammy and Holli, Robyn Carr, Kelly, Jackie Kessler and Jana DeLeon for their support throughout the writing process. And of course a big thanks to Marcy and Claire for everything that it took to get these books out there.

And finally, much love to my husband and children for putting up with deadline madness and me flying out the door after dinner with my laptop. I love you very much and am so blessed by your love and support.

Prologue

Wherein Our Heroine Considers Her Options

Victoria Gardella Grantworth de Lacy, Dowager Marchioness of Rockley, had a problem—and for once, it didn't have to do with vampires.

Well, that wasn't precisely true—it did, in an oblique way. There really wasn't any part of her life that had nothing to do with the undead.

Ever since her great-aunt Eustacia had informed Victoria, two years ago, that she was the next in their long family line of Venators—vampire hunters—Victoria's life had become filled with the red-eyed undead and their gleaming fangs, sharp wooden stakes secreted on her person, and the challenge of appearing normal to the rest of London Society.

Victoria was anything but normal, for she wore a holy strength amulet, the *vis bulla*. The tiny silver cross every Venator wore pierced through their skin imbued them with the extraordinary powers of their calling: speed, strength, and fast-healing capabilities.

But despite her unique skills, Victoria's current problem was of a more common variety for a young woman.

It had to do with a man.

She looked at the rich bloodred gown her maid had pressed in anticipation of tonight's ball given by the Duchess Farnham. It lay spread on the hip-high bed in all of its lush glory. With its low décolletage, clean lines, and understated frills, this was the kind of frock that would, like a magnet, attract a gentleman's attention to her person as he attempted to keep his chin off the floor and his gloved hands to himself.

With her creamy skin and thick, dark hair, full red lips and thick-lashed eyes, the gown would merely be the final touch to a magnificent presentation.

Dressed thusly, with her curling hair piled high to show off her long, elegant neck (which was, at the moment, devoid of vampire bites) and white shoulders, she would cut the kind of figure that would cause Sebastian Vioget's amber eyes to smolder and his fingers itch to touch. His attention would linger on her, heavily, leaving her no doubt of what he wanted to do . . . what, in fact, he had already done on numerous occasions.

And as pleasant as those memories might be, unfortunately, Sebastian Vioget wasn't her problem.

It would have been so much easier if he were.

There was an enthusiastic knock on the door, and then a burst of energy bustled in. Her maid Verbena had springy orange hair that matched her personality: loud, uncontrollable, and colorful. "M'lady, I'm sorry 't took so long t'find these," she said, flapping a pair of soft pink gloves. "They 'ad a stain an' I forgot I took 'em to wash, an' left 'em to dry. Grass stain, from th' party at Lord Fenworth's after yer return from Italy. Didn't want t'come out, an' I thought to m'self, What will my lady wear . . . ?"

Victoria let her maid prattle on. The grass stain was indeed from the Fenworths' fête—when she had had to slay a vampire in the garden. Gloves got in the way when handling a stake, and she'd removed them, losing them in the battle and grinding one under her foot into the grass. But apparently her maid had been able to remove the stain, for the pale pink appeared unmarked. They would look lovely, evening out the sensuality of her garnet-hued gown.

And Max might even notice.

But then again, he noticed everything.

Yet beautiful gowns, intricate coiffures, witty conversation, and intelligent questions made no difference to a man who'd confessed—under duress—that he loved her. But would never, under any circumstances, stay with her. Be with her.

Because he was afraid for her.

Since her mother wasn't around, Victoria didn't bother to stifle her snort.

Afraid for her. *Her. Illa* Gardella. The most physically powerful woman in the world, the leader of the Venators. The woman who had the strength and speed that matched superhuman vampires.

He was afraid for *her*.

Victoria snorted again. It was more likely that he was afraid for himself. Or, more precisely, his heart.

Bloody coward.

He was currently living in the servants' quarters here in this house, which had belonged to her great-aunt Eustacia but now belonged to Victoria. Yet it was only a matter of time until he disappeared again.

Only two weeks had elapsed since they'd been captured by Lilith, the vampire queen, and escaped from her wrath yet again. Frankly, Victoria was surprised Max hadn't slipped away yet—particularly since the last time they'd been alone was when he'd admitted that he loved her—and had then proceeded to leave the room. Flee, more accurately.

He'd taken great care not to be in her presence alone since.

At that moment, she realized that during her wool-gathering, Verbena, who was as efficient as she was verbose, had removed the dressing robe Victoria wore and was now raising the heavy silk gown over her head. Victoria lifted her arms so that she could find the short little sleeves made of ruched and gathered silk. The frock fell smoothly to the floor, where its hem was anchored by two narrow rows of flounces. As Verbena buttoned the gown up over her mistress's corset and shift, Victoria considered her options.

There was no sense in trying to make Max jealous. He'd been encouraging her into Sebastian's arms for months now. Although Victoria had spent her share of time there, she'd realized no more than a few weeks ago that the man she loved enough to spend the rest of her life with wasn't Sebastian Vioget. It was Max Pesaro.

That realization had been creeping up on her for a while, but it had come crashing down upon her un-suspecting head after she'd spent a night in *his* arms. His warm, muscular arms. Against his long, powerful body.

"Yer shiverin', my lady. Can ye be cold? Y' can't be chilled. It's July, and from the size o' my poofy hair, y'can tell how warm 'tis out. I do hope ye aren' gettin' a chill. Nothin' like a chill in the summer, t'make ye miserable, y'know."

Victoria steered her thoughts away from that exceed-ingly active night that had been the culmination—she realized belatedly—of two years of tension between her and Max.

Max, whom she had mistaken for a vampire the first time they met.

Max, who had believed she couldn't be a successful Venator because, when he'd first met her, she was more concerned about gowns and balls and dance cards—and the gentlemen of the *ton*.

Max, who had been there when she slayed her husband, Phillip, after he was turned to a vampire by Lilith the Dark.

Max, who was too damned honorable and unselfish to accept what she knew he wanted.

But she'd at last wrung the confession from him.

I didn't want to love you, but I can't help it. I don't want to be without you, but I bloody well will, Victoria. I'll not go through this again. I'll not risk your damned neck again. It's the way it has to be.

Victoria looked at herself in the mirror, tall and slender, now garbed in a striking gown the color of blood. A circlet of diamonds and garnets adorned her throat, and heavy matching earbobs hung against her white neck.

These trappings weren't the solution to her problem. For a man like Max, she would have to be more subtle. More cunning.

She'd have to appeal to his sense of honor—without appearing to do so.

But . . . She smiled at herself in the mirror. Looking like this certainly couldn't hurt.

After all, even *Illa* Gardella had other weapons besides stakes.

One

Wherein the Marchioness Is Without an Escort

Victoria made certain that her back was to the hallway as she spoke to Verbena. "He's not doing well, not at all," she said to her maid. "It has been a most difficult year for him, losing Aunt Eustacia and then his nephew . . . and now . . ." She allowed her voice to trail off, and smoothed the rich red gown Verbena had helped her don moments before.

She felt rather than heard the cat-footed presence behind her and looked meaningfully at Verbena.

"Poor Kritanu," the orange-haired maid was quick to respond. "An' him losin' his hand that way . . . I jus' don't know. . . . Mona says he ain't been eatin' much and I 'eard him walkin' the halls jus' th'other night, my lady. Jus' walkin' and walkin'."

Kritanu, the elderly man who was Victoria's martial arts trainer and who had been Aunt Eustacia's lover and companion for more than fifty years, had suffered several losses in the past several months—the most recent being that of his hand. It had been cut off when he and Sebastian had been captured by a group of Lilith's minions. Sara Regalado, the leader of the group, had also maimed Sebastian—cutting off the small finger of his left hand.

Kritanu and Max had been close friends for years, ever since Kritanu's nephew, Briyani, had become Max's martial arts trainer. Briyani had been brutally murdered by the vampires a few weeks before Kritanu's injury.

Victoria shook her head as she pulled on the stain-free pink gloves. "I'm quite worried about him," she added for good measure. "I don't know what to do. I just hope . . ." Again her voice trailed off, as if she didn't want to be overheard.

"Another party tonight?" asked Max as he came into the front hallway. "Ah, the busy life of the dowager Marchioness of Rockley." It was hard to tell whether he was coming or going, for he insisted on staying in the servants' quarters at the rear of the house, and therefore rarely made use of the front entrance.

He was sorely underdressed by Society's standards, as was his way—his white shirt was rumpled and his neck cloth slightly askew. The dark breeches and coat he wore were well made but certainly not recently pressed, nor were they at the height of fashion. Tonight, his thick, dark hair was pulled back into what Victoria had come to think of as his pirate look—in a short club at the base of his skull, the hair sticking out from the leather thong like the stiff bristles of a brush. With his swarthy skin, dark brows, and angular features, he wouldn't be considered handsome as much as striking. Imposing. His dark eyes barely glanced over her, as if terrified that by lingering they might be trapped.

"Indeed. Duchess Winnie—of course you've met her," Victoria added with a little laugh.

Max had indeed met Duchess Farnham, one of Victoria's honorary aunts and a bosom friend of her mother, when the duchess had tried her hand at staking a vampire during a visit in Rome. That vampire had been the Conte Regalado, and had been intent on wooing Victoria's mother. Victoria still smiled at the memory of the duchess brandishing a stake the thickness of her wrist.

Although, at the time, she'd been doing everything but smiling.

"The duchess is hosting a dance tonight, and of course I dare not miss it. Especially now that the new Marquess of Rockley has suddenly disappeared. All of London is abuzz with that choice bit of gossip," she said.

Upon his arrival from America to assume his title, Victoria's deceased husband's heir had become the victim of vampires. An undead impostor had been introduced into the *ton* in his place, and had later met the pointed end of Victoria's stake. As there was no body to be found, the new Rockley had been given up as mysteriously disappeared—a fact that both intrigued and worried the peerage.

"Is Vioget keeping you waiting? No doubt he is still fussing with a new knot on his neck cloth." Max sounded supremely bored.

Victoria made a great show of pulling on the lacy shawl that would do little good against a chill in the air—but it was a hot, humid evening in early August and she needn't worry about being uncomfortable. "Oh, no. Sebastian isn't my escort this evening."

"Indeed?"

Though she was turned half away, Victoria felt Max's gaze score over her. Out of the corner of her eye, she saw his expression. He was decidedly displeased.

She wasn't certain if it was because he'd noticed

her gown or because Sebastian wasn't attending her. In any event, it didn't matter. A displeased Max was exactly what she wanted.

"Indeed." She started toward the door. "Good evening, Max."

"Surely you don't plan to attend without an escort."

She paused, then glanced back at him. "Are you volunteering for the honor? You'd have to change. . . ." She raised a brow, looking at him dubiously. "And you might even have to dance."

"Where's Vioget? Foolish of him to allow you to go alone."

"Ah, yes, the man should be protecting his interests, shouldn't he?" Victoria replied coolly. That had been Max's plan: that she should be with Sebastian—in all ways—because, as a born Venator, Sebastian would be able to understand the dual sides of her life and also assist her in the fight against vampires.

Max himself had been one of the most fearsome of Venators, called by choice and not by the blood of the Gardella family legacy, as the other Venators were. But he'd given up his powers in order to destroy a rising demon who threatened to take over Rome.

By relinquishing his powers, Max had also severed the thrall that Lilith had imposed upon him years ago. He'd been freed of her influence, but she was still obsessed with Max. She was certain to be after him again, after she recovered from her recent setback at the hands of Victoria and the other Venators.

But it wasn't so much himself that Max worried about, but Victoria, as he'd admitted during a moment of weakness.

She'll be after me again . . . and again. And she'll use you, Victoria. She'll use you to get to me. I wish I could lock you up, and know you'd always be safe . . . and I know that can't bloody well happen. But I won't be part of it. I won't make it any damn worse than it has to be. I can't do it.

Angry with what she perceived as an illogical argument, Victoria had called him a coward then—a word she could never have imagined attributing to Max. But to her surprise, he'd accepted it. Owned it. And walked away.

The last thing he said to her was an acknowledgment of her insult:

When it comes to risking your life, yes, yes, godammit, yes, I am, Victoria. I'm a damn bloody coward.

And now here they were. Two weeks later. Stalemated.

"Good night, Max," she said, opening the door and stepping out into the balmy evening. Her carriage waited, the footman holding its door open. She didn't look back as the servant helped her into the vehicle, but she felt the weight of Max's stare on her back as if he'd been there, touching her himself.

The Duchess Farnham knew how to give a party, and the *ton* lapped it up. Even when her event was merely a dance instead of a ball, she did it with style and elegance. And when the duchess gave a dance, there were, of course, fewer invitations extended, making them all the more sought after and bragged upon.

Thus when Victoria arrived at Farnham Hall, her sleek midnight blue carriage waited in a long snaking line of arrivals, crossing in front of another long snaking line of carriages passing by the residence in hopes of catching a glimpse of who had been gifted with an invitation this time. The stagnant air and summer heat in the enclosed carriage made her feel sleepy and bored, and she tugged open one of the small windows.

She didn't feel odd about arriving without an escort, for she was as close to the duchess—hence the affectionate, if informal, nickname of Duchess Winnie—as if she were her niece. And also, Victoria's mother, Lady Melly, would already be in attendance, likely with her own escort and longtime beau, Lord Jellington.

Lady Melly, Duchess Winnie, and their other bosom friend, Lady Petronilla, were fairly inseparable, their heads always together, flinging gossip about with great abandon and plotting weddings as if the world were about to end. The three of them were probably the most upset in all of London about the disappearance of the new Lord Rockley, for they had been playing matchmaker with him and Victoria in hopes that she might drop the "dowager" from her title, and become simply "the marchioness" again.

Sebastian had offered to come with her tonight, but Victoria had thought it best to decline. He was well aware of how she felt about Max, but in his words, "I don't plan to be a gentleman about this, Victoria. He doesn't want you—he doesn't want *anyone*—and *I do*." And then he gathered her up into his arms for one of those hot kisses that made her knees weak and her breathing unsteady.

Even now, the memory had the ability to warm her cheeks, making the carriage feel more stifling. By the time Victoria alighted from her vehicle, the mugginess had drawn forth a little line of moisture over her lip. She dabbed at it with a handkerchief and slipped past the butler into the side foyer of Farnham Hall.

There was no need for her to be introduced and attention called to her. Victoria attended this dance because she could not disappoint Duchess Winnie. She'd make an appearance, then leave.

Despite the heavy heat of the summer night and the crush of people, the ballroom was fairly comfortable, and the reason was immediately evident: a row of six French doors had been opened to the garden, and an entire company of servants had been positioned throughout the room with large, palm-leaf fans, which they conducted vigorously.

"At last! I thought you'd never arrive, Victoria," said Lady Melly, swooping upon her with curling gloved fingers. "The Earl of Tretherington is here, and word is, he's in search of a wife."

"Tretherington?" Victoria echoed, looking at her mother with a raised brow. "Mother, please. I'm not about to be courted by a man old enough to be my grandfather."

"But, Victoria," Melly continued, "Tretherington House! It's grander than Westminster, or so they—"

"If you're so enamored with Tretherington House, why don't you set your eyes on him yourself?" asked Victoria. "Then *you* can be Lady T. You might just as well, Mama, for I don't believe Jellington will ever come up to snuff." She rarely called her mother that informal name, but something prompted her to really look at her parent tonight. Perhaps Lady Melly's incessant desire to see Victoria married—again—stemmed from her own loneliness of widowhood.

Her mother was a fine-looking woman for her age. With the same dark, curling hair she'd bestowed upon her daughter and a more curvaceous figure, not to mention a more outgoing personality, she'd had her own share of admirers since her husband's death. One of them, in fact, had been the vampire that Duchess Winnie had been stalking with her ungainly stake that night in Rome.

Victoria had relieved the duchess of her hunt, slaying the Conte Regalado herself. And shortly thereafter, she'd used her aunt Eustacia's special gold medallion to relieve Lady Melly, Duchess Winnie, and Lady Nilly of their memories of that particular occasion.

"I?" Lady Melly looked as though Victoria had suggested she dye her hair green. "But of course not. And, to be sure," she added coyly, looking at her beau, who was eyeing her from across the room, "Jellington has already proposed to me. Six times."

Victoria gaped at her. "Why on earth haven't you accepted? We could be planning your wedding."

Melly tapped Victoria lightly with her folded fan. "But it's so much more fun to plan yours, my dear. What about Mr. Killington? You already have a title, and he—"

"Has no hair, and breath so bad I'd swear it's rotting his teeth. No, thank you, Mother," Victoria replied, back to the formality.

"You aren't serious about that Monsieur Vioget, are you? He hasn't asked you to marry him, has he?" Melly's horror had gone from dying her hair green to shaving it all off and dashing through Almack's naked.

"As a matter of fact, he has," Victoria said breezily. "Excuse me, Mother. I think I see . . ." And she let her voice trail off as she hurried away, grinning at her mother's dismay.

To be fair, Sebastian hadn't actually asked her to marry him. But that didn't bother Victoria one whit. After what had happened with Phillip, who, like most of London, had been unaware that vampires existed— let alone of his wife's calling as a Venator—Victoria had realized that she would never marry again. She couldn't put someone she loved in danger as she had done to Phillip—although men like Sebastian and Max were already in danger by virtue of who they were.

Just as she was.

But she'd also recently realized that, as *Illa* Gardella, and the last of the direct line from Gardeleus, the first Venator, it was incumbent upon her to continue that direct lineage. Certainly, there were far-flung branches of the Gardella family throughout the world, where

Venators born to the family legacy were called . . . but the most powerful of them, and the leader of the vampire hunters, descended only from the direct line. Aunt Eustacia and her brother, Victoria's grandfather, had been the last two directly descended Venators. But he had declined the legacy, passing his powers on to Lady Melly, who had also chosen not to be a Venator, and who now lived in blissful ignorance of the undead.

Victoria had received two generations' worth of Venator skills, and now that Aunt Eustacia was gone, there was only Victoria.

"Why, Victoria, how lovely you look tonight!" exclaimed Duchess Winnie. Victoria blinked, wondering why she hadn't noticed her before nearly running into her, for the duchess had chosen a frock in a bright tangerine hue. It blazed like a beacon among the softer pinks and blues and greens of the other attendees.

And right smack in the middle of the duchess's massive bosom was an equally massive silver cross.

Victoria stared at the pendant. She knew the duchess had been known to carry garlic and to wear crosses in an effort to stave off potential vampire attacks, but this was absurd. Duchess Winnie, like the rest of London Society, didn't know that the undead even existed beyond the fertile imagination of John Polidori. His story, *The Vampyre*, had taken London by storm a few years ago, and from that had evolved the fashionable superstition of vampires.

Little did most of London know that vampires weren't like the mysterious, elegant Lord Ruthven portrayed in Polidori's work, but bloodthirsty demons who tore into humans with no remorse. Victoria had seen the remnants of vampire attacks, and it wasn't pretty.

"That is a lovely cross," she ventured to the duchess.

Winnie clapped her hand over the ornament. "I'm

taking no chances," she said in a low voice, her row of chins wobbling as she looked over the guests. She leaned closer to Victoria, bringing with her a subtle whiff of . . . garlic. Tinged with hyacinth. "The rumors about Rockley's disappearance claim that it was a vampire that took him. If the Marquess of Rockley can be attacked in his own home by one of those creatures, then no one is safe."

Victoria looked at her. "Where on earth did you hear such a thing?" The Venators took great pains to keep the rest of the world ignorant of the undead in order to protect them. And when someone did see or hear something they shouldn't, Aunt Eustacia's special gold medallion was used to hypnotically remove the offending memories.

"Why, from Nilly's new friend," said the duchess. "He told us in the utmost confidence."

"Lady Nilly's friend?"

"Ah, but I've forgotten! You already know him, Victoria, and in fact, here they are. Nilly!" The duchess waved, the underside of her arm jiggling enthusiastically as the bracelets at her wrists jingled.

Victoria turned to see the slender, flat-bosomed, pale-as-a-wraith Lady Nilly approach with her new friend.

He had blond hair, round cheeks, and a cleft in his chin. Dressed as befit his station, he looked elegant in a boyish way, although, as Victoria had cause to know, he was a few years older than her own twenty-one.

"Good evening, Victoria dear," trilled Nilly. She seemed to be clutching his arm as though she were afraid he'd fly the coop.

But she was in no danger of that, for the man bowed deeply to Victoria and took her hand, raising it to his lips. "How enchanting to see you again, Lady Rockley."

"I don't know *how* I could have forgotten that you two have met," said the duchess with exaggerated surprise. Victoria noticed the waggle of her eyebrows as she looked conspiratorially at Nilly.

"Indeed we have," Victoria replied, then turned to the gentleman. "George Starcasset. I certainly didn't expect to see you again." Her voice was glacial.

No, she certainly hadn't. The last time she'd seen George, he'd been ushering two hostages, in the form of Max and a bloody, one-handed Kritanu, out of the room where Victoria had slain a group of vampires. George was a member of the Tutela, the secret society of mortals that protected and served the undead.

"I'm certain you didn't," he had the grace to say. And when she looked at him, she saw a bleak sincerity in his eyes that had replaced the bravado she was used to seeing there. "But I needed to see you. Will you dance with me?"

Victoria would have rather taken a spin around the ballroom with Beauregard, the great vampire who'd tried to turn her undead, than George. But Lady Nilly and Duchess Winnie looked as though they were about to explode with pleasure at the handsome, albeit boyish, young man who was not only titled but also wealthy, and who was clearly attempting to charm Victoria.

She could see no gracious way out of the mess, so she took his arm. And at the very least, she could lecture him about spreading rumors of the undead among unsuspecting ladies of the *ton*. The last thing she needed was Duchess Winnie out trying to stake a vampire again, and Lady Nilly inviting one into her bedchamber. She was under the impression that vampires were romantic.

"What are you doing here?" Victoria demanded as George spun her into his arms.

"My God, you look lovely tonight," he replied, unable to keep the bald admiration from his voice. He stepped them into the waltz, still looking at her as though every other thought had evaporated from his head.

Victoria knew from past experience that he was easily distracted, and that he wasn't the most efficient of villains. The two times he'd tried to capture her, he'd been abysmally inept with aiming a gun, binding with ropes, and other nefarious activities. She had absolutely no fear of him. Not even an inkling. The biggest emotion he raised in her was flat annoyance, which was what she felt now.

But before she could open her mouth to speak again, he looked up from her half-exposed bosom and into her eyes. The admiration was gone, replaced by fear.

"I'm in trouble, Victoria. I need your help."

Two

Wherein Our Heroine's Services Are Engaged

"I find it exceedingly ironic that you should ask me, of all people, for help," Victoria replied. She tried to keep the sarcasm from her voice, but, based on the abashed look on George's face, she didn't quite succeed.

Yet he forged on, showing a resilience she would never have expected of him. And for once, he wasn't looking down the front of her bodice. "Daresay it's mad, but there's no one else who could be of assistance."

Victoria concentrated on the waltz for a moment, if only to keep from laughing outright at his presumption. He'd spent the last year trying to capture her for a variety of villains, including vampires and a demon. And that was after he had sneaked into her bedchamber—and bed—one night and tried to kiss her. Of course, he'd been foxed at the time, and goaded on by a mischievous Sebastian . . . but still. Despite her concentration, she wasn't able to keep a smile in check.

"Should be the last person in the world to turn to

for help," George muttered, "after you killed my sister, but there's nothing for it."

"That's what I do to vampires, George. I stake them," Victoria reminded him drily. "And you—you protect them, and serve them. I cannot imagine how you think I might, or should, assist you."

"They're all gone, y'know," he told her. "Since you ruined Lilith's plan to kill King George, she's gone away and taken them—most of them—with her." His lips twisted grimly. "There's where I need your help."

"What? Is there a vampire that hasn't gone with Lilith that you'd like me to chase away?" Victoria thought she was making a jest, but when his face dissolved into shock, she realized her flippant comment had hit the mark. "Is that it? Truly?"

George tightened his hand at her waist, pulling her toward him to redirect their path from a collision with another couple. "Sh'won't leave," he admitted. "I was . . . er . . . attached to her a bit, but her demands are getting too much. Need her gone."

"Her demands? For drawn curtains to keep out the sunlight? And for fresh blood, of course. Does she have you snaring rabbits or catching mice? Visiting the butcher?" Victoria felt the giggle bubbling up inside her and swallowed it back as she thought of George running to and fro betwixt the butcher and the attic to check mousetraps. It was so unusual in her world, in the battle of mortals versus the undead, that she encountered a situation in which she found amusement.

Then her eyes narrowed and all humor fled. "You'd best not be bringing her humans, George. If you are, I'll kill you myself." It was a bluff; of course she wouldn't kill George. He was a human—a member, albeit an insufferable one, of that race she was charged with protecting, no matter what the cost. "No, perhaps I'll tie you up and set her on you."

He swallowed and managed an uncomfortable smile. "Too late for that, Victoria." He released her hand to pull the tall, starched collar of his shirt away from his neck. Beneath were four angry red bite marks. Fresh enough that the inside of his collar was smeared with dark red.

"Aside of that, only brought her two people—" He must have felt Victoria tense up beneath his hands, for he continued quickly. "They were willing. I swear it! Wanted to see what it was like, y'know." He leaned forward, a sudden leer showing his teeth. "Y'dear friend Lady Fenworth wanted to go, Victoria."

"Lady Nilly?" Victoria didn't doubt it for a moment. The twittering old lady had been fascinated by vampires—or at least the romantic legend of them—since Polidori's book.

George seized the opportunity to press further. "If y'don't help me, I'll take her to visit Maybelle." He seemed to think his pronouncement a perfect occasion to examine Victoria's décolletage more closely.

"Maybelle?" Victoria missed a step and nearly trod upon George's foot—something she hadn't done since her first year out in Society, when she was putting all of her Venator strength behind her sharp, little heel into the toe of the obnoxious Lord Beetleton. She didn't feel the need to do so in this case, although it was a close call. George was still ogling her cleavage.

"You aren't perhaps speaking of Miss Maybelle Felicity-Underwood, who was rumored to have run off to Gretna Green with her fifth cousin?" she said, poking George in the back of the neck with a sharp fingernail.

"The very same," replied George. Now he had the grace to meet her eyes, and as the music tinkled to an end, he kept his arm around her waist, drawing her off to the edge of the dance floor. "Lots of rumors as of late 'bout people running off, see? Better say that than to put about that they were lost at sea, hmm, Lady Rockley?" This was the first time he'd used her title, and it was purposeful.

Victoria kept her face devoid of emotion and allowed George to propel her toward the main foyer of the house. His reference to the story Victoria had given out to explain the death and disappearance of her husband, Phillip—that he'd died while on a ship—reminded her of the evil Bemis Goodwin. Goodwin had been a Bow Street runner and the brother of a vampire she'd slain her first year as a Venator. Goodwin had been bound and determined to turn her over to the authorities for murder, and he'd very nearly succeeded in getting her thrown into Newgate.

The problem in Goodwin's case—and in any case involving the death of a vampire—was that there was no body to be produced. Only a dusting of smelly ash remained after an undead was staked. Thus, a story had to be created to explain the sudden disappearance of people like Phillip, and then the new (impostor) Marquess of Rockley, along with Gwendolyn Starcasset, George's sister, and now, apparently, Miss Maybelle Felicity-Underwood.

"And so you wish me to help rid you of Miss Maybelle, who has now become undead, and who, through someone's meddling, has dragged her fifth cousin's presumably good name into the fray. Pray tell, George . . . how did that come to pass?"

She stopped at the edge of the ballroom, and glanced at the foyer beyond. Guests were still arriving, despite the fact that there were more than three dozen already here. Firmly she pulled her arm from his grip and stepped away, looking up into his pale blue eyes.

"Her fifth cousin is a swine and a fool, and is most likely at the bottom of the Thames with the fish," replied George airily.

"I suppose that to mean Miss Maybelle partook of a generous portion of his blood before disposing of him. Or did she have you do it?"

He had the grace to look away. "He was a swine," George repeated, petulance in his voice.

"But a man, nevertheless. I happen to know a few of those swine type of men myself." She looked at him meaningfully. "But I've never gone so far as to feed them to the fishes—or the undead." She pursed her lips, rather enjoying the moment of watching George squirm. Of course what he'd been party to wasn't amusing at all, and if ever a man deserved a comeuppance, it was George Starcasset.

In fact, the only reason she hadn't yet walked away from him and left him to deal with his vampire guest on his own was the very real threat that he might involve Lady Nilly.

"Did you have something to do with her being turned undead?" she asked again.

He smiled nervously, his cheeks rounding like crab apples. The softness made him look more like a boy than ever. "Mm . . . She was curious, and so Gwennie helped . . . and next thing, she had red eyes and fangs. And," he added, swallowing, "an attachment to me."

Victoria's brows rose. "And what did dear Sara Regalado have to say of that attachment? The two of you seemed to be rather intimately acquainted when you were escorting her about Town."

Sara Regalado had been a powerful member of the Tutela, often to the extent of sacrificing willing and unwilling human life. Her father, the Conte Regalado, had been the Tutela's leader in Rome before being turned into a vampire and attempting to woo Lady Melly.

Sara was dead now, but she'd figured significantly in Victoria's adventures in the last year, initially by befriending her in Rome and then announcing that she was engaged to Max. That engagement had turned out to be a foil Max created so he could infiltrate the Tutela.

At the beginning of the summer, Sara and George had turned up together in London. This was after disappearing in Rome, during a battle in which Max had killed the evil demon Akvan, who was also their master.

"Thought it quite amusing, if you must know," George admitted. "Loved to watch Maybelle feed."

Victoria nodded knowingly. Sara had been overly fond of watching the undead drink blood—from both a distance and her own participation. "On you, of course."

He looked away, grinding his jaw so hard that his chin shifted and creaked audibly. "Finished with vampires," he muttered, then looked back at her. "Will you help rid me of her?"

Victoria looked down at her magnificent gown. Since she'd become a Venator, fashion had been low on her list of priorities . . . but the frock was new. And the loveliest gown, after her wedding dress, she'd ever owned. And Verbena would scold. She'd hate to tear it, or get it stained. Yet . . . it had been two weeks since she'd seen a vampire. Her stake fingers were beginning to itch. Not to mention the fact that the whole situation with Max had left her in a constant state of frustration.

It would be a simple task. Perhaps she could even stake Maybelle, then return to the dance before anyone knew she'd gone.

"There will be conditions," she told George sternly.

His eyes sprang round and hopeful. "You'll do it, then?"

She nodded once, then began to tick off her requirements. "We will take my carriage. You shall alight from it at your residence and draw Maybelle out to me in my vehicle. Tell her whatever you wish: that you've someone to feed on or whatnot. Once she's safely in the carriage, I will dispatch her for you. And then," she said, glaring at him, "you'll stay away from the Tutela, and the undead. If I find that you've become involved with them again—even *thought* about going about in the moonlight—I *will* kill you."

He was nodding emphatically. "Of course, of course."

She looked at him long and hard, and saw only sincerity and hopefulness there. At least for now, he was good for his word. "And if I choose to, I'll collect on this favor at any time, and in any manner."

"Agreed." His moment of begging over, George allowed his attention to slip down toward her bosom once again.

Victoria sighed. "Then let us get on our way."

"Tonight? You'll do it tonight?" He looked as though she'd offered to tear off her gown right there.

"Of course. Do you think I shall stand for you to bring any other people for her to feed on?" She started for the entrance, and he trotted after like an earnest pup.

Max scanned the guests in the ballroom beyond, taking care to remain at the edge of the grand foyer of the duchess's home. The last thing he needed was one of those mercenary Society mamas to get him in her sights as a potential husband for her skinny, pale, spotted, or talkative daughter—despite the fact that he wasn't a member of the *ton* or even the Italian peerage. It seemed as though any unmarried, ambulatory male (and even some who weren't) who had access to Society gatherings was considered a potential husband.

He would have preferred to stay in tonight, knowing that Victoria was out and unlikely to disturb him in the *kalari*, the room set aside for martial arts training. He'd thought to ask Kritanu to work with him, hoping to take the man's mind off his grief—but then he'd had to attend to this.

Blast it. Where the hell was she?

It wasn't as if that bloody red dress—what there was of it—wouldn't stand out, especially among the washed-out pinks, blues, greens, and yellows that clustered around the room. Christ.

Good God. What was the duchess wearing? It was shockingly . . . orange. And the soup of *eau de toilette* scents was strong enough from here . . . what would it be like in the thick of things?

He was going to have to skirt the side of the dance floor and make his way out to the patio in search of Victoria.

Just as he was about to move, he caught a few words of conversation behind him: ". . . in that red dress."

Max turned and pinpointed two men who were chuckling lasciviously together, shoulder to shoulder. One of them was the butler, whom Max had refused to allow to announce him, and the other appeared to be a groom or footman.

"Lucky gent t'ave that in 'is 'ands," said the footman, who, based solely on the appearance of his full, glistening lips, Max decided was the more vulgar of the two. "Looked ripe f'the pickin'."

Max stepped toward them, and the two men straightened from their not-quite-muttered conversation.

"May I help you, my lord?" asked the butler.

Max was not a lord, per se, but he forbore to correct the man. The higher his perceived position, the better his chances of getting the information he required. Of course, there was always the option of slamming their two heads together. "Were you speaking of Lady Rockley?"

The butler drew himself up taller—even taller than Max, but several stone lighter and certainly not as quick on his feet. His Adam's apple bobbed above the high collar of his shirt. "What of Lady Rockley?"

"I'm in search of her." The two men remained silent, the footman looking slightly ill at ease; truly, he was little more than a boy. But when Max had been that age—sixteen, perhaps seventeen—he'd already been hunting vampires for more than a year. On his own and without the grace of a *vis bulla*.

"I'm not certain—"

Max stepped closer. "I suggest," he said, pleasantness oozing from his voice, "that you desist in prevaricating and tell me where she is. And," he added, his tone dropping low enough to make the footman's eyelashes flicker, "I suggest you also cease from speaking about the marchioness in such unflattering terms."

The butler swallowed. "She left some time ago, my lord. With . . . er . . ."

"Yes?"

"A blond man," the footman offered, obviously wishing to be of assistance in an effort to dispel Max's obvious anger.

A blond man. Vioget?

"Did she go willingly? That is, was she agreeable about leaving? So early?"

The butler nodded, his face blaring hesitation. He obviously wasn't certain if Max was angry or pleased that Victoria was gone. That made two of them. "She . . . er . . . was smiling and laughing a bit just before they left, my lord."

Definitely Vioget then. That was good. Perhaps they'd made plans to meet here, and Victoria had contrarily chosen not to tell him. That would be no surprise.

"In whose carriage?" Not that it mattered. Vioget would make use of any vehicle, and soon that rich red dress would be crumpled in a pile. Or torn, under eager hands. Its fabric was delicate enough to split at the slightest strain.

"My lady's, my lord. They went out to her carriage."

Max stepped back, satisfied. Yet . . . something itched deep inside him. He ignored it and turned to leave. It really wasn't terribly urgent that he see Victoria tonight.

But what if it wasn't Vioget? What if she'd left in a carriage with another man?

"The man . . . how tall was he? What else did you notice of him? His name?"

And then there she was. In front of him.

"Max?" Her voice lifted in surprise as she stepped through the door, into the foyer. There was, indeed, a blond man with her. And it wasn't Vioget.

What the hell had she been doing in her carriage with George Starcasset?

Max tore his attention from Victoria and focused on her companion, but not before he noticed her hair was a bit off-kilter and one of her gloves was missing.

Max turned a cold gaze onto Starcasset. The man didn't even attempt bravado, which was no surprise. After all, he didn't have a gun in his hand to give him ballocks. A tinge of red flushed over the man's round cheeks, and he gave a little bow. "Signore Pesaro," he said formally. "We've just returned."

"I see that." Max didn't trust himself to say much more. There were too many people around, and he'd likely end up with his fingers around the man's throat—which would be a great blow to his reputation for control.

Where the hell was Vioget? Why wasn't he at this blasted dance, protecting his own interests?

"Max, what are you doing here?" Victoria asked, moving closer. She was looking at him with sharp eyes that held not a hint of shame, and, quite likely—bloody *hell*—a bit of smugness. Blast. "Perhaps you had an urge to waltz after all?"

"I came to see you on a matter of some urgency," he said, duly pushing from his mind the one and only time they'd waltzed. He didn't like to dance, but he was damn good at it, and the glow of pleasure—not to mention surprise—in her eyes at the realization had been worth the ridiculous display. He glared at Starcasset. "Alone." *In a carriage.*

No.

Victoria's red lips tipped up at the edges, revealing the collection of tiny dimples around them. "Of course, Max." There was that knowing edge to her voice, that allure, as she looked up at him as if she knew—she *knew*—how bloody uncomfortable he was.

Damn and blast. He should have left London weeks ago.

He should have found Vioget and sent him here tonight.

He should have merely lifted his brow and looked down at her with an arrogant expression and asked if she was ready to hunt vampires now, or if it was more important to finish off her dance card.

But it was so much harder now. After. Since.

There was so much hanging between them.

Victoria slipped her arm through Max's before he could react, and she pressed her hip, torso, leg, all alongside him. "Good night, George," she said coolly, as if she weren't fairly melting against Max. Bloody hell. "Remember our agreement. I will keep my promise."

"Of course. Thank you again, Lady Rockley."

"Let's go," snapped Max, easing away from that red dress and the woman in it. As he turned, she bumped closer, and he saw, for the first time, a thin streak of red along her neck. "What the hell is this?"

Without thinking, he touched it, and saw that it was a thin scratch that oozed blood, half hidden by her hairline and around the back of her neck. Not a vampire bite.

Before she could reply, he grabbed her by the arm, angling her away from him, and started them toward the front door. "Get her carriage," he snapped at the goggling footman, who fairly pissed his pants, presumably at the expression on Max's face.

"My God, Max, you don't have to be so rude," Victoria said.

He ignored her. And Victoria, for once, closed her mouth and said nothing while they waited for the carriage.

The carriage. The small, dark, closed carriage.

Bloody hell.

Three

In Which Our Heroine Dredges Up a Past Event, to the Dismay of Her Companion

Victoria climbed back into the conveyance she'd alighted from only moments before. The scent of May-belle's ash still hovered in the air, and she swore she heard Max sniff as he slipped in after her.

She hadn't even pulled all her skirts up and into the carriage, saving the hem from being trod upon or caught in the door, when he pushed past and sprawled on the opposite seat, settling in the center of the bench in an arrangement that clearly indicated his desire for solitude there.

The footman closed the door, and Victoria heard it latch in place. Inside, the interior felt dark and close. Her corset suddenly felt more restrictive.

"You're losing your touch, Max," she said, sinking into her own seat across from him. She took her time smoothing the skirt over her legs, perversely allowing it to whisk against his pantaloons, which, in the way of fashion, were held neat and straight by narrow straps beneath his feet.

He raised a brow in question, his face half lit by the small lantern that hung in the corner above Victoria. Of course he'd choose the side that wasn't as well illuminated.

She took the brow quirk as an invitation to explain. "That message," she said, gesturing at his long, sprawled body, "doesn't have your normal subtlety."

His lips moved in what looked like a suddenly checked smile.

"In fact," she continued, "it's a rather clumsy and obvious shield against something you wish to ignore." She drew off the single glove she still wore and looked expectantly at his stony expression. Her throat had dried, and she swallowed gently, trying to ignore the sudden . . . awareness . . . between them.

"Are you going to tell me what you were doing with George Starcasset, or are you going to continue to look for meanings that aren't there?"

"Since you were the one who sought me out, on a matter of some urgency, I should think you'd be more eager to share your news. What on earth was so important that you braved a Society dance fraught with—what do you call it? Social frivolities?" One of her slippers was very close to his shoe. She edged her foot over slightly, just enough to touch him, and waited.

"Brim and Michalas have left," Max told her. The other two Venators had come to London to help Victoria, Max, and Sebastian foil Lilith's plot to kill the new King of England.

"For Rome?"

He shook his head, and moved his foot. Away from hers. "Back to Paris. We received word tonight that another demon was sighted. They went to conduct an investigation."

Victoria considered him for a moment. Wheels crunched and ground along the street below, and the floor beneath her feet rumbled. The lantern above her jolted, swinging its light gently from side to side, casting larger, then smaller, larger, then smaller, shadows over his face. "And?" she asked when he said nothing further.

"And Kritanu thought that you should be advised immediately."

Victoria smothered a smile. And thus Max, who was so biddable and who adored social functions, leapt at the chance to join her at the duchess's party. Even for Kritanu, who was as close to him as an uncle?

Not, as he himself would say, bloody likely.

"So why was it necessary for me to leave the dance?" she countered. "If that was the extent of the news."

"Your hair is mussed, you're missing a glove, and there's a streak of blood on your neck," he replied. "You look as though you've just returned from some sort of assignation. A violent one."

"As it happens, I have." Of course her hair was askew. She'd not quite gotten the technique of pulling the small, hidden stake from her coiffure without messing it up.

"And along the way accosted a vampire? Or was that the purpose of the meeting?" He seemed to relax more, settling those wide, square shoulders against the velvet squab behind him. "You might wish me to believe that you had a tête-à-tête with George Starcasset, but the thought is utterly ridiculous."

"If I were to have an assignation in a carriage, it would most definitely not be with George Starcasset."

His elegant fingers, spread over the back of the seat, straightened. Then curled. "Viog—"

"Nor would it be with Sebastian," she continued coolly, refusing to drop his gaze.

"Victoria—" His voice was strained. Laced with anger, real anger. He looked away, out of the window. His fingers relaxed again.

She wanted to reach across the gap between them and grab those shoulders and shake him until some sense filtered down through that stone-filled, honor-bound, *cowardly* skull of his.

And she could do it, too. She was so much stronger than he.

But what good would it do?

Silence, full and heavy, sat in the carriage with them.

"This reminds me of the night we had to go to Bridge and Stokes," Victoria said after a moment. "Do you remember?"

"I remember," he snapped, still gazing out the window. "We had to save your husband from a vampire attack."

She took the opportunity to shift in her seat, arranging herself subtly, so that the small lantern light fell just so, cutting a swath of pale gold over the front of her gown. "I had to change in the carriage, remember? Into men's clothing, because it was a men's club, and of course I couldn't enter dressed as I was."

"My memory is perfectly clear; you needn't review the details."

"Then I'm certain you recall having to unlace my corset—"

"Victoria." Now he looked away from the window. "What are you about?"

She couldn't make out the expression in his eyes; they were muted by shadow. But by the set of his mouth, she knew he was angry. She knew how his eyes would glare, flat and black and cold.

"I've always wondered about something," she continued as though he wasn't looking murderously at her. "When I was undressing, and you were sitting shoved back in the corner, studiously looking out the window, or with your eyes closed as you claimed . . . did you peek?"

She heard what sounded like a stifled snort or strangled cough. Then . . . "Of course not."

At that moment, the carriage eased to a halt, and Victoria realized in dismay that they'd arrived at Aunt Eustacia's town house already. Max fairly leapt to his feet, looming like a full-winged bat in the small enclosure.

But although he stood in such a way that did not permit her to rise as well, he didn't leave. Instead, he turned to face her, looking down from his half-stooped position. His hands moved to the wall above her head—a position of power that he must have felt he needed—and he looked down, his feet spread on either side of hers.

For the first time since they'd climbed into the vehicle, she could see his face clearly. Emotionless, sharp, closed. So empty it made her heart ache.

Her head tipped back, her neck cradled by the top of the cushion. Her fingers twisted in the shadows, burying in her thin, silky skirt, and her heart thumped audibly in her chest. At least, it was audible to her.

"Max," she said. Whispered. Begged.

"I can't, Victoria." His voice was just as unsteady, but deep. And low.

"You *won't*."

"Don't be a fool." He'd regained control, and his words were clipped, cool. "You are obliged to do what's right for the Venators—just as I am. And what's right, Victoria, is for you to be with Vioget. A man who is your equal, who can stand at your side and doesn't have to hide from the bloody queen of the vampires."

"Max—" she began.

But he spoke over her. "Victoria, understand. You are the last of the Gardellas. You have to do what's right for them, for the world. It's your duty, your calling. You can't ignore that because we"—here his voice dipped even lower—"spent the night together. I told you then, it changes nothing."

"Coward!"

"Good night, Victoria."

He snapped open the door and was out before Victoria could respond.

She pulled to her feet, suddenly frustrated to exhaustion. How could a man who did what he'd done, faced what he'd faced . . . made the decisions he'd made . . . be such a bloody coward?

Then all other thoughts fled as Max's head came back around into the carriage. His eyes were fierce and dark as he reached forward to grab her by the arm.

"Victoria. Wayren's gone missing," he said, dragging her from the vehicle so quickly that she lost a slipper.

Victoria caught her balance once her feet were on the ground. At the same time as she assimilated Max's words, she registered the fact that Sebastian and Kritanu, whose arm was curled up to hold something close to his body, were standing next to the carriage. All three of the men appeared tense and concerned.

"What?" she said sharply, ignoring the damp on her silk-stockinged foot. "What's happened?"

Wayren was a woman of an indeterminate age—she looked older than Victoria, but much younger than Lady Melly, yet she'd been Aunt Eustacia's friend and mentor for more than fifty years. The keeper of the Venator library, records, and many other secrets protected in the catacombs of Rome, she dressed like a medieval chatelaine and always carried a leather satchel that held many more books and manuscripts than could possibly fit.

She had been a source of information, advice, and guidance to the Venators for as long as anyone could remember. Yet no one knew very much about her.

"Inside," Max said, looking around sharply, his hand over Victoria's elbow. "Who knows what's lurking about?"

Moments later they were gathered in the small study, and Kritanu, who was still a bit awkward with his missing hand, told them what he knew. He sat, his spry, seventy-year-old body straight, his wiry legs bent in their customary loose trousers, ankle stacked above ankle. The small burden he'd been holding outside was revealed to be a bundle of white feathers with a single beady eye peeking out. A pigeon.

"I have not seen Wayren today, but I thought nothing of it," he said, glancing at Victoria.

When Wayren visited London, she took her own accommodations, their location unknown to the rest of them. She required her privacy and a place to study, but she often visited the house where Victoria and Kritanu—and, for the time being, Max—lived. "When Brim and Michalas received their summons back to Paris, they left straightaway. Max and I felt that you should be notified immediately, and Wayren as well. We sent a message to Wayren, and Max went to inform you."

"You sent Myza?" asked Victoria, looking at the bird in his lap. "But she returned without a message?" Myza, one of the many pigeons the Venators used for communication, was the one Wayren preferred.

"No, Myza was not here at the time. That is how I know Wayren is in trouble, for Myza returned with the bird I sent. Her wing is injured." He gently stroked the top of the pigeon's head with one of his five remaining fingers. The quiet bird's eye blinked and looked about sharply.

Victoria looked at Max for confirmation of her thoughts. He nodded, and she felt an uncomfortable chill descend on her. If Wayren's pigeon was injured, it was likely she was also in trouble.

"Myza can lead us to where she is," Max said. "If she can fly."

Kritanu nodded. "Indeed, that is what Sebastian and I were discussing when you arrived home. The bird is hurt, but seems eager to leave, and I can only believe she wishes to take us to Wayren. She will be able to hop a bit, and I'll help her."

"We've also sent the other bird off with a message to catch Brim and Michalas and bring them back. They left under an hour ago, and could not have gone far," Sebastian said.

"Good, but we cannot wait for them. It will take only a moment to change," Victoria replied, then slid her glance delicately over to Max. "I'd prefer not to do it in the carriage."

Max's mouth quirked, but he didn't smile. "Then be off and get it done."

"What a shame," Sebastian said as Victoria sailed past. "I rather like that gown." But even he, the consummate flirt, still held worry in his expression.

Wayren missing, perhaps injured . . . this was something they'd never had to contend with before. She'd always seemed so protected, so above the violence and struggle in which the Venators were engaged. The idea that she, the wise, serene, ageless woman, had somehow fallen prey to some evil was unsettling.

True to her word, Victoria was quick to use Verbena's assistance to change from her luscious red gown into clothing that was not only cooler, but also much less restrictive. Like Kritanu, she wore loose trousers, but of a dark brown color, and a man-style shirt she'd had made to fit her female curves. Her corset loosened, her slippers exchanged for heavier shoes, her person well armed, she hurried down the stairs, working her loose hair into a thick braid. She'd not wanted to take the time for her maid to do it; the sense of urgency had begun to grow.

"Mounts are being brought around," Max said as she reached the bottom.

She nodded in agreement with his assumption. Following a hobbled bird would be much easier on horseback than in a carriage.

Outside, the air was still comfortable, and a wide swath of stars helped the moon light the sky. Yet threads of dark cloud threatened to creep over the half-moon and weave into the Milky Way, creating in her a sense of unease.

Kritanu elected to remain behind, partly because riding one-handed at the speed with which they hoped to move would be difficult; but also in the event that Wayren, Brim or Michalas should return or some other message arrive.

They started off, Myza being turned over to Max for assistance. The pigeon, whose eyes now seemed to burn with purpose, also acted as eager as the rest of them to be off and fluttered into the air ahead of the party. Lofting awkwardly into a low tree branch, the pearl white pigeon paused, then launched herself to another tree.

She flew a bit, then scuttled back toward Max, who caught her gently and held her until she was ready to fly again. As they made their way along the street of town houses, carriages rumbled by, bringing members of the *ton* to and from theater engagements, fêtes, and other events. Despite the hour, hacks and wagons transported members of the lower classes along with their wares, but as Victoria and her companions followed Myza, the streets became less populated, narrower, and more eerie.

They'd been following her stop-and-start rhythm for more than thirty minutes when Myza turned and fluttered back into Max's large hand. She sat there, neck stretched up, head tilting, looking around, and Victoria found herself nudging her horse up next to them. Her leg brushed against Max's as she maneuvered near him, watching the bird as she gave a soft, throaty coo.

Suddenly, the soft beat of wings and an answering coo announced the arrival of another pigeon. And then the *clip-clop* of rapid horses' hooves as Brim and Michalas appeared from around a corner.

Myza and the new pigeon, who was called Thrush, seemed to be having some sort of avian conversation, and at once, the second bird flew up into the air and began to circle around them. Then it swooped down and nipped Max on the ear, fully gaining his attention and understanding. They would follow the uninjured pigeon, who would receive navigation from Myza.

Making much better time now, the five of them and one pigeon thundered through the streets, following the speedy Thrush away from the more populated areas. Often, Thrush had to stop and circle back, flying just above Max, because the horses had to follow a less convenient route—by road. At last, after more than an hour of hard riding south of the Thames, they reached a small graveyard at the edge of a dark-windowed village.

Black iron spikes fenced the cemetery, studded with masonry columns taller than Max. In the moonlight, what had been bone white stone gleamed from beneath eerie black moss and dirt stains. A stand of trees cast long shadows from the north side of the graveyard, mingling with the gray and ash colors of the headstones.

Thrush circled now, silent as the bats that darted and dodged around with him, sending sweeping black shadows over the horses and their riders. Victoria urged her mount closer to the fence, looking for the gate. It was clear from Myza's reaction that Wayren was nearby. The pigeon had raised her head, warbling quietly, and attempted to take flight.

Max released her, and the pearly pigeon settled in the low branch of a tree, unable to get enough height with her injured wing to fly over the fence.

As she searched the enclosure, Victoria heard the others separate, some riding in her wake, the others starting in the opposite direction to circle around and meet her. Once she reached the west side of the fence, Victoria saw a small mausoleum near the north side, buried in the thick thrust of shadows.

The hair lifted at the back of her neck—not the same chill that portended the presence of a vampire, but a different, uncomfortable feeling. At the same moment, she came upon a small gate, barely a man's width if he should move sideways, between two of the stone columns.

She was off her horse as Sebastian thundered up, and he swung himself off to land light-footed on the ground next to her.

One brief glance told them the gate would need to be forced open, or the wall must be scaled. The iron bars were topped with spikes much sharper than necessary for mere decoration; they looked wicked enough to slice through flesh and even bone, given enough force. Forcing the gate would be the most prudent option.

Victoria and Sebastian examined the gate more closely as Max and the other two Venators rode up, having circled the rest of the graveyard.

"No other entrance," Max said. "It'll have to be here. Any undead?" Of course, he could no longer sense the presence of a vampire, unlike the rest of them.

"No," Victoria replied, stepping away from the gate to look around. Her attention focused on their target: the low, squat building cloaked in shadows only fifty yards away. "But something. Something . . ." Her voice trailed off, and she paused as she drew in a breath.

No.

She sniffed again, and her stomach pinched. An unmistakable scent of malignance and death simmered under that of moist peat and horse sweat.

Victoria looked up and met Max's eyes, then looked at Brim. The tall, ebony-skinned man who wore his *vis bulla* through the corner of an eyebrow had lifted his head as if to scent something on the air as well. He nodded and looked at her, his dark eyes black pits.

Demons.

Not every Venator could sense the presence of fallen angels, or demons, but Victoria and Brim were both capable of recognizing the malevolent scent that lurked beneath everything else.

They would need swords along with stakes, then, for demons had to be beheaded in order to be completely destroyed. Being prepared for any eventuality, the Venators had armed themselves not only with stakes, but also with firearms and swords, which hung from the horses' saddles.

At that moment, a low screech tore Victoria's attention to Sebastian and Michalas, who'd used their Venator strength to work an iron hinge loose from its hasp embedded in the masonry. As they pushed, the long-abandoned gate creaked and moaned as they worked to free it. When Brim, the bulkiest of them all, added his muscle, the gate gave another long, low moan as it bent nearly double. Still attached by a lower hinge and by its heavy metal bolt on the opposite side, the gate had now been rendered impotent and scalable.

After retrieving the sword from her saddle and buckling it around her waist, Victoria scrambled over first, using Sebastian's offered hand for stability. As she slid down to the other side, she eyed the mausoleum, watching for any sign of movement.

All was quiet except for the faint shuffles of the others as they joined her inside the cemetery wall.

Victoria stepped toward the building, and as she drew closer, more of its details became apparent. The structure stood no taller than the midpoint of a single story, with a low peaked roof and plain, blank sides. Perhaps half the size of a carriage house, the mausoleum was situated with the stand of trees curling around and behind it.

Beneath her feet, the ground was soft and damp, littered with stones and larger rocks, embedded brick boundaries outlining family plots, and tufts of grass poking out. As she drew closer to the building, the faint scent of demons grew more discernible, though not strong enough to clog her nostrils. Something stirred in the air. Not a breeze but . . . something.

Then she saw it. Above the low pitched roof of the mausoleum, not far above her head: a faint swirl of . . . fog? Smoke?

No, the threads were too dark for fog. Or smoke.

Her throat tightened, and she swallowed hard.

Thin clouds of black whispered in and out of the glowering trees, tangling like tendrils of hair above the mausoleum. Circling.

Victoria stopped and felt someone behind her. She turned. It was Sebastian, who was looking up over the mausoleum just as she had. Her heart thudding, she grasped his arm as she waited for the others to draw near.

When they came closer, Victoria sought Max's gaze in the meandering light. His face held the same arrested expression as hers. "What is it?" she asked, looking at him, but speaking to them all.

Max shook his head, his lips pinched. Sebastian moved closer to her, murmuring, "Whatever it is, it's not vampire."

Victoria looked at Brim, whose face was wary. With terse words, she sent him and Michalas around the mausoleum in one direction, and she, Max, and Sebastian went the other way in search of an entrance.

They found it, well cloaked by two overgrown cedars. The door was set half below ground level, accessed by four rough, narrow steps.

Victoria glanced up at the swirling black mass above them. It seemed nebulous, for it hadn't changed, nor did it seem threatening. But it moved and writhed, barely visible in the shadows of the trees, hovering like an eerie warning over the roof, beneath and among the tree branches.

She shivered. She'd met many demonic and undead threats in her two years as a Venator, but this was particularly disturbing—partly because it was unknown, but also because it was apparent that whatever it was, it had something to do with Wayren.

A shadow appeared close by and had Victoria reaching for her sword, but it was only Brim and Michalas, completing their circuit of the mausoleum.

She noticed that Brim, too, had a hand on the sword at his belt.

Everything was strangely quiet. Tense, and quiet.

Victoria lifted her foot to take the first step down toward the mausoleum door, but Sebastian curled his fingers around her arm and slipped in front of her. She allowed him to without annoyance, for she knew he made the gesture not because she was a woman, but because he loved her. Victoria followed him.

The small alcove at the bottom of the stairs was only

large enough for one person to stand, and so of necessity, she remained on the bottom stair, her head level with his as he looked at the door. She watched as his damaged hand, the left one, felt along the solid wood bound by metal, and then heard the soft clunk as he found the iron latch. Victoria felt a shift behind her and realized Max was standing on the step above, towering over them both from his vantage point.

More dull clanks, and a soft creak, and then Sebastian had the latch loosened. The door opened without the reluctant groans of the iron hasp of the gate, indicating that this latch had been used more frequently.

Sebastian glanced up at her as if to ensure everyone was ready, and then returned his attention to the door, pushing gently against it with a widespread hand.

The heavy, metal-bound planks moved reluctantly, and it was so quiet that the faint scrape of wood over the gritty stone floor was audible. Shadows moved above Victoria, changing the faint illumination, and she assumed it was because Brim and Michalas had drawn closer as well.

Then, she realized with sudden horror that the shifting darkness wasn't from the others gathering closer. She looked up, eyes wide, as the air began to move. She felt it against her cheek, a rising breeze.

The mass of dark clouds above now writhed faster and harder, curling above them, swirling and twisting, sinking like a vortex. It happened so quickly, all at once they were engulfed by the spinning air, the black fog, as it cloaked them in cloying darkness.

Victoria couldn't see, but she felt Max behind her, grabbing her shoulders from above, her long, thick braid flailing like a whip, and Sebastian suddenly warm and solid in front of her. If anyone spoke or shouted, the sound was snatched up in the whirlwind and destroyed, for all she could hear was a roaring in her ears.

The air, cold suddenly, smelled ancient—ancient and deathly, like rotting bones and aged flesh. The chill was unbearable, biting and sharp, stinging her face and skin through the fabric of her clothing.

Black filled her eyes and ears, buffeted against her, pushing and battling her trousers like wind against sails. Something screamed high and long in her ear—or perhaps in her mind. She felt Max hovering over her, touched Sebastian, kept her fingers around the useless sword.

Suddenly, the wind whipped hard enough to rip a tree branch from above, and it crashed down onto the group of them. The branch tumbled away, leaving Victoria scratched and her head aching though she'd not borne the brunt of its weight.

The demonic cloud surged again, louder and darker now. Victoria pushed at Sebastian, shoving him toward the open door even as Max tried to pull her back. She shouted, but couldn't even hear herself, and so she shoved Sebastian with all of her strength, leaping after him.

Helped by the black gale force, they tumbled down through the door into the mausoleum.

Four

A Dark Battle

Victoria slammed into Sebastian when they hit the ground, then tumbled onto the rough, cold floor. The wind whipped above her, but the roaring in her ears had eased.

She staggered to her feet, hand on her sword, trying to make out details in the furious, dark world. For a moment, she had an impression of dim illumination, and perhaps the outline of shapes near the floor. Something warm touched her—an oasis in the fury—and she grabbed Sebastian's hand. His grip closed around her hand, strong and solid, anchoring her, as someone—Max?—crashed to the ground behind them.

And then suddenly, the horrible fog seemed to scream in rising desperation, whipping and buffeting even stronger and harder, filling her ears and nose and needling her skin . . . and then all at once, it stopped.

Everything became still.

The door was closed. Had Max done it?

Victoria released her grip on Sebastian and looked around, still mistrustful of the sudden peace. The faint gleam of illumination she'd discerned became a small blue-tinged glow in the far corner of the small chamber. It cast a pearl gray frost over the bare stone walls, blackened by mold and age. A large ash-colored crypt rose low in the center of the room.

"Max?" she said, more to try out her voice in the sudden silence than anything else.

"Brim and Michalas are still out there," he said by way of reply. His voice was low and taut in the quiet.

She wondered if the closing of the door had subdued the curdling fog, or if it merely waited outside, battling harder against Brim and Michalas.

"Victoria." Sebastian had moved away from her, and now crouched near the corner where the dull bluish light shone.

The urgency in his voice had her hurrying past the waist-high crypt to join him, hand on her sword. He stood as she drew closer, revealing that the glow seeped from beneath the wall, and appeared to be curling into the darkness of the chamber. Tendrils of the eerie bluish light coiled up, snaking around Sebastian's boots and legs, writhing up against the wall . . . then dissipated as if losing strength.

Victoria's and Sebastian's eyes met, that odd glow giving his tanned skin a peculiar pallor. She read the worry in his gaze, and knew it echoed her own.

"A door," she said. But what was behind it? Another hurricane of fury? Wayren?

Max moved up to join them, his face stark and taut. "Let's get it open."

Without further discussion, the two men turned to the wall, feeling along with their hands in search of a crevice or gap in the doorframe, while Victoria moved farther away, searching for some other opening.

A hiss of satisfaction in the silence drew her back over to Max. "Here—Vioget, push . . . there."

And then a portion of the wall moved slightly, one side canting inward, and the one nearest Victoria edging out. She braced herself, waiting for an angry burst of foggy blue light. The hair on the back of her neck rose as more coils slipped through the crack, draining into the room through the narrow aperture. Silent, like insidious smoke.

She looked at Max, nodded for him to continue, and the door moved again, levering out of position until it left a gap wide enough for someone to pass through.

Now the chamber glowed with blue and gray smoky light, and the air began to whip up. Victoria heard the roar as it gathered its strength, filling the room, seeming to swell and writhe with fury. A dusty, musty evil smell filled her nose, and an ice-cold sting again pummeled her face and skin through her clothing. The wind swirled against her, pounding and deafening.

She ducked, dodging into the gap, and heard a vague shout behind her. Past the door, she found herself stumbling into another chamber filled with the thrashing blue smoke. It glowed as if possessed.

The illumination was enough to reveal the walls, etched with dark shadows. In the center, dark blue flames roared toward the low ceiling. The smell of death and malevolence was stronger here, the snarling rush of wind louder.

Victoria stayed near the ground where she had more stability, and inched toward the twisting blue flames. The ferocity around her charged and buffeted onto her back and the top of her head, but it was marginally quieter near the ground. Her sword dragged next to her as she moved along, the other accoutrements in her pockets sagging toward the floor.

She'd seen sapphire-colored fire like this once before, when Max had destroyed Akvan's Obelisk—a
demonic shard of obsidian imbued with malevolence.
Whether this pyre of flame protected another such evil
item, or something else, she didn't know.

But she would find out, for she believed it had to be
related to Wayren's disappearance. And it was impera-
tive that they save Wayren, for she was the Venators'
mentor. There were other Venators to replace Brim and
Sebastian and even Victoria, *Illa* Gardella . . . but there
was only one Wayren.

The stone floor burned beneath her fingers, but it
was an odd sensation. Icy heat seared her fingers and
crept through the trousers into her knees. It burned
hot, then immediately blazed cold on her flesh.

Despite the pain, she kept moving toward the flames
as the faint thread of shouts reached her ears. There
was no sense in trying to call back to them. . . . They
wouldn't hear her.

And so far, though the snaking, twisting fog and
cloud was loud and malicious, it hadn't attacked or
seemed able to injure her. She kept crawling.

Finally, the flames roared next to her, and she could
see that the fire burned in a ring.

And in the center of the ring was a pale, lifeless
body.

Wayren.

Her long blond hair lay spread over her torso and
on the ground, and her face was turned toward Victoria. Her eyes were closed, and she was not moving.

Rearing back onto her knees, Victoria glanced behind her and could see nothing but faint shapes moving amid the blasting smoke. The blaze reached the
ceiling, and when she looked up, she saw more shapes
flitting and skittering through the tips of the flames
like large bats or birds. The shapes were amorphous,

yet more solid than the smoke and fog that continued to envelop her.

The fire was too tall for her to try to jump over, or come down from the ceiling, even if she were able to get high enough amid those ugly black shadows. The only way to get to Wayren was through the blaze.

Victoria pulled to her feet, unsheathing her sword. The wind continued to batter, tearing her hair from its braid and sending long locks flying into her face, and around her shoulders and torso. It flicked into the blue flames, caught, and sparked, sending Victoria stumbling back, struggling to stuff her loose hair down inside her shirt. The last thing she needed was for it to catch fire.

When she'd subdued her curls as much as possible in the ferocious vortex, she stepped forward again and swung the sword, slicing it through the evil blaze to see if it would allow the metal to pass. As it swished through, cutting into the flames, something stunned the metal blade, and it vibrated in her hands.

The trembling was so strong that she felt it all the way up her arms and into her torso. She swung again, and again the vibration caught hold, and this time a hot sizzle followed it, slamming into her body.

Victoria stumbled back and stared at the flames, breathing heavily, wondering briefly if Max and Sebastian had followed her into the room, or if something had stopped them.

She looked at Wayren again. The woman hadn't moved, but Victoria didn't think she was dead. If she'd been killed, why protect the body with this prison of fire? There'd be no need. She *had* to be alive and able to be saved.

But how? *How?*

In frustration, Victoria swiped her blade again, and this time, it was even harder to drive it through the fire.

The wind nearly knocked her off her feet, and it blared in her ears, drowning out everything, even the crackle of flame. Her hair swirled again, coming loose from the collar of her shirt.

The strength of the flames was increasing, incensed by her attempts to battle it. She had to make a choice. She had to get to Wayren, even if it meant going through the fire.

And then she remembered that deep pocket of her trousers in which she carried a bottle of holy water. Pulling it out, she removed the cork and, still huddled near the floor, splashed a bit of the water up and into the flames.

They hissed and leapt back, turning sunny yellow and cowering for the briefest of moments ... then roaring back with a vengeance, angrier and louder and hotter.

That was it.

Victoria gathered herself up, holding the sword in front of her, and backed up several steps. She bumped into someone behind her, and his hands grabbed at her. She heard her name carried away on the wind, though it was shouted into her ear.

"Wayren!" she yelled back, trying to make him—it was Sebastian—understand. She lifted up the bottle of water and shoved it into his face so he could see it, then turned away, knowing that the blaze was growing stronger with every moment of delay.

Tearing away from him, she dashed through the thick, churning smoke and hurricane-force wind, splashing the entire contents of the bottle just as she leapt into the flames.

The yellow lull allowed her to clear the flames and tumble onto the ground near Wayren, and the force of her jump sent her lurching into the woman's legs. But the flames remained in their circle around them, and it was eerily quiet within the enclosure.

Victoria scrambled over next to Wayren's face and touched her cheek. It was warm, and she moved her hand along the woman's neck to feel for a pulse. She felt nothing. *Nothing.*

No.

She smoothed a hand over the prone woman's torso, praying to feel the shift of breath. Just as she did so, Wayren moved beneath her. A slight movement, not even a breath, but a little shift. Almost a shudder.

"Wayren," Victoria said urgently. She felt again for a pulse, but could feel no sign of life at Wayren's neck or wrist. Yet her body was warm and felt . . . alive.

Victoria heard a distant shout and looked over to see Max and Sebastian on the other side of the flames. Their faces were muted by the swirl of angry blue fog, and whatever Max was shouting at her was lost in the whirlwind.

He gestured sharply and she looked up, then immediately dove to the ground, covering Wayren.

The heavy black shapes had become solid ones, with burning eyes of red and orange, and they swooped and skulked. She saw the flash of a claw and the gleam of a long, curved fang, and Victoria reached for her sword.

Standing in the middle of the blue flames, she struck out at the nearest black shape as it dove closer. Her blade went right through it, and a blast of frigid cold swept over her. Staggering back from the force of it, Victoria nearly fell into the blaze behind her.

She caught herself in time, using the tip of her sword, and looked back over at Max and Sebastian. They were gesturing to each other, and she couldn't tell what they were doing.

A black shape swooped again, and Victoria watched for its eyes, measured, and struck again with her sword, aiming for the neck area.

Reaching up, her arms made a long, high arc, and

the blade sliced into the black being. It disintegrated into a burst of smoke. Then another one, and another, swooped down harder and faster, stirring the calm air amid the flames.

One of them scored her arm and shoulder with its claws, and the other rushed over—and *through* her . . . God, *through* her!—sending her stumbling once again toward the flames. Cold shudders paralyzed her for a moment as Victoria collapsed to the ground. Her stomach pitched, and nausea trammeled through her, her muscles weakened and shivering. She struggled to breathe, fought to steady the dizziness that crushed her to the stone floor. Her fingers had loosened over the sword, and she had to focus hard, so *hard*, to close them again. The weight of the heavy hilt steadied her a bit, and she groped at her belly to touch the two *vis bullae* beneath her shirt.

Several long moments she lay still, hunched away from the swooping shadows, praying that neither Max nor Sebastian was foolish enough to try to join her. Especially Max, who acted as though he still wore the *vis bulla*.

The last thing they needed was for all of them to be trapped within this wall of flame.

When she was able to regain control of her movements, she raised her head and crawled back toward Wayren. Staying close to the ground, she looked beyond the flames and toward Max and Sebastian. They were foggy, but she saw that they were holding something up in their hands.

It looked like they each had a bottle. Holy water?

Sebastian shouted something, and Max made hand signals, and Victoria nodded back to them. She gathered up Wayren's warm, limp body over her shoulder, staying as close to the ground as she could, and dodged another swoop of the black demons.

Max raised his fist and shook it. . . . One . . . two . . . *three*.

The arms of the two men thrust out in unison. Victoria heard the sizzle and hush of the flames as they cowered low, yellow, and bright, and she launched herself into and through the path they'd made.

She crashed into Max, and they fell to the ground. Once again, she was back in the midst of the raging wind, where sound was drowned out and the force of the smoky fog battered at her.

Still holding on to Wayren, Victoria began to scramble toward the door, keeping the limp body cupped near her own.

Before she'd moved very far, however, strong hands pulled at her. Max's face was there, suddenly, close to hers, and he gestured sharply with his head in the opposite direction.

She nodded, knowing that Max had an unerring sense of direction . . . and she didn't. Suddenly Sebastian was there, too. The three of them huddled together over Wayren, protecting her, and, with Max leading the way, stumbled, clustered together, through the deafening, blinding, stinging storm.

The black shadows slung down low, gouging with very definite claws. One of them caught in her hair and pulled, nearly lifting her off the ground. It felt as though the top of her head would be torn off.

She cried out and released her hold on Wayren, grabbing at her own hair and trying to pull up her sword without slicing into her companions, but before she could do so, she felt Sebastian move next to her. Suddenly, her head was released, and she saw the angry curls of the disintegrating demon. Pain still screamed over her scalp, and she was certain half of her head was bald, but she had scarcely any time to recover before another swoop and the cut of sharp talons over her shoulders and along her back.

Max and Sebastian fared little better. They bumped and moved and struggled against each other, protecting Wayren as they tried to beat off the demonic creatures. Victoria found herself trying to shield Max as well. And she noticed, even in the blur of movement and muting fog, that he moved more slowly and heavily than she and Sebastian. She tried to stay close to him, protecting his back and shoulders from the swerving demon shadows.

Somehow, Max found his way to the levered door through which they'd come. Victoria tripped as they went through, catching her shoulder against the corner, and one of the horrible creatures slammed into her back.

She lost her hold on Wayren again, and felt the full force of the shadowy wraith push her very substantially into the stone wall. Her head slammed into stone, sending a ringing into her ears that squealed over and beyond the loud roar.

Someone pulled on her, and she stumbled along, suddenly aware of the warm liquid seeping through her clothing and the dripping on her arms making her hands slippery and sticky.

It was darker here, in the first chamber they'd entered—not because there was less of the glowing blue smoke, but because there were more of the horrible black shadows. They seemed to have multiplied. But Victoria and her companions moved on toward the door, compressed around Wayren.

At last they reached the outside entrance. They were so closely knit together that she felt Max's movements as he reached for the door, pushing at it, and Sebastian close behind her. When he raised his arm with his own sword, he shifted against Victoria, and she felt the thrust, the arc of each movement. She was aware of the weight of Wayren, the warmth of her body, the silk of her hair, and the stone wall against her cheek. . . .

And suddenly, they were falling through the open door, and the roaring noise softened, the musty stench of malice eased. The fog lessened, and the black shadows skittered up and away.

The door had opened. They were on the steps outside.

Five

In Which Max Takes the Long Road Home

Being outside did not wholly protect them from the heavy black shadows and the swooping, swirling mass of fog, but it tempered the ferocity of the storm contained by the small building. Brim and Michalas must have been waiting nearby, for as soon as Victoria and the others spilled out of the door, they helped pull them to their feet.

Yet, out here, the shadowy creatures with claws and burning eyes had more room to dive, with gouging fangs and grasping talons. One grabbed Victoria by the shoulders, lifting her feet from the ground. She relinquished her hold on Wayren, groping for her sword.

She sliced up and through the demon, feeling that nauseating cold again, but also finding her mark. As she fell back to the trampled grass, she looked up and saw the moon glinting through the roiling fog.

If they got out of the graveyard, they'd be safe. Or at least safer.

She hoped.

Max alone was holding Wayren now, bent over her, presenting his back to the threat above as Brim and Victoria battled back the demons.

If they could fight their way toward the gate . . . would the walls of the cemetery confine the demonic fog?

Sebastian and Michalas had the presence of mind to close the door of the mausoleum, and together they battled it shut. The wind eased, and the spill of shadows stopped, though a faint tendril of blue smoke curled stubbornly through a crack. The fog ebbed and quieted a bit so that they could at least see one another. Blood streamed down Brim's cheek, and Sebastian had a long red welt over the side of his face.

"This way," Victoria shouted, pushing at the hair caught in her mouth, and started toward the gate before the door could burst open. It shuddered and trembled.

The wind whipped up again as they reached the gate, and a billow of black engulfed them. Victoria heard the shriek and scream of its fury, and she turned to Brim. "Holy water!" she shouted.

As he ran, Brim dug deep into his coat and pulled out a bottle, and a large silver cross. The wind buffeted and whipped, sending another tree branch crashing onto the ground. The missile, which was as thick around as a man, barely missed slamming into Brim and just grazed his shoulder. He offered her the bottle, but she turned to Max, who still huddled over Wayren.

Victoria's hair thrashed around her face like a weapon, and the gust of blackness nearly sent her into the wall. Something wet trickled down her cheek, and warmed her neck. She had to get Wayren out of here, and there was only one way to ensure her escape. She grabbed Max's face and lifted it to look into his eyes. "Take her. Take Brim. Go. We'll distract."

She shoved him toward a sprawling bush, and he slid under it with his burden, but not before she saw the look he gave her. *Be safe.*

Brim joined him, armed with holy water, and Victoria, Sebastian, and Michalas began to inch away from the bush and the gate, battling at the evil forces.

Victoria didn't know what sort of perception the malevolence had, but the swooping shadows, at least, seemed to be able to tell where to dive and strike. If they could at least draw their attention away, perhaps Brim and Max could slip out of the gate safely with Wayren.

Max watched Victoria slip away, her face streaked with blood, dark hair plastered in the sticky mess. The back of her shirt was dark with more blood and torn to shreds.

He forced his attention to Wayren, who'd stirred more than once in his arms, and looked over at Brim, who crouched next to him and for once didn't appear to be enjoying the battle.

Wayren had to be taken away from the demons that drained her of her strength and power before it was too late. It was possible yet to save her, for she was already showing signs of life now that she'd been removed from captivity.

If Victoria's plan to distract the demons by battling them worked, they'd have only a few moments to make a dash for the waiting horses, on the other side of the bent gate.

Max's lips flattened. He knew why she'd chosen him to take Wayren. He was the weakest of the group, no longer protected by the *vis bulla*.

Victoria would never have tried to protect him before.

And she'd chosen Brim . . . who could not only sense vampires, but demons as well.

What a warrior—and a leader—she'd become.

Something pinched deep inside him. Anger, frustration. Self-pity.

Then he realized it was time. With one last glance toward her, with her lethal blade and impractical mass of long, dark hair, Max slid out from under the bush, carrying Wayren against his chest. Ignoring the painful gouges in his back, he ran, hunching head and shoulders over his burden as the creatures swooped and dove.

Brim was behind him, and though Max didn't dare glance over his shoulder as he stumbled toward the gate, he knew the big black man was slicing with sword and splashing holy water in their wake.

The iron gate shone under the moon and stars, clearer now as they were away from the foggy black smoke. He leapt and glided over it without pause, using the half-flying *qinggong* skills Kritanu had taught him.

Once over the broken gate, Max didn't hesitate but lifted Wayren over his horse and untied the reins looped over a tree branch. A quick glance told him that Brim had made it to the gate, but just as Max leapt into the saddle, he saw with horror that Brim, who had put one foot onto the curved metal, was suddenly engulfed by the black shadows. They pelted down on him, talons shiny and red eyes bright, and the man crumpled to his knees, devoured by the shadows.

Christ. Max looked back, knowing he couldn't return, knowing he had to get Wayren to safety. Every bit of his being needed to return, begged to go back and help . . . to save Brim . . . and Victoria. *Victoria.*

She would be next.

Yet he knew what had to be done; he'd lectured Victoria about it often enough.

You can no longer think only of yourself, of your needs

*and desires. You must recognize the far-reaching conse-
quences of your actions.*

And that was why he had to wheel the horse around
and slam his heels into its flanks and ride pell-mell back
to town, back to the house where Kritanu waited . . .
back to where Wayren would be safe.

And it was also why he *must* leave London.

He shoved Wayren forward so she sagged, propped
against the horse's neck, then leapt off. He couldn't do
it, by God.

Twenty jarring, running steps took him back toward
the cemetery gate, where the black shadows pitched,
and dove against Brim. Sword in his hand, Max noticed how his arm screamed in pain and realized he
was streaming blood. Ears ringing, he reached the
damaged gate in time to see Brim's arm rise from beneath the writhing black. The gleam of his sword sliced
through the air as Max joined the fray, sending one of
the attackers into swirls of dark fog.

Raising his own weapon at one of the swooping
birdlike creatures, he lunged at the amorphous neck
area. The blade arced through the evil black shadow as
though through a fog, and a streak of cold paralyzed
him.

Max staggered, his arms trembling with the sudden
overwhelming chill, and he fought the dip of his belly
as he staggered against the stone wall. But he raised
that sword again, feeling the scream of pain along his
arm as another demonic shadow dove into him. Claws
dug into the back of his shoulders, gouging in the same
wound, drawing forth a deep, guttural cry of pain as
he turned again. The sword was heavy, but Max aimed
well. . . . He whirled around and whipped the blade
through the being. Stumbling back, he saw it burst into
dark, fizzing curls.

Breathless with exertion, nearly blind with pain,

Max lunged forward again. Unable to rise from the ground, Brim nevertheless fought to beat back the never-ending crowd of shadows, slashing up and out with his sword. Despite the blood streaming from him, winging through the air with every movement, Max fought hard . . . but not as quickly and powerfully as Vioget, whose blade suddenly appeared, slashing and gleaming like stars winking in the night.

The blond man had arrived like the cavalry, leaping into the fray, moving with speed and assurance despite the continuing attack of the shadows. Max's movements, though lethal and strong, came slower and with less power, and when he and Vioget came face-to-face, the other man said, "Go! Take her and go."

Blood streaked his handsome face, but determination—and a bit of satisfaction—twisted his lips. After so many years away from it, he'd come to love the battle again.

Max made one last vicious slash, marking a shadowy target, and said, "Bring her back. This time."

Vioget's eyes met his, and a flash of anger dissolved the satisfaction there. He knew Max was referring to when Vioget's grandfather, the vampire Beauregard, had nearly turned Victoria—and Max had been the one to bring her back. Sebastian alone couldn't have done it.

Then Max whirled away, ducking under another darting shadow. He slashed above him with the sword, missed his mark again, dammit. He was growing weary . . . and he felt that blast of nauseating, paralyzing cold stagger him. He nearly fell, saw the red eyes and bared teeth of the demon as he tried to regain control of his sword—but Sebastian was there, with his gleaming silver blade, saving his bloody life yet again.

As the creature disintegrated into a foul-smelling tangle of coils, Max ran unsteadily toward the horse, where Wayren still slumped. A foglike tendril teased after him, cold and musty.

Dammit. *Dammit.* Had his delay, his coming back, given the demons a chance to find Wayren?

Max used the *qinggong* he had mastered to fly forward and leap onto the horse. Gathering up the reins, he slipped an arm around Wayren, huddling her back against him, and slammed his heels into the flanks below. His mount surged forward with a great leap, and Max bent low, closing his eyes for a moment to banish the agony that coursed through his body.

After no more than a pace or two, he looked behind him.

He saw the roiling black cloud that was still somehow contained by the walls of the cemetery, except for a few slender tendrils. He pulled back on the reins, ignoring the agonizing pain in his back and arms. The frantic horse fought the bit, needing to charge ahead . . . but Max forced him around, turning on the road to look back again.

The black cloud pitched and rolled, clear below the night sky lightened by moon and stars. It crept beyond the boundaries of the cemetery, slowly, as if searching. Max could hear the rising of the wind as it crooned eerily. . . . It sought something. It knew Wayren was gone.

Bloody hell. He'd never seen anything like this. Ice settled over him as he stared back.

Something unaccountably evil burned here. Something that, he feared, would change everything.

At that moment, Wayren moved. She shifted, groaned, and Max's attention came back to her.

"Wayren," he said as she lifted her head as though trying to waken from a dream.

Her eyes fluttered, but they didn't open, and she seemed to sag further in his arms. Bone white in the silvery light, her face stretched taut and still like porcelain.

She was ill, gravely weakened by this permeating malevolence. If she was to survive, he had to get her away.

Max looked back toward the cemetery one last time,
then kicked the horse again. And they were off.

Dawn reached up from behind the line of London
rooftops by the time Max returned to the town house.
Wayren had moved, awakening enough to sag back
against him and grasp the horse's mane with weak fingers. His body, shaky from loss of blood, ached with
every movement. Black dots and long, slender shadows danced before his eyes. The memory of every
sword slash, every swipe of the blade replayed in his
mind. Every stumble, every missed arc, every time
he'd been too slow . . . too weak.

He tired more easily, hurt too strongly, bled too
damn much.

She'd been right to send him away.

He rode directly into the small stable, pounding on
the wall to awaken the groom as he slid to the ground.
No one was there to see his knees buckle and him stagger before catching himself, still holding Wayren.

The groom, a bulky, redheaded young man named
Oliver, appeared, and Max tossed the reins to him. No
explanation was needed.

Inside the house, Kritanu waited. Lights shining in
the windows told Max that the elderly man hadn't left
his vigil since sending Brim and Michalas after them.

Words weren't necessary; the grave condition of
Wayren, who attempted to stand but needed to lean
against Max, spoke for itself.

"I've sent word to Ylito," Kritanu said quietly, helping Max settle Wayren into a large chair. "The birds fly
fast; perhaps we will hear by tomorrow if he has any
wisdom."

The birds did indeed fly quickly, helped, Max knew,

by the same holy power that protected and strengthened the Venators through their *vis bullae*. Ylito, the hermetic who dabbled in herbalry, alchemy, and other spiritual elements, was likely still in Rome. But with the assistance of the message pigeons, he could share any knowledge that might help Wayren.

"Max." She spoke at that moment, her voice low and weak. "Sit." Her hand shifted in her lap as if too weak to make the full gesture.

He didn't want to sit. He wanted to go back out, get a fresh horse from somewhere, and fly back through town, over the Thames, to that demonic cemetery so that he could drag Victoria to safety.

Damn. What a bloody mess he'd become.

Weak. Indecisive. Battered.

"Sit," Wayren said again, more strongly now. "Before you fall."

Kritanu, who'd stepped away to give the butler, Charley, some murmured orders, turned to the large cabinet that sat in this small parlor. As he fumbled with its latch, using his one hand, he asked, "What happened? Victoria? The others?"

Max shrugged and felt a renewed twinge in his shoulder. His knees trembled. If he didn't sit soon, they'd leave him no choice. If he did succumb and sit, he'd not stand again. "Fighting the demons that took Wayren. The others held them back so we could get away."

Kritanu turned from the cabinet, and Max saw that he held the Gardella family Bible. An ancient tome, made up of hand-bound pages yellow and brittle with age, this book held the names of those called to the Gardella Legacy—both Venators born, as Victoria was, and Venators chosen, as Max was.

Had been.

Damn Lilith.

She'd taken everything from him.

Max gave in. His knees bent, and he slid into one of the chairs, using his grip on its arm to give his acquiescence an appearance of grace.

He watched as Kritanu brought the Bible to Wayren and rested it, open, on her lap. It dwarfed her, hanging over the edges of her slender legs and dirty, torn gown. She placed her hands on it, closed her weary eyes, and Max watched as color began to seep back into her face.

Her pale lips moved silently, flushing slowly with pink. Her fingers stopped trembling and the tension in her face eased.

Suddenly she opened her eyes and looked at him with clear gray-blue orbs. "Thank you, Max. I know how difficult it was for you to leave."

"I was ordered to go."

She opened her mouth as if to say something else, then paused, tilting her head to the side like Myza. Her eyes glittered brightly and she exchanged a quick look with Kritanu, who'd received a bowl of water from Charley and curled his maimed arm around it. In his other hand, he held a soft cloth. It dripped, and some pungent smell wafted from it.

Wordlessly, Max took the cloth and buried his face in it, inhaling whatever herbal decoction it had been steeped in, scrubbing away the blood and grime. Every muscle in his body ached, yet they gathered beneath his skin, demanding to be put to use, taut and ready.

He couldn't sit here. And wait.

And wait.

He rubbed his face harder.

"Thrush has returned."

Wayren's quiet words brought Max's hands down and his face from the damp cloth, which had cooled in the interim. Then he heard a soft clinking tap at the window, but Kritanu was already there, unlatching it and pushing it open.

If Thrush had returned . . .

Max felt jittery and cold.

"I cannot find a message." With only one hand, Kritanu couldn't easily remove the small tube from the bird's leg; but instead of bringing it to Max, he offered the bird to Wayren.

Hell. Did he look that bad?

Wayren looked up from the pigeon. "There is no message."

No message.

Max started to rise, but Wayren glared at him, raising a hand. It was surprisingly steady. "Be still. Thrush would not have left Myza alone. They had nothing with which to send a message."

Was he that damned transparent?

He remained in his seat and tried not to look toward the window, tried not to appear as though every bloody creaking board in the house snapped him to attention.

"Max, it's time that you returned to the Venators."

Despite the hollow of pain and pounding anxiety in which he sat, Max heard and understood Wayren's words. "It's impossible," he said, taking no care to hide the bitterness. Lilith had made certain that when he broke her hold over him, he would be unable to become a Venator again. Her bite, enhanced by a special salve that bound him to her, had tainted his blood. "You know it. And without a *vis*, I am nothing but a liability."

"Indeed. You were quite the liability tonight," Wayren said drily.

Max lifted his eyes to meet hers, and his sharp retort remained unspoken. Nevertheless. "My blood is tainted by Lilith. I cannot pass the Trial again, even if I should wish to try."

"You don't wish it?"

To become whole again? With all of his being.

And yet . . . never again.

"I won't go back . . . to that."

Wayren looked steadily at him. "Ylito has been studying your blood," she said as though he hadn't spoken.

"My blood?" Then he remembered. He'd sliced his arm open during that black ordeal in Roma. Victoria had needed blood in order to help fight back Beauregard's blood as it attempted to turn her undead. Because his blood was not of the Gardellas, it was useless, but . . . "Ylito kept it?"

Wayren nodded. "That was why I asked for you to give some, even though we did not believe it could be used for Victoria. I asked Ylito to study it, to see if Lilith's taint was real. Or if she lied."

He didn't ask. Max closed his mouth.

The Trial to become a Venator for one not called by the Gardella Legacy, one without the blood of the family in his veins, was a life-or-death proposition. Max had not cared about dying the first time he'd undergone the test.

In fact, he'd fairly wished for death. Yearned for it, for years.

But now.

He wasn't afraid of it.

He just . . . didn't want it. Yet.

He looked at Wayren and read the answer to the unspoken question. "Ylito believes there is no taint," she said, reaffirming his thoughts.

Just then, his keen ears recognized a new sound from the front of the house. Max surged to his feet, ignoring the rush of light-headedness and the renewed flow of warmth down his arm, moving toward the foyer.

Flinging the door open, he saw the shadowy figures

sliding from their horses. The big, burly Brim, moving slowly, but on his own, thank God. The tight strawberry blond curls of Michalas as he dismounted his horse.

There was another person turned away, pulling a limp body down from a horse.

Max hurried down the steps . . . without appearing to hurry. Hiding his fear.

The figure turned, steadying the inert bundle, and Max saw that it was Victoria, bloody and wild-faced, helping Sebastian stagger toward the house.

Six

An Unwelcome Summons

"Wayren?" asked Victoria as soon as she saw Max coming toward her. She didn't have to ask the other question that had burned in her mind all during the long ride home. Though his face looked haggard in the early dawn, and she could see bloodstains all over his clothing, he was walking. Limping, moving slowly, but walking. Thank God.

Thank God.

"Recovered," he said.

The tension drained from her, then surged back.

They were safe. For now.

Victoria saw Max's attention shift to Sebastian, who sagged against her, an arm around her neck while she steadied him with one around his waist. She suspected he was exaggerating his weakness just a bit, for his fingers had been tracing little designs under her braid for the last fifteen minutes. The gentle caresses sent shivers skittering over her shoulders, and down along her arms, reminding her that Sebastian, unlike Max, had no problem with intimacy.

At least with her.

When they left the cemetery, Sebastian had been unable to walk on his own, due to a deep slash from hip to knee. Though his face had creased with pain, his eyes gleamed with delight when she suggested that he ride pillion with her so that she could keep him balanced on the cantering horse. His leg was still bleeding; she'd felt the warmth of his blood soak through the back of her left trouser leg as they rode.

And though his leg was immobile, his hands had not been. Settling at her hips, those strong fingers had curled around them like the handles of a teacup as he leaned gently against her wounded back.

Max turned away, moving toward Brim, leaving Victoria and Sebastian to make their way up the three steps onto the front stoop. Kritanu waited in the doorway.

The sun seemed to move suddenly, and all at once, clear yellow beams shone between rooftops and chimney peaks as though the earth's lamp had been turned brighter. Victoria found it difficult to believe that only hours before, she'd dressed to attend Lady Winnie's dance and had walked down these very steps in that crimson gown.

Now it felt as though many things had changed, in some indefinable way.

Inside, Victoria went directly to Wayren, who, though she appeared fully recovered, did not rise when they came into the small room.

"Thank you," she said to Victoria, extending her slender hands.

Victoria took them, feeling the warmth, the peace that always came with Wayren's touch. She didn't know as much as she'd like to about the woman. But based on what she'd seen of her at the hands of the demons, she felt as if she'd learned quite a bit tonight. She shook off the older woman's gratitude. "It was Max who got you to safety."

Wayren's fingers tightened over Victoria's, and their eyes met. "It was both of you. You had to let him go . . . and he had to go."

Victoria felt a sudden unexpected flush warm her face, and an automatic desire to pull away. The feelings were still new to her, and so deeply buried that it felt uncomfortable to have them spoken of so easily. So openly. Yet Wayren understood how difficult it had been to send Max away, where she could no longer watch over him . . . and how, at the same time, she'd known he was the one she could rely on to succeed in taking Wayren to safety.

"What happened?" Victoria asked, easing her aching body onto the floor next to Wayren. She was strangely loath to release the woman's hands, though her muscles reverberated with the remnants of battle. She ached, she bled, she trembled . . . yet the protective *vis bullae* had ensured that it was so much easier than it could have been.

"They took me when I wasn't expecting it," Wayren said simply. "I had gone to an old graveyard to see to . . . something. Not the one in which you found me, I don't believe. But it's a bit of a muddle in my mind. The black shadow demons pummeled me, flying into me, weakening me so I couldn't call on my power, cutting off my resistance."

Victoria nodded, remembering the feel of those winged creatures shoving into her body, through her, leaving her cold and paralyzed, and shuddered. It was a miracle Wayren hadn't been killed.

But . . . she hadn't been breathing when Victoria found her. No heartbeat. Yet . . . she moved. Lived.

"Max explained how you found me. Thank God for Myza." Wayren looked over, and Victoria noticed for the first time that Kritanu cradled the small bird against his body.

"Who or what was it?" Victoria asked. She felt Sebastian brush against her as he limped to a chair nearby, his hand lightly touching the top of her head.

Wayren looked around the room, her serene face grave. "Brim, Michalas . . . you returned to help. Thank you. And Sebastian." She looked at him steadily, then nodded. "My thanks." Her eyes lingered on him a bit longer than necessary, then slid away. "Fallen angels. Demons. They took me. . . . For what purpose, I'm not yet certain. But the very fact that they dared to touch me . . ." Her eyes looked like cool moonstones for a moment, clear and colorless, as she faded into silence.

Suddenly, she seemed to come back to herself. "I am tired, Victoria, and you must have your injuries seen to. All of you. And some rest. I am safe here . . . and it will keep until we've all had a chance to rest."

Victoria pulled slowly to her feet, her hand squeezing, then finally releasing Wayren's. "I'm glad you'll stay here tonight," she told the older woman. "We'll all rest easier."

The draft that Kritanu had given him leeched away some of the agony radiating through Max's body, though it pained him to admit it was needed. But it was.

His muscles trembling, his salved wounds still oozing stubbornly, he changed out of his dirty clothes, all the while grimly considering Wayren's request.

Become a Venator again.

He'd not need the bloody draft if he did. He'd not need to step aside and let a faster, stronger Vioget save a comrade. He'd have no reason to leave.

Yet he couldn't bear to stay.

Even if he got his Venator capabilities back, he couldn't. He couldn't trust himself to be strong enough, to do the right thing.

To share her.

Pouring the still-hot water into the basin, Max felt a wave of steam rise. He splashed it on his face and chest, gasping at the sudden twinge of pain when he moved his arms too vigorously in his ablutions, and pausing to catch his breath.

His face was buried in one of Kritanu's lemon-scented towels when there came a knock at the door. He flung the door open, startling the twitchy red-haired servant, Oliver. The groom who'd taken his mount earlier tonight had obviously been pressed into other service within the small household.

"Beg your pardon, sir, but my lady wishes you to attend on her," Oliver said most correctly.

Max glowered at him. "My lady?" Wayren or Victoria?

Oliver looked confused for a moment, then recovered, offering, "Lady Rockley." Apparently, he didn't consider Wayren a lady, which wasn't surprising. Only the Venators—and the evil ones—knew what she was capable of.

Max wadded up the towel and tossed it onto the table. One end flipped over the side of the basin, landing a corner in the water. Blast it. Could she not leave him be? He pulled out his last clean shirt and tugged it over his damp skin, where it seemed to stick everywhere. Just as his head emerged from the opening, he heard the man add, "She awaits you in her chamber."

Max stilled, his hands crushing into the soft linen. "Her chamber?"

Christ.

Then he centered on the whirl of thoughts—and,

damnation, the *images*—that bit of information invoked, and extracted the most palatable one. Victoria's face had been dead white and her clothes soaked with blood. Was she injured more severely than he'd thought? She'd never released Wayren's hand during their short meeting in the parlor.

Max opened his mouth to ask Oliver, but the young man had scuttled off, leaving the door ajar.

There was nothing for it but to "attend to her."

His mouth closed grimly, his jaw tight, he set off, certain that whatever he found, it wouldn't be to his liking.

When he reached Victoria's chamber, his peremptory knock produced no response. Max waited for a moment, then knocked again, a bit harder, and the door edged open. Hell. Was he supposed to go in?

Blast it.

He'd not hesitated entering her chamber a few months ago when he first came back to London. He'd been uninvited then.

And now it was morning. Filled with light, which meant exposure. And few shadows in which to hide.

Max pushed the door open, his attention going immediately to the bed. It was empty.

He stepped inside and closed the door, firmly, behind him, looking around the chamber. Early-morning sunlight filtered through the nearby tree branches, casting the small room in a soft warm glow. The bed lay pristine and made, high off the ground, with a bumpy white coverlet. The dressing table was situated near the entrance to what must be a small dressing room. The mirrored table held an array of ladylike items—and a few that were not so ladylike: perfume bottles, combs, brushes, jewelry, stakes, holy water vials. . . .

He paused and looked more closely, seeking a slender blue-tinted bottle. No. It was gone. The potion that he knew Victoria drank in order to keep from getting with child. Aunt Eustacia, and now Kritanu, made it for her. But it was gone, and he knew that Victoria had made good on her promise to stop taking it.

Max did not want to consider the implications of that fact, and he turned abruptly to examine the rest of the room.

The fireplace held a neat stack of kindling ready to be lit should the weather turn chill or rainy. A chair in the corner near the floor-to-ceiling drapes would provide a good, distant seat from any other furnishings or activity in the room; it was the same chair in which he'd sat when he'd visited her chamber before. This morning, the windows had been flung open, and a soft breeze filtered through them.

Where the hell was Victoria? Had she sent for him or not?

Suddenly, he heard a faint . . . *splash*. Water.

Max looked past the dressing table toward the dressing room and swore. Under his breath.

She was taking a bloody *bath*.

He turned, ready to flee, when the chamber door opened and in bustled Verbena, the poof-haired maid. She carried a load of linens and didn't appear surprised to see him.

And now it was too damned late for him to slip out without being noticed.

"Oh, an' there y'are," the maid said, bustling past him. "S'sorry t'keep ye waiting, my lord, sir," she added, her skirts sending a glass bottle clinking against another on the table as she hurried into the dressing room.

Where Victoria was bathing.

Christ. Almighty.

Max considered making his escape anyway when the chamber door opened again and in limped Vioget.

He hadn't even knocked.

And he looked exceedingly pleased with himself as he came into the room dressed no more formally than Max himself, in trousers and an untucked shirt. Vioget never went about in such dishabille. He likely thought he'd not long be attired at all.

Fully aware of Vioget's penchant for carriage seductions, Max couldn't keep his mouth closed. "You're a bit out of your element, Vioget. There's not a carriage in the vicinity."

He had to give the man credit; he eclipsed his shock almost immediately. "What are you doing here?"

"Likely the same as you," Max replied smoothly, sinking into the chair in the corner. "Responding to our ladyship's beck and call. Unless you weren't beckoned and are calling uninvited?"

"I was referring to your presence in London, not in this chamber," Vioget responded.

Max looked away. Bloody damned good question. If he'd leave, Victoria would have no choice but to be with Vioget.

Now that she wasn't drinking from the little blue bottle.

He eyed Vioget with a mixture of loathing and candor. For all the man's faults, Max knew Sebastian cared for Victoria and would protect the woman who feared little and needed no protection—at least, overt protection.

If only Max would get out of his way and allow him to do what both men wanted Vioget to do.

"She attended a ball without an escort last evening," Max said. "And left with none other than George Starcasset. Perhaps if you were a bit more attentive, I could leave you to your courtship."

Vioget's fist tightened, and for a moment, Max thought he might use it. His glance flickered down to the clenched fingers, then back up to meet Vioget's eyes. *Yes.*

Just then, he heard the quiet scuff of bare feet and the soft swish of clothing. Victoria entered the chamber, fresh from her bath. Her face flushed from the heat, her eyes bright, she brought in a waft of something spicy and exotic. She was properly clothed in a neck-to-floor robe. Only her bare toes peeked out, and in light of the fact that both Max and Vioget had seen—touched, tasted—considerably more than those slender digits, it seemed ridiculous to focus on that immodest display.

"Ah, so you're both here. Good." She sat on the edge of her bed, high enough off the ground that her feet didn't quite touch. "I'm sorry for bringing you in here, but there was no other place for us to talk. Wayren is in the parlor, and I didn't want to disturb her . . . and Brim and Michalas are sleeping on the floor in the *kalari* room. The house isn't large enough to accommodate so many people." She raised her chin, as if challenging him to argue that they could have met in the dining room, or . . . somewhere. Else.

In the most surreal moment of his life, Max realized he was about to have a strategy meeting with Victoria and Vioget in her bedchamber.

Someday, perhaps, he would find it amusing.

"Brim and Michalas aren't invited?" he drawled. "What a shame." Her hair fell in a dark cascade over one of her shoulders, and he remembered her scream as the clawed demon had lifted her by the scalp.

Victoria looked at him, and hell if there wasn't a glaze of smugness in her expression. "I apologize for the informality of the accommodations, Max," she said. "I realize you'd prefer to be anywhere but here."

Bull's-eye.

She turned to Vioget, who'd selected the chair in

front of the dressing table, turning it to face the rest of the room. "How is your leg?"

"Verbena assisted Kritanu, and I do believe that between their efforts, I'll be able to retain that limb, at least." Vioget's smile held a bit of self-deprecation, and Max's attention flickered to the man's left hand—which was missing two knuckles of his little finger, thanks to a particularly bloodthirsty woman named Sara Regalado.

"I never doubted that," Victoria said, shifting on the edge of the bed. The hem of her robe gapped a bit, revealing a slice of the gown beneath it.

Max recognized it. Unfortunately. The fabric was the same pale lilac as the lacy, satin-skirted night rail she'd been wearing the last time he'd ventured into her chamber. The one that left little to the imagination, as the bodice was made purely of lace. At the time, he'd complained, telling her to cover up the ghastly gown . . . but he suspected in retrospect that she'd realized it wasn't because of the design that he'd insisted. Hell.

"Perhaps I should take a look at it, Sebastian. Just to make certain," Victoria was saying. She leaned forward, and the front of her robe gapped a bit, giving a hint of shadow and textured lace.

"Perhaps we could get to the matter at hand," Max said crisply. "Then I can excuse myself and the two of you can examine each other's injuries to your hearts' content."

He found it a bit more difficult to sound bored and annoyed today. And when Vioget gave him an arch look, Max merely ignored the smugness in his face.

It really would be best if he took himself away and disappeared. For good.

At least then he'd not have such trouble making decisions. And sticking to them.

Victoria drew the edges of her robe closed and straightened in her position. Her face grew serious. "I spoke with Brim before he went to sleep—his injuries were very severe, but he'll be all right. Thank you, Sebastian." She glanced at Vioget, who raised a brow at Max.

"Pesaro got there first. Credit where it's due. Shall we?"

"Of course. Max." She nodded at him, and he recognized a decided frost in her eyes.

Good, she was still annoyed with him. Best to keep it that way.

"Brim agreed with me that there has never been any kind of attack like this, that we know of. However, when he and Michalas were in Paris just before coming here, they had been investigating a rise in demonic activity. And there was, from one source, the report of an eerie black cloud forming over a cemetery."

Brim and Michalas had left off their investigation in order to assist Victoria to foil Lilith's plot to kill the king a few weeks ago.

Max straightened. His mind had moved from frivolous matters like lacy lilac night rails and on to more important topics. And he didn't like where his thoughts led. "Wayren's divine powers were rendered useless by those demons," he said. "If we hadn't gotten there in time, she may have been destroyed. She was in Paris before she came here," he added meaningfully.

Victoria looked at him. "I suspect that's what they were after."

"Of course." He let the impatience thread his voice. "That must mean—"

"There's something greater afoot. Demons rising."

Their eyes met, and Max felt an uncomfortable stirring in the pit of his belly. Vampires were a serious enough problem, but an uprising of demons—great numbers of them released from the pits of Hell—would annihilate both mortals and undead. Demons—angels who had fallen from grace long ago—and vampires were immortal enemies, just as mortals and vampires were.

Max and Victoria had faced demons in the past—one or two at a time, and of the lower rungs of power. But the demonic activity in the cemetery tonight had been like nothing else: smarter, sharper, more dangerous than Akvan or even Lilith.

"Wayren understands the strength and power of demons better than anyone. Of course they would attempt to incapacitate her before surging to power. Unless she was their target."

"But where are they coming from?" asked Vioget, who'd been watching the two of them. "Demons cannot just rise from Hell. They have to be released. Somehow, somewhere."

"Not by Lilith," Victoria said, glancing at Max.

He stifled a snort even as an uncomfortable shiver rippled under his skin. "Of course not. Lilith would never consort with demons. She hates them."

"But she asked you to destroy Akvan's Obelisk, knowing that it would call him back to earth," Vioget said pointedly.

"One mere demon is of no consequence to Lilith. And Akvan was little more than a thug. These . . . these are different. A whole different caliber of evil."

Victoria was nodding. "They are. Something's changed." She looked almost frightened for a moment. . . . Then it was gone. "I'm sending Brim and Michalas back to Paris, as I want them to see if they can find any more information about the events there. And whether they've continued since our experiences here—in other words, are the demons moving about looking for . . . something . . . or are they in more than one place? In the meantime, I would like us to visit the cemetery again. During the day. And armed with much holy water."

Max gave a short nod, then rose. The meeting was over. He hurt. He was exhausted. He wanted to get far away from the two of them. "Very well."

Victoria slid off the bed, her feet making a little thump, muffled by the rug. "I hope it wasn't too much trouble for you to attend me, Max," she said stiffly.

Before he could turn, there was a knock at the door and it opened. Verbena stuck her head in, eyes wide and blue. "S'sorry to interrupt, my lady," she said. "But . . . Kritanu is calling for Monsieur Vioget."

Max felt Vioget's eyes flicker to him, then to the door. As if Max had somehow arranged such an interruption. He tightened his lips. If anyone had arranged anything, it was Victoria. Not Max.

And if Vioget didn't understand that, then perhaps he was not wholly prepared to handle Victoria.

Max looked at her, noticed that while she wasn't looking at *him*, she was looking extremely innocent. Blast it. Blast her.

"Pardon me," said Vioget, standing abruptly. He gave a little bow to Victoria. "Are you quite finished?" he asked.

She looked directly at him and replied, "For now. But I will be here if you wish to return."

Max blinked and nearly missed the sharp look Vioget sent toward him. He edged toward the door, ready to make his exit. Vioget stepped aside, quite willing to let him pass.

"Max."

He turned, his fingers tightening. Their eyes met, and he knew she wasn't about to let him leave.

Vioget could delay no longer without looking the fool, and so he left, leaving the door ajar behind him.

Victoria walked over and closed it, brushing against Max as she did so.

He steeled himself, remembering those moments in the carriage. She'd looked up at him, everything written on her face that he knew was also engraved deep inside himself. "What is it?" he said, his voice hard. Angry.

Why did she persist?

"Thank you for taking Wayren last night. I knew . . . you were the only one I could trust to do it."

"I was the one you had to protect."

"I knew you were the one who would succeed in bringing her back, Max. *Vis bulla* or no. We spoke last night. She told me she asked you to return to the Venators."

"I won't." The words were out of his mouth before he could consider them.

"As she told me." She stood there, far enough away that he couldn't reach to touch her—if he'd wanted to—but close enough that he could smell the remnants of her bath. "You don't have to risk your life and become a Venator again. It matters not to me."

Max snorted. "I risk my bloody life every damn day, Victoria. As if that fear would keep me from the Trial."

"Ah, that clears things up for me, then." Her voice grew cold, and she turned slightly away. A damp curl clung to her bruised cheek. "It's not fear of death. It's that if—*when*—you succeeded in reinstating your Venator powers, then you would have no excuse to leave. No reason to hide. To shunt me off on Sebastian. Isn't it, Max?"

He opened his mouth to speak, anger driving through him. He didn't want to talk about this. "You should cut your hair."

She looked at him in surprise, but accepted the

change of subject. "I've thought of it. It's too long and dangerous."

That was not the response he'd expected. He didn't like it.

Damn it to Hell. He didn't like anything right now.

"Max, you're right. As long as Lilith is obsessed with you, there is an added danger."

He narrowed his eyes at her, an uncomfortable feeling rising inside him again.

"So I've decided to take matters into my own hands." She smiled. It wasn't a seductive smile, or even a pleased one. It was feral. Bestial. "Once I'm sure Wayren is safe, I'm going to find Lilith, and kill her."

Seven

Wherein Sebastian Swears Off Women

Sebastian did not return to Victoria's chamber after all.

He thought to have had his mount saddled in order to take himself off to the rooms he let while in London, but something drew him back to the sitting room. He had a compelling desire to see if the Gardella Bible, about which he'd heard so much, was there. An odd thought, to be sure . . . It certainly wouldn't be sitting out, and, furthermore, why did he feel the need to see it? It had never occurred to him to care before.

Nevertheless, that persuasive thought directed him to the small room when he would have left the house, plagued by other unpleasant thoughts instead.

Though Victoria had said that Wayren was resting, she seemed to be waiting for him. He would have backed out of the room if she hadn't fastened those all-seeing blue-gray eyes on him from her half-reclined position on a chaise.

"Sebastian. Come."

"But you're weary." Something niggled uncomfortably inside him, something that told him he would be happier if he left.

"Please."

Before he realized it, he was limping into the sitting room, as though drawn by some invisible thread. Wayren had always unsettled him—from the first time he met her, years ago, when he first learned of his Venator calling . . . to less than six months ago, when he was discovered sneaking about in the Consilium, the secret headquarters of the Venators in Rome.

Yet she seemed to mean him no harm, and unlike Pesaro, she had no condemnation in her eyes. They were peaceful. Serene.

And perceptive. His self-deprecating charm would be out of place in the face of such bald honesty and sincerity.

"Do the dreams still plague you?" she asked as he began to sit.

Startled by her question, Sebastian froze, half poised above the seat cushion. "Dreams?" How could she know?

But as soon as he thought it, he knew the question was foolish. Wayren knew many things—of past, present, and future. Of truth and deceit, of promise and threat.

Her weakness wasn't knowledge. Wayren's limitation was her inability to change what she knew—or portended. Or even, sometimes, to simply divulge her information.

She didn't respond—merely looked at him. Sebastian allowed himself to sink into the chair. Devil take it. He should have left when he had had the chance. But now he had become entwined.

"I dream of Giulia, if that's what you mean." Sebastian could hardly believe he'd admitted it aloud. The dreams he had of the woman—girl, really—he'd loved all those years ago were a private thing. By admitting it aloud, he felt as though he tainted those nocturnal images and memories—at least, the pleasant ones. Yet he was compelled to speak honestly and without prevarication.

Wayren nodded. "Tell me about the dreams."

Sebastian looked down at his hands. His fingers trembled in his lap. "I dream over and over again of the moment when I saw her . . . and realized she'd been turned undead. Her eyes turned red for only a moment, then dissolved back to normal mortal ones."

Normal mortal ones that he saw every time he looked at Giulia's brother. Max Pesaro.

"Your antipathy for him has not affected your work as a Venator . . . now that you've returned to us," Wayren said quietly. It did not surprise him that she knew the trail on which his thoughts had gone. "I find that commendable."

Antipathy? What Sebastian felt for Max Pesaro went deeper than antipathy. It had been Max who'd taken Giulia—as well as their elderly, crippled father—to the secret society of vampire protectors, believing that the Tutela could help prolong their lives. Even give them immortality, through the vampires.

Giulia, beautiful and gentle as she was, had always been a sickly girl, unlike her twin brother. Pale, delicate, and with a persistent cough that worried those who loved her.

In his more generous moments, Sebastian almost understood Max's intent, naive as it had been: to protect and save his family.

But that empathy usually dissolved when Sebastian reminded himself that because of Max, he'd not only lost the woman he loved, but had been forced to send her to Hell by slamming a stake into her heart. Giulia had been the second vampire he'd slain, and she became the last undead he killed . . . until last autumn in Rome. Nearly fifteen years later.

Sebastian realized he'd been silent for too long, and looked up to find Wayren's eyes focused on him. Patience limned her gaze, patience and sympathy.

"I dream it over and over: that her eyes turn red and her fangs . . . extend . . . and then moments later, she returns to normal. A mortal. Unchanged. But I slay her anyway. I slam that stake into her heart even as she opens her mouth to plead with me." He swallowed. "And then the dream shifts, so I don't see if she turns to ash . . . and I wonder if I was mistaken . . . if I was wrong, and she hadn't been undead. And if I killed her for no damn good reason."

He didn't care that those last words came out tight and low and hard, that fury burned through him. Moisture stung the corners of his eyes and he closed them tightly.

And now he was about to lose the second woman he loved. To the man he hated.

"It is said that those turned undead have souls damned for eternity upon the destruction of their physical body," Wayren said. Her voice remained easy, soothing. And despite the turmoil inside, the anger and pain, Sebastian felt a vestige of peace slide over him. "And that is why you turned from the Venators for years, is it not? The belief that you had no right to send any soul to its eternal damnation."

"Yes. How could I make that judgment? How would I know who was . . . deserving? For if they had been good in life . . ." To his great mortification, his voice cracked with emotion. Sebastian swallowed and forced himself to go on. "If they had been good, and blameless in life, and then unwillingly or unwittingly turned undead . . . how could I thrust eternal damnation upon them?"

"You believe that there might be hope for those undead." Wayren did not ask a question; she stated a fact, a hope that had been buried so deeply inside Sebastian that he'd never really allowed himself to think it. Let alone to bring it to life by putting it into words.

Emboldened now—or, perhaps only dispirited—by her question, he looked at her. "Is it possible?"

Her eyes remained clear; he could read nothing there. But she replied, "Anything might be possible, Sebastian. I may know much, but I do not know all. I suspect that divine judgment considers many factors that we cannot comprehend. And that all we can do here is what we are called to do. No matter how difficult it might be."

Sebastian sagged back in his seat. An answer that was no answer. He stood, brushing self-consciously at his rumpled shirt. "Thank you, Wayren."

Her smile held a tinge of amusement and a bit more of sorrow. "I thank you, Sebastian. I know it was difficult for you to return. And to have this conversation with me."

At this, he allowed his lips to quirk on one side. "I've had many difficult conversations with women in the last weeks," he said, recalling the moment when Victoria attempted to tell him what he already knew: that she loved Max in a way that she'd never love him. "I begin to think that it would be best for me to avoid females until such a time as when my luck has changed."

"I am sorry for your pain," she said. "Sometimes, it is through pain that one discerns one's true path."

Sebastian would have liked to return with a quip about figurative stakes through the heart, but something stopped him. He closed his lips and bowed, relieved to quit the room.

"We couldn't find you anywhere," Lady Melly shrilled.

Victoria shifted her position slightly so that the high pitch of her mother's voice didn't go so *directly* into her ear. As she was sitting next to her, that was a bit of a feat, but she did the best she could. "I was there for a time, Mama," she said, then glanced at their hostess. "The duchess saw me, indeed."

Victoria had managed a brief nap after her bath and subsequent meeting with Sebastian and Max in her chambers, but she was still weary and achy. The only reason she'd left the house to join the triumvirate of ladies for an early tea was because the alternative would have been hosting them at her house.

At least here it was possible for her to make an escape.

"Lovely dress, my dear," Duchess Winnie said, leaning forward to take up a little biscuit topped with strawberry preserves and a dollop of cream. Despite the fact that she'd hosted a dance the night before, it was her pleasure to have her dearest friends over the following day in order to scale through every bit of *on dit* or gossip that might have occurred. And aside of that, it was a well-known fact that her cook made the best, most unique biscuits and sweets. "A bit scandalous, to be sure, but you aren't a virginal debutante anymore, are you?"

Lady Melly shot her a silencing glare and turned back to Victoria. "But where did you go off to? I never got to talk to you, and I intended to have Jellington introduce you to Davington's heir, just returned from the Continent."

"Mama," Victoria began, but it was to no avail.

"Never say that you still harbor the idea that you might have an attachment to that Monsieur Vioget," Melly said, her spoon clinking noisily as she stirred her tea. "Why, he wasn't even there last night, and I just could not abide that your second husband should be French. And not of the *ton*. I simply would not permit it."

"But, Melly, you cannot ignore that he is a handsome gentleman," said Lady Nilly, who'd just returned to the room.

In light of her conversation with George Starcasset last evening, Victoria couldn't help but examine the long, papery skin of Nilly's neck for vampire bites. Unfortunately, Lady Nilly was wearing a wide choker that, as Victoria knew from personal experience, could work very well to hide fang marks. "What a lovely cameo," Victoria said.

Her rising from the sofa, which she shared with her mother, had a dual purpose: one, to get her away from the shrill voice, and second, to examine the brooch . . . and its wearer's neck.

"Oh, do you like it?" asked Nilly, moving closer so that Victoria could see.

Victoria lifted the (quite ugly) cameo of a . . . well, she wasn't certain what it was, but it wasn't immediately recognizable . . . from the hollow of Lady Nilly's throat under the guise of examining it more closely. As the wide lace lifted, Victoria saw that there were no marks on her mother's friend's neck, and allowed the cameo to settle back into place.

And now Victoria had no choice but to settle back into her place.

"And the other thing," Lady Melly continued as though there'd been no interruption in her lecture, "I was certain you'd find it fascinating to hear that they have notified the new heir to the Rockley estate."

"Indeed?" In spite of herself, Victoria was mildly interested. "After they'd searched so hard and long for James Lacy, I thought it would take much longer to locate the next in line."

"But no, Victoria, for it wasn't that they didn't know who the heir was. . . . It was where to find him," Melly told her archly. "Surely you knew that."

Victoria didn't have the heart to tell her mother—who had memorized the lineage of every noble family in England—that her interest in Phillip had not extended to learning every branch of his sparse family tree. She'd been much less interested in his wealth than his generous and caring personality.

Blast. A tear pricked the corner of her eye. Would she never be able to think of Phillip without that happening?

"He has been living in Spain for the last ten years," Melly told her. "But of course, now that the current marquess has disappeared and has not been heard from in weeks, the worst is believed to have happened." She frowned thoughtfully. "What bad luck those de Lacys seem to have. Pardon me, dear," she added hastily, realizing she might be infringing upon her daughter's grief.

"He's not the only one to have disappeared quite suddenly," Lady Nilly said, lifting a biscuit genteelly to her lips. "Didn't your friend Miss Starcasset—who was to marry the Earl of Brodebaugh—also go missing? After he was found dead in his own parlor?" She shuddered, but bit into the biscuit with gusto. Cook Mildred's strawberry-cream biscuits were not to be missed for any reason. Since the berries were only in season for a short time, one could not squander the opportunity.

"Ah, indeed," Victoria replied, wondering if Nilly had learned of that information about Gwendolyn through her interactions with her brother, George. "But, though I dislike spreading gossip"—she looked pointedly at the ladies three—"I do have it on good authority that Gwen has eloped with an exceedingly unsuitable man."

It was gossip, but a better tale than the truth. And even Victoria, for all of her virtuous activity hunting the immoral undead, was not perfect. She still felt the sting that her good friend, as a vampire, had planned Victoria's demise simply because it had been Victoria—and not Gwen—who'd caught the eye of Phillip de Lacy, Marquess of Rockley, when the two girls debuted into Society. If the gossip behind Gwen's disappearance was juicier than the oranges she'd had in Rome, Victoria figured it was only fair.

"Indeed?" Duchess Winnie's eyes widened. "How unsuitable?"

"We can talk about that later," Lady Melly interrupted, though the gleam of interest burned in her expression as well. "But I was telling Victoria about the new Rockley heir, which I am certain she will find most interesting. Of course, no one is *certain* what happened to the previous Rockley, our dear James, but since he's disappeared without a trace, the lawyers have gone on to find the next in line in the event that he doesn't return. Mr. Hubert de Lacy will arrive in London next week, so they say, and I believe it would be most fitting for the Marchioness of Rockley to attend his welcome-home ball." She looked at her daughter. "He is a widower of five years, after marrying a Spanish girl and staying there on her family's land after the war. A bit longer in tooth than your dear Rockley, Victoria, but as my mother always said, 'what's in the pocketbook before the measure of teeth' . . . or something of that nature."

"Welcome-home ball? The man is not already here,

and you've planned a welcome-home ball?" Victoria could not help but roll her eyes, but she took care to keep that unladylike expression out of her mother's sight.

"I'm not hosting the welcome-home ball, my dear," said Lady Melly with a gush of surprise. "If anyone in this family should be doing so, it would be you. But as you're doing your best to deny your societal duties, I suppose I can have nothing to say about it. The party is being hosted by Viscount Rutledge, as he and Mr. de Lacy knew each other at Oxford . . . or somewhere from their youth." Her eyes narrowed as she looked at her daughter. "I do hope you will make an appearance so you can at least meet the presumptive new Rockley."

"Mama, I'm not going to marry again, so you can cease and desist in attempting to fling me at every bachelor who shows his nose at court. And aside of that, Rutledge has a son only ten years my junior, so if he knew de Lacy at university, they must be of an age. If I were interested in marrying again, it wouldn't be to a man fifteen years my senior!"

She stood. "I must be going—but, Mama, if you should like to plan a wedding so much, why do you not put Lord Jellington out of his misery and marry him?"

"Yes, indeed, Melly," Lady Nilly jumped in. Victoria wasn't certain if it was because the lady felt sorry for *her*, or because she was such a romantic that she wanted to see her friend wedded off again. In either case, Victoria rejoiced in the diversion, edging toward the door.

"Indeed *not*," said Melly. "I—"

"But why not, Melly?" the duchess put in, spraying crumbs with abandon. "It would be such fun, and Jellington is simply besotted with you. Has been for years."

"I have no interest in getting married again," Melly replied, for once on the defensive herself.

"But think of the *gown* you could wear," Nilly sighed, pressing a hand to her nonexistent bosom.

"And the *food*," added the duchess. "I would even loan you my Mildred to do the wedding luncheon."

Victoria felt the doorknob under her hand and turned it silently. Melly was no longer looking at her, but had become wholly distracted by the bombardment of her friends.

Taking the rare opportunity of her mother's inattention to slip out, Victoria eased through the door, her mother's shrill refusals ringing in her ears.

Their volume and pitch made her particularly relieved to be out of direct range.

Once out the front door and in her carriage, Victoria had a decision to make.

A great part of her wanted to simply return to her comfortable bed and sleep a bit longer. Although her *vis bullae* provided her with fast healing and other protection, she still had injuries that made her weak and sore.

But going back to the town house meant that she could come face-to-face with Max, and after their conversation this morning about Lilith, she wasn't certain she wanted to see him. As expected, when she announced her intention—a rather logical one, she thought—to hunt down the vampire queen herself, Max had not accepted it.

There was no need to relive the scene that followed, the lethal tone to his raised voice as he told her how foolish she was.

He would not listen, no matter how calmly she spoke, reminding him that it was her *responsibility* to rid the world of vampires, and that destroying their leader would be a great victory that would likely lead to a serious annihilation of the undead.

Perhaps in retrospect, she should not have told him anything at all until the deed was done.

Victoria sighed. Perhaps by telling him her plans, she had merely achieved the result of driving him from London all the more quickly.

As she shifted on the seat, rearranging her skirts, her hand brushed against something hard and metal. Curious, she picked it up—a small coin that she recognized immediately. Her mind flashed back to the evening before, when George Starcasset had sat in this very seat and fumbled with something jingling in his pockets.

Very interesting. Perhaps . . .

She realized the carriage had stopped at the end of the drive, waiting for her direction. Opening the window, she made her decision and called up, "The Claythorne residence, in St. James."

Several minutes later, upon arriving at George Starcasset's family home, Victoria sent Oliver, acting as footman, up to the door with a card for George. Fortunately, her carriage—having been inherited from Aunt Eustacia along with her London town house—was unmarked, and thus unidentifiable to any random passerby—or neighbor.

Moments later, the footman returned with the news that George was at his club, Gellinghall's. This information being what Victoria expected, as well as the most expedient way to find out which club George frequented, she ordered her groom to drive the carriage over to Gellinghall's.

Upon arrival at the gentlemen's club, she again sent Oliver to call for George. Not more than ten minutes later, she was rewarded (if one could call it that) by George's arrival at the door of her carriage.

"I trust you were discreet in your leave-taking," Victoria asked, although it wasn't of great concern to her whether George's companions knew it was the Marchioness of Rockley who called him away. The only reason she cared to protect her reputation any longer was because she wished to avoid as many lectures from her mother as possible.

She smiled to herself as George settled into the seat across from her. It wasn't lost on her that she had no desire to avoid superhumanly strong demons and vampires in the dead of night, but went out of her way to escape seeing her mother in a sunlit parlor.

"Do hope this is important, as I was winning, first time in two weeks," George said by way of reply as he settled in the seat across from her. "Come to collect your favor already?"

Victoria shook her head. "No, I came for information. What does the Tutela know about the increase in demon activity here, and in Paris?"

"Haven't talked to anyone in the Tutela—"

"Save it, George. You were fumbling with the coins in your pocket on the way to your house last night, and dropped one of the Tutela markers in this very carriage. I sincerely doubt you'd be carrying one if you hadn't been in recent contact with them." The Tutela used coinlike metal disks as tokens of identification for entrance to their secret meetings, as Victoria had cause to know. She'd nearly been mauled at a Tutela meeting in Venice, after having gained entrance by presenting her own token.

She forestalled any further excuses by handing him the coin.

George, well caught out, pursed his lips. The expression made him look more like a spoiled boy than ever, with his cheeks pudging out and his round chin smooth and shiny. "To be truthful, Victoria," he said, glancing sidewise at her to see if she objected to his use of her name, "the undead have been well aware of something perking beneath the surface in the last months."

Along with his reticence, George had also abandoned his affected speech pattern common to many of the *ton*'s dandies. These facts had Victoria sitting straighter against the back squabs of the bench and watching him sharply.

"What do you mean?"

"They're frightened, if you want the bloody truth. Lying low, hiding. 'S why Lilith was so quick to leave London, and took the rest of them with her."

Victoria contemplated him thoughtfully. She'd assumed that Lilith had taken her minions with her and retreated somewhere to lick her wounds after having been bested by the Venators. Was it possible that there was more to it than that?

"What else do you know? I want all of it, George."

He shifted against the cushions and loosened the neck cloth that had been tied in an intricate knot that even Sebastian might have envied. "I don't know much, to be sure. Just that there's something might happen, and the vampires ain't too pleased with it."

Demons and vampires, both creatures of Hell and minions of Lucifer, were lethal enemies. The demons, who were angels who had fallen from divine grace aeons ago, claimed Hell for their own because of their longstanding alliance with Lucifer, the most powerful of the demons.

But Lucifer had wooed Judas of Iscariot to his side after Judas's betrayal of Jesus Christ, contending that he'd never be forgiven for his actions. He induced Judas to hang himself, and promised that he'd make him the father of a powerful new race. Thus Judas was the first of the vampires—immortal creatures who were half demon and half human, immortal, and destined to take from man in order to subsist.

Thus, the struggle between the demons and vampires for Lucifer's favor over the millennia had been vicious and violent.

"What else? You've given me nothing worthwhile, and I've interrupted your card game," Victoria said. "What's going to happen? What are the vampires doing about it? And when?"

George shrugged. "Don't know."

Victoria bared her teeth in a false smile and leaned forward, grabbing his wrist with her fingers. "That's all you have? After I did you the favor of eliminating your houseguest?" She tightened her grip slowly, and felt his bones shift beneath it.

"Stop," he gasped before she'd hardly squeezed at all. "I don't know, but I know someone who might."

"Take me to them."

George flickered a look at her, then sagged back in his seat, a decidedly sulky look on his face. He rapped on the roof and leaned toward the window to shout directions up to the driver.

When he was finished, he sat back in the corner, looking speculatively at Victoria. He opened his mouth to speak, his expression shifting from sulk to interest, and she raised her hand, palm out.

"Don't bestir yourself, George. I'll toss you from the carriage if you even think to make an inappropriate remark . . . or suggestion."

The sulk returned, and she had to bite her lips to keep them from quirking. He looked as though he'd just had his favorite toy taken away.

His directions took them to an area fairly familiar to Victoria from her first days as a Venator. The dirty, poor, and dangerous neighborhoods of St. Giles were where, for a time, Sebastian had owned and operated the Silver Chalice—an establishment that had catered to both mortals and undead. She hadn't been to St. Giles since shortly after Phillip died, when she went to look at the ruins of the Chalice, which had been destroyed when the vampires came after Sebastian and Max.

The streets looked the same during the day as they'd done at night: crowded, dark, close, and strewn with offal and other refuse. Beggars, thieves, and whores populated streets that weren't known for producing honest tradesmen or crafters.

George glanced at Victoria, as if to measure her reaction to this dangerous place, but she had no reason to be frightened. Her strength and speed worked just as well against mortals as it did against the undead.

When they alighted from the carriage, he lingered close by her, and Victoria had to prod him—roughly— to keep him moving. Reluctantly, he led the way down an alley so narrow that nary a beam of sunlight made its way into its depths. At last, Victoria became impatient with his reticence, and despite the fact that her hem—which only brushed the tops of her shoes— dragged through the muck, she grabbed him by the arm and propelled him forward.

"Here," he said at last as they reached a wretched-looking door in the back of the dead-end alley. Low, warped, and with dirt and mildew decorating the wood, the entrance looked much less inviting than even that of the Silver Chalice had.

Of course, Sebastian Vioget had run a clean and well-ordered pub, so that was no surprise.

The back of her neck did not feel cold, nor did she smell anything like demons lingering above or below the environment's normal stench. She sensed nothing to fear, no trap, nothing out of the ordinary.

Victoria didn't bother to knock. She kicked at the door, and it splintered easily. George could have done it himself. She glanced at his round face and pudgy gloved hands. Perhaps.

He lingered again, but she snagged him by the arm and yanked him behind as she ducked through the door. Inside, the small space looked just as miserable as its exterior suggested, with broken crates and sparse furniture in shambles. Dark, dank . . . and empty.

Before Victoria could turn to George to demand an explanation, he shrugged off her grip and walked to the center of the room. Turning around in a circle, looking about him in dismay, he said, "They're gone!"

Eight

Wherein a Frothy Pink Confection Leaves Little to the Imagination

"It's worse than we thought, isn't it?" Victoria asked as soon as she saw Wayren's face. She'd been summoned to her presence the moment she walked in the door of the town house. It was already late in the afternoon the day after they'd rescued Wayren from the cemetery.

So many things had happened since Victoria had left for the dinner dance in her red dress, less than twenty-four hours earlier.

The older woman nodded and gestured for Victoria to sit. "The fact that those demons had not only the power, but the insolence, to attack me . . . It has weighed heavily on my mind since yesterday."

Victoria sat, regarding the taut expression on Wayren's face. Her aura of serenity faltered, yet strength glowed in her eyes. Whatever evil they faced, it would not be simple or weak.

Not for the first time, Victoria acutely felt the loss of her aunt Eustacia, and simultaneously, a wave of relief and affection for the wise, peaceful woman in front of her.

Wayren seemed to understand, and she reached for Victoria as she often did, closing her fingers over her wrist. As always, tranquillity seeped into her and the leaping of her nerves settled. *We'll do this together.*

"What have you learned?" she asked, slipping away from Wayren's grip, unwilling to cause the woman further weariness.

"As you have remarked, the demonic activity you experienced at the cemetery is unusual, and carries a malevolence that has not often been experienced on this earth. Those demons were from true fallen angels, Victoria. Not merely creatures that have been imbued with the spirit of evil, as Akvan—and other demons you've previously faced. The fallen angels have great power, and are not so simpleminded as those of Akvan's ilk."

Wayren shifted in her chair to reach toward her ever-present satchel. "It's my belief," she said, pulling a crackling parchment tube from the depths of the bag, "that these demons are escaping through the Midiverse Portal." She slipped square glasses on and unrolled the brown paper.

"The Midiverse Portal?" Victoria repeated. "Portal . . . like an entrance?" She frowned, yet that uneasy feeling continued to build inside. This was so different from anything she'd encountered. She felt rather like she had when she first began hunting vampires: nervous, unsettled . . . yet determined. "From where?"

Wayren nodded. "Yes, indeed." She settled in her seat, her slender hands moving as she continued. "An entrance from Hell, Victoria. These demons once were angels, and roamed freely throughout the earth and heavens. When they fell from divine grace, and decided to follow Lucifer, they were banished from Heaven and

Earth and sent to Hell with their new master. They cannot move easily onto this earth. They can only gain access through certain passages. Or portals. They've all been sealed for millennia, but it seems as though one has been opened. Or at least, the seal is broken."

"Fallen angels," Victoria repeated. "Why would they want to harm you?" But even as she spoke, a little shiver traveled up her spine.

"Because they know me. Because they know I am here to help you. And because once, countless aeons ago, I knew them." She nodded at the question in Victoria's face. "Because they fell . . . and I did not."

Because she didn't *fall* . . . ?

Prickles exploded over her shoulders as Victoria looked at Wayren, aware of the shock and sudden comprehension that must be washing over her face. That simple statement explained so much about this woman, who never seemed to age. Who seemed to be able to be anywhere she was needed, whenever she wanted to be. Who knew so much about everything.

And how she could fit so blasted many books in a satchel that was too small to hold them.

Victoria wondered absurdly why an angel would wear reading glasses.

Wayren merely smiled at her, as if she knew what she was thinking, and replied, "We're not perfect either."

At that moment, the door to the parlor opened, and Max came in. Victoria couldn't help but notice the weariness in his demeanor and the strain around his eyes. Doing the work of a Venator, without the blessing of a *vis bulla*, took a great toll on a man.

She wondered if he knew that Wayren was an angel; then she realized. Of course he did. It seemed as if Max knew everything.

He probably assumed *she* knew.

Max flashed a glance at her, but said nothing. Instead, he took a seat near the cabinet that housed the Gardella Bible. "Wayren," he said by way of greeting.

She smiled at him, but by the tightening of Max's mouth, Victoria knew that he, too, saw the cracks in her calm facade. "I was just telling Victoria that I believe the demons we've been encountering here, and those in Paris, are escaping into our world through the Midiverse Portal. It's in Romania, in the mountains," she said, tracing a half-moon fingernail over the rigid parchment. "And . . ." Her voice trailed off as she became absorbed in whatever she was reading.

"And their target is Wayren," Victoria finished tightly. "Perhaps others, but Wayren for certain."

"Did you go to the cemetery today?" he asked sharply.

Victoria shook her head. "No, I meant to, but—"

"I did. There is nothing there any longer."

"You went alone?"

His mouth tightened. "In broad daylight, Victoria. Even I am in no danger in bloody broad daylight."

They lapsed into silence, stress zinging in the air between them. Before now, the last words he'd spoken to her had been in anger and frustration in her bedchamber, punctuated by the slam of the door. He'd acted only as she'd expected, and, in fact, anticipated . . . but there was no sense in keeping her plans from him.

If he knew she was going to go after Lilith, he'd either be moved to go with her, or try to find a way to keep her in London—or at least otherwise occupied. Either way, they'd be together and she'd have the chance to wear down the resistance he'd erected.

But deep in her heart, she knew that until Lilith was gone, Max would not be wholly free.

Of course, any plans she had to find the vampire queen must be delayed until the demons were contained. Wayren's safety was of paramount importance.

"Yes," Wayren said, breaking into the charged silence as she looked up from her reading, "it's as I feared. It must be. The portal has either cracked or somehow been opened, for the only way those types of demon could find their way out beyond the protections that have kept them locked in Hell is through that opening."

"How do we close it, then?" Victoria asked.

"I believe . . . there is a crystal . . . an orb. . . ." Again Wayren's voice trailed off as she closed her eyes, little frown lines appearing between her fair brows. Then, reaching blindly, she slipped her hand inside the battered satchel and rummaged around, her lips moving silently. After a moment, the scrabbling stopped and she withdrew a small book, hardly larger than Max's palm.

"It would be in here," she murmured and flipped through brittle pages. Victoria saw scrawls from a language she didn't recognize, as well as drawings, stains, and ink blots on the yellowed paper. "Yes, as I thought." Wayren looked up suddenly, her eyes clear and sharp. Removing her glasses, she folded them neatly on top of the open book. "There is a crystal, Tached's Orb, that can be used to seal the portal."

"Do you know where it is?" Max asked.

"The orb is inside a pool at the base of Muntii Făgăraş—near Lilith's hideaway." She cast a quick glance at Max, and Victoria recalled with a start that he had gone there voluntarily—and perhaps involuntarily as well.

"However, the pool is enchanted," Wayren added. "So one cannot simply reach in and retrieve the orb."

"But if we get the orb, we can lock the portal? How?"

"And there is no other way to seal the entrance?"

Max and Victoria spoke at the same time, then fell into silence, looking at Wayren.

"I know of no other way to close the portal," she replied, "but I will continue to study it. Time is precious, for the longer the portal is cracked, the more evil will penetrate this world. And the weaker we shall be."

"And the more you will be in danger," Victoria said.

"So our most efficient course of action is to determine how to breach the pool at Făgăraş," Max said.

Victoria stood. "I was with George Starcasset today, and according to him, all of the vampires have fled England—even the ones who don't love Lilith and who stayed behind when she left. They're frightened of something, and I wonder if it has to do with this influx of demons."

"Perhaps you ought to ask him," Max suggested smoothly. "I'm certain George is a font of information and will be able to tell us something even Wayren doesn't know."

Victoria looked at him, but the surge of anger that had begun to rush to her cheeks faded. Max might be arrogant and sarcastic, but he wasn't normally petulant. "Perhaps I shall," was all she said, and walked, queenlike, from the room.

"The pool at Muntii Făgăraş?" Sebastian repeated. He looked at Victoria, his lovely lips turning in a twisted smile. "I suppose it might have been too much to hope that you came to my rooms for something other than information."

She almost took a step back from the doorway, but stopped herself. "It's not the first time I've come to you only for information." Indeed, she'd left Wayren and Max at the town house to come directly here to speak with Sebastian.

"To my great dismay," he agreed. "Do come in." He gestured into the small, spare chamber that he leased while in London.

He looked tired, nearly as tired as Max. Although his shirt was pressed, and his hair combed back in rich, tawny waves, Sebastian had an appearance of underlying rumpledness. He wore no neck cloth, nor a jacket, and his boots, though clean, didn't shine as they normally did.

"Yes, I know about the pool. And it's no secret, at least among the undead, how to breach it. According to Beauregard, it's Lilith's creation, you know," Sebastian said, gesturing impatiently for her to sit. "And is hidden not very far from where she hides in the mountain."

The only place available was a small wooden chair, or the bed. When Victoria chose the chair, Sebastian gave another of those wry smiles. "Of course," he said. "The fool me."

"Will you tell me about the pool?" she asked after a moment.

There was no question—she cared for Sebastian deeply. He'd done much for her, offered her pleasure and escape over the difficult last years. With his own particular skill, he teased her, taunted and angered her . . . always seeming to know what she needed in order to help her clear her head. To alleviate the stress or tension or fear she struggled with.

Why couldn't she love him?

"I will," he said. His voice carried low, and she looked up to find him standing in front of her chair. She'd forgotten the question, and for the moment it didn't matter.

Something snapped in the silence, so real, it was almost audible. Sebastian took her arms and pulled Victoria to her feet, there, flush in front of him. She allowed him.

"You didn't really think," he said, holding her wrists down between their bodies, "that you could come to me, here, without repercussions."

Her heart slammed in her throat. Warmth billowed between them, and Victoria pulled one of her hands away. One. The other one . . . He tightened his fingers around it so that she felt the pad of his thumb digging into her flesh. It would likely bruise.

"I told you," he said, leaning forward to her cheek, "that I have no intention of being a gentleman about this." Now there was a layer of anger in his voice.

"I came for information," she said. Even to her own ears, she sounded breathless.

"You came for more than that, Victoria." He was still close enough that his breath heated her temple, and his leg brushed against her gown.

Had she?

No.

No.

"You're pining for a man who cannot be what you want. And need," he said, and his lips brushed her cheek. She turned her face away, swallowing hard . . . but she didn't step back.

Was it curiosity that had driven her here? Petulance? Confusion?

"Sebastian," she said just as he turned his face.

"Victoria," he murmured, then kissed her. Roughly.

Yet her eyes sank closed, and she opened her mouth. Their tongues tangled in that hot, sleek way, reminding her how skilled Sebastian was at seduction. Very skilled. Very willing.

Then his kiss altered, becoming more coaxing, teasing, urging; she could feel the change in the way he touched her. As if he knew what this meant . . . could mean. He traveled to the sensitive spot on her neck, kissing and nibbling down to the curve of tendon into her shoulder. Her knees weakened.

His hands gripped her shoulders now, tightly but not painfully, and suddenly Victoria felt the nudge of a bed against the back of her leg. And as if to forestall any argument, he returned his lips to cover hers at that moment, pulling her up tightly against him, trapping her legs between his and the mattress. With one little tip, they'd be sprawled on the blanket and pillow.

She separated her mouth from his, and turned her face away.

"Sebastian, it's not . . ." She drew in a deep breath, felt her breasts move against his chest and the long line of his legs against her. He'd not loosened his grip; in fact, his fingers tightened into her shoulder.

"Victoria," he said. His voice came out rough and with a decided edge. "You came here. To me."

"I know, Sebastian. I really . . . came for information."

"You never come only for information."

"I did this time." She pressed her palms against his chest. His skin burned warm through the linen.

"You know I don't give information without compensation," he said. His voice was tight, and his eyes angry.

Victoria looked up at him and recognized the pain in his face. She hated that she was the cause of it, but it couldn't be helped. If she had any question before, she did no longer. "I'm sorry, Sebastian."

Now she stepped to the side, away, putting space between them. Her heart still slammed in her chest, but it wasn't the right kind of slamming.

It just wasn't.

A rumpled Victoria returned to the town house late that evening, tired and dejected. Despite the unpleasantness of their confrontation, she'd obtained more information than she'd hoped from Sebastian.

His knowledge had no doubt been obtained through the relationship he'd had with his grandfather Beauregard. Sebastian was able to answer several questions, and as a result gave Victoria enough to begin to formulate a plan. But the situation was not a hopeful one. It would mean long travel and danger, but worst of all, they would need Lilith's cooperation.

Which was impossible to imagine.

To make matters worse, when she walked into the front entrance of the town house, Max was there. She had no idea what would cause him to be standing in the foyer, perhaps he was merely passing through—but he was the last person she wanted to see at that moment.

Apparently, the feeling was mutual.

His eyes scored her more sharply than usual, disdain pronounced in his expression. "Don't expect me at supper tonight."

Surprised at the venom in his voice, she paused in her intention to sail past him, up the stairs, to the sanctuary of her chamber. "You're going out?" she asked, suddenly aware of the burn of moisture at the corner of her eyes. No, not now.

Not in front of Max.

She drew in a deep breath, brought herself upright, and clasped her hand over the newel post. The sting abated, but her throat felt scratchy.

"I have matters to attend to," he replied. Still just as bitterly. His face looked as though it had been sculpted from some harsh gray stone.

"As you wish." She turned away and started up the stairs without a backward glance. Her eyes filled with angry, furious tears, and the inside of her nose began to tingle.

Perhaps she ought to let him go.

Perhaps it would be best. For both of them.

Victoria fell asleep in her clothing on top of her bed, waking only when Verbena brought her a tray much later that night.

Amid clucking and *tsk*ing, the maid helped her mistress to remove her rumpled gown and insisted that she eat the meal of cold chicken, bread, tomatoes, and cheese. Victoria felt marginally better after her nap and a good meal, yet an angry, itchy sort of internal grumbling continued to nag at her.

Even after her bustling maid finished brushing out her hair for the night and helped her dress for bed—she had no social engagements tonight, and apparently there weren't any vampires left in London to hunt—Victoria hadn't relinquished her mood. Half of her wanted to curl up and sob, over what, she wasn't certain . . . and the other part would have loved to come face-to-face with a pack of vampires.

She'd annihilate them.

Verbena's twittering began to grate on her nerves, and at last Victoria sent her maid away for the night—which apparently was the right thing to do, as Verbena confessed that she and Oliver had planned for a drive to Vauxhall Gardens.

"Then be off with you," Victoria said, noting that it was only eleven o'clock.

Perhaps all she needed was a bit more sleep.

And she did, for a time, dreaming of black-smoke demons and red-eyed vampires and dark-eyed men.

But after a while she woke to a cool moonbeam shining through her window, lighting the room as if it were a gray-and-blue-tinted day.

The thought that had been worrying, grumbling, grating in the back of her mind now came out to the fore with full force: Perhaps she ought to let Max go.

Victoria sat up, slid off her bed, walked over to her dressing table. Her face shone ghostly in the mirror, her thick dark hair falling over her shoulders, brushing past her elbows, her eyes dark almonds alongside the bridge of her nose. A faint sheen of moisture dampened her upper lip, for the heat of day still lingered.

Perhaps Sebastian was right. She was pining for a man who couldn't give her what she wanted. Who didn't want, or need, anyone.

She looked at herself in the mirror for a long time and at last made her decision.

If that was what he really wanted, she'd let him go. But the way he'd looked, as he stood over her in the carriage after the dinner dance, spoke otherwise.

Perhaps it was time to force his hand. One way or the other.

Rising from the stool, she whisked off her simple white night rail and pulled from the wardrobe a lacy shell pink gown. The fabric weighed little more than a whisper, and fitted her breasts like two lace hands . . . then fell free, in a sheer pink glaze from her bodice to the floor. Her two *vis bullae* glinted behind it, at her navel.

Victoria left her chamber silently and padded through the small town house to the rear, where the servants kept their rooms. Then she climbed up a flight of stairs to the next level, where the heat lingered even more heavily.

Her gown swirled around her, light as smoke, as she came to a stop outside Max's room. The crack under the door showed no illumination, but it was well after two o'clock in the morning. He was either sleeping or out. And since there weren't any vampires in London anymore . . .

Victoria opened the door and saw the same moon-beam splaying over his bed. Empty. Unslept in.

He wasn't there.

Victoria backed out of the room, her stomach twisting uncomfortably, her palms suddenly damp.

She felt foolish.

Back down the stairs she went, and kept going down to the ground floor. She found herself near the kitchen at the back of the town house. She wasn't hungry, but walked through to the front of the house, now wide-awake and alert. Suddenly she realized why.

The hair on the back of her arms lifted, and she slowed her careless movements into something silent. The sound had been a soft clink, or a dull scrape, perhaps.

Not a vampire—she didn't feel a chill. It could be Kritanu or Charley or . . .

Victoria drew herself up tall and continued along the corridor to the sitting room. Her heart pounded.

A yellow glow shone from under the door, faint and unassuming. She turned the knob and pushed it open.

Max sat in Aunt Eustacia's favorite chair near the piecrust table on which her stakes had lain. A short glass with liquid that glowed amber in the lamplight gave testament to the dull scrape Victoria had heard, and the fat decanter next to it, the clink. He raised his face, half of it burnished gold from the lamp, and the other melding into shadow. His white shirt, with a loose neck cloth draped around his shoulders, glowed in the dim light.

"What do you want?"

She stepped across the threshold and stood close to the wall, feeling anger . . . and something else . . . bubbling through her. Her fingers gripped the edge of the door, but she moved to stand in that beautiful, broad moonbeam from the side window. "I couldn't sleep."

His glance flickered over her, and she saw his mouth compress. "Go away, Victoria."

"Max."

Then he looked at her, straight on, and she was knocked nearly breathless by the venom in his expression. The same bitterness he'd had earlier that afternoon. That same deep, flat anger he'd had when she drugged him with *salvi* three weeks ago.

"You've settled things with Vioget. Why are you here?"

There was no use wondering how he'd known she'd visited Sebastian; she'd accepted that about him long ago. Max knew everything.

"Ye—" she began, but he didn't wait to hear the rest of it.

"Get. Away." His words were little more than a breath.

She took a step closer, and felt the whisper of fabric around her legs. She knew what he saw, with the white glow behind her: the froth of pink gauze outlining her from torso to toes, the heavy bundle of thick curls cascading down her back. Victoria had no illusions about the image she made.

She needed all the help she could get.

"Max, I went to your chamber, looking for you."

"Obviously." Those dark eyes scraped over her, somehow managing to be cold and yet arrogant. "I've no interest in Vioget's leavings. Or is it that you don't want to know your child's patrimony?"

So he also knew that she had stopped taking the potion. Again, that was no surprise to Victoria. She'd told him it was her intention, and Max, being Max, would confirm it. But his other accusations . . .

"Sebastian's leavings?" She gave a short laugh, trying not to let that cold voice penetrate too deeply. "Max, don't be—"

"Or was that someone else's mark on your neck?" He'd not raised his voice this whole time. It came out quiet and flat. Cold.

Victoria reached reflexively to her shoulder, where Sebastian had indeed left a small mark earlier today.

Max couldn't have seen it now, for her hair covered it. But this afternoon . . .

"This is the last time I'll say it. Leave."

His eyes looked like black pits with a faint glitter in their centers. Though the glass of whiskey sat next to him, he never lifted a hand toward it. Instead, she saw that his fingers curled around the arm of his chair.

"Or what?" she countered. "You'll make me?"

They both knew what had happened the last time he had laid angry hands on her. Angry hands that had turned to passionate ones.

"I'm leaving London. As soon as the sun rises."

She glanced toward the window. The sky still boasted stars and moon, but a faint essence of lighter blue could be seen in the east. Victoria gave a brief nod. So be it.

But she had something to say first.

Later, she was never certain how she managed to keep the emotion from her voice, the shock and grief that he would have left without telling her, without saying good-bye. How she kept her words steady and as cool as his. But she did.

"Sebastian and I have settled things, but not in the way you thought we should." She looked directly at Max. "You're mistaken on many fronts. I've not been with him since Rome, Max. Since . . . you and I . . . went to the Door of Alchemy." Since Max had kissed her, flat up against that damp, rough stone wall.

Little had she realized, but that had been the defining moment.

He didn't respond, merely sat unmoving, his gaze as flat as ever.

"But if you leave, I will be with him. And there will be no question about the paternity of my child." There. She couldn't keep a bit of bitterness, a hint of mockery from her voice.

Silence stretched for a moment, and at last she understood that he was Max, and that Sebastian had been right about him.

Victoria turned and walked out of the room. Head high, but stomach churning.

Her hand was on the newel post at the base of the stairs when she heard her name.

She turned and Max stood in the doorway of the parlor.

The expression on his face made the bottom drop out of her stomach and a sharp quiver snap through her, leaving her knees weak, her palms damp. A small lamp in the foyer illuminated his eyes, hot and heavy and calculating.

"I've changed my mind," he said quietly, a hand moving to pull the untied neck cloth away from his collar. Slowly, deliberately, his eyes moved over her. "And when we're finished, Victoria, you won't remember your own name . . . let alone Vioget's."

Nine

In Which Our Heroes Accept Their Mission

Her heart thumping madly, her stomach fluttering, Victoria drew in an unsteady breath as Max moved toward her. She'd never seen this expression on his face: the hot avidity in his eyes, the set of his mouth more gentle than harsh and grim.

"You've ... changed ... your mind?" Her words, unnecessary and completely absurd, considering the way he was looking at her, came out breathy and feeble. And very unVenator-like.

She stood on the second step, her hand still curled around the top of the newel post, and when he reached the bottom of the stairs, they were face-to-face. Instead of reaching to grab her to him, to devour her, Max surprised her by moving so that they were flush and he was sliding his hands along her torso to close them over her hips.

He bent, not to her mouth, but to the side of her neck just below the ear—a place that, when his mouth touched it, quite literally made pleasure shoot through her in all directions. Her fingers trembled over the banister. Her eyes closed. He pressed his lips to that strong tendon at the side of her throat, moving them, slow and warm and thorough, over her skin. Little bumps rose everywhere, and she reached out, her hand landing on his solid shoulder.

She felt the brisk flutter of his eyelashes against her cheek and heard the sound of her own breath as though an ocean rushed through her ears. All from a gentle, purposeful kiss.

At last.

She felt the emotion well up inside her, and tears sting the corners of her eyes. So different, this flood of warmth, of *rightness*. No guilt, no furtiveness, no . . . rushing.

When his mouth closed over hers, she tipped toward him on the edge of her step, leaning against his warm chest, her hands planted at the tops of his shoulders. Pulling him close.

Where he belonged.

There was no urgency, no ferocity between them . . . but the kiss knocked her breathless, stole her reason, weakened her knees. It was deep and long, and as if he had all the time in the world.

As if the sun wouldn't soon be rising and pouring through the sidelight windows, illuminating and warming them.

As if he couldn't ever grow tired of matching his lips to hers, tasting and sliding in an easy, sensual dance. His hands slid up into her heavy hair, lifting it from her warm neck, holding her head cradled so the kiss could go deeper.

Damn him. He was right. If he kept this up, she *would* forget her own name.

As if reading her mind, he pulled away, but not before his mouth curved in something like a smile against hers. As if he were well pleased with himself.

"Perhaps," he said—and his voice wasn't quite as steady as normal, thank God—"we ought to move somewhere a bit more . . . comfortable."

Her hands slid down over the front of his shirt, and she felt the firm muscle beneath, heating the cotton. And the mad pumping of his heart.

"What?" she managed to say, stepping backward up the stair behind her, tugging on his shirt so that he would follow. "Not here?" As jests went, it was another feeble attempt.

His lips, full and soft now, stretched into a bit of a smile. "Neither staircases nor carriages lend themselves to a terribly thorough experience." His eyes were still hot. "And I intend to be very thorough."

Victoria nearly tripped on the back hem of her gown, but he was there to steady her. She had to work hard to swallow, yet her own mouth curved into a delighted smile. "It's about time, Max." Her voice came out in a purposeful purr, her hands still planted on his chest. But inside, she was a riot of warmth and relief. This was him. This was *Max*. This was what she'd always wanted.

His response was to lift her in his arms and take the rest of the stairs swiftly and easily. As he climbed, she felt his muscles slide and shift beautifully around her, and dipped her face into the hollow of his shoulder. Pulling the shirt away, she found warm skin that smelled like Max and tasted like him, too.

By the time they reached the stop of the stairs, he was breathing a bit harder—and not because of the climb. At the top, he allowed Victoria to slide down from his grip in a swirl of gossamer silk and lace. His hands moved over her breasts, covering the lace, and then suddenly his palms cupped her bare flesh. Thumbs found the hard and sensitive points of her nipples, followed by that hot, slick mouth.

Her world became a slow, swirling vortex of pleasure, of gentle, purposeful hands, sleek mouths tangling and tasting, warm skin, and the insistent *need* tugging at her . . . then more and more urgent, demanding.

Before she realized it, the bed materialized beneath her, and she felt the soft linen on her bare skin . . . the warmth of his body as he moved next to her, his hands and mouth never stopping from their inventory. She arched up when he moved down to take the *vis bullae* into his mouth, and heard the soft click of the metal against his teeth . . . and then nearly cried out in surprise when he moved lower.

A strong hand was planted gently on her belly, thumb twisting around and amid the strength amulets, kept her steady, but writhing as he kissed and licked and stroked until the only sound in her ears was the rush of her own breath. And then the little gasps of her rising pleasure.

Max brought her over the edge and stayed with her while she trembled against him, biting her lip to keep from crying out, fully aware of a slender tear trickling from the corner of her eye. Then he was next to her, warm and sleek, lining up alongside her torso as she reached between them. When she wrapped her fingers around him, he closed his eyes with a sigh.

But then moments later, he removed her hand, gently but firmly, and covering her mouth with his, settled over her. His weight felt blessedly solid and warm, and she pressed her curves up into the solid planes that made his torso, imprinting herself on him, holding him close.

When he slid fully home, she closed her eyes and thought . . . *at last*.

Giulia came to him in his dreams . . . in a more real way than she had for many months.

Sebastian didn't know if it was the amount of brandy he'd consumed, or the fact that he'd finally accepted Victoria's decision.

Either way, when he woke, it was to reach blindly for Max's sister . . . only to find her no more substantial than Victoria.

Who had gone to Max.

Max's sister.

Max's lover.

Sebastian gnawed on bitterness, there in the breaking dawn.

The remnants of the dream still clung to his consciousness, and he closed his eyes again, trying to bring them back. He touched her long, dark hair—just as thick as Victoria's, but without the curl. He looked into her Pesaro eyes, felt the warmth of her body next to his as he'd never done in reality.

In his dreams, he missed her. Grieved anew. And pined over the fact that it was he who'd ended her undead life, who'd sent her to eternal damnation.

And yet, in his dreams . . . her dark eyes were clear, uncondemning. Tender. Even . . . hopeful.

When he woke, Sebastian stared at the scarred, smoke-tinted ceiling in his cramped, impersonal room. What now? something asked in his mind.

What now?

"Say my name."

"Max."

Victoria closed her eyes. She might not be certain exactly where she was, or what had happened to that whispery pink gown, or even whether the glow from the window was moonbeam or early dawn . . . but one thing she knew for certain was the man next to her.

Her mouth curved beneath his as he bent to kiss her yet again. The scrape of his whiskers had long ceased to bother her tender skin, and her own musky taste lingered on his lips and tongue. His body was long and warm and very, very powerful. Very skillful.

Very welcome.

"And you are?" he murmured against her mouth, settling into her in a lovely, deep slide. Again. Oh, yes, again.

Victoria caught her breath, arching a bit closer to the hair-roughened skin pressed against hers. She spread her hands over the smooth slide of muscle on his back. Her world had slowed from a taut, frantic whirlwind to one slower, more deliberate.

She barely remembered to answer him. "I'm . . . Jane?"

His cheek moved, and she knew he was smiling.

Max smiling. A wonder.

But then her thoughts evaporated as that smile eased and they began to move together. His mouth against her neck, his face buried in her hair. She felt the warm rush of his breath and felt a whisk of lashes against her temple as pleasure rose inside her . . . higher, stronger . . . and then she slid over in a long, undulating wave.

She felt his quiet groan of completion against her cheek, and her eyes slid closed . . . and her long, loose, sated body eased into sleep.

Victoria woke sometime later. Even though her eyes were closed, she felt the burn of sunlight on them, and she knew it was well into the day.

She lay still for a moment, aware of the warmth of Max's body next to her, afraid to open her eyes and find . . . whatever would be the results of the night before. The last time—the only other time—she and Max had been together thus, she'd awakened to a man with regret and bald fear blazing across his face.

She didn't think she could accept that again.

She didn't think her heart could.

A knock at the door had her eyes flying open, despite her intentions otherwise; but before she could respond, the knob turned, and it began to open.

In the bed behind her, Max growled, "Get out," and Victoria saw the door jerk slightly open—as if someone jolted in surprise—and then whip shut, as if that same person was mortified. She smothered a chuckle. That would give Verbena something to talk about.

For days.

Girding herself, she turned her head to find Max's dark eyes regarding her.

"Good morning . . . Jane," he said. A slight twitch moved the corner of his mouth.

No regret. No fear. Even . . . a bit of humor? Victoria began to feel warmth bubble inside her. "Good morning. Do you have one foot on the floor, ready to dash off?" She kept her voice light, yet she realized that she was holding her breath.

"Is there a reason I should dash off? The return of a husband or lover?" he asked, his voice light . . . yet . . . yet . . . she felt an underlying *edge* to it. Subtle, but present.

"No." She sat up. The coverlet fell away, drawing his attention . . . and his fingertips . . . to her bared torso. "Max," she said, as his long, elegant fingers brushed gently over her skin, "I want you to know that . . . it was never like this with Sebastian. What I mean to say is, he never . . . we never slept. Or woke. Together. It was always much more . . . furtive with Sebastian."

"Hmm," said Max, in a decidedly un-Max-like tone, "should I be offended that you do recall his name after all?"

But then the glint of humor ebbed, and his face grew serious. "I preferred not to think about what did and didn't occur between the two of you."

"Nothing," Victoria said, noticing the way the white sheets appeared so crisp against his dark skin, "like what happened last night."

"Nothing?"

"Well, perhaps . . . some of the mechanics were similar," she replied, with a tug of guilt. It had been much more than mechanics with Sebastian. But they hadn't left her feeling as sated, as content . . . as fulfilled . . . as she did now.

Max slid from beneath the covers, and Victoria turned to watch his tall, graceful body. The silver *vis bulla* still hung from his areola. She remembered in a burst of clarity the way the smooth, warm metal had clinked against her teeth last night and the extra surge of power she felt from it.

Mmm.

But as Max scanned the room, Victoria smothered a smile. Having been married, she was well used to men's early-morning needs and gestured Max toward the chamber pot in the dressing room beyond.

While he was gone and she took advantage of the privacy for her own needs, Victoria wondered not for the first time what had changed his mind. Not that she'd spent a lot of energy mulling over it during the activities of the night . . . and morning. But it worried her.

Max had been pushing her at Sebastian for months. He'd been ready to leave last night, and Victoria had no illusion that he'd have returned.

But she'd said something that had changed his mind, for Victoria knew that the sheer pink night rail hadn't done the job on its own, and she suspected that what had tipped the scales was the confession that she'd not been with Sebastian in months.

I've no interest in Vioget's leavings.

Or is it that you don't want to know your child's patrimony?

That had to be it. He'd made comments before about her long line of lovers, and he'd thought she meant to dally with them both. She hoped last night's confession had set him straight.

When Max came back into her chamber, he stood in the doorway for a moment lacing his simple trousers. Victoria swallowed, her throat suddenly dry. She forgot her intent to confront him about his decision to stay. Those sleek muscles, the broad, square shoulders, the dark hair dusting swarthy skin . . .

"Did you learn anything from Vioget yesterday?" he asked without preamble.

Victoria looked sharply at him, but she saw nothing but normal interest in his expression. Ah. Back to the matter at hand. "He says we need the Rings of Jubai," she replied, feeling his gaze follow her as she pulled on a thin robe. "He also told me that Lilith has protections on the pool at Muntii Făgăraş so that no one can breach the water."

"And the rings? To trade with Lilith so we can get the orb?"

Victoria shook her head. "Lilith had them made—five copper rings that she gave to her most powerful Guardian vampires. According to Sebastian, when all five are worn on one hand, they allow the hand to reach safely into the pool."

Max's face had become more serious and intent as she spoke. He nodded once. "Vioget's information is usually accurate. At least his years with Beauregard have brought us some advantage."

"We have two of the Rings of Jubai," Victoria said, more to herself than to Max. "One Sebastian retrieved from Lilith's underground lair last month."

"I recall," Max replied drily. Indeed he should, for Victoria and Sebastian had intended to trade the ring for Max's freedom if there was no other way for him to escape from Lilith. "And the other is in the Consilium."

"Sebastian tells me a third is somewhere in Prague."

"Prague? I haven't been there in years," Max said. "Does Vioget know where?"

"He claims he can locate it. He's already agreed to go with me." She looked at him. "And you . . . if you wish."

Max straightened and looked out the window. His dark hair hung, rumpled and thick, framing his face, brushing the sides of his neck, making Victoria want to touch it.

But she wasn't yet confident enough to do so. Max could just as easily pull back as allow it.

"I must find a vampire," he said, still looking out the window. His jaw seemed tight, and the beam of sunlight scored his high cheekbones.

Victoria's eyes narrowed, but before she could respond, a knock on the door startled her. She turned. "Yes?"

Orange hair poked bashfully around the corner, followed by Verbena's pert nose and sandy eyelashes. "Would ye be wantin' somethin' to break the fast? Eh . . . I thought y'might be hungry. It's nearin' to noon."

Victoria checked her smile as Verbena glanced balefully at Max, who, in his disheveled, shirtless state with the set look on his face, did look rather intimidating.

"Yes, indeed," she replied to her maid, choosing to answer for both of them.

But she hadn't forgotten Max's statement . . . one that sounded almost as if it had been wrung from him.

As soon as Verbena quit the room—after having rested a tray laden with food on the dressing table—Victoria simply raised a brow at Max. And waited.

"For the Trial," he said. "All of the vampires have

quit London, but I need one if I'm to undertake the Trial again."

Suddenly assaulted by a variety of emotions, Victoria fell to examining the victuals brought by her maid. Fear . . . a sudden thrust of fear, accompanied by a thrill of excitement . . . and the soft nudge of some other gentler emotion. Tenderness?

"Max," she began.

But he held up his hand, turning at last from the window to face her. "I'd already decided, before . . . last night." Was it her imagination, or did his voice falter a bit at the end? Grow a bit husky with memory? Or was it merely wishful thinking? "But if we're to go to Prague, and find the rings . . ." He stopped. His mouth tightened and she saw, even felt, the ripple of tension settle over his body. "I presume Lilith has the other two."

Victoria nodded. According to Sebastian, Lilith had managed to retain only two of her rings. When she saw the expression on Max's face, her stomach turned into a ball of lead.

They would have to find some way to retrieve the last two Rings of Jubai from the vampire queen—either by her cooperation, for the protection of her race as well as theirs, or by violence.

And she knew if Max survived the Trial and became a Venator again, he'd be in the thick of whatever it was.

If Victoria thought that things with Max would change completely after he divested her of that pink froth (which, incidentally, Verbena had found crumpled beneath one of the tables at the top of the staircase . . . in two pieces), she was wrong.

It felt as if they wore new clothing that didn't fit quite right yet.

Offering a vague excuse, Max left the bedchamber shortly after Verbena did, grabbing up a chunk of cheese wrapped in crusty bread and casting a lingering look over Victoria as he slipped out the door.

He didn't kiss her . . . though she could tell he wanted to.

She sighed in exasperation after he'd gone. He was definitely not comfortable with this new arrangement. However, she stretched and smiled and rolled onto her stomach to bury her face in the sheets, inhaling his scent still imprinted on the pillow . . . taking a rare moment in her stressful life to simply enjoy something that most people took for granted.

Soon enough—tomorrow—they'd be traveling post-haste to Prague, and then on to wherever Lilith was, and there would be little time for pleasure of any kind.

If it wasn't enough that Victoria suddenly felt odd in her skin around Max, she also had to contend with her mother, for Lady Melly called not more than two hours later.

"My dear Victoria," Lady Melly said, frowning at her daughter, "whatever is the matter with you?"

Victoria blanched a bit, her hand moving to her neck as though to feel for . . . what? Vampire bites? Love bites? "What do you mean, Mother?"

"Why, you look as though you can barely walk. Did you have a fall?"

Victoria's face warmed and her hand fell from her throat. "No, indeed. I'm simply a bit . . . tired."

"Well, you certainly don't look tired," Melly said, eyeing her critically. "You look . . . well, if I didn't know better, I'd think . . . *well*."

Was that a flush settling over her mother's cheeks?

"Mother, I'm sorry that I don't have time to visit, but I was just leaving."

"Leaving? Are you making calls? Perhaps I'll go

with you . . . but you aren't dressed for calls, Victoria. You simply cannot wear—"

"Mother," Victoria interrupted, gesturing at Charley to call for a carriage that she didn't really need. Desperate circumstances required desperate acts.

"I'm not making calls. I have to meet with Aunt Eustacia's barrister," she explained, thinking quickly. "It appears I might have to travel back to Rome to attend to business there." That, at least, was true . . . the business being retrieving the copper ring from the Consilium. But from there, it would be on to Prague.

"You are going *to* the barrister, instead of him calling here? Why that's simply not done, Victoria! Not by a marchioness, indeed not. And where are your gloves? I daresay—"

"Mother," Victoria said, enunciating clearly, "I must not be late for my appointment. Was there something you wished to speak with me on?"

"Why . . . why . . . and did you say going to Rome? To handle *business*? But, Victoria, that's why you have a barrister to manage all of the inheritance from your aunt. There's no need for you to dirty your hands with that. Speaking of which, where *are* your gloves? And"—her voice became more strident as her daughter opened her mouth to respond—"aside of that, the apparent Marquess of Rockley has arrived in London this day . . . which was why I hurried over to notify you."

"Thank you for that pertinent information, Mother," Victoria said drily. She glanced longingly toward the door.

At that moment, it opened and Max stepped in.

Lady Melly looked at him. Up at him. And she took a step back. A slight one, but a step nevertheless. Her attention darted to Victoria, as if to measure her response to the imposing man who'd just entered her home uninvited.

Melly had met Max only briefly over the years that he assisted Aunt Eustacia, and Victoria wasn't certain whether she even remembered or recognized him.

"Your carriage is waiting, my lady," Max said in the driest of voices. There was no mistaking him for a footman. Victoria saw a glint of humor in his eyes, and she lifted her chin in an effort not to smile.

"I'm sorry, Mother, but I simply must go. Do give the marquess my best wishes." She paused with her hand on the doorknob. "I shall likely be leaving for Rome tomorrow."

"Tomorrow?" Lady Melly shrieked.

Victoria winced.

Max grimaced, and Victoria slipped past him through the open door. Her mother's words followed her like the screech of an owl, and Victoria dimly registered something about a welcome ball for the presumed marquess.

"You must give him my regrets, Mother," she said over her shoulder, certain that Melly would at least seize upon the excuse to speak to the marquess if she didn't have a daughter to thrust at him.

To Victoria's surprise, Max followed her to the carriage. He spoke briefly to the groom, and then stepped inside. The door closed, and as the vehicle started off with a gentle lurch, Max settled in the seat . . . across from her.

Apparently, old habits died hard.

For a moment, the only noise was the rhythmic clopping of hooves on the cobbled street and the faint creak of the carriage springs. Victoria studied him, feeling as though at last she'd earned the privilege of watching him as long and as hard as she wished.

As he often did, Max gazed out the small window, giving her little more to look at than the profile of a strong, straight nose and solid chin, now clean-shaven. And his mouth.

Her own mouth dried just a little, as she remembered with perfect clarity all of the wonderful places those lips had been, and all of the breathtaking things they'd done. Victoria's belly did that little flip that settled into a warm tingling through her limbs, and she swallowed.

"Rather a shame to hitch up the horses for a drive around the block," she commented drily, breaking the silence at last. "But I knew that, short of leaving the house, I'd not escape from Mother."

"I thought perhaps you might have another use for the carriage."

Victoria looked sharply at him, but he still peered out the window. She couldn't tell from his profile whether that glint of humor . . . or heat . . . was there in his eyes.

But heat definitely warmed her cheeks.

"Such as?" she asked.

He lounged back into a corner of the blue velvet squab, resting an arm along the top of it. At last he turned to look at her. A dangerous glint lingered in his dark eyes, but he merely replied, "A visit to Fleet Street? Don't you need some fripperies or furbelows for your trip to Roma?"

"Why, Max, do you mean to say you wish to go shopping with me?" She batted her eyelashes coyly. "How unexpectedly accommodating of you."

Max's response was a snort that sounded suspiciously like "Like hell," but those beautiful lips tightened as though trying to keep from smiling. "I had plenty of bloody shopping when I courted Sara."

"Ah, yes, you would have done." Now Victoria

couldn't hold back a smile. She no longer cared about Max's false courtship with Sara Regalado, and could find humor in the thought of him dutifully following the fashion-conscious Italian girl from shop to shop. Max would do anything in the name of duty.

Anything.

Victoria sobered. "Max, you don't have to take the *vis bulla* again. It doesn't matter to me."

His face stilled, matching hers in seriousness. "It does to me."

"I don't want anything to happen to you," she said, unable to hold the words back. Blast. She sounded like a weak woman! She, *Illa* Gardella. Was this what love did?

Max gave a humorless laugh. "The feeling is quite mutual, Victoria. But the fact is, something is much more likely to happen to me if I *don't* take the *vis*."

He was right, of course. Max wouldn't stop fighting vampires without the power of the *vis bulla*, and so far his lack of Venatorial strength hadn't kept him from being coveted by Lilith. Only three weeks earlier, Lilith had had Max in her possession and Victoria and the other Venators had helped him to escape.

"And to you," he added. His dark eyes settled on her, and she felt a burst of warmth. And fear.

This emotion, this tingling, sparking connection that bound them frightened her—it was strong yet uncertain.

And the future was frightening, for she couldn't imagine it without Max.

"Max," she began, but he cut her off.

"What you fail to understand, Victoria," he said, his voice low, cool, "is that I now have no choice. I will go through the Trial, and I will succeed."

"Are you saying that I've forced you into it?"

"Of course not." His mouth flattened.

"Why did you decide to stay last night?" she asked boldly.

"I was previously . . . Well, I had no desire to share you. With anyone."

As she had suspected. "You thought that I would linger in Sebastian's bed and then come to you?" Victoria wasn't certain whether to be angry or insulted. So she kept her voice steady.

Max's eyes turned flat and black. "You forget that I've observed you and your various beaus over the last two years. You never seemed to settle on one for long."

She could have allowed the righteous fury to burst forth, skewering him with her words, but Victoria sensed something unspoken beneath his comments. Something he masked very well. So she chose bald honesty. "I never have. Until now."

The belligerence in his eyes died. His mouth relaxed. But he didn't speak.

"Max," she began, unsure what was about to come from her mouth . . . and then her breath trailed off. Because he was looking at her again like he had last night . . . through hot eyes filled with intent and boldness.

"I begin to see the attraction of carriage rides," he said, and reached forward to close his fingers around her wrist. "The rhythm, the privacy . . ."

She saw the flash of a decidedly wicked smile before she flowed across the divide, into his arms.

"Most definitely the privacy," she murmured after a moment, pulling a bit away from the long, sleek kiss. "No Verbena to interrupt us. Poor girl," she said, paused for a lovely little mash of lips, then continued. "She's half terrified of you anyway . . . and you bellowed at her this morning."

He smiled against Victoria's mouth, his fingers already loosening the buttons at the back of her gown. Efficient in everything he did, of course.

Then suddenly, he stopped and gathered her close.

One strong hand curved around the back of her head, fingers sliding into the loose knot there, palm cupping the base of her neck, and the other at the center of her back, where the gown had begun to gap open. "Victoria," he said into her ear, barely audible, "I can't let anything happen to you. I simply cannot. That's what I meant by having no choice."

She pulled back, looking into his eyes. "I've made the same choice, Max. Don't you understand?"

He turned away, his face becoming rigid. "I almost wish you hadn't. *Almost*," he added sharply, before she could argue.

Now he moved away, putting space between them, tilting her off his lap and into her own corner of the seat. "It's you that doesn't understand, Victoria." He grabbed up her hand, closing his strong brown fingers around hers, covering her slender white hand with his broad, square one. "You called me a coward once."

"Twice," she reminded him.

The flicker of a smile ticked at the corner of his lips. "Yes, then, twice. And it's true. I am a coward. I've fought this for so long—"

"How long, Max? Since you peeked at me changing in the carriage?" Victoria couldn't resist.

Again, that involuntary twitch of lips. "Long enough. And I've already told you, I had no desire or reason to peek." Then the sobering mood returned, this time laced with underlying anger. "Be quiet and let me say this."

He glanced out the window. "The hardest thing I've ever done was when I . . . executed Eustacia. I loved her like a mother, a leader, a mentor and a friend . . . and she ordered me to kill her."

"You had to, Max," Victoria said earnestly, her fingers tightening inside his. "You had to in order to get close enough to the vampires to destroy the obelisk."

In fact, Aunt Eustacia had ordered Max to sacrifice her in order to prove his loyalty to the vampires.

"Goddammit, I know that, Victoria. Of course I had to—it was the right thing to do. One life sacrificed in order to save countless others. I hated myself for doing it. I loathed the fact that I had to . . . but I did. I didn't hesitate. I did what bloody well had to be done."

He turned from the window then to look at her, bleakness in his eyes, austerity in his face. "But if it had been you? I couldn't have done it. Do you understand? *I could not have done it.*"

He pulled his hand from hers. "That's what I'm afraid of, Victoria. A choice like that."

Ten

In Which Sebastian Acquires Reading Material

Sebastian knew the moment Victoria walked into the town house parlor that things had changed.

He'd been conversing with Wayren, sitting yet again in this little room that continued to tug at him whenever he came to Eustacia's home. During the short time he'd been here, waiting for Victoria's return, his attention had been drawn over and over to the cabinet that held the Gardella Bible.

More than once, he'd thought to ask Wayren if he could look through it—after all, he was a Gardella, somewhere centuries back in his mother's family tree.

But then Victoria breezed in, dressed in a simple gown of pale blue that didn't begin to do her justice. For pity's sake, he'd seen maids better dressed. She was gloveless, and her rich, inky hair sagged low at the base of her skull, curls flying in little springs from her temple. And she was followed by Max Pesaro.

"Sebastian," she greeted him. "Have you been here

long?" She took a seat at one side of the empty sofa, and Pesaro sat there as well, but at the other end, well away from her, as though afraid of catching something. Though from the look on his face, he'd already been close enough to do so.

Devil take it. How was he going to travel to Prague with the two of them?

He realized with a start that Victoria had asked him a polite question that required a suitable response. "I haven't even been here long enough for Charley to have brought tea," he replied. "Although I'm not entirely certain that the request was made, so perhaps that isn't a good measure." Taking care to keep his voice light and casual, he added, looking directly at Max, "I understand you went for a drive. How did you find the carriage's accommodations?"

"Cramped," he replied coolly, but with a measured look that confirmed everything Sebastian had suspected.

He transferred his attention to Victoria, whose cheeks had tinted a charming pink. Or it would be charming if it didn't have to do with Max Pesaro. He gritted his teeth—for whom had he to blame for the topic but himself? But he'd had to know for certain, and now he did. Yet they both looked . . . well, certainly not as if the carriage ride had been as pleasant as it could have been.

Keeping his insouciant smile in place, he replied, "What a pity. I've never had a complaint about such—"

"I've received word from Brim and Michalas," interrupted Wayren.

Sebastian allowed his smile to fade as all attention turned to her. He had information as well, but it would wait for a moment.

"They've arrived in Paris. Two more demons were dispatched, and all seems to be quiet for the moment.

Yet we know it's only a matter of time before more slip through the portal, and we haven't any time to waste. They received my message about the Rings of Jubai—thanks to Sebastian for that bit of information—and have suggested that they go to retrieve the ring from the Consilium, then meet up with us in Prague." Wayren looked at Victoria. "If you agree."

"Yes, of course. They can be to Rome much sooner than we can, and it makes the most sense to split up. We have the pigeons to communicate."

Sebastian noticed that she didn't look at either Pesaro or himself to confirm her decision. How far she had come from the first time he'd met her, when she'd attempted in vain to hide her femininity by wearing men's clothing to the Silver Chalice, then had nearly forgotten to offer a gentlemanly handshake.

Since then, she'd grown bold, beautiful, strong, and intelligent.

Worlds different from his gentle, serene Giulia, who nevertheless had had a fiery side when it came to her gardens.

He remembered the first time he'd met her, the sister of his acquaintance Max. The two boys had trampled two basil plants and a rosemary bush in an effort to peek through the window of a house sharing the same courtyard, where a beautiful young signora tended to stand whilst changing. Giulia had given them both the sharpest side of her tongue, a tartness he rarely remembered experiencing after that first time. Although, to be sure, it was those big, dark eyes that had captivated him—not the signora in her shift—so perhaps his memory was faulty.

Sebastian caught himself and looked back up to find Wayren gazing at him. He swallowed and fixed that charming smile on his lips, and realized with gratitude that no one else seemed to have noticed his lapse.

Max and Victoria had exchanged their own sharp words about whether horse or carriage would be the more efficient mode of transport, with both of them acknowledging that horseback would be the best choice. Which left Sebastian to wonder exactly what they'd disagreed about.

Then suddenly he was drawn back into the conversation by something Victoria said to Wayren. "A vampire? You're in need of a vampire? What can an undead tell you that I cannot?" he added with an unabashed grin.

"It's more what he can do," Pesaro replied. "Unless you wish to oblige me by allowing me to drain your blood, then stake you."

"It would certainly be interesting to participate in the *attempt*."

"He needs a vampire's blood for the Trial," Victoria said sharply. "Max is going to take up the *vis bulla* again."

Devil it, so he was. Sebastian pursed his lips, considering the implications of such an eventuality. Max with a *vis* would certainly be a welcome addition to their team when it came to closing the Midiverse Portal and retrieving the other Rings of Jubai. And Sebastian grudgingly admitted to himself that Victoria would be that much safer in the man's company, if that was where she wished to be.

And there was always the tantalizing possibility that Pesaro wouldn't live through the Trial.

"There are no vampires in London right now," he said. "I'll be most happy to assist you to find one in Prague. Ah . . . perhaps . . . perhaps you could use Katerina." He smiled with genuine humor for the first time that day.

"A paramour of your grandfather's, I presume," Pesaro responded drily.

"Of course. In fact, there's quite a story about how she came to be sired by Beauregard, if you will permit me to tell it, for it has bearing on our quest."

"Sired by Beauregard," mused Pesaro. "But with Beauregard dead, she is then locked in obeisance to *his* sire . . . which was Lilith, as I recall."

Sebastian saw the flash of unease in Pesaro's eyes, and much as he might abhor the man, he had some compassion for him in this case. The bond of Lilith's thrall, and her obsession with Pesaro, had been a bane to the man's life. And even Sebastian, who'd lived among the undead for a time, didn't care to contemplate some of the things Max had had to endure when he was with her.

"Yes, Lilith was Beauregard's sire, but the connection had become very weak. He was a Guardian vampire, but she did not trust him with one of the Rings of Jubai. He turned on her centuries ago, so I am not certain how strong Katerina's bond would be with Lilith."

"Ah yes . . . Beauregard was a power-hungry one, wasn't he?" Pesaro replied.

Sebastian didn't reply. Before Beauregard's attempt to turn Victoria undead, against his grandson's wishes, Sebastian had loved the vampire. Staking him to end his attack on Victoria had been almost as difficult as staking Giulia those years ago.

"Sebastian, you said that you had learned some other information," Wayren said, once again interrupting his thoughts. He felt as though she not only broke into his musings, but knew exactly what they were . . . or at least, had a sense of them. The canny look in her eyes seemed to support that.

"As I was about to say, the story of how Katerina became sired is an interesting one and it is germane to the task at hand."

"Then perhaps you could proceed with the story," Wayren encouraged.

Sebastian leveled a look at Pesaro. "I think I shall keep you in suspense. The pertinent information is that she has one of the Rings of Jubai. It was given to her by Germintrude, one of Lilith's other Guardian vampires, in an effort to sway her loyalty from Beauregard. Which didn't work, but she did keep the ring. If you need the blood of an undead, and we need the ring, it would be expedient to combine the two tasks. And then you can have the pleasure of killing her, after . . . how many days of fasting will it be?" he added with relish.

"Three," Pesaro replied. "We leave in the morning." He stood and, with the briefest of bows to Wayren and Victoria, left the room.

Torn between the hope and dread that Wayren would also go, leaving him alone with Victoria, Sebastian remained in his chair. But Victoria rose first and turned to him as he, too, politely got to his feet. "You will go with us, then?"

Did she truly think he wouldn't? That he'd leave her to Katerina and Lilith—for they'd have to face her, too, at some point in order to get the other two rings—and close the portal without his help?

Had he not proven himself yet?

But he held back these thoughts and nodded. "I'll be here before daybreak." He would have started for the door, but Wayren's quiet voice stopped him.

"Sebastian, if I could have a word with you."

The hair lifted at the back of his neck. Could she not have had that word with him earlier? He wanted to leave now. To get out of this house, where Victoria would go upstairs to her chamber and be joined by and with a man he loathed. How could she love him, the cold bastard?

"If you'll excuse me," Victoria said, hurrying from the room.

Sebastian preferred not to think about where she was going.

Instead, he turned to Wayren, not entirely sure that a conversation with her would be the lesser of two evils.

"If you want to see the Gardella Bible, there's no reason to hesitate."

"Is it blasphemous to say that I greatly dislike it when you do that?" he said wryly, turning toward the cabinet.

Wayren gave a soft laugh. He couldn't ever remember having heard it before—quiet, gentle, spritely. "No indeed. I've heard much worse over the centuries. Sebastian, do you know what you're looking for?"

He had to shake his head. "No." Honesty compelled him to speak with forthrightness. "I feel as though I'm waiting to find out what will be asked of me next."

The heavy handle twisted easily, levering downward and unlatching the door of the cabinet. Inside, the Bible sat, large and smelling of age. He pulled it out, sensitive to the crackling, browned pages and the faded ribbons that marked places in the great tome.

"The first pages of that Bible were scribed by the sisters who lived with Rosamunde in Lock Rose Abbey. Rosamunde, the mystic who wrote many pages of personal revelations before being called to the *vis bulla*."

Sebastian nodded, carefully opening the heavy cover. His education of Venator history was sketchy and incomplete, due to his many years away from them. But he had heard of Rosamunde, and he had seen the painting of her in the Consilium. Serene and oval faced, Lady Rosamunde Gardella had seemed much less imposing than a Venator should be.

"In the front of the book are listed all of those called

Illa Gardella," Wayren continued. "And in the back are named all of the Venators. Your name is there, as well as Max's."

And in between, Sebastian found, were faded pages of cramped medieval text of the New and Old Testaments, many of which were decorated with large illustrations, their colors long since washed out. These pages had been bound and rebound, and bound again into this much newer leather cover.

Beyond those crackling medieval texts, he found, were more pages of cramped writing in a different hand. Each one signed with a large, ornate *R*.

Here Sebastian paused. His hands hovered over the page, and he felt compelled to stop and read.

Feeling Wayren's interested gaze on him, he looked up and saw understanding there. "Rosamunde's writings. Of course. Would you like a copy of your own?" she asked.

Sebastian watched as Wayren reached into her ever-present rugged leather satchel and shuffled around inside. At last, she withdrew a sheaf of papers. Not nearly as aged as those he held on his lap, but crinkling and loosely bound with a leather thong stitched up one side.

"Perhaps you will find what you are looking for in here," she said, offering them to him.

Sebastian carefully closed the Bible and reached for the papers. When he touched Wayren's hand, a peaceful warmth slipped along his arm and settled inside him.

"Perhaps I shall."

Victoria slept alone the night before they left for Prague, and, of necessity, the nights following.

The journey left little time for sleep. Once they crossed the Channel, she, Max, and Sebastian sat a-saddle from sunrise until past sunset. Wayren did not ride, but she had her own methods of travel and would join Brim and Michalas in Rome and then the rest of them in Prague.

In fact, Victoria was relieved that Wayren would not be traveling with them. Knowing that she'd been a target of the demons once before left her uneasy, and she thought it would be best if Wayren were safely in the Consilium.

"But I will be there in Prague for Max's Trial," the blond woman told Victoria, after agreeing to go to Rome as quickly as possible. "I must be there to ensure that all goes well, and to make certain that he is well prepared."

Victoria had no reason nor desire to argue. She felt confident that Wayren would be safe now that she was on her guard against the demons, and until they could meet again in Prague. She wanted Max to be ready for the life-or-death task ahead of him as well, and she vacillated between begging him not to take the chance and understanding why he must. He felt it would help to protect her—as well as himself. She couldn't argue with that logic or sentiment.

In fact, after her conversation with Max in the carriage back in London, Victoria had little time to speak with him privately. His bleakness and underlying anger left her cold and uncertain . . . and frightened.

It wasn't a matter of him not caring for her, loving her.

It was a matter of him caring for, and loving, her too much. So much that he could be tempted away from his duty if her life was at risk.

At last she understood why he resisted being with her. Making her a part of his life. He was afraid she would affect his decisions, his honor, his duty.

And perhaps . . . perhaps she should be as thoughtful and hesitant.

But she could not. She'd found what she wanted, and if she had to live the life of *Illa* Gardella—a life of sacrifice and danger, duty and necessity—she wanted Max to be part of it.

The night before they left for Prague, after she left Sebastian in the small sitting room with Wayren, she'd had one last private moment with Max in the *kalari* room.

The broad, mat-carpeted chamber housed a variety of weaponry as well as piles of cushions and pillows. Kritanu used them for protection when he worked with Victoria, training her in the martial art of *kalaripayattu* and on the Chinese fighting method of *qinggong*, the half-flying, half-gliding ability that Max had mastered.

Victoria and Max had used the generous cushions for a wholly different purpose only a few weeks ago.

When she opened the door, Victoria found Max standing at the slender weapons cabinet that held Kritanu's extensive collection of blades.

Despite the fact that she moved silently, he turned when she came into the room. He held an odd-looking sword that curved from blade through hilt, and with his bare feet, thick dark hair, and swarthy skin, he reminded her of a fearsome pirate. His expression supported the comparison.

"Three days of fasting?" she asked, imitating his habit of getting immediately to the point as she walked across the room to him. "And then what?"

"Three days of fasting and prayer, while you and Vioget obtain the Ring of Jubai," he corrected her. "I know time is of the essence, but the process is not unlike that of the knights of old when they were ready to take their vows. Three days on my knees, and then locked in a room with an undead. Only one of us will survive that meeting."

Victoria felt the ground shift beneath her feet and the walls tip.

She'd heard about the Trial before, but never having had occasion to witness it, she hadn't known the details other than that it was a life-or-death proposition. Max would never have spoken of it, and no one had attempted the Trial since she became a Venator. It was an exercise that Wayren, not *Illa* Gardella, managed—and now that Victoria understood who Wayren really was, it made even more sense.

"You have to fight a vampire after no food or sleep for three days? In a closed room?" Even she, with her two *vis bullae*, would be hard-pressed to succeed in that.

And even though they were in a hurry to close the portal, a one- or two-day delay in Prague wouldn't make much of a difference if they had Max back with them in full strength. Especially when it came to facing Lilith and finding her lair.

But what if he didn't succeed? Oh God. Then they would be without him. . . . *She* would be without him. After all of this. Victoria swallowed and looked up at him. "Max," she began, trying to find a way to speak her worries that he would understand . . . and not find insulting, but he interrupted.

"Did you think it would be a simple task?" he asked derisively. He replaced the *khukuri* knife and latched the cabinet. "Only four others have ever succeeded."

"But, Max . . ."

"Stop with the histrionics, Victoria. It's not becoming to *Illa* Gardella. Do you think your aunt Eustacia begged Daclid not to take the Trial?"

"Who?"

"Before she loved Kritanu, when he was merely a young man sent to train her, Eustacia loved a man named Daclid who believed he could wear the *vis bulla*. He attempted the Trial and did not succeed, as have many others over the centuries."

He didn't give her any relief; his face remained closed and hard. "There is no guarantee of my success, even this second time."

Victoria struggled to gather her thoughts, which seemed to have splintered into uncollectible shards with these revelations. The last time she'd felt so taken off guard, so out of her realm, was when she witnessed Eustacia's beheading by the man who stood before her. "How do you get the blood if you stake the vampire? What is that for?"

"We get the blood prior to the battle—I'm allowed assistance with that because that isn't part of the Trial," he added with self-deprecation. "Just enough blood to soak the *vis bulla* in it."

He stood in front of her, so close her skirt brushed the tops of his narrow feet. "But that doesn't come into play unless I succeed in leaving the room alive. That part of the Trial, incidentally, comes from the battles in the Colosseum. You know of the men thrown to the lions for sport . . . but after dark, they might be thrown to vampires instead. A crowd of Tutela and vampires would watch for their enjoyment."

Victoria didn't want to think about what Max would have to face. Not with him standing there, close enough that she could see the individual whiskers starting to emerge from his chin, and the steady pump of heartbeat in the side of his throat. But nor could she be ignorant of it. She had to know. She was *Illa* Gardella. "And if you leave that room alive?" she prompted.

"The blood-soaked *vis bulla* is pierced through my skin—just as it was yours. The difference is that I, not of the Gardellas, take it drenched with undead blood as well as holy water. That's the final test. I either live, and have the power of the *vis*, or I die from the combination of evil and holiness piercing my flesh."

And then Victoria understood it all. "If you succeed in any of it—all of it—it's by . . . by divine will."

"Of course. Just as your calling is."

"Max, you—"

"Don't." He spoke through teeth clamped tightly.

So she didn't. She surged into him instead.

His arms came around her with a fierceness she hadn't expected, a strength that told her he wasn't as dispassionate as he pretended.

She felt, for the first time, an edge of desperation in his touch, and knew that the same fear echoed in her own actions. The faint tremble in her fingers as she dragged him as close as she could, the way he pressed his temple against hers in a singular, frozen moment as their hearts beat together, their breaths mingled. The way they dragged the other to the floor seconds later, pulling haphazardly at clothes, lifting, shifting, yanking them away so that they could be flesh to flesh again.

They came together with ferocity, without finesse or hesitation. And when they finished and found themselves in a sweaty heap, limbs and fabric tangled and twisted, Max opened his eyes and looked down at Victoria.

Her heart seized up, began to flutter and swell, and she opened her mouth to tell him how much she loved him, how she couldn't bear it if something happened . . . perhaps even to beg him not to attempt it.

But he spoke first, sending all of her flowery thoughts scattering. "Stay away from me until after, Victoria. I need no distractions. Do you understand?"

She nodded, her head cradled in his large, warm hands, the weight of his body gentle against hers. She moistened her lips, drew in her breath to argue . . . then nodded again.

The corners of his eyes crinkled the slightest bit, just enough for her to know that he recognized her struggle to acquiesce.

They rose, righted their clothing, left the room, and went separately to their chambers.

And the next morning, they left for Prague.

Eleven

In Which a Vampire Is Taken in by a Pretty Face

Max found it infuriating that he couldn't shake the dreams. Nearly every morning, the remnants lingered throughout his first waking hours, leaving his stomach tight and hands shaky, and the images swimming in his memory.

One would think that sleeping only four or five hours each night after a grueling day of riding, and then bedding down in small, rented rooms with Vioget and Victoria—one too close, and the other too damn far away—that he would be too exhausted to dream.

But, alas, no.

He staggered awake from the nightmare, his hand still gripping the sword to slice off Eustacia's head— and the image, not of hers, but of Victoria's face, turned toward him, awaiting the fatal blow.

Max rolled off the thin bed and pulled slowly to his feet, heart still pounding, fingers still shaking. When he turned groggily and slammed his temple against a low beam in the dingy little room, he didn't bother to hold back a bellowed curse. At least the blow helped to knock the nocturnal wisps from his mind.

Victoria looked at him curiously, but had better sense than to say anything. They'd fallen into a bit of a routine in the morning, the three of them. Max and Sebastian dressed quickly, then left to saddle the horses and find something to break their fast while Victoria prepared to leave.

Of necessity, for both riding astride and sharing a room with two men, Victoria had dressed in men's clothing since crossing the Channel.

And she'd cut her hair.

Rather, Max had cut her hair.

They'd argued about it on the first morning, in Normandy.

"You'll need to hide your hair better if you think to pass as a man," Max had told her. Breeches and a shirt and coat were all good, but they'd been fashioned for the sharp angles of a man's body, not the curves of a woman's.

"Cut it off, then," Victoria told him, lifting the rope of a braid and letting it flop against her shoulder. "You've already told me I should."

"But no, you needn't go to such an extreme. Tuck it inside your hat or coat," said Vioget from across the room. "It would be a shame to cut such lovely curls. Why, when they're unbound, they reach nearly to your—"

"Waist. How crude to mention it," Max cut him off. Their eyes locked and antipathy flared.

"I'll do it myself," Victoria snapped, yanking the braid taut with one hand, and reaching to her waist for the knife. The blade glinted suddenly in the early dawn. "Bloody damn fools."

"No, wait," Max said, grasping her wrist. He hesitated . . . but in the end, it had to be done. "Let me. You'll cut yourself."

A bloody weak excuse, but she relaxed her arm and allowed him to remove the knife from her fingers. His hand settled on the top of her warm head. Before he could think twice, reconsider, he sliced the long, thick plait right at the base of her neck.

The braid fell away, sagging in his hand, and he watched dark curls spring up softly around the tender skin of her neck and shoulders. She turned, tipping and tilting her head as though loosened from some great burden and smiled at him. "It feels so light."

"A bit safer, too," he said, unable to keep from staring at Victoria with the mass of soft, rumpled tresses that fell into her eyes and face and made her look as though she'd just risen from bed.

"And very, very lovely," interjected Vioget. "Not boyish at all."

"Then what was the point?" laughed Victoria.

None too gently, Max smoothed what was left of her hair back into a low tail. "This," he said, fastening around it the leather cord he would have used for his own hair. "Wear a hat, and you'll look like nothing more than a young man."

"A very pretty one at that," agreed Vioget. Who always seemed to need the last word.

Now, after more than a week of rapid travel, Prague loomed ahead. The orange-red roofs of close-set buildings burned bright in the lowering August sun behind him, and the wicked-looking black spire of the unfinished St. Vitus's Cathedral jutted above the sea of terra-cotta roofs. Beyond, across the sparkling Vltava, Max could barely see the dual towers of Týn Church.

"I presume you know where to find Katerina," he said, turning to Vioget.

"Most assuredly."

Max nodded and gathered up the reins to his horse. "I will leave that to both of you, then. You'll find me at Týn Church on the evening of the day after tomorrow." He'd already begun his fast this morning, and would be on his knees in the cathedral before the sun completely set. That would suffice as his first day of fasting, according to Wayren.

Vioget looked as though he meant to say something, but for once held his tongue. Max glanced at Victoria but couldn't allow his attention to linger. "Be safe," was all he said, and urged his mount forward.

Whatever she replied was lost in the scattering of rock and rubble beneath his horse's hooves as they leapt forward.

Max didn't look back.

Victoria watched him go and resisted the urge to kick her own horse into a gallop after him. She'd see Max again in three days, and before then, she and Sebastian had to find the vampire Katerina. She couldn't afford to be distracted or worried. There would be time for that later, she told herself. Nevertheless, she watched him grow smaller on the road ahead of them with a pervading sense of loss.

She and Sebastian rode in silence for a time, and the city's features became clearer even as the lowering sun cast longer shadows in front of them. Through the trees she caught glimpses of the single bridge crossing the Vlatava River, and Victoria watched closely for a sign of Max's tall figure. But it was growing dark, and the riders all looked the same to her.

Victoria shook herself mentally and tightened her resolve. There were important matters to be dealt with, ones that could have far-reaching impact if she didn't succeed. She looked at Sebastian and asked, "You're quite certain this Katerina has the Ring of Jubai?"

He looked at her, a grin tipping the sides of his mouth. "It would have been a waste of time to bring us here if I weren't, would it not?" He shrugged. "According to my grandfather, once Katerina obtained that ring from Germintrude, she never took it off. It was her way of spiting Lilith, I think."

He pointed to the snaking river and the single span over it. "The Stone Bridge," he told her. "Katerina was turned because of that bridge."

"You did claim to know the story," Victoria said, glad for the conversation to keep her mind off Max. Why did he have to ride ahead of them? They were still going to the same place.

"I do know the story, perhaps better than any other mortal," he told her. "Perhaps if I tell you, it will distract you a bit—hmm, Victoria?"

His sidewise look made her heart pang quietly, for he wasn't completely successful in hiding his own hurt.

"It's a beautiful bridge, is it not?" he asked with a gallant sweep of his hand. "When the sun rises, it casts a lovely burnished glow over it."

She could see people and carriages moving across the bridge, which stood in the river on ten arches that made it look like a graceful centipede. At the leg of every arch, statues rose on either side of the bridge. Other than that, the span was unfettered by wall or decoration. Simple, clean, elegant.

They drew nearer, and Victoria looked up at a single ornate spire that rose atop a hill above them. "Prague Castle is there," Sebastian told her. "And that is St. Vitus's Cathedral, which they have been building off and on since the thirteen hundreds. It's still not completed."

"And what of Katerina?"

"You're not interested in the history of Praha, as the natives call it?" Sebastian asked. "I'm merely attempting to fill your mind with something other than worry."

"I'm not worried. Not at this moment."

Sebastian looked at her. She realized how dark it was getting, for she couldn't see the details of his face, or the gleam in his eyes. "Perhaps you should be, Victoria."

"What do you mean?" Fear seized her. What did he know? Something about Max going off alone?

And then she stopped herself. She very nearly stopped her horse, too, there in the middle of the road. What a fool. What a fool!

She was doing exactly what Max had warned about, had worried about. She was allowing her fear for him, her thoughts of him, to overtake everything else.

There were demons to fight. A horrible, unfamiliar malevolence that she'd never faced before . . . that had dared to abduct Wayren.

And Max . . . Max was more than capable of taking care of himself. She shook her head and felt the hair loosen from its tie at her neck. A chin-length strand fell into her face, and she brushed it back impatiently.

"Now there's the Victoria I know," said Sebastian airily, as though he'd watched her pull herself together.

She saw that they were just at the approach of the bridge. Great statues guarded the arched entrance tower.

"As I'd begun to tell you," he continued as their mounts clopped onto cobblestones, "when the bridge was built, the masons added egg yolk to the mortar to make it stronger. People from all over the country sent eggs here to Praha in order to assist. And," he added with a smile as their horses took the first steps onto the bridge, "one particularly helpful town thought to hard-boil the eggs before sending them in order to keep them from breaking during the journey."

Victoria saw the glitter of lights ahead and along the

bridge, but the orange roofs and cream-colored buildings had turned gray in the low light. She looked over at Sebastian. "They hard-boiled them?"

"Ah, so you were listening," he said. "I thought perhaps I'd lost you. Yes, indeed. According to the tale I heard, the eggs weren't so helpful for the mortar, but they were a fine snack for the builders."

She gave a short laugh and at the same moment felt a familiar chill over the back of her neck. A vampire, perhaps two.

A surge of energy swept through her as she reached for the stake she kept inside her boot. When she rose upright in her saddle, she caught Sebastian's eye and saw that he'd armed himself similarly.

With a quick sweep of her gaze, she identified the undead as a handsome young man near one of the statues. He rode on a large horse and smiled down at a woman who lugged a heavy basket on wide leather straps over her shoulder. She was well past Victoria's age and, in the lantern light, looked haggard and tired. She'd be no match for a superhuman undead, but, given the option, the vampire would probably prefer fresh, younger blood.

Such as Victoria's.

With a telling glance at Sebastian, she pulled the tie from her hair and yanked the edge of her cloak down over to hide her breech-clad legs. Then, urging her mount forward, she brushed past the vampire and his intended victim.

"Pardon me, sir," she said, looking at the vampire, pulling his attention from the older woman. She saw and felt the spark of interest when she stopped just beyond him and turned as if in need of help. Her English speech identified her as a stranger, and Sebastian had stayed far enough back that it wasn't evident that they were traveling together.

The vampire, fickle as she expected him to be, directed his horse away from the older woman and toward this more attractive prey. Victoria watched beyond him as Sebastian moved toward the woman and alighted from his saddle. He'd make certain she got safely away.

"May I help you?" he asked, in accented English.

"Yes, oh, thank you for speaking English," Victoria stammered. "I'm a bit lost, you see, and I was hoping you might help me to find an inn for the night."

From her perspective, it seemed that any self-respecting vampire with a dram of common sense might question how such a ripe plum of a victim would fall into his lap . . . but this particular undead appeared to have no suspicions about the serendipity of the situation. In fact, his eyes lit with unholy glee, seemingly unaware that his other prey had begun to walk along.

"But of course," he replied. "Let us cross the bridge and get to the Town Square. There are many rooms for let there."

And many dark corners into which a victim could be dragged and sucked bone-dry.

"Oh, thank you," Victoria replied, wishing that she could simply slam the stake into him right here. But it would be rather difficult to explain how a man suddenly disappeared from his saddle and turned into a puff of musty ash. Too many people wandered about.

But the moment they reached a dark corner—and, ironically, they would both be intent on reaching such a locale—Victoria's stake would find its home if he wasn't able to tell them where Katerina was. And even if he was.

"You're lost, you say? Where are you going?" he asked, keeping his horse next to hers along one side of the bridge as though to block her from any other passersby.

Victoria turned away coyly. "For tonight, I wish only to find a place to sleep. In the morning . . . well, in the morning, I shall meet my friend." Not her best lie, but the vampire seemed patently uninterested in anything but guiding her into a dark corner.

In fact, he didn't flicker an eyelash over her vague, rather silly story. This undead was definitely one of the less capable vampires she'd ever met. It just went to show what Aunt Eustacia had always told her. There were smart vampires and foolish ones, silly ones and frightening ones . . . but regardless of their personalities, every one of them was evil and bent on one thing: drinking human blood.

By now they'd crossed the bridge, walking their horses under the gateway toward Old Town.

Victoria found the area on the eastern bank of the Vlatava much closer and darker than the west side, from which she and Sebastian had approached the city. Connected buildings, creamy white ones with the familiar orange roofs, butted up along narrow, twisting cobble streets. Row after row of houses connected ten or twelve in a row of varying heights and widths. Many had lights burning in the windows, but they were obscured by curtains or shutters, and the illumination gave little to the shadowy streets.

When Victoria and the undead moved far enough from the bridge, she eased her horse into a particularly shadowy corner and stopped. "Oh dear," she said, pretending to fuss with the bag attached to the back of her saddle. The vampire moved closer, and when she looked up, she found red eyes burning next to her face.

"I don't think you're going to need a place to sleep tonight," he said, reaching for her arm. "But if you insist, I can certainly provide accommodations."

"I don't think that's a good idea," Victoria said calmly. "I seek Katerina. Where is she?"

"Who are you?" he asked. But he didn't move away.

"I'm looking for the Ring of Jubai. Does she have it?"

"Who are you?" Now he pulled back, his eyes fading a bit in surprise.

Impatient with his repetitive response, she grabbed the front of his coat. And then Sebastian appeared just behind the vampire, blocking his horse into the corner with her.

The vampire, who was, in the end, too foolish to look more than a bit alarmed—but not truly frightened—turned at this new presence.

"Ah, I thought that was you, Antonín," Sebastian said in a liquid-smooth voice. "I suggest you remove your hands from her if you wish to see another sunrise. Or . . . pardon me. I meant to say . . . sun*set*."

Antonín released Victoria, his eyes definitely no longer as pink. "Vioget?"

"Alas, but you don't seem pleased to see me at all."

"No, I should say not. And Katerina . . . I don't believe she would welcome you either, considering the last time you were here." Then he swiveled back to Victoria, and she could see calculation in his face. "And who is this that you protect her so vehemently?"

"This is *Illa* Gardella. I don't think she is in need of my protection, Antonín." Sebastian's voice held a wave of humor.

"*Illa* Gardella. The woman Venator." He shifted in his saddle. "But I thought she was dead. Killed in Rome last year."

"You have faulty information, for as you can see, I am alive and well. If you take me to Katerina . . . or, better yet, obtain the Ring of Jubai for me, I may perhaps allow you to see another . . . What was it, Sebastian? Sunset?" She leaned closer and got a whiff of undeadness. "Or perhaps I will not."

"Is she at the tavern?" asked Sebastian.

"Not at night," Antonín replied. When Sebastian made a face of disbelief, he continued. "I've no reason to lie! Her quarrel is with you, and most likely I'd be rewarded if I brought you to her. But I can't get the ring for you. She's never removed it since Germintrude gave it to her. She thinks it will help bring her husband back to her someday." He wrapped his reins in preparation to go. "Katerina is a bit . . . mad."

"That is an understatement," Sebastian muttered.

Victoria glanced at him, wondering exactly what he hadn't told her. It wouldn't be the first time Sebastian hadn't been completely forthcoming. Nevertheless, they'd find Katerina and retrieve the ring. And if the vampire was slain in the process, Victoria would locate another undead for Max's Trial.

Perhaps even this unfortunate one here. In fact . . . that might not be a bad idea after all, she thought, looking at the vampire in a new light. Why should Max meet a more powerful vampire like Katerina when this one would suit just fine?

"Follow me to Josevof, the Jewish Quarter," said Antonín, backing his horse up.

"Mmm . . . perhaps you would be so kind as to allow me," said Sebastian without moving from his path. He reached over and grabbed up the reins from the vampire, wrapping them loosely around his wrist. "I do hope you aren't offended, Antonín, but I don't trust you one whit."

The undead gave a bit of a chuckle, and Victoria saw the flare of pink again in his eyes. The tips of his fangs touched his lower lip. "Of course not. Now shall we be off?"

Sebastian and Antonín led the way with Victoria close behind them in the narrow warren of streets. They passed by the famous astrological clock that looked down on the Town Square, a relatively wide-open area that offered relief from the close streets blocked by three-story buildings. As it was only ten o'clock on a pleasant summer evening, people were scattered about, walking and talking. Victoria noticed Antonín's wistful glance at more than one isolated couple.

He was probably wishing he hadn't been so easily distracted from the simple woman on the bridge.

Her own gaze lingered on the ornate entrance to Our Lady Before Týn, the cathedral in which Max was presumably on his knees. She hoped. Victoria felt Sebastian watching her as she looked toward the grand building, which reared up over the square and could be seen throughout the city. Brushing the sky, two ornate spires lifted in dual points.

"One tower represents the masculine of our world, and the other, the feminine," Sebastian said in her ear. He still held the reins of Antonín's horse. Victoria realized that she'd stopped, and was looking up at the asymmetrical towers. "That's why they're different. Do you wish to look inside?"

"No." *Yes.* "Let's get the ring."

"As my lady wishes."

They left the Old Town Square behind them, Victoria riding past the church without another glance. The unencumbered area gave way again to the winding, narrow streets, which became quieter and darker as they left the city center behind. The back of Victoria's neck shifted with chill, and she knew that undead lurked about. But though she and Sebastian exchanged measured, meaningful glances, they didn't detour to investigate.

"Klausen Synagogue," said Antonín at last, flourishing his hand toward a simply faceded building. After the detail of the cathedrals and other structures in the Town Square, this gleamed like smooth cream under the moonlight. "Behind it is the old cemetery. Katerina usually stays within, waiting for the odd mortal to venture through the graveyard."

"You will show us where," Sebastian said, dismounting from his horse while holding both sets of reins.

Victoria and Sebastian remained close to Antonín as he led them past the synagogue and beyond the gate of the cemetery. She'd never seen anything like this dark, shadowy space jumbled with tombstones.

The headstones erupted from the earth as though pushed up by some great internal force, so close together there was very little space to walk between them. Off-kilter, tipping, broken, the thousands of headstones clumped in a small space reminded Victoria of the hair on a cat's back, rising in all directions.

She found it nearly impossible to navigate between them without stepping on graves, lifting her foot over a grave marker, or even finding grass on which to trod. The space held an eeriness, yet an overriding sense of peace as well.

"Twelve thousand people buried here," Sebastian said quietly. "Most of them on top of each other, in layers upon layers." He stood near her, occasionally offering a gentlemanly hand to help her over a jutting stone.

"Where is Katerina?" Victoria asked, realizing the back of her neck hadn't changed in temperature—as it would if there were another vampire nearby.

"I don't know. She should be here," Antonín insisted, leading them on, deeper into the center of the cemetery. Victoria saw a grave that looked like a large stone bed, complete with head and foot, and at about that moment, she realized the air had begun to stir.

Not a breeze . . . no, not even the chill that lifted hair at the back of her neck when she sensed the undead. Victoria lifted her face, flaring her nostrils to draw in the scent on the air.

A blast of chill swept over her as she smelled it . . . and felt the air's movement grow stronger. She looked at Sebastian, read the recognition in his eyes, and turned back to their vampire companion. "What is it? Why have you brought us here?" she demanded, her hand falling to the sword at her side.

But he seemed just as shocked as they, his red eyes wide and frightened. "I . . . What is this?" he cried, stumbling backward over a jumble of headstones.

He tried to run away, but Sebastian caught him by the arm, slamming him into a nearby headstone. The vampire fell as Victoria's hair lifted and swirled in the rising breeze. "What is it?" Sebastian demanded.

"I don't know! On Lucifer's sword, I swear it. . . . I don't know!"

Victoria drew her sword, looking up to see that the scattering of stars and the half-moon had become little more than a dull glow behind a billowing black cloud.

Again. No, not again.

Chill that had little to do with undead presence battled through her body, freezing her fingers and slowing her reflexes. One look at Antonín's face told her that no matter what trap he'd led them to, he hadn't expected this.

"Stand up, you bloody fool," Sebastian roared, yanking the vampire to his feet. "You'll stand with us or see the end of my stake."

"But they're . . . demons," he said, his voice distorted by the rising wind. The horribly familiar black clouds stewed above them, wind tossing Victoria's short hair wildly. "They'll kill us."

"Or I will," Victoria muttered, turning away from the ridiculous undead as the first swipe from the black-clawed, red-eyed creatures scored over her scalp.

She cried out and swung up with the sword. The

blade sliced through, and ice shivered along her weapon, through her arms, and up into her body.

Staggering, Victoria stumbled into a tombstone and fell, crashing into another nearby stone. She screamed in rage and arced the blade up again. Fallen leaves and old sticks lifted from the ground, battering against her like pummeling fists. She pulled to her feet, using the point of her sword against a moss-covered stone, felt it scrape metal against rock, and battled back at the black demon.

Another swipe, and she slowed further, slicing the wraith's head while accepting the paralyzing cold that trammeled through her body. Sebastian bumped into her and their backs came together. His warmth bled into her, and she was able to move again.

"Idiot," he shouted at Antonín, who cowered down between the cluster of stone markers. Sebastian swiped up with his own blade.

Digging beneath her coat, Victoria ducked as another black creature swooped close again. A small jug hung at her side, protected by a snug leather holder and a strap that went over her shoulder. She pulled it out, feeling Sebastian struggling against the demons above her, protecting her as she worked the cork free.

"Ready," she called over the rising gale, turning toward Sebastian. He struggled for a moment, pulling out his own store of holy water as she sliced at one of the black creatures. Again the unbearable cold shocked her, staggering her.

Sebastian caught her arm before she lost her balance on the unsteady ground and spilled her holy water. They looked at each other for a moment, barely able to discern the other's features in the maelstrom of leaves and fog, gauging the moment.

"Go!" shouted Victoria, and they both whirled,

winging the holy water from their bottles up and around into the hurricane about them.

Sizzling sounds, fizzing and even a scream of rage . . . The winds settled as the water spewed into the clouds and onto Antonín, who'd remained huddled against one of the taller gravestones.

Victoria considered leaving him, but instead, she grabbed him by the sleeve and dragged him haphazardly behind her as they dashed around and through the cluster of headstones. She had to swing up with her sword only once more before they found the cemetery entrance. The cold wasn't as daunting as before, but it slowed her enough that she gasped in pain.

Once they were out of the cemetery, as before, the demonic cloud lost its strength and remained behind them, rumbling and gurgling wickedly. Then, as Victoria watched, it swirled into itself and settled into the darkness below.

"Did you have to do that?" Antonín cried.

Victoria turned and saw that the holy water had caught him straight in the face. His skin had peeled away, leaving one of his eyes sagging in its socket. He held a hand to his destroyed flesh, but seemed less concerned over that than the mass of evil they'd left behind.

And indeed, as before in London, they'd left it behind, weakened by the holy water.

Or it had chosen not to follow.

Victoria wasn't sure which.

She shivered and whirled at the vampire. Before he realized what had happened, her stake was poised over his chest and a great handful of his shirt was clumped in her fist. "What kind of trick was that?"

"No trick, no trick!" he cried. "I swear it! Do you think I would have gone into that if I had known?"

"If you don't take us to Katerina—" Sebastian began, but Victoria interrupted.

"No, he'll come with us now, and we'll find Katerina in the morning. When the sun is risen." She bared her teeth at the vampire, furious. "We're in need of undead blood, and he looks more than willing to share."

Sebastian nodded and helped Victoria bind the undead's hands together behind him.

"I've never seen anything like that," he whined. "I've never seen it. I swear it. I heard something. . . . Just let me go, and I'll take you to Katerina."

"You heard something?" Victoria repeated as they climbed back onto their horses. She glanced back over the cemetery and saw that the angry cloud had all but dissipated. She hadn't noticed the malingering fog when they'd arrived at the cemetery, although she'd been more distracted, having expected an ambush of undead . . . not one of the frightening demons. "What do you mean, you heard something?"

"Recently," Antonín said, "there have been incidents. . . . I've heard about them. And Katerina seemed to be a bit worried about her cemetery. I didn't lie about that," he added defensively. "She usually *is* there at night. But I didn't know. It was horrible." He shuddered. His vampire countenance twisted with fear, made all the more grotesque by the ragged flesh near the one side of his mouth.

Victoria ignored his last statement and looked at Sebastian. Her rising worry was reflected in his set face, even though she couldn't see the details of his expression.

More demons—demons that even frightened the undead.

Demons that had driven a powerful vampire from her cemetery lair.

That realization as much as anything else worried her. Vampires hated demons, but they didn't fear them.

At least, they never had before.

Twelve

Wherein Sebastian Is Reminded That Hell Hath No Fury

"The only way you'll get the ring from Katerina is by killing her," said Antonín companionably, apparently having recovered from the unexpected demon attack. His face had also begun to show signs of healing, the peeling skin falling away to reveal fresh baby pink flesh beneath.

Victoria swallowed a drink of wine from where she sat on the edge of the bed and replied, "I don't anticipate a problem."

She'd kept Antonín out of sight and quiet while Sebastian found a room at a small inn, and now the three of them had settled into the chamber for the night. At least, she and Sebastian had settled in. The vampire was well and truly trussed in a corner, yet he seemed to be feeling rather talkative.

"I wouldn't mind something to drink," he said at that moment. "Perhaps a wrist or arm?"

"Don't be ridiculous," Sebastian said, looking up

from a sheaf of curling papers. A dusky blond curl fell from his forehead and into his eyes, reminding Victoria that he still had the ability to make her insides go soft.

"I'm thirsty. Unless you wish to offer me even a drink of wine if you won't give me a wrist? You could hold the cup." His voice lifted in a bit of a whine.

Victoria ignored him and looked over at Sebastian, wondering not for the first time what he was reading. He'd pulled the pages out more than once during their trip, even late at night, often sitting in the small circle of candlelight to pore over them, while she and Max pretended to ignore each other.

Or, at least, she pretended. She didn't know about Max.

"She's not so easy to kill," Antonín persisted.

Victoria looked at Sebastian. "If I give him something to eat, perhaps he'll stop talking."

He glanced up, and she noticed that the gleam of humor was missing from his eyes. "You could knock him on the head, too," he said. "Or, better yet, stake him. We don't need him to find Katerina."

"But I have other plans for him," she replied, looking at the vampire speculatively. The more she thought about it, the more pleased she was with the undead candidate for Max's Trial. Max could take him blindfolded and with one hand behind his back, even without a *vis* and after three days of fasting.

"I see." Sebastian looked back down.

Victoria had traveled since dawn, and had slept little for the last ten days while they journeyed, so she was tired. She'd ordered a bath earlier, using another chamber for privacy. More than a week's worth of grime and dirt had layered her skin, and it was the first chance she'd had to wash in more than a small basin.

The window of their room faced east, toward the

sun that would rise in a few hours, and toward Týn Church, which stood on one of the city's central hills. She found her eyes continuing to stray in that direction, and she had to pull them back. More than once.

Perhaps she ought to try to sleep, especially since tomorrow, when the sun was up, they would go after Katerina. But something bothered her, niggled at the corner of her mind.

She wasn't worried about sleeping with Antonín in the room—he was bound tightly, wrist to ankle, and tied to the post of a heavy bed on the floor. He was going nowhere unless she released him.

Which was probably why he continued to talk. "She's a bit mad, as Vioget has cause to know."

Victoria glanced at Sebastian, who didn't flicker an eyelash. He reached for the cup of wine and drank without lifting his eyes from the pages.

"She won't take off that ring, either, because she hopes it'll be a bargaining chip to bring back her husband."

"Is her husband dead?" Victoria asked in spite of herself.

"He was one of the architects trying to repair the Stone Bridge five hundred years ago. It fell apart after the king threw the queen's confessor into the Vlatava because the priest wouldn't tell him whether the queen was cuckolding him. Someone decided he should be sainted for that, too."

"So Katerina's husband was repairing the bridge?"

"Trying to. It kept falling down. Lucifer had been delighted by the murder of the priest, and he amused himself by continuing to destroy the bridge every time they thought it was going to stand. Finally, Brughard, Katerina's husband, made a deal with him and agreed to give Lucifer the soul of the first creature to cross the bridge after it was repaired."

"He gave his wife's soul?" Victoria asked. No wonder the vampiress was mad.

"Not intentionally." Antonín sounded annoyed. Perhaps she had ruined the suspense of his story. "He finished the bridge, and told the workers to release a cock to cross over first. But Lucifer sent Beauregard to bring a message to Katerina that her husband had been injured. She fled from her house and ran across the bridge, and was the first to cross. Thus she lost her soul, and Lucifer gave her to Beauregard to sire. Which of course he did."

So that was why Katerina wasn't very fond of Sebastian. His grandfather had tricked her into becoming a vampire. "But what about Brughard?"

"She turned him herself, but he was slain some years ago." Antonín's gaze drifted to Sebastian. "By a young Venator staking his first undead."

At that, Sebastian looked up, brushing the hair from his face. "Why don't you put a stake into him, Victoria? He's beginning to annoy me."

"And so now her husband is damned to Hell . . . not a bad thing in my book, of course, but apparently Katerina meant to keep him alive for a lot longer."

"She thinks the ring will bring him back?" Victoria asked. "How?"

Antonín shrugged as well as he could, bound thus. "I said she was mad. But she believes a bargain might be struck with some holy or divine entity. She gives them the ring, and her husband is rescued from Hell."

"There is no way to rescue an undead's soul from Hell," Sebastian spoke suddenly. His face looked grim in the low light. "Once an undead drinks from a mortal, he's damned for eternity."

"I have heard otherwise," replied Antonín loftily. "Lucifer doesn't like it one bit, but he's had to release more than one of the vampire souls he's collected over the millennia." He nodded knowingly. "It's never a pleasant time for us, of course. Lucifer is—"

"Give him some wine and shut him up," said Sebastian suddenly. Victoria was struck by how much he sounded like Max at that moment—sharp and terse. Perhaps he was as tired as she felt.

Or perhaps there was something else bothering him . . . besides the reminder of what he'd done to Giulia. And Burghard.

She rose and found some *salvi* in her pack. The potion worked quickly to put mortals to sleep, but she wasn't certain whether it would affect an undead. However, she was willing to try.

Antonín was thirsty, and gulped the wine she held to his mouth. When she pulled the cup away, he looked up at her with hopeful red eyes. "How about a bit of something else?" he asked thickly. "Your wrist . . . I could make it easy and quick."

"Why would I do anything for you?" she asked, although a thought had been teasing her mind.

"Because I'll tell you how to get Katerina. The way to get to her." His voice lowered, and he glanced at Sebastian as though afraid he would hear.

"The same way you took me to her lair at the cemetery?" Victoria said.

"I didn't expect those demons to be there."

"You said you'd heard about the demons, stories. How long ago did you start hearing about them?"

"More than a month."

"Is Katerina frightened, too? Or merely inconvenienced?"

"She is frightened. All of the undead are frightened. There's been nothing like this before." His eyes were fastened on her white wrist, showing from the cuff of the clean man's shirt she'd donned after her bath. "Please. Just a bit. It won't hurt you."

Victoria didn't reply. "Is it true that an undead soul isn't damned if he didn't drink from a mortal? Is it true?"

Antonín looked at her, and she allowed herself to meet his eyes. The tug of his thrall, weak though it was to someone like her, tickled around her, and she allowed her breathing to grow heavy. Yet she was aware of everything. She knew she could blink, could turn away at any moment. "Is it true?" she asked.

Phillip. Oh, Phillip, I've always believed it was true.

What if it isn't?

She allowed Antonín to lure her, to tease and pull and to think he was gathering her in with his strength. She felt it, felt the curl of warmth and pleasure slip under her skin . . . but not completely. Raising her arm, she watched his attention move to her wrist as though it slogged through water. The gleam in his eyes burned hot and red, and his breath whistled from behind his teeth and fangs. Warmth . . . softness . . .

"Victoria!"

Sebastian was there suddenly, and Victoria turned in surprise.

Before she could react, he pulled her from the vampire, jerking her up and away from where she'd crouched. The heat still simmered in her veins as she caught herself from falling. She steadied her staggered breath, dragged in air from between her lips.

"What are you doing?" he demanded over Antonín's cry of annoyance.

She glanced briefly at the vampire. She'd known exactly what she was doing, but she wasn't about to explain it to Sebastian.

"Isn't it enough that you had to bring him here? And now you do this? What are you trying to do?"

"Sebastian," she began, the last remnants of the vampire's thrall slipping off her like a silken shroud.

His fingers dug into her arms, and she pulled away with such force that she bumped into the table. The pages he'd been reading fluttered onto the floor, but before she could bend to retrieve them, he caught her shoulders.

Not so roughly this time, he closed his fingers over her. "Is it that you didn't trust me?" he asked. "Or that you didn't trust yourself?"

Then she understood. They would have been alone in the chamber with Max gone; Sebastian thought she'd brought Antonín as a chaperone of sorts. "It's neither, Sebastian. You know that."

She stooped, pulling away from his grip, and picked up the papers from the floor. "What have you been reading all this time?" But when she saw the ornate *R* on the bottom of one page, she didn't need him to tell her. She recognized Rosamunde's sign. "Do you find them fascinating?"

But Sebastian had turned away. Victoria set the manuscript on the table, and as she took a step toward him, she heard a choking, snorting noise from the corner. A glance told her that the *salvi* had worked, and Antonín was snoring with alacrity.

"It's hard enough," Sebastian said, looking out the window that framed Týn Church, "to be here. In Praha, with you. Both of you. Stay away from Antonín. Don't tease him. You don't know . . . you don't know what you looked like, Victoria. Just now. Your eyes half closed, your face like that . . ."

She swallowed. Her throat constricted roughly, audible in the quiet moment. She had had a purpose; she would have let Antonín feed from her, just a bit. She had a reason.

But she didn't have to explain it to Sebastian.

"I told you that I wouldn't be a gentleman about . . . it . . . ," he said, still looking out the window. "And so if you brought Antonín here because of that, I suppose I cannot blame you."

Victoria couldn't hold back an angry snort. "Sebastian, the day I use a vampire as a shield from my own desires is the day I'm finished as a Venator."

"Your own desires?"

"There's no arguing the fact that we've been together, that there is attraction and affection between us. I wasn't pretending. But I've no intention of acting on it again."

"I told you I wouldn't be a gentleman about it," he said again, in a steadier voice. "But I was wrong. I don't think he's worthy of you, Victoria. And I don't like the way he has acted toward you, in the past and during this trip. But you've made your choice, and if he makes it through the Trial, I'll leave you be and wish you well."

But if he doesn't . . .

The words hung there, unspoken. But they both heard them, and they left Victoria cold.

If he doesn't.

"I'll go in first," said Sebastian, his hand wrapping around Victoria's arm to stop her. "Katerina will be suitably distracted, and then you can take her by surprise."

They stood in the narrow passageway known as Goldsmith's Lane. Prague Castle reared up beyond its stone wall, which made one side of the street. Tightly packed houses had been built flush against the stone enclosure, and another row lined the other side. This created a crooked little lane barely wide enough for two horses to pass through, side by side. The houses themselves were tiny, but decorated with colorful shutters thrown open.

The sun shone boldly down, more than halfway across the sky, but still high enough to burn hot and cast short shadows. People passed by on their way to and from the castle, the goldsmithies, and on other errands. Victoria and Sebastian had stopped in front of Number 75's pie-sized stoop, but their destination did not lie through that red door.

Instead, a small staircase led down to a door directly beneath Number 75. The top of the flight was framed at the street level by an iron gate to protect unwary passersby from tumbling down the hole—a necessity in such a narrow thoroughfare. The subterranean steps reminded Victoria a bit of the entrance to the Silver Chalice.

"And if Katerina isn't there?" Victoria asked, although she was quite certain Antonín had been telling the truth about the vampiress's location, for Victoria had promised him a reward when they returned if he had. He'd licked his lips hungrily and nodded enthusiastically, knowing that he had no chance of leaving the inn during the flush of sunlight.

Little did he know she had other plans for him.

"Unfortunately, I can fairly assure you that Katerina is here. We've met in this location before."

Sebastian slipped past her and started down the steps, the iron gate clanging in his wake. Victoria was left to wonder in just what manner he'd "met" Katerina. At least she was certain they hadn't been lovers.

Her stomach pitched when she considered the possibility of a mortal and a demonic undead being intimate. Black spots danced briefly before her eyes, and a definite nausea churned in her belly. That thought crept too close to those moments with Beauregard, in his chamber, when he drained nearly all of her blood . . . when she was helpless and under his thrall, wrapped in pleasure and sensuality . . . images that remained soft and vague in her mind, memories that she couldn't allow herself to contemplate.

She didn't know. She didn't want to know.

And then there was Max. And Lilith. And her control over him, her obsession with him. The flat expression in his eyes could hide much horror.

Victoria swallowed hard, shoved the thoughts away and concentrated on the chill at the back of her neck. Stupid to allow her mind to open to such repugnant ideas. They only served to weaken and distract her.

And she wouldn't wait any longer.

None of the pedestrians on the street around her seemed to notice when she lifted the latch on the iron gate and slipped through, then down the steps. It stank of urine and damp, and she found she needed to take care to avoid stepping on unpleasant substances as she descended. It certainly no longer reminded her of Sebastian's clean and well-run Chalice.

The stairs went down below the earth, down, down, down so far that no sunlight filtered down the spiral stairs. When at last the steps ended, she saw a single horse symbol carved on the wall in front of her, next to a door. The Lone Horse.

The black door had an old-fashioned string latch. The string hung outside, and she pulled on it to lift the small wooden bar inside. The door opened with only a gentle shove, grating across a packed-dirt floor.

To her surprise, Victoria found herself in an establishment more than reminiscent of the Silver Chalice. Wooden tables and chairs lined the space, all fashioned of scarred, smooth, hand-worn maple. Lamps burned from the walls, and a fire in one corner brought a bit of warmth to the underground chill. The place smelled like sweat, damp soil, ale, and . . . blood.

There was no mistake; Victoria definitely knew bloodscent. Several patrons sat with various cups of libation in front of them, and she didn't need to look closely to know what the beverage of choice was. A piano stood in the corner, being badly played by a woman with wheat-colored hair. A small counter laden with bottles edged up into the corner of the room, with a man tending to them. The low ceiling was lined with heavy beams between which Victoria could see roots growing.

And the back of her neck felt as though a pack of ice sat there.

Vampires everywhere.

Most of them looked up, showing burning red or pink eyes, lifting a lip to display the point of a fang. None of them, fortunately, glowed red-violet. Victoria wasn't in the mood to fight an Imperial vampire, the type that was the oldest and most powerful of the undead. She wanted to make this a simple exercise: Get the ring, slay Katerina if necessary, and get back to Antonín.

One of the vampires made the mistake of standing up and lunging for Victoria as she looked in the other direction. A quick shunt of her stake arm, and the foolish creature poofed into dust.

"That wasn't a very polite way to greet a newcomer," Victoria said to the room at large.

The lustful faces that had risen to look at her—fresh, young blood that she was—immediately dropped to look down at the cups on the tables in front of them, as if hoping that by ignoring her, she would ignore them.

For now she would. But only because she had other matters to attend to.

And as she swept the room with her gaze, she saw what appeared to be those other matters in a far corner. Victoria cast a sharp look at a vampire in her path. He moved and she scooted past him to the dark corner where Sebastian seemed to be attempting to extricate himself from a bit of difficulty.

"But, Katerina, *chère*," he was saying as Victoria approached. "Can we not let bygones be bygones? It was more than eight years ago."

"Eight years?" repeated a tall, stout woman; presumably Katerina. She'd backed Sebastian up against the wall with a meaty hand, stabbing a finger in the middle of his chest. Though Sebastian had a stake in his hand, she didn't pay it any attention. "Eight years ain' barely a *breath* ago for someone living forever, Sebastian Vioget."

"But surely you didn't truly miss those casks—"

"Casks of the best French brandy? Casks I paid overmuch for?" shrieked Katerina, drilling her finger into his chest. Her nail must be sharp, for Victoria saw red blossom beneath Sebastian's snowy shirt. Yet his charming smile didn't falter. "You're knowing as well as I that calf's blood is all well and good for the likes of some customers, but the ones who pay well are expecting something even better. Are you knowing what business I lost when I couldn't serve them?"

Sebastian gave a little laugh. "But I see that business is flourishing now. And aside of that—"

"I do hope I'm not interrupting," Victoria said in unapologetic tones as she pushed over to stand next to them.

Katerina turned, but did not remove her hand from Sebastian, who gave Victoria a rueful smile. "Who are you?"

"I am *Illa* Gardella, and I'm here because you have something I require."

"If it's him," she said, with a jerk of her head at Sebastian, "you have to wait a moment until I'm finished."

"Now don't be silly, Katerina," said Sebastian, moving quickly and smoothly to get out from under her grip. "You know I prefer not to hurt a woman, but I will if I must. I intended to apologize, but if you won't accept it, then it's none of my concern." He smoothed his rumpled coat and brushed off dirt that had crumbled onto him from the ceiling above. "As far as I'm concerned, you owed me those casks."

Katerina, who had been blessed with a full head of black hair and pancakelike breasts during her mortal days, glared at him, her hands on her hips. She stood more than a head taller than Sebastian, and the top of her skull brushed the ceiling . . . hence the dusting of dirt that followed her every movement.

"I swore if I ever laid eyes on you again, I'd be squeezing every last koruna from you to pay for that brandy." She tightened her ham-sized fists as though to put her words to action. "It was a years' worth of income for me to buy them. And you taking them off with you to London was a dirty trick."

Victoria decided it was time to intervene. The vampiress was massive in size and height, and with her pink eyes and poison-tipped fangs, she wouldn't be an easy target. But Victoria had handled worse threats.

"You can settle your accounts with Sebastian later," she said, giving him a sidewise glance, "but for now you can give me what I came for."

"And what might that be?" The woman turned and focused her attention down, heavily, onto Victoria. Her pink eyes tried to capture Victoria's gaze, but in vain.

"The Ring of Jubai that you have in your possession."

Katerina began to laugh, a loud, uproarious sound that boomed in the small room and shook even her flat breasts. "And what makes you think I'd be considering giving it to you?"

"Because you don't wish to join your husband in a pile of dust." Victoria showed her stake and looked up boldly at the woman.

Sebastian winced behind her, and rolled his eyes. Victoria ignored him; perhaps his tactics might have been to charm the ring from Katerina. But Victoria intended no such thing.

Katerina lifted her hand, shoving it at Victoria, knuckles facing out. "Then it will have to be over my pile of dust, for the ring's not going anywhere without me."

And indeed, she spoke the truth. Only a slender line of copper gleamed on the vampiress's ring finger. Flesh covered the rest of it, puffing over and around it like rising bread dough. The only way to get it off would be to kill Katerina, for, as Victoria knew, the only material that survived a vampire's dissolution into ash was copper. Everything else would disintegrate along with the undead, which was precisely the reason Lilith had crafted her special rings of that metal.

"As I don't intend to go anywhere . . . and as my patrons would be sorely missing me . . . I think you might perhaps be leaving empty-handed. If you leave at all." Katerina bared her teeth, showing large ones that looked like yellow tombstones.

Victoria saw the warning in Sebastian's eyes at the same moment as prickles rose at the back of her neck. She whirled to face two tall vampires just as they leapt at her.

Her timing was a bit off, and the force of their bodies slammed her into a nearby table. Victoria bumped her head on a corner dulled by years of use, and used the momentum of her fall to roll under the heavy wooden trestle. Ignoring the pain, she reached up and grabbed the long, slender leg of the vampire nearest her and slammed a fist into the back of his knee.

He collapsed, and as he fell, Victoria erupted from under the table and shoved a stake into his chest. The dust poofed in her face as she pulled to her feet, her breath faster but by no means labored, and she swung around to kick out at another attacker. Pushing, whirling, punching, shoving . . . she found the thrill of the battle coursing through her in a way she had been missing for a while. The spray of spilled drinks, the dull sound of wood crashing into flesh, the smell of undead ash, the satisfaction of seeing the vampire's red eyes widen just as the stake thrust home . . . this was her world. Her moment.

This threat, of corporeal demons who lunged and shoved and kicked, was one she was well used to combating. She found herself slipping into her familiar *kalaripayattu* moves, ingrained by hours of practice with Kritanu. She used her strength and speed to upend a vampire, to knock another into his companion, to slam an elbow up into the chin of still another and then, each time, to finish it off with a stake to the heart.

Exhilarating. Exhilarating and—not simple or easy by any means—but familiar.

Out of the corner of her eye, she saw Sebastian join the fray, battling directly with Katerina. One of his wrists had been captured by the massive woman, and Victoria saw that he was doing everything to free himself but shoving a stake into her chest.

With a wave of exasperation at his sentimentality, Victoria finished off a sixth or seventh undead attacker and, grabbing the arm of yet another vampire, flung him out into the cluster of his companions. As the vampires tumbled to the ground, she turned and, with one sleek movement, shoved her stake into the back of Katerina's torso.

The pike slid in, Katerina froze, and Sebastian cried out. . . . Then, as Victoria pulled back, the vampire stilled and poofed into a dark cloud of dust.

The clang of metal told her where the copper ring dropped from the vampire's person, hitting a wooden table, then falling silently to the dirt floor, and she dove after it.

Sebastian followed, and they found themselves face-to-face under the table. "I would have done it," he protested immediately.

Victoria snatched up the ring and allowed him to help her surge back to her feet. She turned, bracing herself for a renewed onslaught, and found that the few remaining vampires had begun to flee. "Well. That was simpler than I expected," she said, looking at the empty pub.

Sebastian pushed past her, stepping over a splintered bench as he made his way toward the counter, now vacated. He moved behind it and gave her an impudent smile as he raised a dark bottle to examine its label. "I don't believe she'll miss this at all anymore," he said, pouring a generous draft into a glass. "Care to join me in a victory drink, Victoria?"

She navigated her way through the debris and selected a stool next to the empty counter. "I do believe I shall."

Thirteen

In Which We Observe Venators in Their Natural Habitat

Sebastian was well into his cups by the time he left Goldsmith Lane. He certainly wasn't staggering along the street—indeed, he was much too refined to make a fool of himself in such a manner.

But the fine—*very* fine—brandy Katerina had kept for those "special" customers had put a sort of glaze over the world, over the dull throb of emptiness in his middle and the remnants of dreams that continued to linger and tease. It softened the edge of unpleasantness . . . and aside of that, it was *damn* fine brandy.

Perhaps even better than the Armagnac from which he'd relieved Katerina all those years ago. It was a shame she'd never forgiven him for that transgression, but, as he'd said, she rather owed him. It wasn't his fault her daughter had seduced him.

However, Katerina hadn't quite seen it that way, and had been furious with him for not "keeping his dillyjohn packed away," as she had termed it. So Katerina had set a bunch of undead goons on him in retribution and caused a riot that destroyed half of the Lone Horse. Not to mention Sebastian's arm, leg, and a few ribs.

Yes indeed, she'd owed him for that, and those casks had been a nice little start to his proprietorship of the Silver Chalice.

After Victoria left the Lone Horse, Sebastian had taken it upon himself to hunt around in the hidden storage room to see how much of this brandy was left. Perhaps he'd take the rest back to London, or wherever he thought he might settle after things were done with the Midiverse Portal, and open another establishment.

Having ascertained that there was, in fact, a nice store of various libations hidden away, Sebastian finished his last drink and left the tavern.

Though it was late in the afternoon, once he was outside of the dark place, he had to blink rapidly in the glare of sunshine. The great towers of Týn Church rose in the distance, high over the city across the river. He looked away. Victoria hadn't given a reason for leaving the Lone Horse, but he knew where she'd gone.

As he made his way back to their inn with nary a stumble, he wondered when Wayren and Brim and Michalas might arrive in Praha, or whether they would all attempt to meet up on the way to Muntii Făgăraş. Sebastian had no desire to visit Lilith's mountain lair in Romania, but in the last year, he'd become accustomed to doing things he preferred not to do.

Staking vampires, including his grandfather, was one.

Loving a woman who had to be coaxed into a kiss—or more—every time.

Fighting his arse off against paralyzing demons.

Even seeing Katerina poof into a pile of dust had raised melancholy in his mind.

Or perhaps it was the brandy.

No. It was more than the brandy. For all her faults, Katerina had been kind to him once upon a time, and it had been Sebastian's fault that her husband was no longer living undeadly by her side.

At least now they rotted in Hell together.

The thought made his belly swish. Maybe he *had* had too much of the brandy.

Giulia in Hell. Sent there by his own bloody hand.

Was there no way to change that? To save her soul?

Of course not. He'd wondered and wished and hoped for years for some way to change that. What was done was done. Ashes to ashes . . . and in this case, ashes to ashes to Hell.

Damn. The brandy. Bitterness rose in the back of his throat, and Sebastian had to swipe the back of his hand over eyes that watered from the bright sun.

When Wayren had given him the papers written by Rosamunde Gardella, Sebastian felt certain they would contain something important . . . something that he needed to know. Some kind of message for him. After all he'd been drawn to them so strongly, there had to be a reason for it. And all the dreams, coming stronger and clearer than ever.

Was it just because he'd lost Victoria that Giulia had come back to haunt him? Had his relationship—such as it was—been simply a distraction from Giulia and her memory?

But so far, though he'd pored over them night after night so that the words seemed to be burned into his brain, there'd been nothing that spoke to him on those brittle, cramped-character pages.

Rosamunde prophesied Eustacia's death in Rome:

The golden age of the Venator will find rest at the foot of Rome.

She'd foretold of Victoria's near-turning by Beauregard:

And the rising daughter shall find herself blemished, and malevolence will fight to reign within. Yet the strength of a pure heart may overcome this test.

There was another passage that seemed to stick deep within his mind, but it meant nothing to him:

And in the new world shall be a savior who carries the deepest taint. A long promise shall the savior make, and in the end those for whom he lives will be saved.

In his sober moments, and in those early-morning hours when the words slipped around in his mind, Sebastian thought that perhaps it spoke to him for a reason. Might he be meant to go to America—the New World? He certainly carried a deep taint.

But a savior?

That couldn't be him. Pesaro, perhaps—the damn hero who never shirked from his duty. The man who hadn't a sensitive bone in his body.

Perhaps Pesaro was the savior and he would go off to America for some "long promise." And leave Victoria for Sebastian. He smiled grimly. Then the bloody bastard could be as heroic as he wished, an ocean away.

Sebastian swallowed, tasting the strong flavor of brandy again. He had had too much. But it was day, and a bit of a nap would leave him clearheaded by evening.

The door to the chamber he shared with Victoria—*shared with Victoria*; of all the blasted lies, teases!—opened easily, and he stepped over the threshold with a slight shuffle.

And stopped short.

Blood. He smelled blood.

The vestiges of the brandy fell away as he took in the scene: Victoria, pale visaged, sprawled on the bed, her dark hair plastered to her face . . . Antonín's face buried against her, his jaw moving as he drank . . . long and deep.

The scent of iron filled Sebastian's nose, and red tinged his vision. With a roar, he leapt across the room, grabbing up the vampire by the hair, somehow remembering not to yank him away from her flesh before his fangs slid out.

"Sebastian, no!" she said, lifting herself from the bed. He saw blood trickling down her white arm, a stake in her other hand, and surprise in her eyes, heavy lidded and soft. He managed to stop his hand from slamming the stake down into Antonín's chest just as she lunged up from the bed, surging toward him.

"What the bloody hell are you doing?" he shouted, realizing belatedly that the vampire was still bound helplessly, hand and foot. That he'd been feeding from her wrist, and she had a stake at the ready. Revulsion swamped him as he understood. He grabbed her by the shoulders, his fingers driving into her soft skin.

"Sebastian," she said, struggling in his arms. But he held her tightly, with every bit of strength he possessed, anger and disgust mingling with desire and fear. "Stop!"

"Victoria, I don't understand. Why? What are you . . . ?" His voice trailed off, and he swallowed. Then shoved her away so hard she lost her balance and fell onto the bed.

He wanted to join her. Sebastian turned away, the nausea churning deeper.

She stood up, her beautiful face tight and perhaps

a shade guilty. "I'm sorry to frighten you," she said calmly, watching him closely. "I didn't mean to."

"I didn't know that you'd become fond of . . . that," he said. Horror, mingled with the taste of brandy, rose in the back of his throat. . . . He knew well how it felt to have fangs slide in, the pleasure-pain of blood drawn long and slow from within . . . the sensuality of it, the light-headed eroticism. But Victoria?

She glanced at Antonín, then back at Sebastian. "I thought," she said in a low voice. "I thought if his blood had some Gardella blood mixed with it, it might . . ." Her voice trailed off as understanding washed through him.

Pesaro. She'd done it for Pesaro, for his damned Trial.

Sebastian felt his lips move crookedly. "Well, now . . . what an interesting thought. Though I doubt Pesaro would thank you for your interference."

"You mustn't tell him." Victoria stood, swiping at the ugly marks on her arm. Hell, they were deep, and her face looked pale. She staggered a little. How much blood had she given?

"You fool," he said, turning to rummage through his satchel. Salted holy water would help to heal the marks.

But she was weak. He saw it in the depths of her eyes and the paleness of her face.

Yet he couldn't blame her. For wasn't he also a fool for love?

Later that evening, word came by pigeon that Brim and Michalas had arrived in Prague, so Victoria and Sebastian went to meet them near the Stone Bridge. Brim embraced her as soon as she approached, surprising her with his affection and strength. Then the massive black man showed her the ring they'd brought from the Consilium.

"And now we have three of the Rings of Jubai," Victoria said. "But the last two will be the most difficult to obtain. Lilith won't give them up easily."

"It's in her interest to stop the demons," Michalas said firmly, shading his eyes against the last shot of sunbeam spearing low between the red roofs. "Surely even she will understand that—especially if we are the ones taking the risk."

Victoria grimaced. "I'm not confident that Lilith will see it that way. But we'll get the rings. And then Sebastian will lead us to the pool at the base of her mountain."

"And hope that they work to breach the enchantments therein," he said grimly.

She replied, "Your grandfather would have known. I presume that's why he wanted the ring that was hidden beneath London, because he knew how valuable it was."

Sebastian nodded. "And the Midiverse Portal is less than two days' ride from the pool, so if all goes as planned, we might be there in a week."

"Wayren stays safely at the Consilium until she is needed here." Brim looked at Victoria, understanding in his eyes. "And so we stay for another day?"

She nodded. "Until after Max's Trial. Then we'll be five strong and off to Muntii Făgăraş." She couldn't help but glance toward Týn, up on the hill, and when she looked back, she caught the exchange of glances among the others. Wayren would arrive on the day of the Trial by her own means in order to conduct the event, but until then, there was nothing to do but wait until tomorrow evening.

"Well," Brim said, "the sun is setting, and I can think

of several ways to pass the time." He flexed his massive arm and smiled menacingly.

"I know of a place that has good brandy," offered Sebastian.

"And what about food?"

"If it's food you want, I can take you to a suitable tavern." He glanced quickly at Victoria. "Not the Lone Horse."

"And after that . . . some other amusements might be in order," said Michalas. "Victoria, you'll join us, won't you?"

She nodded, realizing that her other option was to go back to the chamber with a snoring Antonín and stare out at Týn, or to hunt on the streets alone. Perhaps another night she might opt for the latter, but tonight her friends were offering companionship as well as a distraction.

And she realized she wanted both.

Hours later, Victoria sat in a large, loud, but dingy establishment with the three other Venators, who'd imbibed a generous quantity of brandy or ale or wine—depending on their preference. She, too, had had enough wine to take the edge off her worry, and found herself relaxing and enjoying the companionship of three others who lived the same dangerous, duplicitous life she did.

The tavern catered to mortals, but there were vampires mingling about, which was part of the attraction, according to Sebastian . . . and the reason he, Michalas, and Brim had slipped into their cups. Every time a vampire walked into the place, all four of them noticed, of course. And then the wagers began.

"He'll go for the young man over yonder. Easy, and near the door."

"I think not. See how he's watching the server girl? It'll be her."

"No, no . . . see how he's looking at the ones throwing dice? He'll slip into the game and lure the winner away later. . . . Then he'll get the winnings, too."

And then . . .

"She's got her eye on that big guy by the wall."

"No, see how she's looking at the two over by the counter? The one with the red hair, mark my words."

"She's just dropped something—the bald one's going to pick it up, and that will be his death wish."

Coins of all denominations clanked and clinked into a small pot on the table until the vampire made a move to lure his victim out of the pub. Then the winning Venator collected his spoils, slipped them into his pocket, took a stake out . . . and followed.

The rest drained their glasses and poured another round.

After a while, vampires stopped coming into the eatery. Perhaps word had spread that those who did found themselves quickly turned to ash.

"It's still early," Michalas said, digging out a pair of dice. He tossed them on the table. "Who's first?"

"Vioget and I," said Brim, raising the eyebrow through which his *vis bulla* glinted.

Sebastian sighed, rolled his eyes, and sat up as though quite put-upon. Yet Victoria saw the gleam of challenge in his gaze. "I accept."

Victoria watched with interest—all of these pastimes were as new to her as visiting a men's club and watching them at cards.

Michalas rolled the bones. "Ten." He laughed and looked up at the other two. "Good luck."

Brim and Sebastian shoved to their feet, sending glasses clinking, and rushed out.

"Where are they going?" Victoria asked.

"I rolled a ten. . . . Now it's a race to see who can get ten vampires and get back here first."

"Ten? Each?" Her eyebrows rose, and she stifled a laugh. "Are there that many undead left in Prague? We've been a bit busy."

"Ten each, and the last one back buys a round." Michalas settled back in his chair and sipped from his beverage of choice—wine. They chatted amiably for a time, and after a while he said, "Ah, here's another one."

Victoria felt the telltale chill on the back of her neck and saw the undead come through the door. "Yours or mine?" she asked.

"I'll take him."

"No, wait," she said. "I'll do it." She stood, feeling the gentling effect of the wine, and made her way casually toward the vampire.

He stood near the counter of the bar, sipping something from a cup. Even though she was innocently looking away, Victoria felt the moment she caught his attention. She could imagine the picture she made— clearly a woman who was dressed in men's clothing, for she'd left her hair unbound and removed her jacket in the warm evening.

The vampire stood tall, nearly as tall as Max, she realized as she came closer. His shoulders were broad, and despite the scar that cut along the edge of his jaw, he was a handsome man. And, she was fairly certain, a Guardian vampire. But she wouldn't know for certain until his eyes began to glow.

"Well, well," he said in a liquid voice that somehow penetrated above the dull roar of the eatery. "What is a lovely lady doing in such an ugly place?"

Victoria resisted the urge to roll her eyes. Instead, she gave him large, innocent ones and replied, "I was supposed to meet my brother here, but he hasn't arrived yet."

"Your brother?" The interest in his voice ebbed.

"He was supposed to meet me yesterday evening," she said. "But he's late."

The vampire laughed, showing normal teeth. "I should say that is the case. How much longer do you intend to wait for him?"

"I don't think he's going to come after all," she said ingenuously. "I'm thinking it's time that I went home."

"By yourself? The streets are dangerous at night," he said, leaning a bit closer.

What woman didn't know that? "I'm not afraid." That was the truth.

"Perhaps you might like an escort?" he asked.

"I think not," she said, giving him a coy smile. "I don't usually walk with strange men." She rested some coins on the counter to give the impression that she had approached so as to settle her account. "Good night, sir."

She was nearly out the door when she felt the chill at the back of her neck intensify. A knowing smile tickled her lips, and she slowed her pace so that he could catch up to her.

But just as she stepped onto the crooked street, she saw Sebastian and Brim approaching. Both were moving quickly, obviously to see who could win the wager.

"Victoria," said Sebastian as they slowed next to her. She felt the scarred vampire move past her and slip into the shadows. Neither Brim nor Sebastian made any attempt to follow him. Instead of going into the pub, they stopped at the entrance next to her.

"I'm very sorry," said Brim. "I've made a mistake."

"A mistake?" Victoria frowned.

"I was looking for my tenth vampire, so I could win this wager with Vioget," Brim explained. Victoria felt

Sebastian's eyes on her, and an odd chill went up her spine. Why was he looking at her that way?

Max. It had to be about Max. What had happened?

She swallowed and realized Brim was continuing his explanation. She forgot about the vampire and listened.

"I couldn't find one, or sense one anywhere, and so I kept looking. I'd found the first nine rather quickly. But then, nothing. At last, I came to a small boarding-house and felt an undead was nearby. I found him. In one of the rooms, sleeping. Just as I staked him, I realized he was—"

"Tied up," Victoria finished, her heart sinking.

"Tied up," Brim repeated.

So Antonín was gone.

She glanced toward Týn and nodded slowly.

That, she supposed, was what she deserved for attempting to interfere with divine will.

The gentle hand on his shoulder brought Max to reality.

He blinked, focused, swallowed, then breathed. A long, shuddering, deep breath.

The stones beneath his knees had long ceased paining him, but the moment he moved, the agony screamed along his joints. His legs felt leaden at first, and then as he moved them, nasty prickles traveled up and down and into his buttocks and down into his toes.

Colored light beams of red, blue, and gold glowed in the massive church nave, shining through stained glass and spilling over the altar and arches and pews. By their angle, he surmised that dusk was near.

The end of the third day.

Always knowing, always perceptive, Wayren had touched his shoulder to draw him from the deep meditation, then eased away to allow him time to come back to himself. Now he turned and saw her sitting in a pew beneath a low arch, where the only illumination was a few alms candles. For a moment, he saw a shimmer of light around her in the dusky church, and then it was gone.

He moved stiffly next to her and sat for the first time in three days.

"You're here," he said.

"I am indeed."

"Do we have the third ring?"

She gave a brief nod. "We do. Now to finish here and to retrieve the other two from Lilith."

He couldn't think about that now. Not yet. One moment at a time. One task at a time.

Wayren seemed to understand, and she touched his hand, her fingers soft and cool against his rough ones. A surge of power sleeked through him. Power and peace. "You're feverish. Are you ill?"

He shrugged. "I've been. A bit."

She offered him a flask of water, and he drank. He'd never tasted anything more pure, more cold and clean. The heat burning through his limbs eased a bit, but it still raged beneath. He was ill and bloody weak. Yet he had work to do.

"Did you ask Ylito what he thought?"

Wayren nodded. "He agrees that you should not remove the *vis bulla* during the battle. There is no reason to, and yours is a special situation. Never have we had a Venator need to pass another Trial, wearing his own *vis bulla*. You do have your own back, don't you?"

Max shoved away the memory of the exchange with Victoria, when she had returned his *vis bulla*, which she'd secretly been wearing, and he had given her back her own. Which he'd been wearing. "Yes." He looked at Wayren. "Did you discuss with him the other matter?"

"He agrees that it would do no harm to try, Max. Normally, of course, we have the blood from the vampire waiting, with the *vis bulla* soaking in holy water. After the vampire is dead, then the *vis* is taken from the holy water and dipped in the dead vampire's blood and then pierced through the flesh of the Venator. That is when the truth will out: either death or life as a Venator.

"But in your case, since you already wear the *vis*, Ylito believes you may be able to miss that step and finish the Trial sooner. We'll pour holy water on the amulet before the battle. If blood from the vampire is wiped on the *vis* during the battle, it may indeed reactivate your Venator powers."

"Or it may not."

"Or it may not."

Either way, the result would be the same. If it was meant to happen, it would happen, whether during the battle with the vampire, or after.

Max knew that he didn't want to kill a vampire only to die afterward.

He didn't want to die at all, he realized, for the first time in a long time. For the first time since he could remember.

But he might. And he was prepared. He stood. "I'm ready."

Fourteen

The Trial Commences

When he walked in, Max didn't look at Victoria.

She supposed she wasn't surprised—after all, this was Max.

But what if he never came out of that pit again? What if this was the last time she'd see him? And he wouldn't look at her.

Victoria dug her fingers into the palm of her hand and tried not to notice how gray he looked in the face, beneath his olive skin. How exhaustion pinched his mouth and lined his eyes. A sheen of moisture glazed his forehead and cheeks. Was he ill or simply worn down?

He moved easily, yet lacking the grace she was used to seeing from a man who could waltz like a creek flowing over rocks, or lift his feet and glide through the air while wielding a sword as though it were an extension of his arm.

She assumed he wore nothing but his breeches for

safety purposes—for the same reason she'd cut her hair: to give his opponent nothing to grab on to—but for the moment, the sight of his square shoulders and powerful arms made her mouth dry. The *vis bulla* at his areola shone against dark skin and the hair on his muscular chest and arrowing down his belly. His feet, bare and wide and brown, moved silently across the room, taking him past her. She saw the brand of the Tutela on the back of his shoulder, a stylized, wiry canine burned into his flesh in an unforgiving reminder of his youthful mistake. He carried a stake. And as she watched, he poured a small vial of water—holy water, probably—over the silver *vis*, then drank long and deeply from a skin that Wayren handed him.

Victoria knew better than to speak, to move toward him. But couldn't he even look toward her for a moment so that she could let him see how much she loved him?

Her fingers tightened against the trousers she wore, her knuckles scraping over rough wood. A splinter shot into the tender skin there, but she welcomed the discomfort. A distraction.

Brim sat on one side of her, and despite the fact that they weren't touching, she felt compassion radiating from him. On the other sat Sebastian, stiff and removed.

Just in front of where they sat on rough wooden benches, an iron grate rose from ceiling to floor, separating them from a shallow ditch. Lit by a torch at either end of the elliptical space, the gated space reminded Victoria of a shallow version of the pit in which Lilith had thrown her less than two months ago. Then, it had been Max who sat helplessly and watched as she fought for her life . . . and then for the life of Sara Regalado.

Victoria didn't know how or when Wayren had arranged for the Trial to be here in this abandoned building. It didn't matter. What mattered now was the large, scar-jawed vampire who paced in the space, waiting for Max to join him.

The vampire happened to be the one Victoria had lured out of the tavern last night—so very different from the creature she'd hoped Max would face. He was a Guardian; she'd been right about that, damn it. And because of the games the Venators had played the night before, they'd either scared off many of the undead or whittled their numbers down to nearly nothing . . . and this tall, strong undead had been the only one they'd been able to find for the Trial.

The next thing she knew, Max clanged the grate's door open and jumped down the shallow incline, his stake black and lethal in his hand. He landed with a bit of a stumble, catching himself, and Victoria closed her eyes.

Three days of fasting and lack of sleep . . . no *vis bulla* . . . How could he be anything but weak and slow?

But he'd done this before.

Her eyes had opened, and she watched, trying not to wonder what Max thought about being on display for them all. Whether he was aware of anything but the powerful undead he faced.

Beyond the grate, she saw a blur of motion. Victoria found it hard to tell who launched first, but both were fighting for their lives.

And only one would walk through that gate.

Victoria found it a small consolation that, should the undead be the one to do so, she'd meet him there with her stake.

As always when he fought, Max cut everything from his mind, his awareness—everything but the battle. The hand to hand, the strikes, the rhythm, the timing.

Despite the fever that burned beneath his skin and parched his tongue, the exhaustion that wanted to weight his limbs and slow his movements, he met the vampire's assault readily.

Draw blood first.

He swiped viciously, but the undead dodged and slammed Max against the iron grate. It clanged loudly, echoing in the space, and Max whirled around just as the powerful vampire launched at him, eyes burning pink.

A bloody Guardian. A large one.

The room spun around Max, spewing dots of lights before his eyes, but he surged up and toward the vampire, slicing the stake's point at his face, along his arm. Not deep enough. No blood yet.

Not enough strength, even, to lift himself through the air in *qinggong.*

Look away from the eyes.

Max ducked another assault, hooking the creature's leg to pull him off balance. He was damn big, and frighteningly strong, and he fell hard. But he pulled Max with him, slamming his head against the dirt floor. Something pinged at the back of his skull, but then Max felt the vampire move with him, grabbing for him, and he kicked him off.

Free from the deadly weight, he rolled over and surged unsteadily to his feet. He sliced up and out again, catching the vampire's hand in a deep gouge. Bright red blood spilled at last, but as Max swiped his right hand toward it, the undead slammed him in the stomach.

The stake fell from his hand as everything ceased. The world stopped, darkened, became nothing but a desperate fight to pull a breath back in. Even the strong hands at his shoulders . . . the hand pulling roughly, jerking his head aside to bare his neck . . . they were barely more than dreams as he struggled . . . to . . . breathe. . . .

Pull . . . it . . . *in.* . . . God . . .

The pink eyes came close. Fangs gleamed, Max couldn't move. His lungs wouldn't move. The fever made his body shake weakly even as it fought for air. The pink eyes burned, beckoning, trying to lure him in.

Then Max gasped a bit, and with a sudden whoosh, the oxygen flooded his lungs, and renewed strength swept over him. The vampire lunged down, and Max whipped himself around, twisting to the side and using his momentum to bring the vampire with him. Slamming him to the ground, Max twisted and reached for the streaming blood on the vampire's hand.

But instead of blood, he found only dirt. He leapt to his feet, bracing himself to face the vampire once again.

They squared off against each other, breathing heavily. Max tried to ignore the floor tilting beneath his feet, the trembling in his fingers and knees, the heat burning through his body, the shimmering lights before his eyes.

But the fever sapped his strength even more, and he found it difficult to draw breaths.

He was not going to bloody die.

What the hell was he doing?

Sebastian had seen more than five missed opportunities to slam the stake into that vampire's chest . . . but Pesaro hadn't taken any of them.

Instead, he swiped at him. *Swiped.* At the face, the arm, the hand.

Was he *trying* to die?

Sebastian divided his attention between Pesaro—who, for all his obvious weakness, still showed more skill than he would have expected—and Victoria, who sat like stone next to him.

If Sebastian was wondering what had addled Pesaro's brain, she had to be thinking the same. Or worse.

And Sebastian realized he didn't know whether he wanted the man to succeed or fail.

Now Max's stake lay on the floor of the shallow ditch, out of reach, and the vampire was barely wounded, flinging blood with his every movement.

Sebastian felt his own heart racing, energy surging through his own veins as man and undead clashed again. The room was silent but for the slap of flesh against flesh, of grunts and groans, and the occasional dull clang against the iron grate.

Pesaro made a sudden move and shoved the vampire off him, then followed with a well-placed kick. Sebastian watched, waited for him to scoop up the stake and slam it into the open chest, but again, instead of doing so, Max moved forward with his bare hand as though to touch the undead.

He staggered away, his hand red with vampire blood, and the undead surged toward him again. Pesaro blocked him, but the creature came after him again and slammed him to the ground. They fell in a tangle, Max's head crashing into the iron bars as they tumbled onto the floor with an ugly thud. Sebastian heard the dull clang, and an uncomfortable chill washed over him when Pesaro didn't move.

The vampire struggled to his feet, and Max shifted slightly. His eyes opened. Sebastian saw those dark eyes look toward them for the first time; he saw the way they moved over Victoria. She tensed next to him; he could feel her gathering herself up and he heard the soft gasp. She read Max's expression as well as he did.

It all happened so quickly after that. The vampire moved, fangs bared and eyes burning pink; Pesaro lay still, one hand splayed over his chest as though to protect it and the other curled up behind and beneath him. His stake lay out of reach against the wall.

Sebastian knew what was going to happen—he knew it, but couldn't believe it—and he did the only thing he could do.

As the vampire launched himself for the fatal strike, Sebastian pulled Victoria toward him and smashed a kiss onto her lips.

Fifteen

In Which Our Heroine Finds Herself Between a Rocky Wall and a Hard Place

By the time Victoria extricated herself from Sebastian, it was over.

She shoved him away, stunned and furious, and terrified by what she'd missed. In the back of her mind, she knew what he'd meant to do—to distract her from seeing the final blow, shield her from the last strike.

But how could he?

Brim and Michalas had moved while she was disengaging herself from Sebastian, and now they stood between her and the iron grate. Her knees felt weak, but Victoria rose and made herself move forward. Because of that, because she simply couldn't believe it was over, it took her a moment to recognize the smell.

Ash. Undead ash.

Then the iron grate clanged, and suddenly there was Max.

Standing on his own, sweaty, bloody, scraped, but standing. On his own. Tall, imposing, blood-streaked . . .

and without a hint of the exhaustion she'd recognized the moment he walked into the room. *Thank God*.

The vampire had disintegrated, its dust tufting in the air, and Max held a stake in his hand. Not the long black one he'd carried in, but a shorter one.

The one that had obviously done the job.

Relief and a blaze of joy surged through her, and she pushed between Brim and Michalas to reach Max's side.

But he didn't look at Victoria except when his eyes accidentally skipped over her on their way to Wayren.

"You succeeded," the older woman said to Max. "Congratulations."

He nodded, and a smile, tinged with relief, lit her face. She handed him a jug from which he drank, long and deep.

Victoria watched a slender rivulet of water trickle down Max's jaw and throat and over the ridges of his bloody, sweaty chest. When he stopped drinking, he handed the jug back to Wayren and accepted a cloth.

He wouldn't look at her.

Victoria stood there, right in front of him, and he wouldn't meet her gaze. Wouldn't even allow his eyes to skim over her.

She stepped back, all of the relief and joy at his success dissipating into confusion and hurt. Her mouth went dry, and her fury with Sebastian rose anew. He'd eased away, sort of behind the others, as though ashamed of his actions. As well he should be.

What had Max seen, as the final blow of the vampire came toward him? Her in Sebastian's embrace—whether willing or not, he wouldn't have known. It would have been the last thing he'd seen. What did he think? That she'd rushed into Sebastian's arms the moment it looked as though all were lost?

Victoria felt a surge of annoyance with him. With both of them.

Max wasn't smiling, not quite, but the lines around his mouth and eyes had relaxed a bit, and even though he wouldn't look at her, Victoria recognized the strength emanating from him, and a sort of rightness about his person. She could see, without being told, that he'd regained his powers, that the *vis bulla* empowered him again.

But he hadn't finished the Trial. How could that be?

Her silvery hope filtered away. He still had to undergo the last part, dipping the *vis* into holy water, then vampire blood, and then reinserting it.

But she realized Max was talking to Brim and Michalas, explaining. "Ylito agreed that I should try to wipe the vampire's blood on the *vis* during the battle, and it worked."

"I saw that you put holy water on the *vis* just before," Brim said, nodding. "I didn't realize it was for any other purpose."

"Your abilities and powers are restored?" Michalas asked.

Max nodded. "Fully restored." He poured a healthy slug of water onto his head, wiped his darkly stubbled face, then took the rest of the jug and dumped it over his chest. All without sparing a glance at Victoria.

Despite her confusion and annoyance, she bit her lip and felt that familiar fluttering in her belly. She watched as he toweled himself off, removing much of the dirt and blood. Muscles flexed and shifted smoothly, and now they glistened with water.

As he accepted the clean shirt Wayren offered him, there was again the accidental, sketchiest of impersonal glances over Victoria. His gaze barely touched her, and they weren't even the flat black eyes that she'd expect him to have after seeing her and Sebastian in an embrace. . . .

Impersonal. As if he didn't know her.

Not angry at her defection. But as if he had no feeling whatsoever.

A sudden flash of worry coursed through her, and she didn't speak after all. When he'd lost his Venator powers a few months ago, Max had also lost his memory. With the help of Ylito's foresight and planning, however, he'd regained his memory almost immediately.

But was it possible that now that he'd restored his powers, some of his memory had gone away?

No. Of course not. He seemed to remember everyone else.

Victoria almost stepped forward, her pain turning to annoyance. She was *Illa* Gardella. She could say something to him, *make* him respond to her . . . but in the end, she didn't.

Not here, in front of everyone, would she take on the possible razor edge of his disdain. Her unsteady fingers and queasy stomach told her she wasn't strong enough right now.

So, rocked off balance by Sebastian's actions and Max's cool impersonality, she settled into herself and remained uncharacteristically quiet as they left the abandoned building.

The moon rose high and fat, casting its blue-silver glow over the creamy buildings, darkening the red roofs to black once they were back on their horses. Victoria rode alongside Brim and Sebastian while Max and Wayren lagged behind, speaking quietly. Michalas brought up the rear.

Somehow they made their way back to the inn in which they'd let rooms, all without Victoria speaking to Max, or even having more than the chance to watch him, to confirm that beneath the grime and blood he truly was recovered.

But she didn't really have any question. . . . She'd seen it in his eyes, in his bearing. Yet the base relief she felt at his success waned into dismay. Had Sebastian's actions sent her relationship with Max back to where it had been only two weeks ago?

The dismounting and stabling of horses happened smoothly and quickly, and beneath her swirling thoughts, Victoria got the impression that plans to eat, drink, and celebrate—and the need to leave early the next day for Munţii Făgăraş—were being discussed. She didn't care. She merely moved silently as they made their way across the small yard to the entrance, trying to decide if she should be furious, joyous, or simply hurt.

When they clustered inside the inn, Max somehow slipped up behind Victoria and grabbed her arm. Hard.

Taken by surprise, she turned, but, though his fingers closed tight around her lower arm, he said nothing. He wasn't even looking at her. He was looking at Sebastian.

It happened quickly. A look passed between the two men, an instant, silent exchange, and the next thing Victoria knew, a door had opened and Max propelled her into a chamber. She had the wherewithal to recognize it as the one she and Sebastian had shared with Antonín.

Max closed the door with a deliberate clunk of the latch, his hand still gripping her arm. Anger welled up, and Victoria opened her mouth to speak as she tried to pull from his hold—but he was too strong, and he used the force of her aborted movement to whip her around.

The next thing she knew, Victoria was shoved up against the rough stone wall. Max followed, his long, strong body pinning her there as he covered her mouth with his. He released her arm at last, sliding his hands around to hold the back of her head as he molded into her from mouth to chest to hip to thigh. One strong leg slipped between her trousered ones, and she was completely imprisoned.

It took Victoria a bare second to comprehend, and her brain and body to catch up to the sudden onslaught. Then she closed her eyes, sagging gently against him as his heat and scent and strength surrounded her. Max was back.

One long, deep, ferocious kiss later, he pulled away enough to let her catch her breath and to adjust position. He captured her wrists and spread both wide above her head, clasping them with large hands as he kept her in place against the wall with the pressure of his hips and straddled thighs.

Deliciously dazed by the assault, she blinked and swallowed, realizing that her breathing sounded as though she were fighting a battle. Her lips throbbed, her face burned from sharp whiskers, and the imprint of his body left no illusion about how much he desired her.

His own breathing was unsteady, his beautiful lips full and very, very mobile, his damp hair in deep waves against his unshaven cheek. He looked down, and their gazes met.

And . . . she saw everything there in his dark eyes that she needed to see.

"Don't you dare stop," she said. "Or I'll kill you myself."

At that, as if he too had needed to see validation, his eyes gleamed hotter and the set of his lips changed, quirking and relaxing in a way that made her stomach plunge and her mouth dry.

Now Max turned from fierce to languorously intent and deliberate. He released her wrists, but moved in to imprison her head in place against the wall with another staggering kiss while his hands tore quickly and efficiently at the clothing between them.

He worked the button of her man's shirt collar, yanking at it until it gave way and tumbled to the floor. His fingers slid down into the opening as her breathing quickened, feeling the warmth of his flesh against hers as he slipped and tugged and pulled at the gentle breast bindings she'd taken to wearing.

As her shirt and the strips of cloth fell away in tatters, he never removed his mouth from tasting her lips, her cheek, her jaw . . . even the soft spot beneath her ear.

That lovely curl of desire flooded her from her center out to each limb and digit. Warmth and relief, mixed with urgent need and rising pleasure, set her to sighing against him. Pinioned by the kiss, she felt his hands slide up to cup both breasts, thumbs fanning briefly over their hard nipples, pausing to stroke the tips just firmly enough to send more sharp, lovely little tingles curling through her belly and lower. Then he grabbed up her wrists again, holding them crossed above her head with one hand so that her knuckles brushed the rough masonry.

His hand slipped down beneath the loose waist of her trousers, his fingers quick and sure. With a few deft movements, he slicked and slid, surprising her into the sudden tumble of orgasm, right there against the wall. She trembled against him, and felt the movement of his cheek against her face as he smiled into the curve of her neck—in satisfaction, no doubt.

She didn't care. She didn't care at all, especially as, with those long, elegant fingers, he flipped open the three buttons of her trousers' fall. The waist thus loosened, the trousers slipped down, and he helped them . . . and she realized she'd begun to tear at his own waist, pulling the fabric from its button fastenings.

He lifted her into position, and she locked her legs around his waist, feeling the rough prickle of stone and masonry against her bare back as he settled into place. And then he thrust deep . . . and paused, holding her against the wall, pressing as intimately as one could press, delaying the lovely rise of pleasure for the moment as their breath mingled roughly in the silence.

Then he took her hand and pressed it to his chest, curling her fingers around the *vis bulla* there, warm from his skin. She felt the sharp surge of power and, along with it, a surprise increase in pleasure so that she gave a little gasp. His mouth, tight with control, eased into a quick smile; then, with a meaningful look in those dark eyes, he slipped his fingers between their bellies to press against her amulets.

An erotic shock sizzled through her, and her gaze flew up to meet his dark, knowing one. "Don't let go," he whispered.

With another smile, he closed his eyes and began to move again, at last. Long, deep, satisfying strokes matched the little sizzles of power from the tiny amulets. She cried out softly into his shoulder at the peak, and felt him catch his breath just as he moved one last time and then stilled, shuddering against her.

Quiet, tangled breaths, hot, damp bodies, little quakes of pleasure. She smiled inside herself, and against Max. *Max*. At last.

He gathered her close now with his arms, pulling her away from the wall, splaying his large hands over her bare skin, gritty with mortar. Max helped her settle back on her feet, and moved with her toward the bed. Not about to give him the chance to slip away again—who knew what went on in that mind of his? For all she knew, this had simply been a way to put Sebastian in his place for the trick he'd pulled.

No. She didn't believe that. She'd seen the look in Max's eyes, the look that had blazed there once before when he saw her rise free from Lilith's pit of hell. Yet . . .

He tumbled her onto the bed, a narrow, lumpy affair, then stood over her for a moment. Max looked down with eyes that had become inscrutable again, and she thought, *Here it is. Now he'll make the excuse, call it duty, draw upon Lilith. . . .*

"Victoria," he said, his voice rough. She gathered herself up at the tone, ready for it. . . . Then, instead of speaking, he came forward, down to her, his hands settling on either side of her, pressing into the thin pallet. And he kissed her.

His lips moved over hers, soft and sensual this time, tracing the contours of her mouth as gently and thoroughly as one might sculpt soft clay. She could scarcely breathe . . . the kiss was so exquisite in its long, slow melding and tangling of lips and tongue, the scrape of teeth, the gentle suction. It seemed to go on and on, and her world spiraled around her into this imprint, this learning of gentle mouth to gentle mouth.

After a long while, he moved. Propping a knee on the bed next to her, Max smoothed his free hand up along the side of her throat to play in her hair, lifting her face closer to his. Then he released her mouth. "Perhaps I should have bathed first, but"—he kissed her again—"I was bloody damn tired of waiting for you."

Victoria nearly laughed in relief, understanding now that earlier, just after he released her from that heated moment against the wall, what she'd seen in his eyes was . . . not uncertainty—no, Max would barely comprehend that emotion—but perhaps a bit of regret or discomfort for the rough-and-tumble way in which he'd taken her.

She lifted and met his mouth halfway, her kiss telling him that she didn't care, that his sweaty male scent and damp, hot body were home to her. Home and Heaven.

And she wanted more.

Sebastian watched the door close to the chamber he and Victoria—and Antonín—had shared, and turned away. Michalas and Brim seemed to be merely surprised and amused as Max dragged Victoria into the chamber, unaware of any undercurrents. But Wayren's all-knowing colorless blue eyes snagged his.

He pulled away from her gaze, but not before he recognized the look therein: perceptive, and perhaps even satisfied. Perhaps.

What was missing was condemnation, judgment. At least from Wayren.

Victoria had given him enough of that in her steely, furious look, and she had avoided him since. Alas. Perhaps one day she'd understand what he'd given her, besides a long, hot kiss.

And Pesaro. In that brief, measured look before disappearing with Victoria, he'd sent both acknowledgment and warning. Acknowledgment of Sebastian's purpose in the bold move—but of course not a hint of gratitude. And warning as well.

The warning had been unnecessary.

Even now Sebastian wanted to bristle at the man's arrogance . . . but the desire ebbed and faded into something emptier. The trip to Muntii Făgăraş to retrieve the last two rings, somehow, from Lilith would be a long one, now that Pesaro had returned to the Venator fold and staked his claim.

That thought gave him a needed distraction. Was Max's reinstatement bound to be a blessing or a curse when dealing with Lilith?

*   *   *

"Are you going to tell me what happened?" Victoria asked, soaping Max's broad, square shoulders from where she knelt behind him.

The much-needed hot bath had been ordered some time ago, and though he'd settled with a great groan into the steaming water, she still felt the urge to touch him. There was nothing, she found, like the feel of warm male skin slick with lemon-rosemary soap and water.

He craned his head to look at her. "You haven't figured it out for yourself?"

"Obviously you had something planned, because you missed at least five chances to stake him," she replied archly. "And I understand now that you were intending to finish the Trial by getting the blood on the *vis bulla* that you were already wearing . . . but why? You could have killed that vampire in one or two strokes instead of nearly getting killed yourself."

Max snorted. "Nearly killed? You're mistaken. I was not in any danger of dying by the hand of that vampire, Victoria. I knew exactly what I was doing. I had to get blood on the *vis* and then twist the ring around into my skin, and wait for it to empower me again. It took a few bloody moments for that to happen."

"Well, you looked as though—"

"And looks can be deceiving, can they not? Speaking of which, Vioget's . . . er . . . shall we say . . . added incentive for me to survive was completely unnecessary."

Victoria sat back on her haunches, water dripping all over her lap and streaming down her arms into the rolled-up sleeves of the shift she'd donned. "I rather hoped you'd been too distracted to see that."

"I was meant to. Was that not the purpose?"

"Not by me."

"Indeed not, although, from my vantage point, you didn't seem terribly vexed at his actions. I know why he did it. He had the audacity to think I needed his help."

From any other man, that might have sounded like so much bravado, but coming from Max it sounded just about right.

Before she could reply, Max slid down into the water, submerging his head completely. This left his knees and a good portion of his powerful legs angling up from the oval wooden tub.

When he reappeared, it was with a little surge that slopped water over the sides, sending a renewed wave of rosemary and lemon scent into the air. His hair was slicked back away from his clean-shaven face, its ragged edges plastered to the sides and back of his neck.

"I was vexed with Sebastian," she said. "I didn't want you to think . . . well—"

Max shifted in the tub, splashing water yet again, so that he was half facing her. "I knew you'd been with him for three days while I was at Týn, Victoria. And so did he."

"Nothing happened."

"Of course it didn't."

"Then why wouldn't you even look at me when you came in for the Trial? And after? Especially after. You acted as if I didn't even exist."

Max's look was a combination of pity and satisfaction. "That bothered you, did it? The truth was, Victoria, I needed no distractions before the battle. You of all should understand that. And after . . . well"—he lifted that arrogant brow of his—"I knew it was only a matter of time before I had you exactly where I wanted you. There was no need to be exchanging pining, lovesick glances or tearful embraces after the Trial. I had other things on my mind."

She swallowed hard at the look that blazed back into his eyes. Apparently, he had other things on his mind now, as well.

"Max," she said, leaning toward him over the edge of the tub, "I'm so glad you're safe. And a Venator again—only because it will help keep you that way."

He kissed her briefly, but then she felt his lips settle into a familiar firm line. "You know that Lilith will be pleased as well."

She felt as though a bucket of cold water had been tossed over her. Lilith did prefer Max as a Venator. She claimed it made it much more interesting to try to subdue him. "You're not going to disappear again, are you? Leave me under the guise of protecting me?"

"Victoria, you know that this"—he swept his arm to encompass them, the room, the piles of clothing on the floor—"doesn't mean anything's changed."

"Yes, it does," she said sharply. "You're a Venator again, Max, and yes, you have your precious duty back. But things have changed—"

"I *meant*," he said, his loud voice overriding hers, "that nothing outside of *us* has changed. The rest of the world." He moved again, and again the slop of water. At the rate things were going, Victoria would soon be as wet as he.

She calmed a bit, but still, she gave him a look of mistrust. "Max, you have to promise that you'll never leave like that again."

"I'm not going to promise that, Victoria."

She turned away, shocked at a sudden sting of tears, the sharp pain in her belly. She wanted to respond, but she didn't trust herself to speak.

"Victoria," Max said in a slightly gentler voice, "you can't promise either. The future could require anything of us, and what's the point of making promises that we may not keep?" He reached for her, tugged her peremptorily toward him so that the edge of the tub bit into her ribs. "I don't want anything to happen to you, Victoria. I'd die first. . . . Do you understand?"

She pulled out of his grip, but remained next to the tub. "That's the easy way out, Max. Dying and leaving the other to live on. Alone."

"Have I not admitted I'm a coward when it comes to you?"

She glanced at him, at the black expression on his face: skin stretched taut over his high cheekbones, nary a hint of softness near the corners of his eyes. His mouth that had, moments before, been full and sensual, was now thin and pursed.

Yet, much as it pained her to hear the words, she knew he was right. Aunt Eustacia, and then Max, had been telling her for two years that duty had to come before personal wants and choices. The good of many would always win out over the safety or love of a few. It had to.

It was part of being a Venator—especially for Victoria, who was *Illa* Gardella. Despite her love affair of fifty years with Kritanu, Aunt Eustacia had understood. That was why she'd ordered Max to execute her.

But if it had been you instead of Eustacia? I could not have done it. Do you understand? I couldn't have done it. That's what I'm afraid of, Victoria. A choice like that.

And if she had any intelligent bones in her body, she should be afraid of the very same thing.

Neither of them had spoken, and there was only the tinkling sound of lapping water and the arrhythmic drips from the side of the tub. Then Max moved and pulled Victoria over the edge and into his lap, shift and all, closing his arms around her as the water enveloped her in a softer embrace.

"You won't agree with every decision I make," he said. "And God knows I won't agree with you. But I know you can take care of yourself, Victoria. I've seen it, much as it turned my insides to pudding when you came sailing down from the rafters during the battle with Nedas. Among other instances."

The warm water lapped gently over her cotton shift, and Victoria settled against him, resting her face on his damp neck, smelling the fresh rosemary on his jaw. "Your insides were pudding?" she asked, smiling, tangling her fingers in the wet hair on his chest. She lifted his *vis bulla* and felt a shock of power.

"Indeed. More than once."

"Like when else?"

He shifted her slightly, settling her sidewise onto one of his thighs so that he could untie the lace at the neckline of her shift. "When you appeared unexpectedly at Regalado's art show that first night in Roma."

"Did Sara know who I was at that time?" The cotton shift was glued to her body from just below the breasts, down into the water, and she lifted her rump a bit so Max could tug it up and over her head. It landed on the floor with a damp splat.

"I don't believe she did; she knew of Eustacia, of course, and that there was rumor of another female Venator. But since you'd been in mourning for the year since Rockley died, the gossip among the Tutela and undead had died down."

"You acted so cool and angry that I didn't know what to think. Even later, you never gave the slightest hint that you were anything but a member of the Tutela."

"The last thing I expected to see was you, when Sara introduced you as her new friend." His hands had become busy now, and she felt a renewed rise of lust as he bent to one of her breasts. She admired the long, strong width of his neck and the swath of dark hair, just beginning to dry. His fingers moved to sift through the duo of silver amulets at her navel.

"Well, you hid that fact quite well. And when else?" she asked impishly. "When I had to change in the carriage, and you had to unlace my stays? I know you peeked, Max. Admit it."

His tongue caught the sensitive tip of her nipple, making her jolt with pleasure, and then he swirled it around languorously. She sighed and arched toward his mouth, her hand sliding down into the water between his legs.

"When else?" she asked, closing her fingers around him, smiling with satisfaction at his sharp, indrawn breath.

"Hmm . . . ," he said, vibrating against her breast, then lifting to look thoughtfully into space. "There were too many times. And I'm certain," he said, lifting her suddenly from the water, "that there will be many more times to come."

Quickly and easily, he settled her in place and slid inside with a smooth movement. Anything she might have said . . . or even thought to have said . . . became lost in a damp whirlwind of pleasure and rhythmic splashing.

Sixteen

The Negotiation

Max refused to feel guilty, though the emotion nicked at him like the tip of a blade. It nagged, but he ignored the incessant prickles and focused on the journey ahead.

This was the only damn way, the most efficient and only certain way to get the rings from Lilith. He of all people knew what she wanted. He knew how to manage her insofar as she could be managed.

Victoria didn't.

The simple fact was, aside from him, the other thing Lilith wanted more than anything in the world was Victoria—Eustacia's prodigy and *Illa* Gardella.

He glanced at Vioget, who rode next to him. They, along with Michalas, had left Prague just as dawn broke, Max slipping reluctantly from the chamber where Victoria still lay sleeping. As well she should be. It had been a very busy night after that bath. And during.

Hell. His fingers were still unsteady. Damn, and his

palms grew damp at the mere memory of those last hours.

He didn't know whether there'd ever be a repeat of a night like that again. Now his belly soured, and he thrust away thoughts of the future. One step at a time, one moment at a time.

Victoria would be damn furious when she woke to find him gone, even more bloody angry when she realized what he meant to do. His lips flattened, and he corralled his determination. Max had made his decision as he always did—the right one, the only one. He understood the repercussions.

She bloody well would have to understand and accept it. Just as he had.

She had to close that portal—and sooner rather than later, for next time there might not be a chance to rescue Wayren. Or beat those demons back.

There was no better way. She'd have to accept that.

Victoria was *Illa* Gardella, and she was bloody damn smart. After she got past the anger, the shock, she'd understand.

She might never forgive him, but she'd understand why.

The burn of rage and pain hadn't subsided in the least since she left Prague, nearly a week ago.

Victoria rode like a fiend, stopping only for a few short hours of rest each night, driving Brim to keep up with her pace despite her increasing weariness. Wayren had returned to Rome at Victoria's strong suggestion—where she might remain safe in the Consilium. They could call for her if she was needed, but Victoria wanted to take no chances with Wayren's safety now that the Trial was over.

And Sebastian and Michalas had gone with Max.

She'd alternated between fury and relief that he'd

taken them with him. He wouldn't face Lilith alone—
but how dared he circumvent her and sneak off into the
night with two Venators. Michalas she could perhaps
understand, for he'd worked with Max for years . . .
but Sebastian as well?

The hope that she and Brim might overtake the others
kept urging her on, but no matter how quickly they traveled, there was no sign of them, no word from anyone
who might have seen the trio along the way. She wasn't
even certain where Lilith's lair in Muntii Făgăraş was, a
fact she was sure Max had used to his advantage.

She didn't want to think about what else he'd done
to get the advantage. Making love to her, lulling her
into complacency . . .

Promise me you won't leave like that again.

I'm not going to promise that, Victoria.

No indeed. She had no illusions; Max had known
exactly what he intended to do even then. Likely before they'd even arrived in Prague. In fact, she suspected he'd known from the moment he learned that
they would need to obtain two rings from Lilith. Stupid, foolish Victoria not to have predicted his pattern
of thought herself.

So, knowing that she'd never allow it, he'd taken the
decision from her.

Damn him.

And then he'd left Brim to meet her when she came
out of the chamber that still had damp marks on the
floor, and to detain her from leaving right away. At
least Max had had the courtesy to leave a note for her.

*I'm the best person to deal with Lilith. I will obtain
the rings. She won't give them up easily.*

And, as he reminded her further, in the heavy, masculine scrawl that perfectly matched his arrogance, he

could have resorted to the same trick she'd done to him only a few weeks ago—using *salvi* to render her deeply asleep so that he could make his escape. That simple comment was meant to remind her that she too had made a similar choice, and that he'd eventually come to accept it. Forgiveness was another matter.

Forgiveness, acceptance . . . those were too far away for her to consider right now. All Victoria wanted was to find Max, to lay eyes—and hands, *furious* hands—on him and show him that there was another way.

There had to be.

But Max had planned well, which was no surprise, and by the time Victoria and Brim reached the foothills of the Romanian mountain that held Lilith's lair, they'd encountered no one who'd seen the three Venators. And they could go no farther, for neither Victoria nor Brim knew how to find the hidden place.

"Sebastian didn't seem to know exactly where the magical pool is," Victoria said, shielding her eyes against the sun rising over the mountain in front of her. They'd slept from midnight until four o'clock, then risen and gone as far as they could. "He didn't tell me its name or any other information, other than that the orb was hidden inside."

"Max said that they would find us when they had the rings," Brim told her. "You look like you've not slept in a week, Victoria. Perhaps since we can go no farther, you should rest for a bit."

She *was* exhausted. And heartsick. And furious. All of which had kept her from getting any good sleep since leaving Prague. She didn't want to rest, to waste time that could be spent searching for Max. Dragging him out of whatever situation he'd tried to put himself in.

But aside of all that, Victoria was a practical woman, and she knew Brim spoke the truth. She would be no good to anyone if she didn't take care of herself; even Venators couldn't go on forever at the pace she'd set.

She agreed to take a room in the village nearby, and, with one last glance out at the stark mountain rearing up to block the yellowing sky, she slept well and deeply while Brim kept watch.

The room felt stifling. Dark, warm, and red . . . red everywhere: in the burning fires, the cloth-draped furnishings, the dark wall hangings. Crimson swirls on maroon, twisting about cabernet and scarlet. Sebastian felt as though he'd entered a furnace. And the smell. Roses. Strong and sweet, laced with evil and desire.

"And to what do I owe the pleasure of your company, my dear Maximilian?" Lilith's eyes gleamed with pleasure. They glowed red, pure, vibrant red, and the burning irises were rimmed with blue as befit her station as Queen of the Vampires, daughter of Judas Iscariot.

Sebastian glanced at the man in question, wondering yet again how he managed it: the impassive, haughty expression that belied no discomfort even as the vampire queen's obsession oozed through the chamber, cloaking it like heavy velvet. The way she looked at Pesaro made Sebastian's skin crawl, and he wasn't even the object of her gaze.

The three Venators had been met outside of the secret entrance to Lilith's lair and brought directly in to this private chamber of hers. Of course both Pesaro and Sebastian had been recognized by her guards, and none of the undead had made any attempt on them, although they had relieved them of their stakes. This left Sebastian distinctly uncomfortable, being deep in the lair of the most powerful vampire in the world. The fact that all three of them wore the protection of the *vis bulla*, as well as larger cross amulets and some small vials of holy water secreted on their persons, was small comfort.

Not that he hadn't been deep in the midst of a group of undead before, but in those situations, he'd always had the protection of Beauregard. But by causing his grandfather's death, Sebastian had declared himself firmly in the camp of the Venators, and he no longer had the freedom to balance between the two sides.

Lilith looked exactly the same. Her long, impossibly bright coppery hair fell like burning Medusa coils over her shoulders and the pale, blue-veined skin revealed by her vee-necked bodice. Her gown looked more the style that Wayren would wear than Victoria, for it flowed long and simply against her slender figure. Lilith had obviously been an attractive woman near thirty when she was turned undead by Judas, but what had been ethereal beauty had turned into cold, marblelike skin and gaunt features. Even from where he stood, Sebastian could see on her cheek the five dark freckles that formed the shape of a crescent moon.

"I see you've redecorated," Pesaro observed. "I don't recall it being so interminably red the last time I was here."

"I find it quite comfortable, Maximilian." Lilith's voice came out in a sort of purr that made nasty little needles prickle along Sebastian's spine. "I'd be pleased to show you what I mean."

He'd met Lilith before, of course, but every other time had been brief, and in the company of the powerful Beauregard—or, most recently, in a vicious battle beneath the streets of London. Sebastian wasn't frightened of her, but, as anyone—mortal or undead—would be in her presence, his vigilance was at its peak.

He glanced at Pesaro, watching for signs of discomfort or weakness. Good Lord, the man must be made of stone. He showed no sign of revulsion, though he must feel it the same way Sebastian did. To be sure, Max had been around Lilith much more than he had. . . . How could he have willingly returned?

To be the object of her obsession, to have been sequestered with her in a cloistered place such as this . . . how could the man have not gone mad?

"You're aware of the growing demonic activity," Pesaro was saying. "The Midiverse Portal is open, causing a threat to both my race and yours."

"Don't say you've come to protect me, my pet?" Lilith spoke like a simpering woman, but the glint in those dangerous eyes spoke otherwise. She had more cunning than any woman he'd ever met.

"You could interpret it that way, if you wish," Pesaro replied coolly. He stood square in front of the chaise on which the vampire queen half reclined, as if to draw her attention to him, and keep it from the others.

Sebastian wasn't quite sure how he felt, being thus shielded. But he took the opportunity to examine the chamber and its contents, seeking anything that could be an advantage. To his dismay, he realized nothing in the room was made from wood, so there would be no opportunity for makeshift stakes. He noted stone chairs and tables covered with an abundance of cushions and pillows, along with the chaise, which was made from slender golden rods lashed together. Bamboo, he thought it might be called.

Nothing in this room that could harm an undead— no windows to allow sunlight in, no swords to behead a vampire.

What the hell had Pesaro been thinking to bring them in here, unarmed?

"Your vampires are threatened as well as my people. They've been attacked by the demons, and run from their hideaways. That isn't news to you," Pesaro had continued.

"No, of course not." Lilith sat upright and for the first time dropped the sultry expression that she'd adopted the moment she saw Max.

"Surely you don't plan to step aside and watch them continue to slip from the portal into your domain here on earth."

"It amuses Lucifer to watch us battle among ourselves," Lilith said. Pale, bluish lips, which had once been full and sensual and likely a luscious red, twisted. "I've dispatched armies, but they've not been as successful as I hoped."

"So here you sit, hiding in your lair?" Max said, a note of challenge in his voice. "I expected more from someone with your power. From you."

"But, my dear Maximilian . . . don't you see? I've barely lifted a finger, save sending a few of my most worthless minions—and here you are. You and your companions. Saviors, one and all. For mortal and undead alike." Her eyes narrowed in delight. "And you cannot think that I'd decline your offer for assistance."

Sebastian looked sharply at his companion. Hell. She'd been expecting them.

Instead of appearing taken aback, Pesaro lifted his chin, looking down at the vampire queen with an air of arrogance. "That's precisely why I've come."

"And here I thought it was because you missed me, my dear, mortal Maximilian." Lilith rose smoothly, sending a renewed swell of roses wafting through the air. Sebastian thought he might choke.

In an instant, she'd moved in front of Pesaro, her silky forest green skirts dragging across the floor in a short train. The vampire queen stood as tall as Max, taller than Sebastian himself. She reached for Pesaro, the sleeve of her gown sliding back to reveal the pale, blue-veined flesh of an impossibly thin arm. Looking at the unfortunate man, trying to capture him with her enthralling gaze, she curled her skeletal hand around the back of his neck, fingers sifting through the dark hair that brushed his collar.

How could he abide those hands on him? Had she enthralled him so easily with her gaze?

Sebastian watched sharply, his heart pounding harder, and exchanged a glance with Michalas. They had agreed—or, rather, been informed—that Max would handle Lilith. But now . . .

Pesaro continued to stand still, without even the hitch of a breath, despite the brush of bone-white flesh against his much darker skin. Sebastian watched in horrified fascination as her hand trailed down around the collar of his open shirt and along the length of his arm to grasp his wrist. She touched him as if he was her possession, as if she knew every ridge of every muscle in his body, every hair on his head.

It wasn't until this moment, watching the sordid pantomime in front of him, that Sebastian fully understood the sacrifice Pesaro had made in coming here.

And in leaving Victoria behind. Safe.

Damn. Grudging respect for Max Pesaro was not one of Sebastian's favorite emotions.

He could see that Lilith had her long fingers closed around Max's wrist, and then her fangs came out as she reached for his jaw with her other hand, pressing her body intimately up against his.

"You cannot know how pleased I am that you've returned to me," Lilith said, reaching up to touch Max's cheek with a sharp nail.

That was when he moved. Suddenly, sharply, efficiently.

One moment Lilith had him in her grasp, seemingly overpowered, ready to sink her fangs into his corded neck . . . and the next, Max had her caught neatly by the wrists. He bared his teeth in a humorless smile and then shoved her away from him. "I think not."

Sebastian braced himself for a furious onslaught from Lilith and the four vampires he'd spotted, lurking deep in the shadows and behind the draped wall hangings.

But to his surprise, Lilith caught her balance, remaining on her feet, and instead of fury blackening her face, he saw delight. Pure, unadulterated delight . . . followed by a bit of confusion.

"You've returned," she said in wonder. "You've returned as a Venator, my dear Maximilian." She smiled, and the bald lust in her expression made Sebastian's belly tighten unpleasantly. "I thought it was impossible, but . . . here you are."

"Obviously your taint in my blood could not withstand divine will," Pesaro replied.

Lilith pursed her lips into a little moue that Sebastian might have found intriguing if it weren't on her. "I shan't complain, Maximilian. To have you back in such magnificent form . . . I must admit, I was a bit bored with the mere man you'd become."

"Anything to destroy your hold on me."

"That is what makes you endlessly fascinating to me, my pet. In all my centuries of nonliving, it's you who've intrigued me to no end."

"Now that we've established your . . . er . . . fascination, if I might be so bold as to use the word . . . perhaps we might get on to business," Pesaro said. "We've come because we need the two Rings of Jubai. As you know, the Midiverse Portal has cracked or somehow been breached, and the only way to close it is with Tached's Orb."

"Of course. But you need all five rings to reach inside the enchanted pool," Lilith replied thoughtfully. "I fixed that truly well, did I not? Unfortunately, three of the rings are lost, which has precluded me from doing the same."

Pesaro didn't speak, and it was only the breath of a moment before the vampire was looking up at him in surprise. "And you have the other three? In your possession?"

"We need only the two rings. It will benefit your race as well as man."

"And you think that we should join forces, Maximilian? Mortal and undead? To save the world from those nasty demons?" With a crafty, sidelong look, Lilith turned. Her movement was an energetic swish, molding her skirts to the boyish curves of her emaciated body.

Sebastian had a sudden mental image of how that body would appear naked, and he swallowed hard. He hoped to God Pesaro had never been faced with such a travesty. But, he realized, it was an unlikely hope. Dear God.

"As I said, it would benefit both of us."

"And so you expect that I might simply give you the rings, and allow you to rush out and save the world?"

"It would save you from losing more of your followers—at least to the demons. After all," Pesaro added with a lift of his chin, "we dispatched quite a few of them in Prague only last week. Your numbers are growing fewer."

Lilith paced, her gown swirling, her gaze continuing to return to Max, and then skittering quickly over to Sebastian and Michalas. The very touch of her attention on Sebastian sent a disgusting chill over his body, and he wondered again how Max had become so inured to her.

"And what of *Illa* Gardella?"

Pesaro remained silent.

Sebastian felt Lilith's rising frustration, and he glanced at Max. Max had made it clear to him and Michalas that they were to allow things to unfold as they would without interfering.

Lilith walked toward Pesaro again, reaching for his arm. This time, she seemed prepared for him to react, and he moved easily to block her reach. They faced each other for a moment, ironically, like lovers whose embrace had been thwarted, and then Lilith stepped back.

"I'll give you the rings . . . but I want something in exchange."

"The safety of your race will be your prize. We'll take the risks, fight the battle. You need do nothing but watch."

Lilith laughed, a low, knowing one. "Very nice try, Maximilian. You know what I want."

A beat of silence. Sebastian felt tension lift in the room.

"And if I refuse?" Max said quietly.

"Then you must find another way to free the orb from the enchanted pool. And while you search, and that fairy-headed angel studies book after book, writ after writ . . . and while you try new ways to breach the glass of that pool . . . more and more demons will slip free . . . and well, now, Maximilian, we both know what would happen then. Your lovely *Illa* Gardella will fight and fight, but the demons will simply keep coming until she dies. Oh, yes, and many others of your race will perish as well. We cannot forget that."

Sebastian couldn't remember ever feeling such loathing, such deep disgust. She was playing them, of course. He looked around the room again, in vain, for something that could be used as a weapon against her. Nothing but the cross around his neck—which would hold Lilith off for perhaps a minute or two—

and two small vials of holy water inside the hem of his trousers.

Damn Pesaro and his blasted leadership and negotiation. They weren't going to get what they wanted, and the three of them had little means to fight against Lilith and her guards. Even if somehow they succeeded, then they'd have to actually find the rings.

Not the best odds.

"So what will it be, Maximilian my pet?"

"Yet another impossible choice you offer me."

"Come now, my dear. It won't be so terrible."

"I do believe it would, in fact."

Lilith laughed. "Again, how you delight me. That lovely mix of pleasure and pain, arrogance and sensuality. How I've missed it." Then she sobered, that cunning look slanting her eyes again. "And if you refuse, and you leave here . . . Of course, I'll let you leave, my dear. I find the hunt a good part of the fun, you know. And now that I know you're truly worth hunting again . . ."

She turned and paced back to her chaise, settling on it once again like a princess who was about to receive a great gift. "If you leave without the means to close the portal, you know what awaits the world. Your race. You won't be able to beat them back, of course. And . . . don't forget your *Illa* Gardella. She'd be in the very middle of it all, wouldn't she?"

"You'd part with the rings, then."

"You know I would. As you say, it would be to my benefit. In several ways. You, my pet, for eternity . . . in exchange for the rings."

Pesaro nodded then, a sharp acquiescence, and it was at that moment that Sebastian realized this had been his plan all along. He'd known he'd never leave, but that he'd need to bargain himself for the two rings.

Sebastian opened his mouth to protest, but Max seemed to know, and he turned to silence him.

"As you wish," said Lilith with distorted kindness. "One moment while I retrieve them for you." She stood with another dramatic sweep of silk and beckoned to a pair of guards, standing in the dark corner. She then moved over to what appeared to be a plain stone wall. But she spoke in an ancient tongue and moved her hand over it. A small door appeared, through which she stepped.

Moments later, she returned, closing the door, which again melded so well into the designs on the wall that Sebastian wasn't certain he'd be able to find it again, even though he'd just seen it open. They would never have found the rings themselves.

But now that they had them, surely Pesaro intended for them to fight their way out?

As Lilith approached Sebastian, offering the two copper rings, he saw the pair of Guardian vampires move toward Pesaro. As Sebastian took the rings from Lilith, he heard the dull clank of metal. Turning, he saw the heavy bands as they were fastened about Max's wrists.

He realized belatedly that there was no way to fight out of the room. They were outnumbered by four Guardians, plus Lilith. They had no weapons, nothing to use for them. And if they tried and failed, the rings would stay . . . and so would they. Either as corpses or guests of the vampire queen.

Neither of which appealed to Sebastian.

As if reading his mind, Pesaro looked at him as the two Guardians pulled him by the chains. "Take the rings. Go. Close the portal. There is no other way."

Seventeen

In Which Sebastian Exercises Unusual Prudence

Victoria couldn't breathe.

"Where's Max?" she asked again. She tried to keep her voice calm. She was sure she succeeded. It was a simple question. It should have a simple answer. *He's coming. He's just around the bend. He'll be along in a moment.*

Sebastian took her arm, turning her to face him, away from the road on which he and Michalas had just ridden in. "Victoria," he said, his voice sharp, "he obtained the rings for us. We have the last two rings. He stayed." He spoke clearly, slowly, and she wondered vaguely how many times she'd already asked, and how many times he'd replied.

He stayed.

Victoria closed her eyes and crossed her arms tightly across her churning belly. *No. Nonononono.*

"We have the rings," Michalas said in a gentler voice. "Lilith gave them up."

But she *kept Max*.

"We—I—have to go after him," she said, her head suddenly clearing. The cobwebs slipped off; the nausea filtered away. Confidence settled over her, and purpose.

This she could do. This was her duty, her task, her calling. She'd come face-to-face with Lilith before. Max must know she'd come after him. He'd planned it this way.

Though her fingers trembled, she drew herself up regally and looked at each of the men in turn. "Michalas, you know the way to her lair now. You can lead me there, and I'll find a way in." She turned to Sebastian, who'd opened his mouth to argue. "I know we have the five rings. You and Brim can go and retrieve the orb while I free Max."

"We have guests," Sebastian said, his thick blond hair riffled by a breeze. He'd not stopped looking at her, a mixture of pity and understanding in his gaze. "Lilith sent some of her own to assist."

Victoria turned and saw three heavily cloaked figures standing in the shadow of the small inn where she and Brim had rested. That explained the chill at the back of her neck, the sensation she'd barely acknowledged when she realized Max was not with Michalas and Sebastian. Every other thought had fallen away when she realized he wasn't there.

Now she accepted the presence of vampires, well covered to protect themselves from the lowering sun.

"They're to return the rings to her when we've finished with them," Sebastian told her.

A sizzle of relief tickled her. "And Lilith will release Max then? She's holding him only as a hostage?"

He shook his head. "That wasn't part of the arrangement."

Her stomach pitched again. "Then it will be as I

said. Michalas and I will go to free Max, and you'll go to the enchanted pool."

Sebastian drew in his breath to speak, but Victoria turned away and approached the vampires. They stood in a tight cluster, careful not to allow any part of their flesh to be exposed to the sun. Under their heavy black hoods, two of them looked at her with red-violet eyes, and the third with ruby-pink irises. She saw the gleam of a sword falling from the invisible hand of one of the purple-eyed ones. Two Imperials and a Guardian.

Victoria felt a little chill up her spine. "I am Victoria Gardella," she told them.

"We know who you are," replied the tallest of the three, who happened to be a female Imperial. The sword she held, the Imperial weapon of choice, shifted menacingly against the side of her cloak. "I am called Mercy because I show none. Lilith sends a message to you."

Victoria inclined her head to accept the message.

"We three are to take you to the enchanted pool, and then to lead you to the Midiverse Portal. We're to return unharmed immediately after with the rings. If we don't return within a week's time, Maximilian will suffer."

"She'll release him when you return?"

The Imperial laughed. "No . . . Lilith merely promises not to torture him before she turns him undead."

"Simply being in her presence is torture," Victoria said, forcing the words from her dry mouth. "That is no guarantee. Nothing to keep me from turning you to dust at this moment."

The Imperial shrugged, her sword brushing against the cloak of her companion. "So be it. If we three do not return with the rings in a week's time, you can be assured that she'll keep her word."

Victoria firmed her lips and turned away. She had to

get to him. The others could retrieve the orb. They could go to the Midiverse Portal. They didn't need her.

She couldn't leave Max here.

She had to go after him.

Without another word, Victoria turned and went inside the inn. Once in the small chamber she'd used to sleep in, she dug through the long leather bag in which she stored her weapons. She'd go in well armed and fight her way to Max.

She could have Michalas show her the entrance to the lair, and then he could go with the others. They would need the three of them, certainly, to fight the demons escaping from the portal, but they could do it.

She knew they could. They were Venators.

Max.

Victoria brushed angry, sharp tears from her eyes. How could he have done this? He had to have known what would happen.

How could he have left me?

They should have gone together.

A noise behind her drew her upright, and she dashed her hand across her eyes again before turning. Sebastian stood there, blocking the doorway.

"Victoria."

"You can't stop me," she said flatly. "Don't try. I have to go after him. He'd go after me."

Sebastian nodded. "Of course he would want to. But you know Max, and how damn insufferable he is about doing the right thing. He'd rather suffer than be happy."

"I don't know what you're trying to do, but you're not going to change my mind."

He shook his head. "I'm not here to change your mind. He knew you'd go after him. And of course you should, Victoria. I'd come after you. Always."

Another blasted tear stung her eyes. Why now, why

after two years of angst and fear and anger did she have to act like a watering pot every time something happened? Aunt Eustacia had never shed a tear.

"But I wanted to tell you what it was like in there," Sebastian continued, walking into the room. "He was brilliant. I bloody well thought I'd never admit it aloud, but the man was brilliant. And strong. So damn strong. He was ahead of her every step of the way; he knew what she was going to say—and do—before she did it. He'd planned it all."

"Why in God's name didn't you just kill her and get the rings and go?" Victoria burst out. "Why did he have to trade himself? Didn't he know what that would do to me?" She clamped her mouth shut, but her voice had already risen in a high-pitched wail.

"I wondered the same thing, but then I understood," Sebastian said, almost gently. His amber eyes focused on her, a depth of seriousness she hadn't often seen within them. "There was no way to get the rings after she was dead. They were hidden in a little chamber. She touched the wall with her hand, and the door appeared as if from nowhere—some kind of magic, I think. We would never have found the chamber or the rings, and it would have all been for naught."

"But after you got them," she said desperately, "you could have attacked her and left with the rings. You didn't have to leave him *there*!" Now the tears exploded, to her great chagrin and shame, and she knuckled them furiously away.

He opened his mouth to speak, then seemed to think better of it and instead drew her into his arms. She allowed him to embrace her, to settle her head on his shoulder and to feel the familiar comfort of his body, the faint scent of cloves and tobacco. How many times had he done this for her? And this time . . . this time she knew he had no ulterior motive.

He meant only to give comfort. Dear Sebastian.

"Victoria," he said, his voice rumbling in his chest against her ear, "he knew the risk. He was fully aware of the sacrifice he made."

Sacrifice.

Damn Max. Why did he have to be so bloody noble?

"We had no weapons. There was no way to leave unless she allowed it. He knew that. He's been there before. He knew what he was doing, the risk. The sacrifice. There was no other way."

Sacrifice.

Aunt Eustacia had sacrificed herself, too. She'd made Max do the unthinkable because she knew he would. One life given for the safety of many.

Victoria pushed the thought away. This was different. This was Max. Her Max.

She'd free him, or she'd die trying. She didn't want to live without him.

Coward.

Dying is easier than going on without.

I'm a coward when it comes to you.

She pulled away from Sebastian. "Go and get the orb. I'll . . ." Her voice broke. She felt as though her insides were twisting like a rag being wrung out. Harder, tighter, until every bit of feeling leeched away . . . leaving her empty.

She·swallowed, stood upright, and looked straight at him. "I order you to go, as your *Illa* Gardella. Get the orb. Close the Midiverse Portal. God willing, I'll see you after."

Sebastian looked at her. "*Illa* Gardella," he said, reaching to touch her cheek, brushing away a tear. "You are a magnificent woman, Victoria. A brave, intelligent leader. Beautiful and strong." His expression grew intense, and he took her chin to keep her eyes fastened on him. "You are *Illa* Gardella. Never forget that."

He turned her face up and kissed her . . . not on the lips, but on the cheeks—one side and then the other. Then he left the room, closing the door behind him.

She realized then that he'd finally accepted her love for Max.

Turning back to her preparations, she felt a wave of fear again. What if she was too late?

What if they didn't get the orb? If something went wrong, and the portal wasn't closed?

You are Illa *Gardella.*

She was.

Victoria's knees gave way and she let herself sink onto the bed.

You are Illa *Gardella now, Victoria. You have an obligation to the Consilium and the rest of the Venators. You can no longer think only of yourself, of your needs and desires, but of the far-reaching consequences of your actions. Or inactions.*

It's time you learned sacrifice.

Max's angry words came roaring back to her, words he fairly shouted at her during their escape from Nedas, months ago.

Sacrifice.

Bloody damn sacrifice.

Illa Gardella. Last of the line.

Of course. He meant to protect not only her, Victoria, the woman he loved . . . but also her, the last of the line.

Of *course.*

She didn't like it, but she understood better why. Why he'd leave her behind, why he *had* to leave her behind. Why he thought he had to leave her behind.

And she knew she couldn't go after him. At least, not yet.

Not until the task at hand was done.

Duty before desire.

But then. And then she'd do what she vowed to do: She'd find Lilith, and she'd kill her.

And then Max would be free.

The five rings fit perfectly, amazingly, from thumb to pinkie. Sebastian had slipped them all on, one by one, and they snugly enclosed his fingers.

The copper bands, half as wide as the length from knuckle to knuckle, felt surprisingly comfortable. They weren't particularly ornate or unusual—five simple rings, made of braided copper strands, each slightly twisted and plaited differently from the one before it.

He looked over at Victoria, her short hair curling around her pale face. She couldn't see the glow that flushed her cheeks, but he recognized it with a deep pang, and felt another halfhearted wave of jealousy. Unless he was wrong, she carried Pesaro's child, the child who would continue the direct Gardella line.

He wondered if Pesaro knew.

He suspected if he had, he would not only have left her behind, but probably imprisoned her safely somewhere.

Not that Sebastian wouldn't do the same, were he in that enviable situation.

And not that it would have done any good, to try to put Victoria out of action.

Thank God she'd decided not to risk herself going after Max, for the loss could be greater than they realized.

Her eyes wandered briefly to the mountain that rose behind them, and he imagined how the need to go there must drive at her.

But she'd abandoned her plan to go after Max. The portal had to be closed first, and difficult as it was, much as the strain showed in her face and around her eyes, he saw that she'd made the decision. She'd accepted Pesaro's sacrifice. And perhaps she did realize that her duty as *Illa* Gardella extended beyond anything the men could do.

"The pool is there," said Mercy, breaking into his thoughts. She pointed with a powerful hand toward a small outcropping of rock.

Now that the sun had set, the undead had shed their cloaks and moved about with ease. The two Imperials sported swords at their waists, but kept them sheathed.

For Sebastian, such casual interaction with vampires bothered him little. He'd become used to it while living with Beauregard off and on over the years. Of course, this situation was different, yet he had heard Lilith's orders. She'd given her followers direction in the ancient language, presumably unaware that Sebastian's grandfather had taught it to him long ago.

Her instructions were clear: They weren't to harm the mortals in any way until the portal was safely closed. Then they were to get the rings, take Victoria prisoner, and kill the others.

Of course, Sebastian had passed that information along to his companions, who had agreed with him that the undead wouldn't make it to see the Midiverse Portal. They didn't need them as guides for anything but the location of the pool, and here they were.

Now he moved toward the indicated crust of rock formation. The sun had set, but still cast a generous glow from beneath the horizon. That last bit of light would fade fast, and the moon had waned to a generous half circle since they'd left Prague more than a week ago.

He wouldn't be able to see well for much longer.

Victoria and Michalas moved forward with torches to light his way, while Brim lagged behind the trio of vampires to watch for anything unexpected.

Sebastian had insisted on being the one to wear the rings and to dip his hand in the pool, for if he was wrong about the protection of the rings, it was only fitting that he bear the results. And aside from that, he *needed* to do it. The desire was just as compelling as the curiosity that had driven him to look at the Gardella Bible, and he saw no reason to fight it.

He still sought whatever path had been set for him.

The vampires agreed with him, although Victoria argued and wanted to don the rings herself. But Sebastian had stood firm.

The torchlight glinted over the glasslike water. Despite the soft breeze that had kept the day from being miserably hot, even though they were in the foothills of a huge mountain, the water didn't move a ripple. Instead, the surface reflected their tall torches and the last streaks of light in the sky behind him as Sebastian knelt next to it.

Victoria and Michalas stood guard between him and the vampires, in the event they felt it was their duty to shove him—or any of them—into the pool. Although that seemed as if it would be a futile effort, for the pool was hardly larger than a carriage, and likely wouldn't be very deep.

The size of a wagon, but perfectly circular, except for a little bulge on its west side, the pool sat surrounded by flat white rocks built up in layers above and, likely, below the waterline.

"The orb is hardly larger than your palm," Mercy said, moving to stand across the water from Sebastian. "You'll have to feel around for it."

"The water isn't deep," Sebastian replied.

But it was lethal, as they soon found when he poked a stick into its perfect mirror. He felt a faint shuddering of the branch, and when he withdrew it moments later, he saw that the part that had been submerged was gone. The edge of the stick smoked, as if it had been burned.

Sebastian drew in a deep breath and moved a bit closer to the edge. He looked down and saw his face reflected in the surface, perfectly detailed as if he looked in a mirror. The tops of Victoria's and Michalas's heads flanked his shoulders, and the flames of their torches flickered near the center of the image.

With a deep breath, he extended the little finger of his ringless left hand, the one that had been cut off at the second knuckle by the bloodthirsty Sara Regalado. Since it was already maimed, it couldn't get much worse, he figured. He touched the blunt tip to the very top of the water and felt such a searing pain that he nearly screamed.

Jerking his hand back, he looked at the edge of his finger and saw that it was black. The flesh had been burned away where he'd touched the water, leaving a gleam of white bone in the center of the blackened skin.

God Almighty.

He looked up at Victoria, whose face had set grimly. "Let me do it," she said, holding out her hand for the rings.

"No," he said. "It's not for you to do. The rings will protect me." He hoped.

Flexing his right hand, the one with all five fingers still intact—and each one now encircled by copper—Sebastian offered up a little prayer. And he plunged his hand in.

The puddle shifted nary a ripple, but his fingers pushed through with no effort.

He felt the bite of the edge of the water's surface against his arm, like a knife brushing against him, and he pulled his hand back, expecting to see blood.

Nothing. Not even a scratch.

And, oddly, no droplets of water splattered when he pulled out. Instead, it dripped off in heavy spherical drops, like mercury, sliding back into the pool and fading into invisibility.

He looked down and immersed his hand once again. This time, although he felt the cut of the water, he ignored it and began to gingerly seek the orb, unsure what other surprises he might find.

Beneath the surface, the pool felt just like any other body of water: surging, pressing, and wet. Sebastian moved his fingers around, feeling along for anything spherical. He touched a sandy bottom, smooth and without the slime of seaweed or the random bump of stone.

He inched closer to the edge of the water, and felt Victoria's hands close around his shoulders, holding him steady and safe. That allowed him to seek further, and he stared at the image of his face on the water, with Victoria and her dark, tousled curls and anxious expression above and to the side of his.

He focused on the image of them together while using his hand to feel around, looking at her, and himself, his fingers brushing the soft bottom of the pool. He felt something sharp and pointed and paused, running his fingers around it, wishing he had another set of five rings so that he could use both hands to seek.

The object felt pyramid-shaped, heavy, larger than his hand, definitely not the orb. But he wondered what it might be.

Reluctantly leaving it in place, for the vampire eyes watched him closely, he slid his hand around to the right, sweeping farther and farther. As he searched, he concentrated by keeping his eyes focused on Victoria's gaze in the image reflected below.

Having swept through most of the large section of the pool, he slid this time into the baylike bulge on the side. The water was deeper here, and it reached past his elbow when he brushed the bottom.

Then his bare fingers moved something hard and rough, very different from the sandy bottom or a glass sphere.

Then the rough object . . . opened, or gave way, or somehow changed under the pressure of his hand, and his arm slid deeper into the water. Sebastian felt a little *zing* of awareness trip through him as he felt something close around his hand and wrist . . . like sand or the mud of a bog.

He couldn't move for a moment, couldn't pull his hand out, and his breathing caught, his vision spotted.

There was a soft rustle in his ears, deep in his mind, whispering in the back of his head. Sebastian blinked and shook his head, refocusing on the mirrorlike pool where his hand remained immersed. He saw his face on the surface, and Giulia's behind him, her long, dark hair falling over her shoulder and onto his.

Her lips moved. She was speaking, urgently, her eyes big and dark. *Save me.*

He cried out, reached out automatically behind him, yanking his hand from the water and twisting to touch her, flinging the ball-like droplets every which way. They bounced back into the pool as he realized no one was there behind him.

No one but Victoria, who, upon his exclamation of surprise, had pulled him back from the pool so that he tumbled onto his arse on the ground behind him. The black spots in his vision had gone, his hand was unharmed, and the little *zing* of awareness went away. His breathing rough, Sebastian shook his head and regained his focus.

Was he going mad, or had the pool triggered one of his dreams?

She'd never spoken to him like that before. Pleading, begging. *Save me.*

But how. Bloody damn *how*?

"Sebastian." He looked up to find Victoria bending over him, her face close and definitely not like Giulia's, except for the dark hair and dark eyes. Perhaps it wasn't so far-fetched that his mind had played such a trick. "Are you hurt?"

"No," he replied shortly. "I was merely startled."

"What happened? Perhaps I should try—"

"No, damn it. Move out of the way, and let me try again. There's not much more I haven't searched, so if the orb is there, I'll find it." His hand was fine, and though that had been an odd sensation, he was unharmed. He'd never felt as though the pool was sucking him in or meant to drag him down. It hadn't been . . . threatening.

Not threatening, but, perhaps . . . enlightening.

Ignoring the sharp look Victoria gave him, Sebastian moved to the opposite side of the pool and knelt there. The sun had gone completely to bed, and the only light was from the anemic half-moon and the orange cast from the torches. This, along with the position of the mountain behind him now, left the reflection of the pool darker and more indistinct. Just as well. He didn't need to see Giulia crying for help.

Taking a deep breath, shaking his head to clear the cobwebs, Sebastian plunged his hand in once more. This time, the cut of the water hardly bothered him. His fingers moved deftly in this area of the pool, sifting over the soft piles of sand until at last they brushed something hard and smooth. Rounded.

The orb.

He covered it with his hand; it fit into his palm neatly enough, and felt warm and . . . pleasant. Gently tingly, lightly comforting, and solid.

Settling back on his haunches, he pulled his hand out, and there it was. The shining blue Tached's Orb.

Its glow illuminated Victoria's face as she bent closer. It bathed her cheeks and lips, the tips of her curls, with rays of silvery aqua. As he held it, he felt the continued heat of comfort and . . . peace. It was the only word he could think of to describe the well-being that trickled through him.

"Now remove the rings," said Mercy in her grating voice. "I'll have them." Her eyes glowed greedily red-violet, and her fangs poked into her bottom lip. "There is one other item I wish to retrieve from below."

Sebastian thought of the prism he'd touched earlier. "What is it you seek?"

"Take off the rings," Mercy repeated, but then her words trailed off.

Victoria had moved and now had a stake in her hand, and a sword in the other. "You seem to have forgotten your manners, vampire," she said. Her eyes glittered, and Sebastian could see that she spoiled for a fight.

"It's of no use to mortals," Mercy said. "Only to the undead."

"I see no reason to accommodate your undeadness," Victoria replied. "Now move away, and we'll be off to the portal. Or . . . Brim?"

Sebastian looked to see that Brim had, for all of his massive bulk, moved quickly and quietly to capture the Guardian vampire. He held him from behind, stake poised over his undead heart.

Mercy cast a quick glance, then shrugged. "You'll face Lilith's wrath if the three of us don't return."

"Oh, dear. Lilith's wrath? I don't believe I've ever faced that in my life." Victoria moved her head in permission, and Brim slammed the stake home. The damned Guardian never had a chance. "Now do you wish to take us to the portal, or will you be next?"

As the undead dust settled, Sebastian saw Mercy take a step back. The vampire pressed her lips together, fury burning in her eyes.

But Sebastian saw that Victoria wasn't about to forgive her insult, and she whipped out her own stake. Michalas moved quickly as she did so, shoving the other Imperial toward the pool. He screamed as he fell, catching himself on the side. Brim planted his foot in the back of the undead and gave a solid push, quickly removing his foot before the boot burned away.

Mercy shrieked, "Lilith will kill him!"

But Victoria had already leapt toward her, over and away from the pool. Sebastian watched warily, but he also thought he understood why Victoria wanted this battle, here and now. She had to relieve that coiled tension and worry somehow.

The battle was short; whether because it was a surprise or so furious, it didn't matter. Victoria took a few blows, gave some of her own, and then had and took the opportunity to shove the stake through Mercy's heart.

"No more Mercy," she said grimly, standing and dusting her hands off.

Sebastian gave Victoria the orb, and she wrapped it carefully in a cloth and slipped it into an inside pocket of her trousers.

"What else was in the pool?" she asked softly as they stood, preparing to mount their horses.

"It felt like a small pyramid of some sort. That was the only other thing I found," he said. "And I'm not sure what it is. I could take it out, but without knowing what it is or if it has powers, I think it best that we don't. Perhaps Wayren will know, and we can retrieve it later."

"Each of us should take one of the rings then," Victoria said quietly. "The last thing we need is for anyone to get all five of them together again and be able to breach the pool."

Sebastian agreed wholeheartedly and slipped his fingers around the band on his thumb. But it wouldn't move. At all.

"What the bloody hell?" he muttered. He tried to pull another one off, the one that had seemed the loosest. It wouldn't budge, not even to twist around his finger.

The rings were stuck fast to his skin.

Eighteen

A Parting of Ways

She hadn't bitten him yet.

Max leaned against the wall, the silk coverings smooth over the rough stone beneath. His forehead pressed into the cloth, and he felt a long trickle of sweat roll down his spine.

Or perhaps it was blood.

He'd lost track, and allowed it all to ebb into a blur of memory rather than accept the reality.

"Come now, Maximilian," came that hated voice. "Join me. You must be hungry."

Hungry? Food was the furthest thing from his mind.

All he wanted was fresh, cool air. Any color but red. Anything but heat and the sweet smell of roses. And the feel of her hands on his skin.

The wrist manacles clinked as she drew him away from the wall, reeling him toward her. He didn't fight it, but took his time walking toward her, tall and easy.

Max had learned when to fight and when to submit. As long as she remained amused and didn't become frustrated by his power and strength, he had a chance. The balance was delicate.

The problem was, he didn't know how long he'd have to play the game. He could end it all at any moment . . . but there was always hope. Hope alternating with fear.

He didn't want Victoria to come . . . yet he did. And he knew she would.

It was simply a matter of when.

And, oh God . . . whether she'd succeed.

He prayed that she'd do the right thing, and close the portal first.

Please. Do not let this be for naught.

Lilith indicated for him to kneel at her side, and she leaned toward him, her mouth brushing his neck. As always, the revolting sensation of one hot, one cold lip smoothing over his skin made his stomach tighten. Her hands slid up the back of his scalp, threading into his hair.

"I think I won't allow you to cut your hair again," she murmured near his ear, playing with the ends that curled under his jaw. He remained impassive, despite the horrible slithering sensation under his skin. "I do like it long. We'll have to let it grow a bit more."

That was a good sign, then. She didn't plan to try to turn him anytime soon. At least until his hair was the length she required.

Thank God that the hair and nails of the undead didn't grow.

"I know you think that she'll come after you," Lilith said companionably, her fingers smoothing over his chest. She avoided the *vis bulla*, and had forced him to remove the larger cross he'd been wearing earlier.

Now his only protection was the *vis*, and the four

small vials of holy water secreted in each of the heels of his boots. The boots stood at one side of the chamber, near the pallet where he slept. He'd not had to resort to them yet, but once she bit him he would.

"She is *Illa* Gardella, and has other tasks to attend to," he replied coolly. "Unlike you, she is dedicated to protecting her race."

Her nails suddenly dug into the skin of his back, then jerked down, hard. A little warning. He complied by producing a soft groan, knowing it would please her that she caused him pain.

"Why must you be so cruel and cutting? Can you not accept your fate?" she asked.

Now he was certain the trickle down his back was blood. Lilith slipped her fingers through the moisture and brought them delicately to her mouth, licking his blood from each of them as though she'd just finished a frosted cake.

She jolted back and looked at him, her eyes narrowing. Ah. "What is this?" she asked, fury burning in the blue-ringed red. Her lips shriveled into an angry pucker.

"Do you taste it, then?" he asked, shifting away from her. "Did you truly think I'd come to you unprepared?"

"What is it?" she asked, her eyes widening, and the veins in her face showing like blue lines.

"A newly anointed Venator," he replied. "I drank a good portion of blessed water before and after the Trial, and it still runs through my veins."

She hissed at him, her irises impossibly red, her fangs long and wicked. . . . Then her fury eased into a feral smile that bothered him much more than her anger. Death would be so much easier.

"Indeed, Maximilian, pet, you continue to surprise me. I wonder if you shall continue to do so as the centuries progress . . . or if I'll become bored with you."

She pulled him closer and looped a link from his chains high on the wall so that he couldn't move away.

"So I cannot feed on you until your blood is no longer diluted by holy water. How very clever of you to create such anticipation." Her cool, skeletal fingers cupped his shoulders, then smoothed down the curve of his biceps. "There are many other ways to pass the time until then, my dearest."

And so continued the second day of his captivity.

Sebastian sat upright, pulled abruptly from sleep.

Sweat poured off his skin, partly from the blaze of noontide sun pouring from the window of an inn, and partly from the dream that still pounded him. His heart raced, his fingers dug into the fabric around him.

Good Lord, would it never end?

This series of nightmares had come with stronger images and a deeper sense of urgency than the others. Shaking his head to dispel the last tendrils of the dream of Giulia begging him to save her, he drew in a long, deep breath and closed his eyes. What was he to do?

He couldn't help but wonder if it was related to the events of last night, when he stuck his beringed hand into the pool and felt himself sucked into a vortex of memory and images. She'd never begged him to *Save me. . . .* Not until now.

Was it possible that he even could?

Was there some event that might allow him to do so, after all these years?

Or was he simply going mad?

As he lay there, wisps of words and phrases mixed and mingled like threads of smoke in his mind. *A long promise . . . a savior.*

Those for whom he lives . . . shall be saved.

He shoved away the unnecessary blanket that

had stuck to his perspiring flesh and sat up, his heart pounding. Brim, who'd been keeping watch while the others rested, glanced over at him.

Sebastian stood, unsteady on his feet, and hissed, "Rest. I'll watch now."

The rings glinted on his hand as he reached for the pitcher of water. Damn rings. Would they never come off?

What did it mean?

He gulped the water, lukewarm in the heat, and glanced out the window. They'd found the orb last night and left immediately, traveling until late this afternoon. The sun burned hot all the rest of the day, leaving its heavy imprint even on the night, making sleep miserable even when he could turn off the disturbing images.

Giulia's face still haunted him, the phrases paraded around in his mind as though trying to embed themselves like a burrowing worm.

A savior who carries the deepest taint. A long promise.

If she were here, Wayren might be able to interpret the words.

Sebastian looked out the window again, his eyes going to the mountain far behind them. Pesaro, poor devil. How long would it take for Lilith to turn him? Surely she wouldn't allow him to escape again, but he'd fight it.

No one understood that more than Sebastian, the fear of being turned undead. The fear of losing one's soul, having it twisted and perverted . . . and damned, the moment he gave in to the craving to feed from a mortal.

Could an undead resist the burning need to drink? That driving, bullying desire? Could it be ignored, that horrible craving, that demonic taint?

The deepest taint.

A tainted soul?

Sebastian's heart began to pound. The deepest taint . . . a twisted, undead soul.

A long promise.

Good God . . . immortality. Someone who gave up his soul, freely . . . in a long promise.

How long?

His mouth felt as though he chewed on a wad of cotton, and he swallowed hard. His fingers were shaking, and the middle of his belly felt full and unsteady. His head lightened, and a renewed sheen of sweat dampened his forehead.

Those for whom he lives . . . shall be saved.

Save me.

And the reverberation of Rosemunde's prophecy sang in his head like a tune that would not be silenced.

Then, finally, he understood. Those words had burned into his brain for a reason.

And in the new world shall be a savior who carries the deepest taint. A long promise shall the savior make and in the end those for whom he lives will be saved.

It wasn't Pesaro who was the savior.

It was he.

Sebastian rose, suddenly more clearheaded, more purposeful than he'd been for years. Even, despite the task ahead, light in the heart.

Victoria awoke when the sun had lowered enough to blaze directly in her face, angling perfectly through the window. She had been so damn tired, her weariness laced with worry over Max—and though she hated to admit it to her companions, she'd been relieved to rest in the middle of the day.

But now they would move on and perhaps reach

Midiverse by late tomorrow. Hurry, hurry, hurry. The sooner they finished, the sooner she could get back to Max.

She sat up and looked over the room, counting the lumps on the floor—one—and on the pallets. Another.

Who was missing?

Maybe he'd gone to buy provisions. She rose from her pallet and rushed over to look out the window. The shadows had grown long from the lowering sun, but she could still see the road leading north, empty of any travelers.

As she turned back, she saw the note, pinned to the wall by a knife. The paper was folded in half, with a large *V* on the outside.

Victoria tore it off the wall and unfolded it, noting the signature—a large, sweeping *S*—before reading the letter.

She sank onto the nearest bed, the one Sebastian had used, and read it again.

Victoria~

    I've gone for Max. Know that I will always love you though you foolishly chose another. That's why I'm going, no matter what may come. Ask Wayren about Rosamunde's prophecies. Tell her I've made the long promise. Above all, keep yourself and the new Gardella safe.

                                   ~S

Damn and blast.

Damn and blast.

Trust Sebastian to write an adieu that would bring both pain and hope.

She folded the paper once, twice, thrice.

The new Gardella.

Did he know for certain, or was he merely guessing? Or was that simply Sebastian, being wry and amusing?

She'd only recently suspected it herself.

Sebastian, you fool. I need you, too.

Was she going to lose them both now?

She looked back at the mountain, nearly two days' ride behind her, purple-black in the distance, with a swatch of sunlight beaming onto it from between a break in the trees.

Godspeed, Sebastian. Bring both of you back safely.

Nineteen

Of Dreams and Sacrifice, and the Incurrence of a Debt

Sebastian woke just before dawn to find Wayren standing before him.

Or, at least, he thought it was Wayren ... but perhaps it was a hallucination. She seemed insubstantial, and she glowed. Perhaps he was dreaming ... but at least it wasn't a nightmare of Giulia begging and pleading with him. Although if it weren't to be a nightmare, he'd prefer that he went back to the old dreams, where his lover wrapped him in her long, dark hair, and they rolled in a nocturnal bed together ... rather than dreaming about an angel.

It just didn't seem right.

The obnoxious snore next to him told him that the other traveler who bunked in his room was still sleeping soundly. The sun had just begun to peek over the horizon, and he'd be back to the mountain in a few hours.

"Sebastian," said a voice, and he looked over.

She was still there.

"Am I dreaming? Wayren?"

"I'm here. I've come to wish you luck and bring blessings."

He nodded. Whether it was a dream or not, he felt contentment.

Wayren's presence in the past had been a source of discomfort for him when he knew he wasn't being true to his calling or following through on his duty. Now her presence—whether it be real or in a dream—felt like a commendation of sorts, an acknowledgment and a blessing.

"And I came to bring you this. Wear this and don't remove it, and . . . it will help."

Something silver glinted in the dusky light, then plopped onto the bed next to him. A ring, heavy and silver, set with a garnet the size of his thumbnail.

"What is it?"

"It will help you follow through on your intent and keep you strong in the face of weakness. I can do nothing else. The rest is up to you."

He picked up the ring and slid it onto the middle finger of his left hand. "Thank you." He then he looked at her. "And thank you for Rosamunde's papers. They led me here."

"I knew that they would." She nodded, her blond hair shifting with the movement. She paused; then he felt the wisp of a touch on his hand, and still wasn't certain if it was real or imagined. "You'll do well, Sebastian Vioget."

And then he woke up.

The silver ring was on his finger, the sun was blazing just atop the horizon . . . and he was ready to begin his last day of life.

Two hours later, Sebastian stood at the stone crevice that led to Lilith's hideaway.

He had no trouble gaining entrance to Lilith's lair once he showed the five rings to her guards and surrendered his stakes. They didn't attempt to take the silver ring that Wayren had given him, which he wore on his other hand. Sebastian didn't intend for this little meeting to last more than an hour, and he was arriving at the high point of noon.

He was taken to the same room as before, only a short walk down a twisting corridor made of stone.

The chamber appeared the same, and he greeted Lilith calmly. She sat on her chaise, just as she had the last time they'd met. Today, she wore a gown of black, which made her skin appear starkly blue-white.

Sebastian didn't see Pesaro at first. When he did, he needed all his strength not to react. Merciful God.

How long had it been? Three days? Barely three days. And look at him.

Sebastian tore his eyes away from the man, faltering for a moment, struggling to hide his shock as he gathered his composure. Never had he seen a man who possessed such strength and power brought to such depths, such vulnerability. Such emptiness in his eyes, an absence of hope—or even comprehension—in his face.

Would he look that way himself after a day? Two days? Sebastian's stomach roiled, threatening to spill its contents.

Save me.

Sebastian took a deep breath. He looked back at Lilith, careful not to eye her directly and become trapped by her gaze. He forced himself to ignore Pesaro. Things would be different for him. He would make certain of it.

"Beauregard's grandson, how kind of you to join us." Lilith trained the force of her blue-red gaze on him, and though he avoided it, he still felt its staggering weight . . . and the lure. He struggled for breath for a moment, reaching his hand through the slit of his shirt to touch the *vis bulla* there.

A zip of strength passed through him, followed by another breath of power. He was the grandson of Beauregard.

He was a Venator.

"I've come for Pesaro," he said, then took a little breath to collect himself and his thoughts. He had to handle Lilith differently from how Pesaro had. "Why do you not release the poor bastard? He looks as though he can provide little amusement in his condition."

Lilith looked at him through sly eyes. She raised a slender eyebrow and smiled. "I have no intention of releasing him. But now that you're here, perhaps you might stay. The three of us would have such an amusing time."

"What an intriguing thought," he said, making his voice low and liquid. He allowed his eyes to slide slowly over her. If there was one thing he knew, it was how to appeal to female vanity. "But I must confess . . . I don't like to share. I should find him just as intrusive here as I always have."

"Lucifer's staff, you sound much like your grandfather." Lilith gave a low, surprised laugh. "And you look a bit like him, too—around the jaw and chin. And the mouth." Her attention settled there on his lips for a moment. "I was always fond of Beauregard, Sebastian Vioget. It was too bad he angered me back in fourteen fifty-two during that episode in Vienna, or we might have been eternally happy together."

"So that explains why you never gifted him with one of the rings." Sebastian held up his right hand. "But that matters no longer. Bygones shall be bygones, shan't they? And . . . I wear the Rings of Jubai. All of them."

She sat upright, interest gleaming in her eyes. "So you have breached the pool. Did you retrieve the orb?"

"We have the orb, and the portal shall be closed. But Mercy seemed to be more interested in something else at the bottom of the pool."

Lilith's gaze sharpened, and she seemed to understand that her plans had gone awry. "You still wear the rings."

"I do, and shall forever, or so it appears. They cannot be removed."

"I don't believe you. Take them off, or I shall remove them for you."

Sebastian dredged up his most charming, provocative smile. "Is that a threat or an offer, Lilith?" He surreptitiously touched the *vis* beneath his shirt again as he maintained that smile.

"You truly cannot remove the rings?"

"Indeed not. They have fused to my flesh."

She watched him closely as if to read what was in his mind. "Why, then, are you here?" she asked at last, settling back onto her chaise.

Sebastian nodded. "Ah, so now we shall speak frankly. I am here to exchange myself for Pesaro. Apparently you're in need of a concubine who can . . . shall we say . . . keep pace with you?"

Lilith gave a small laugh, but there was a hint of confusion underlying the derision. "And why would I make such a trade as that? You're here, and so is he, and all I need do is give the command, and I'll have you both."

"I'm sorry to disappoint you, my lady," Sebastian said, "but that's not quite right. You see, I am willing to trade myself to you . . . for all eternity, myself and the Rings of Jubai . . . only on the condition that you release Max Pesaro. If you aren't willing to do so, then we'll both be dead in a moment . . . and not only will you not have either of us, but you won't have the Rings nor any way to retrieve the pyramid at the bottom of the pool."

"How do you know about the prism?"

"Mercy told me. She had to be persuaded to tell, of course, when I declined to reach my hand back in and search for it. But when she saw that I could not remove the rings, and that she and her companion—did I forget to mention that the Guardian found himself skewered by a stake shortly after we retrieved the orb? As for Mercy and the other . . . well, they annoyed our *Illa* Gardella. So they are no more, I regret to say. But now you might have me to replace them, if you choose to negotiate."

"What's to stop me from forcing you to go there now and get it for me?"

"This." Sebastian produced a small tube no wider in circumference than the stem of a flower. A simple weapon that had aroused no suspicion in the guards who'd relieved him of his stakes and sword. "I'll shoot the poison dart the moment you move to call for your guards, or do something other than what I ask. Pesaro will be dead immediately . . . for I won't miss. And as for me, I also have my own poison ready. Both us will be dead before you can blink."

"But the rings . . . I can remove them from your fingers after you've died," Lilith said dismissively. Yet he saw wariness in her eyes.

"Perhaps. Or perhaps not. Or perhaps you might attempt burning them off my flesh after I'm dead . . . but then again, the rings might be destroyed in the process. Are you willing to take the chance?" He stepped closer. "And indeed, why would you? I'm offering myself to you . . . Beauregard's grandson. What a coup that will be for you. And, quite frankly, I'm much more enter-

taining than that brooding sod in the corner. I've never
been able to comprehend what attracted you to him.
He cannot be entertaining in the least. While I . . . Well,
you were acquainted with Beauregard."

The words tripped off his tongue with ease. Sebastian had seduced and wooed women for years, and it
was simple to fall back into the pattern. He tried to forget that this was different; that the result of this tête-à-
tête would have far-reaching, eternal effects.

He could make it through . . . one day at a time.

One day at a time of his long promise. And at the
end of it, he'd know it was for Giulia . . . and for Victoria . . . that he'd sacrificed.

"So it is you or neither of you?"

"Indeed. You have little choice, but I do believe
you'll get the better end of the bargain."

Lilith rose from her chaise and paced the chamber.
When she walked over to Pesaro, her hand strayed
down his dark head and over his bowed shoulders. He
made no acknowledgment of her touch, remaining still
and quiet as if in a stupor. "And I'm to believe that you
can dispatch my darling pet at a moment's notice?"

Quickly, he put the tube to his lips and blew sharply.
The dart shot through the air and embedded itself into
the front of Pesaro's shoulder, just below Lilith's own
hand. Max gave no indication he'd been struck, but she
looked at him in surprise . . . and delight.

"Indeed. I trust that was merely a warning? An ex-
ample of your . . . shall we say . . . alacrity?"

Sebastian nodded, praying she wouldn't call his
bluff. In fact, none of the darts were poisonous. He
brandished the little tube. "I have three more in here,
all of which do carry the poison. The next one will kill
him, and then me."

"You give me an impossible choice," Lilith said,
thrusting her fingers deep into the back of Pesaro's

hair. She jerked his face up toward her and bent to nibble languidly at his chin and jaw. "I don't wish to let him go."

Sebastian swallowed, but bestowed one of his most charming smiles. "A difficult choice, but not nearly as impossible as one you gave him only a few days ago. Come now, Lilith . . . you know you will be the better off. That prism alone must be worth giving up the presence of a man who does little but brood and cause you problems. And aside of that . . . you'll have Beauregard's grandson. A Venator. To do with what you will."

Her eyes flickered to him, and again he felt the tug of her gaze trying to wrap warmly around him. She walked back to her chaise and settled back onto her place. "Very well, then. You've convinced me, Sebastian Vioget. I'll accept your trade."

Sebastian felt a wave of relief, but he remained impassive except for the trace of a smile on his lips. He brandished the hand that held the tube. "I'm delighted, but I must ask that you remain in your place until we've finished the details. I wouldn't want any sudden move of yours to be misinterpreted by me, and there to be an accident." He smiled and recognized the begrudging respect in her face.

"Very well. Tell me how this is to proceed."

He kept the tube near his lips as he ordered one of Lilith's lurking guards to unchain Pesaro. She moved to the blank-eyed, bloodied, nude figure of Pesaro and helped him to his feet.

The man staggered, and took a moment to find his bearings. But when he looked up at Sebastian, the cloudiness in his eyes had disappeared, leaving Sebastian to wonder how much of it had been an act to keep Lilith bored and away from him. And he wondered how much he had understood of the conversation.

"What are you doing here?" Pesaro mumbled.

Sebastian understood the question he was really asking—whether Victoria was still alive—and for a moment, one last bit of jealous perversity nearly kept him from answering. The sod would find out soon enough, and be able to spend the rest of his days with her, while he—

But no. This was a sacrifice, and he'd not taint it by base emotions, so he responded, "I'm here in exchange for you. The others are traveling to the portal, and Lilith has agreed to release you in exchange for me."

"Vioget." Max's word sounded like a simple thank-you to anyone who might be listening, but Sebastian saw the sharp question in his eyes. *What is the plan?*

Sebastian merely shook his head, letting the truth show in his own expression. Then, for the first time in his memory, he recognized bald shock—and then gratitude . . . from Max Pesaro?—in his face. The contempt that had long been in his eyes was gone, replaced by something one might think was respect and admiration.

Pesaro gave a short nod, an acceptance that encompassed everything that passed between them. "I'll leave my boots for you," he said. "Miro would want me to do so, I think."

Sebastian understood the message. It was a reminder that holy water was hidden in the heels of the boots. Miro, the Venator weapons master, had created the hollow heels that, in the past, had contained small sticks that could flare into flame.

"Yes, indeed, my dear Maximilian, you are free to go," Lilith said, her eyes skimming over his tall, dark body as if suddenly reluctant to let him leave. "Until we meet again." Her words were a gentle threat, and a reminder to both of them that although Sebastian had bested her this time, she would not allow it to happen again.

That, he was certain, was part of the reason she'd agreed to the trade. The thrill of the hunt and the chase to recapture Max would keep her busy when she became bored with Sebastian. He shuddered. How in God's name would he ever suffer her hands and lips and fangs on him?

For Giulia. For her soul.

He would save her soul, and keep his own clean. And then, someday, they would be together . . . when his long promise was fulfilled.

Pesaro dressed rapidly, his smooth movements belying what Sebastian had at first seen as weakness. Not that he was untouched—no, he could see that Lilith had had her pleasure in a variety of ways, but he was by no means the puddle of skin and bones he'd originally perceived.

"They were less than a day from Midiverse when I left them," Sebastian told him as they, along with the four guards, walked toward the external entrance to the mountain hideaway. He was taking no chances that Lilith might allow Max to leave, only to have him stopped once out of Sebastian's sight—and range of the supposedly poison dart. Thus he'd insisted that he be the one to escort Pesaro into the sunlight. Lilith remained ensconced in her chamber, likely unwilling to risk being anywhere near sunlight in the presence of two Venators.

At the entrance, Pesaro turned to him. "Are you certain?" he asked.

Sebastian understood what he meant. He could walk into the sunlight with him; the four vampire guards would be little match for the two of them if they so chose. "I've made the choice to stay."

"This makes twice now," Pesaro said, speaking of the fact that Sebastian had saved his life for a second time.

And as he had done the first time he acknowledged the debt, Sebastian replied, "I didn't do it for you. I did it for her." And then he added, "Both of them. Ask Wayren." And he saw by Max's expression that he understood: both Giulia and Victoria. For who else had caused the enmity between them?

Then he turned and went back into darkness, leaving Max Pesaro to walk out into the freedom of the light.

Twenty

The Visitation

The fact that the Midiverse Portal was situated in the ruin of an old cemetery didn't surprise Victoria in the least.

In fact, the closer they came to the black-stoned graveyard tucked deep in a rocky valley, the more uncomfortable she became. The air was putrid and heavy and smelled of demons. A decrepit gate and stone wall surrounded the cemetery, having crumbled into little more than a narrow pile of rock over the years.

A bare strain of sunlight filtered from behind a haze of gray clouds, giving the area an unfriendly, melancholy appearance. It felt colder as they approached and halted their mounts on a low hill rise just south of the cemetery. Victoria noticed that the area contained nothing but the gravestones blackened by moss and mildew. There were no trees or grass or any type of greenery.

In the center of the graveyard squatted a low, square

building with a flat, overhanging roof not much larger than a gatehouse. Brim pointed to it and said, "According to Wayren, the portal is next to that building."

In order to close the portal, moonlight had to shine through Tached's Orb onto the opening, according to Wayren's research. Obviously, they would have to come back tonight and hope that the quarter moon was strong enough and bright enough to do the job.

But for now, Victoria wanted to examine the place in the daylight. Unsure of what to expect as they drew closer, she urged her mount forward, the orb jolting heavily in her trouser pocket with every cantering step. She gestured for Michalas to remain on guard, and for Brim to join her, wishing that they numbered more than three.

Who knew what awaited them beyond the stone enclosure.

Her horse didn't like the area, and as they drew nearer, at first he balked and then began to fight Victoria's commands. Taking pity on the beast, she dismounted and sent the horses back to Michalas, moving forward on foot with Brim.

She understood the horse's reluctance as they approached a stone wall that would require nothing more than a few steps to breach. Her hair felt as though it had frozen on end, standing straight up all over her body.

With a look at Brim, she clambered up over the low pile of stone and landed on the other side with a sure-footed jump. Pausing for a moment to see if anything changed, she looked around.

The place was silent. Even though Victoria felt the whisper of a breeze over her cheek, tufting her hair, she heard nothing rustling or moving. Out of the corner of her eye, she saw Brim climb over the rocks. When one rolled soundlessly down the low pile and onto the ground, it was an uncomfortable sight because she could see it, but she heard nothing.

An eerie chill tightened her muscles, pulling her skin taut and ready. She felt for her stake automatically, even though such a weapon would be useless against demons. Her sword hung from its place at her belt, and she had a dagger sheathed against her calf, as well as several small bottles of holy water in various locations.

As she and Brim walked between the gravestones, she noticed that none of them had words or symbols carved on them. Plain, flat stones in row after neat row, without the names of the dead they represented. Other than the growth of mildew and moss, there was nothing to indicate their age, for all stood whole and straight without cracks or breaks or the shifting that came with the movement of earth over time.

The ugly feeling in her belly made her tense and on edge, ready for something unexpected to happen. Yet Victoria didn't hesitate, and moved quickly to the building in the center of the graveyard. As she came closer, she saw that it was windowless and doorless. No chimney, and a flat roof. Circling it from a distance, she found nothing that allowed entrance. The building seemed to have no purpose other than to take up space. Unless it was the portal itself?

Wayren had given little detail—either she didn't have it, or she presumed it would be self-evident. All she had told them was that the portal was near this structure. It took Victoria two circular routes around it, moving closer each time, before she found a slender crack in the black earth.

Was this the portal?

Victoria stood away from it, looking down, wondering if somehow they'd been misled or otherwise mistaken. The crevice ran jagged perhaps as long as a man was tall, and no wider than Aunt Eustacia's walking stick.

Somehow she'd expected to find demons streaming from the portal—which, incidentally, she'd envisioned as an actual doorway. But other than the odd soundlessness of the area, and the pervading scent of musty death, the place felt little different from any other cemetery.

Victoria turned to Brim, who'd continued his circle around the building.

"Anything?" she asked. Her voice sounded hollow and empty in the air.

"No. Is this it?" he replied, beside her now. She could hear him . . . but it was as if they were in a soundless windstorm. His words came to her ears distorted and dull, but audible.

"It could be," echoed her voice. Victoria stepped closer to the crevice, an uncorked bottle of holy water at the ready. She peered down and saw nothing threatening about the crack.

Not a breeze stirred now, and every bit of sound seemed to have been sucked out of her ears. Even her own breathing, faster than usual, had no sound. She tipped the bottle of water, allowing a tiny stream to trickle down into the crevice.

Immediately, a curl of smoke puffed up, angry and black and putrid, exploding in a little poof—not unlike the reaction of a vampire that had just been staked. Victoria jumped back, ready for the onslaught, her eyes fastened on the crevice. But all remained quiet.

Still. Now she knew—at least there was something here.

She looked over at Brim, who'd unsheathed his sword. "Let's go," she said. "Come back tonight."

He gave a short nod, and they turned to make their way back.

Victoria kept watch over her shoulder as they navigated around the gravestones, a simpler process than picking through the piles upon piles of stones in the cemetery in Prague. But though she looked back as they walked away, she saw nothing to disturb the eerie quiet of the plot of graves. No more smoke, no puffs of cloud, no disturbances.

It was that silence, that lingering darkness that bothered her the most.

There was nothing for them to do but wait for the sun to go down, so Victoria and her companions rode back to the small village through which they'd passed on their way to the cemetery. The quaint town consisted of approximately two dozen houses, one inn, and the shops of perhaps four or five tradesmen located directly on the road that wound through it. They settled at the tavern to eat and rest and wait for moonrise—if it came from behind the clouds.

Unfortunately, this time of leisure did nothing but give her the chance to think and worry and stew. While Michalas and Brim sat in the tavern, Victoria brooded so darkly and incessantly, she would have made Max proud.

And that wry thought, of course, brought to mind the man himself and set her stomach to spinning and twisting as it had every night when she tried to sleep. Or anytime she allowed herself to think along that path—which was more often than she wanted.

Her fury with him for leaving her and putting himself in danger had settled into a deep, dark, clutching panic. She'd tried to hold on to the rage, knowing it would help keep the terror tempered if she had that strong emotion on which to focus, but that didn't last.

She knew that if—*when*, God, please—she saw him again, she'd have no problem dredging up that anger and skinning him alive with it . . . but for now, all she wanted was for him to be safe.

But how could he be safe, in the hands of Lilith? Wouldn't her first task be to turn him undead, now that she had him again?

Victoria shook her head mentally. Max would never allow that to happen. She knew that much, and knew that if he'd gone willingly to her in order to get the rings, he'd be thus prepared.

Didn't he know she'd come after him? He must know that.

But he'd also know . . . want . . . *expect* her to take care of the portal first. It would be a travesty for his sacrifice to have been in vain, for her to waste his willingness to exchange himself for the rings in order to close the portal . . . and then not to ensure that it happened.

Oh, Max.

Tears burning her eyes, Victoria shifted in her seat near the smoke-frosted tavern window and in doing so, glanced outside onto the street.

A man caught her attention as he walked along the road, passing several other pedestrians. He was extremely well dressed, at the height of Parisian fashion in fact—an oddity certain to draw attention in a small town in the mountains, hundreds of miles from any city. Yet no one seemed to notice him in his curly-brimmed hat, with a knobby cane, and wearing straight, pressed pantaloons. In fact, he brushed past a woman and her child, nearly knocking into her, and she didn't even seem to notice.

Victoria couldn't take her eyes from him and watched as he crossed the street, approaching the tavern, then passed in front of the window through which she stared.

As he strolled by, he looked through the grimy glass. His eyes met Victoria's for an instant, and she felt a cold, sharp spear thrust through her body, paralyzing her, freezing her breath.

Those eyes . . . blank and black, fathomless and yet burning . . . they trapped her for that moment, until he walked on past and released her gaze.

She was out of her chair the moment she could move. Her heart slamming in her chest, she slapped a hand on the table in front of Michalas and said, "Did you see him?"

"Who?" Both of her companions looked where she gestured, even going so far as to open the window and peer out—but the sinister man was gone.

She explained, finding it difficult to describe exactly how it had felt when he looked at her. Before she could finish, however, she lost patience and said, "I'll be back."

She rushed out the door, leaving them scrambling to dig out a few coins for the meal and drinks.

By the time she got onto the street, the man had long since disappeared. And even though she, Brim, and Michalas asked everyone they passed whether they'd seen a man of that description, no one appeared to recall seeing the man with the curly-brimmed hat and dapper clothing.

Frustrated, Victoria sent Michalas and Brim toward the tavern, directing them to search along that end of the street. She followed a bit more slowly, looking between and around the clustered buildings.

Just as she was about to give up, she glanced between a bakery and butcher shop. And there he was.

He sat on a bench in a small courtyard, as if he'd been waiting for her. Victoria didn't hesitate.

As she approached, he removed his hat in a clearly ironic gesture, revealing pure white hair combed smooth to the shape of his skull. His skin was a darker hue, that of tea with a generous portion of milk, and his eyes . . . those eyes that weren't red and didn't burn, but nevertheless fastened on her with an odd, empty, inhuman light.

"Victoria Gardella," he said in a smooth, dark voice that raised uncomfortable prickles over her skin.

"Who are you?" she asked, leaving the stake in her pocket. She knew whoever or whatever this creature was, a stake would be useless against him.

"Please. Won't you have a seat?" He gestured to the space on the bench next to him, but she made no move to sit.

"Very well, then," he said, and looked up at her with those awful eyes. That, along with the subtle scent of death in the air, decided her: He must be a demon. A very powerful one. "You may certainly stand if that's your preference. I am Adolphus."

She didn't recognize the name, but was more convinced than ever that he was a demon. She could smell it, but very subtly. Which implied to her that he must be a particularly powerful one, if he could mask himself so well.

Victoria remained standing, but silent. Waiting. To demand to know what he wanted would give him the advantage. He'd tell her what he wanted when he chose. For now, she remained quiet, knowing the power of patience.

And, as if recognizing her tactic, the demon gave her a shrewd nod and spoke. Again, his voice sounded dark and yet smooth, lulling and coaxing. "We both have a similar objective, Victoria Gardella. I have information that you might find interesting . . . that you might find useful or valuable."

Again she waited, and again, after a moment, he continued. "Lilith is leaving her mountain hideaway. If you wish to have your chance to stop her, the time is now."

Victoria's heart skipped offbeat for a moment. "Where is she going?"

He gave a negligent shrug. "Somewhere she can't be found. It's too dangerous for her now, and she must bury herself deeply in hiding. I do not know where she's going, only that she is leaving. Tomorrow."

Max. Of course she'd take him with her.

"Why should I believe what you tell me?" True, he was a demon, and demons were the immortal enemies of vampires. But they were also enemies of mortals, especially Venators.

"Because my hatred for Lilith is as deep as yours."

Once more, she merely looked at him, waiting for more . . . even as she wondered and worried and felt her palms grow slick with panic. If Lilith disappeared with Max, she'd never find them again.

"You know what she's doing to him," he said, his voice burrowing into her mind. His lips barely moved, but she heard the words as if he spoke them into her ear. "You can imagine it, because you've felt it yourself. It's all pleasure and pain rolled into one, isn't it, Victoria Gardella?

"You've never admitted to anyone what happened when you were with Beauregard, drinking his blood. Letting him feed from you. You prefer to think that it was a dream, that it never happened . . . how you moaned and cried and drank and writhed. Yet you can imagine what's happening to your lover now, with her hands on him, and the power of her eyes burning into him. You can imagine it, because you've felt the same, haven't you?"

"No," she whispered. But the memories assailed her, red and hot and liquid. For a moment, she smelled the sharp, rust scent and tasted the heavy iron of blood on her tongue, in her mouth . . . sliding thickly down her throat. She gagged, swallowing hard, and realized her breathing had grown deeper, rougher.

"Think about it. . . . Imagine it. And it's so much worse for him. His cries and groans, those long, sleek muscles scored by her nails, punctured by those animal fangs. . . . Think about it, Victoria Gardella. You know the torture. You know what's happening to him." His voice was a lullaby, compelling and rhythmic, as he described in detail what Lilith was doing to Max.

The images played out in her mind as if she were watching them. Her awareness of the demon faded away, leaving only his deep, lulling descriptions, using words and phrases that pulled up sharp, frightening scenes so real she could hear the sounds and smell the scent.

"You can save him, and you can kill her in the process. Isn't that what you want to do? What you *need* to do?" he continued in that lovely, sensual voice. "And I can help you."

"How?"

He smiled, just a bit, showing perfect white teeth. "I know a secret about Lilith that will help you send her to Hell. Others have tried . . . but they didn't know the secret."

"What is it?" she forced herself to say, battling through the images of Max under the hands of Lilith, her blue-ringed red eyes glowing with depravity as she drove her fangs into him.

Victoria fought the image of his writhing, stretching, convulsing body under skeletal white hands that shouldn't have the power to hold him, but somehow could. His eyes, filled with pain . . . and pleasure. She blinked hard, gave her head a little shake, and found herself looking deep into the eyes of the demon.

"You must use a stake of virgin ash," he said, his eyes gleaming with life. "White virgin ash, freshly cut so that there is green just beneath the bark. Stab her anywhere with it, and she will be paralyzed, allowing you to ready for the final blow."

"No," she managed to say, her word sounding soggy. "No."

"Yes indeed . . . Listen to me, Victoria Gardella. Do you think you are the first Venator to want to kill her? And to attempt it? How do you think she has lived all these millennia?" He stood, moving closer to her. "Few know the secret. You can go and kill her now. She'll be leaving and riding under the moon tomorrow night. . . . You can reach her as she leaves her mountain, surprise her. Ash trees grow abundantly on Făgăraș. She will send her army west to fool her enemies, but she and a small contingent of her closest companions will secretly go north."

Victoria felt as though she'd plunged underwater. The world slowed, became murky, and she struggled to think. She could. Save Max.

She could.

"You can go now, on this cloudy night, and be there tomorrow . . . and then return here, when the moon is ready. Quickly and easily," he said. "Simple. And you can free him."

But . . . no. She dug through the haunting images, the caress of his voice, the building desire and incessant compulsion to run *now*. To go *now*. She dug through the need to act now, and focused on the truth: She had work here, tonight if the moon was free . . . and if not, then tomorrow night.

"It will be too late if you delay. She'll be gone for good. She knows of the coming threat."

Victoria had to work to focus on those words, and she grasped the idea, pulling it out of the muddle of images that her brain had become. "The coming threat?"

"You know of what I speak. . . . The portal is merely

cracked now. But when it widens, and the dark ones pour out readily, the vampires will be destroyed. You're here to try and stop the inevitable."

Yes. Yes, she was. She had to close the portal.

Victoria blinked and focused on the building behind the demonic man, at last feeling the slog begin to slip away. It felt as though she was slowly awakening. "I'm here to close the portal."

"You are. But you don't understand that it's not the mortals we come for. . . . It's the undead." His voice remained beautiful and smooth, lulling. "Those are the ones who battle us for Lucifer's domain. The battle between us has raged for millennia . . . and now it will come to your Earth. If you kill Lilith, destroy her stronghold, the battle will not need to be fought. We can retreat to our domain and leave your race free. Do you understand, Victoria Gardella? You can prevent the battle from raging on this Earth if you slay Lilith. If you go today. Tonight."

She felt the sway of the words as they wrapped around her, cocooning her in their sweetness, their logic and illogic, their temptation.

"And then you can close the portal. We will no longer need it. You have the means, don't you? Tached's Orb. Of course it will work, and you will triumph. You have time because you have the orb, the lock. The portal is merely a crack. . . . You saw it today. You saw that no threat comes through there."

His compelling voice went on. "But he doesn't have time, Victoria Gardella. He doesn't have any time at all. You know he doesn't. You feel the moments slipping away like grains of sand on the ocean shore. But you can save him. The others . . . they can close the portal while you are gone."

They could.

Brim and Michalas. They could do it.

But she was *Illa* Gardella.

She awakened, pushing the cobwebs away.

"But I am *Illa* Gardella," she said aloud. "And I will close the portal," she continued, her voice growing stronger. The images faded away with the strength of her words, and she looked at the demon and said, "I'll close the portal, and I'll keep your minions behind it. Begone with you and your temptations. Do you not think I can see how you tempt me?"

She was ready when his lips drew back in a horrible parody of a smile, baring teeth that grew long and pointed in a face that turned cruel and sharp. As he swept his arm, an arm that had become large and powerful, she pulled the bottle of holy water from her pocket, thumbing the cork off.

A blast of wind swept up suddenly, nearly knocking her off her feet with its ferocity. Black fog spun around her, and she was pummeled by the gale as she struggled to draw her sword.

She saw Max suddenly, there before her, and for a moment, she almost believed it. He was real, looking at her through the smoky whirl, his eyes dark and intense.

She steeled herself against the attempt to set her off balance, to distract her. It had happened before—the first time she met a demon. He'd taken the form of Phillip, and the shock and confusion of suddenly coming face-to-face with her dead husband had nearly been her undoing.

But she now knew the tricks demons played, and tore her gaze away, as the blade pulled free of its sheath. She brandished the sword and tossed the blessed water toward the murky shadow of the demon's face as she battled against the wind.

He cried out, and the battering force lessened enough for Victoria to stumble backward, out of the whirlwind. Feeling a brick wall behind her, she pulled another bottle of water and shoved its contents toward him again, swinging her sword as the liquid sprayed.

Wet splashed in her face, blasted back by the wind, and her sword connected with something thick. Max. Again. This time, with horror on his face.

With a shout, she shoved the sword home, and sliced away, feeling as though she were cutting through a bog.

And then, suddenly, everything stilled.

The wind stopped, the fog was erased, and she was alone, panting, leaning against the wall. The demon was gone—whether she had killed him or merely driven him off, she wasn't certain.

But she looked up and saw that the sky had darkened. What little light came from a lowering sun was obscured by clouds, leaving only a dull illumination over the small courtyard where she stood.

There would be no chance to use Tached's Orb tonight, for the moonlight would be blocked. The demon had spoken the truth about that, at least.

Victoria tightened her fingers around the grip of her sword and glanced back toward the south, in the direction of Muntii Făgăraş. Where Max was.

She swallowed as the urge to leave, to go after him, clawed through her anew. How much could she believe of Adolphus?

Anything? Anything at all?

He had spoken truthfully when he claimed Lilith was his enemy. It would be to his benefit if Lilith were dead. . . .

Victoria was standing there, trembling, shaking against the need to go, when Michalas found her.

"I've seen no sign of him," he said, looking at her curiously.

"That's no matter," she replied soberly, wondering

how long she'd been here with the demon. "I found him. He's gone for now." She looked up at the clouds. "There's nothing we can do tonight."

And she returned reluctantly to the tavern for another night of doing nothing while Max suffered.

And possibly Sebastian with him.

Twenty-one

In Which Our Heroine Chafes at the Bit

There was no thought of sleeping that night, for a variety of reasons—the least of which was that Victoria absolutely couldn't keep her eyes closed for more than a moment.

For a woman used to always *doing*, a day and night of sitting and waiting was like a personal hell.

Especially since those hours of nothing, nothing, *nothing!* gave her plenty of time to imagine Max in the hands of Lilith. The crafty demon had pulled all the terrible thoughts and images from the depths of Victoria's mind, from where she'd stuffed them deeply so that she could concentrate on the matter at hand. . . . He'd tugged them free, releasing them into full-blown terror, and now they constantly assaulted her.

Along with those images teased the secret he'd told her about Lilith. Was it true? Could something as simple as a stake of virgin ash paralyze the great vampiress?

Why would he lie about that?

To give her a reason to leave.

Or . . . to give her the weapon to destroy Lilith.

It tantalized her, that possibility.

There were no vampires to hunt in this small town, likely run off by the demons. And now that the sun had disappeared completely, the clouds hung heavy and thick, obscuring the moon so darkly that nary a whisper of a beam escaped. The night sat, dark and leaden, over the cemetery. Even the white gravestones appeared no lighter than the dark ground in which they sat.

Victoria had Tached's Orb safely in her pocket, in the event that the clouds shifted and there was the chance to use it. But for now, she sat on her mount on the same small hill overlooking the cemetery. Watching. Waiting.

Hoping something happened.

The village clustered behind her, close enough that she could hear voices from the tavern, where Brim and Michalas remained. She'd instructed them to stay there, to watch the clouds and to come at the sign of any movement. They were close enough that she could call for them if something changed. But for now, Victoria wanted only to be alone. They tried too hard to be jovial and to keep her mind occupied.

The last time she'd checked the time, midnight was near.

If anything meant to slip through the crevice of the portal, it would be in the darkest part of night. The demon's attempts to entice her away earlier today confirmed Victoria's suspicions that something would happen soon. He'd been so intent on getting her away tonight . . . and though she'd run him off, Victoria was under no illusion that he'd given up.

As she watched, she kept her attention on not only

the small, squat building, which acted as a visual placeholder for the portal, but also on the sky above. The clouds had begun to move, fat and heavy, limned with the silver of a hidden moon.

Hope had Victoria backing her horse up, keeping an eye on the cemetery as she moved back toward the tavern, ready to call for Brim and Michalas. The clouds had definitely started to shift and churn, and at the same time, a darkness gathered below.

The demons.

They were released.

Victoria's heart picked up speed, and she turned her horse now, ready to ride back into the village, keeping her gaze over her shoulder as she kicked the flanks of her mount.

The street was empty and dark, but raucous laughter and warm light spilled from the tavern. Just as Victoria was ready to slide off her horse and dash in to call the others, she saw him at the end of the street.

Max.

Her heart stopped, and she looked again at the unmistakable figure, tall and easy in the saddle, moving quickly down the road toward her.

It was impossible.

It was Adolphus, drawing her away from the cemetery as his demons escaped.

She kicked up her mount and started toward him, glancing back at the stirring clouds and the rising black fog.

It can't be him.

Hope rose; then she pushed it back.

He hailed her with a raised arm, and her heart kicked up a notch . . . then sagged back into ugly despair. He was alone.

Sebastian had gone to save him. Surely Sebastian would be with him if he'd succeeded.

Victoria thought to ignore him. She turned her horse, ready to gallop back to the cemetery and fight the demons there. A wordless shout stopped her, and she saw that he'd kicked his horse to catch up to her in the street.

She saw his face, weary and stubbled, his eyes deep and dark in their sockets, hair hanging in straggles. It was too dark to read his expression—but whatever it was wouldn't be true. This wasn't real.

Pulling her sword free, galvanized by fury driven by her dashed hopes, she swung toward him. If she killed him, would that stop the flood of his minions?

A blow to the neck. A good one.

He dodged, pulling his own sword free in a smooth movement. He gave an exclamation as their blades clashed, startling the horses into skittishness.

Clamping her legs tightly, Victoria held on as the horse stumbled and shifted. Then she blasted out with her sword, aiming for his neck.

The demon pulled back, blocking her every move while making no effort to slash at her.

A glance over her shoulder told Victoria that the roiling black cloud had risen higher at the cemetery, and she noticed a glimmer of moonlight.

Desperate for one last chance, she propelled herself upright in the saddle and brought the lethal sword out and around, in a long, vicious swipe. He dodged at the last minute, and the blade cut into the top of his arm, slicing down and across his coat. "Victoria!" he roared.

The momentum of her strike kept the sword in motion, swinging the heavy blade up and around again in a powerful arc—and then she saw the blood.

Blood.

She barely caught herself before the weapon sliced fully into his side, and that last-minute restraint, along with his quick dodge, saved him from nothing more than a graze down the side of his other arm.

"Christ Almighty. I know you're angry, but—"

"Max!" she cried, in a combination of horror, shock, and disbelief.

"—try to damn near kill me."

"It's really you!" She nudged her horse up next to his, keeping the sword down at her side.

Max reached over and grabbed her by the front of the shirt, hauling her across the divide between their saddles, and slammed his mouth onto hers. She half fell into his lap, her hands clamping over his shoulders—one of which was damp with blood—and kissed him back crazily.

"Dammit, Victoria, what the bloody hell were you doing?" he said after a deep, desperate moment of holding her close, crushing the breath from her lungs. She felt the damp on his cheek as his eyelashes brushed against her skin.

"I thought you were a demon," she said, pulling away long enough to shove her weapon back into its sheath. But before she could lunge back into his arms and touch his face, make sure it really was him, his expression changed.

"Look," he said in a stricken voice.

Victoria saw that he was looking over her shoulder, in the direction of the cemetery. Forgetting her joy for the moment, she twisted around to look.

"Oh my God." Her stomach plummeted as she saw the extent of the writhing, coiling black over the cemetery, and she settled back fully in the seat of her saddle. With insistent knees and the pull on her reins, she wheeled her horse around and kicked it into a gallop.

This was why the demon tried so hard to tempt her away. Adolphus must be cracking the portal open.

Thank God she hadn't listened to him.

Thank God she hadn't slain Max in her confusion.

Max wasted no time in following her. As they stampeded past the tavern, she saw Brim and Michalas already on their way out the door to join them.

Her sword back out of its sheath again, Victoria bent low over the neck of her mount, its mane flying up and into her face, stinging her eyes, as they pounded along the dusty road. The darkness had been relieved by the barest spread of clouds, allowing, miraculously, a tendril of moonlight to shine through.

Victoria took the chance to look up as they galloped and saw the edges of the clouds lined by moonlight, and saw that it was possible . . . a bit possible . . . that they could widen more, and allow even a larger swatch of light to beam through.

Please, God. Give me another miracle.

They could fight back the demons with their swords, trying to beat them as they had in London, and she could pull the orb from her pocket and hope there was enough moonlight to strain through it and close the portal.

As if reading her mind, Max looked over, his horse even with hers. "Do you have the orb?" he shouted.

"Yes."

He gave a grim smile, then turned forward again, his sword ready. Victoria let him pull ahead of her just the slightest bit, remembering with a burst of joy that *he was back.* Max was back, fully empowered, fully restored—except for the wound from her own sword.

And at that moment, she remembered Sebastian. Where was he? Hadn't he gone for Max?

"Where is Sebastian?" she shouted. "Did you see him?"

Max shook his head, dark hair flying. "He stayed. With Lilith." His face remained grim.

He stayed with Lilith? No. Not Sebastian.

She drew in a deep breath, and pushed away the instant fear. *This first.*

And then . . . she'd go back to her original plan of finding Lilith and killing her. This time, she'd be going in to free Sebastian instead of Max.

She only hoped he'd still be in one piece.

As they pounded down the small hill into the stony area that cupped the graveyard, Victoria fumbled in the pocket inside her trousers. The orb felt small and warm from the heat of her body, and she closed her hand tightly around it.

The crystal sphere fit easily into her palm, small enough that her fingers nearly met around its circumference. She wouldn't easily drop it.

The black fog writhed and battered them as they came closer, revealing the same glowing red eyes as the flying wraiths they'd met in London. Leaping over the fencelike pile of stones, still astride the horses, they guided them into the midst of the nasty black clouds.

As soon as they broke the invisible wall of the graveyard, the shadows began to surge toward them. Swords flashing, Brim and Michalas remained close on their heels as Max and Victoria sliced and swung at the sweeping, lunging demons.

She found herself clinging to the horse with only her knees, guiding it deeper into the swirling fog as she protected herself with the sword while holding the orb, ready at any moment to pull it from her pocket and lift it into the moonlight.

Without speaking, Victoria and Max moved in tandem, urging their reluctant horses toward the little building, where the roiling fog concentrated. She watched the sky, ducking red-eyed shadows while looking for the moon, aware of Max's powerful blade slicing and slashing near her.

As they drew nearer the building, the darkness became more complete, the buffeting force of their attackers stronger, colder, more paralyzing. Victoria felt claws scrape over her shoulders, grab at her hair, and set her horse to squealing and stumbling beneath her. In fact, her mount was panicked and stamped desperately, trying to get away, tipping and tilting her off balance as she was badgered from above.

Her sword cut through the neck of a flying demon, and as it puffed into little whorls of black smoke, she whirled to stop another one from latching its claws on to Max's shoulders. The battle became a mess of stamping hooves, the cry of gale-force winds in her ears, the scrape of claws and the rank smell of demons and death ash.

"Victoria!"

She swung her sword up in an arc as she heard her name on the wind, nearly lost in the maelstrom, and looked toward Max. He moved slick and smooth, ducking and dodging, arcing and slashing through a new surge of demons, but she saw what he meant for her to see.

A slender beam of moon shone on the black ground.

At that moment, a shadow swooped close. Her horse gave a sudden, frightened twist, and she lost her balance, tumbling off, managing to keep her sword in one hand and the orb in the other. She crashed onto a gravestone, landing on her side, and it knocked the breath out of her for a moment.

Talons shrieked down onto her, scoring her side, then her back as she rolled off the marker and onto the ground. She gasped for air, fighting the blazing pain in her side as she struggled to stand. The orb still in her hands, fingers closed tightly around it—she'd die before she released it—she staggered against a hip-high stone and shoved herself to her feet on shaky knees.

Something slammed into the side of her head, and she nearly fell again, and then another round of claws and nails, and even a thrashing beak, diving, shooting toward her. Pulling the orb from her pocket, she half crawled, half stumbled toward the shining light, the miracle she'd asked for.

She was damned if she'd waste it.

A loud roar in her ears, and a rearing black shadow came upon her, and at first she ducked . . . but then in the fog, she realized it was Max, pushing his way closer to beat off the hordes of demons as they descended madly. Tucking the orb close to her belly, Victoria slung her sword blade up and then felt the shimmer of liquid in the air, spraying gently over her.

At first she thought it was blood, but then when the blackness seemed to rear back, take a breath, she realized it was holy water.

Max, Brim, and Michalas had formed a circle around her and their swords gleamed and clashed, sometimes even against one another as they battled the wraiths back. Victoria pulled the orb away from the safety of her body and stepped toward the moonbeam, shoving the orb into the glimmer of light as another wave of holy water—this time from Brim—set the demons back, gasping.

The light caught at the bluish orb, and suddenly a cast of blue glowed over her hand and arm, up around and shooting from the sphere. A shriek filled the air, streaking into her head, high and loud and long. She dropped her sword, nearly dropped the orb, as she tried to cover her ears, shaking her head to clear them.

The shriek went on, high and shrill, and she staggered, felt the same responses from her companions as their horses stamped and bucked and reared, hooves slamming down, trying to scatter through the gravestones as they were held in place.

The moonbeam. In an ellipse on the ground, there was a circle of pure light in the brown and crusty grass.

She focused on that, tried to ignore the debilitating scream as the orb captured the moonbeam. She saw that the light shone from the sphere in many directions, and, ready to scream herself in desperation, Victoria moved, trying to aim one of the bolts of blue light toward the narrow crevice of the portal.

The screams roared louder, higher, the wraiths came faster and harder, and the swords above slashed slower and more awkwardly. Someone fell next to her, and the slamming and clattering of hooves against stone and dirt told her that their horses had escaped.

But the black fog began to swirl, tighter and tighter, coiling, and screaming, and she saw . . . Oh, yes! It was being dragged back into the crevice, the red eyes of the wraiths wide and burning, then narrowing as they fought the draw, the pull down back into the depths.

She held the orb, watching that the light never wavered from the crevice, even as another swipe of claws set her to nearly stumbling. . . . She saw smoke curling up, and suddenly, the red eyes were set in humanlike faces as they swirled and whirled into a powerful vortex back into the crevice.

The shrieks lessened, the black fog thinned, dragged below, and she still didn't move, watching the orb send them all to Hell, even though her hand shook and her back screamed with its own pain. This went on and on, and she realized that the demons were not only coming from the whirling smoke around them, but from all over . . . for the sky streaked with dark roiling fog and clouds, even as the moon became more and more exposed . . . burning brighter and stronger through dark gray clouds tinged with white.

Suddenly, in front of her stood the man with empty

eyes and the curly-brimmed hat. Adolphus. His eyes were burning, his teeth long and yellow and sharp, and he was lunging toward her, black and dark and evil. . . . The smell of malevolence filled her nostrils as the careening shriek swelled in her ears, reverberating painfully through her body. And then he shriveled and wrinkled, his face melting into a long, drawn-out image, swirling down into the ground as his lips moved, shouting at her, screaming. . . . And then he was gone, in a nasty coil of black smoke.

And at last, there was silence. The orb still glowed in her hand, but the fog had gone. The black wraiths sucked back down into nothing, and Victoria saw the black crevice begin to smoke harder and faster, thick and musty. Curls billowed up and out, and Max rode forward close to it, pouring holy water down into the crack from three different bottles.

A last puff of smoke, and the ground began to crumble into itself.

The portal was closed.

Twenty-two

Wherein Our Heroine Sets the Record Straight

Victoria actually slept that night.

She made her way to the small chamber while Max sat in the tavern with Michalas and Brim. All of them had wounds that needed to be attended to, but the three men opted to have a few celebratory mugs of ale first.

Victoria wanted nothing but to find a bed and sleep. So tired. She was so tired.

And tomorrow, they would start again and go after Sebastian. And come face-to-face with Lilith.

Her mind whirled and churned as she used a basin of hot water to wash away much of the gritty blood and grime. Then, her back still aching from the deep slash of claws, she tottered to the narrow pallet and was asleep before she knew it.

Max was with the others. Safe, only one floor below her. She could sleep.

Sometime near dawn, she woke to a presence in the room.

At first, she tensed, reaching for a weapon, waiting to see if her neck felt chill to determine if it was stake or blade that she needed . . . but then she realized who it was and relaxed. She felt the narrow bed shift with his weight and the comfort of his warm body ease into the narrow space on the bed behind her. His hand slimmed down over the curve of her side as though to ascertain she was really there, and then, tucking her head under his chin and his arm around her belly, he settled, warm and solid, against her. And they slept.

When she woke, the sun had risen high in a cloudless sky and blasted hot through the slit of a shutter, aimed right at her closed eyes. She moved, felt the aches seep through her muscles, and gritted her teeth. Perhaps she should have put something on her wounds.

Shifting so that the sunbeam wouldn't blind her, she opened her eyes and glanced quickly around the room. The other pallet was empty, and no one slept on the floor. Obviously, Brim and Michalas had found another place to rest last night.

Victoria turned gingerly, nearly falling off the narrow bed, and found Max watching her from very close quarters.

"Good morning," she said, suddenly wishing for a drink of water.

"It is."

"I can't believe you're here," she said, reaching to touch his bruised, cut face. Blood had dried on it, and the stubble from yesterday had grown into full-fledged whiskers. His eyes were so close she could see coppery-brown flecks in the dark irises.

"You tried to kill me. Are you still angry?"

"Yes. In fact, I'm quite furious. But that's not why I attacked you—I thought you were a demon. Now I'm just relieved that you're here. We'll probably fight about it when this is done."

"I'll look forward to it."

"It's not amusing," she said, trying to keep from smiling at the interested glint in his eye. The last time they'd had a ferocious battle, they'd ended up in his bed. "I'm *Illa* Gardella. Your leader."

He had the temerity to snort. "By virtue of your bloodline and family tree, indeed. But that doesn't mean that I don't have a brain and cannot make decisions. And that I don't have vastly more experience than you. Your aunt," he continued louder, overriding her angry reply, "considered me her most trusted confidant. And certainly didn't attempt to overrule my opinions."

"Never?"

"Rarely. She trusted me. You'll have to learn to do so, too."

"I already do, but, Max . . . you cannot just disappear like that."

"It was the only damn way."

"I disagree." Her voice became more strident.

"Then disagree, Victoria. But you cannot argue that I know Lilith better than you—better than any bloody other mortal, to my great dismay. I knew there was only one way to get those rings, and I was willing to take that chance—and not willing to endanger you as well. What did you think? That you could walk in and she'd hand them to you?"

"Of course not," Victoria snapped. Her brows drew together in annoyance. "But she must have wanted the portal closed as much as we did. The demons are her enemies, too. It would have been to her benefit."

Max nodded, his eyes sharp and serious. "Most any sane person would agree. But Lilith knew we would move Heaven and Earth to close that damn portal, so she was in the stronger position. If you had come, she would have had both of us. It was better that she only had me. And I knew you'd come after me."

"But it was a great risk you took."

"Every day is a risk, Victoria. That will never change. Do you understand that?"

She nodded reluctantly, her anger fading. Being with him would be the highlight, the sweetest part of a life that would always be filled with danger. Such was their destiny.

He shifted against her, his long legs tangling with hers. "There's one other thing you must understand. I had to do it to prove to myself that I could. That I could do what had to be done, despite . . . you. How much I care for you. If I couldn't make the right decision, then . . . then I would be no better than Vioget had been for all those years."

"Max." Her stomach fluttered. She drew in a breath to tell him she loved him, too. But once again, he cut off her words.

"And don't think you're going after Vioget by yourself, just to teach me a lesson." His expression sharpened as he looked at her.

Anger flared again, but she tamped it back. Later. For now, she wanted to bask, so she shook her head against the pillow, brushing his warm arm. "No. I might have done that . . . once upon a time, but not now. I'm not quite as foolish as you make me out to be." Those last words came out hard and annoyed.

"I don't think you're foolish. I haven't thought so for a long time."

Part of her wanted to follow that trail of thought, but prudence and worry won out. Time for flirtation and teasing later. "What happened, Max?"

His mouth tensed, and he pulled slightly away to lean against the wall behind him. She realized how small a space he'd squeezed himself into and shifted a bit to allow more room. "Vioget came and offered himself in exchange for my release."

"What?" Victoria sat up and would have tumbled off the bed if he hadn't grabbed her arm. "He offered himself?"

Max nodded. "You must know the rings cannot be removed, and so he proposed an exchange—himself and the rings for my release."

"But why? Why on Earth did you not simply kill her? He came in . . ." She couldn't speak any longer. What sort of addled men did she know, who insisted on sacrificing themselves to the depraved vampire queen? Couldn't they find some other way to meet their objectives? Did they have some sort of hesitation about violence against a female? Even an undead one?

Blasted fools.

"He could have left with me, Victoria. But I think . . . I believe he came for some other purpose. He told me . . ." His voice trailed off, then began again, stronger and rushed, as though to get the words out before he changed his mind. "He did it for you."

"For me." Her stomach dipped and squirmed, and she had to look away for a moment. Sebastian had sacrificed himself to Lilith for her . . . for her happiness. He'd released Max, his rival, so that she would be happy. The very thought made her want to cry. Again.

She met Max's eyes. He added, "Do you think me selfish for allowing it?"

"Selfish?" Max, selfish? "You?" She shook her head. "Don't be ridiculous. And aside of that, did you really have a choice?"

"I could have refused to go."

Victoria snorted, unable to help herself. "And then both of you would have been trapped by Lilith. Both of you selfless, idiotic men. Then I would have had to come rescue two of you."

He moved forward and covered her mouth with his in a firm, solid kiss, as though to drown out her lecture. "Victoria," he said, pulling away after a moment. "There's more, and before you go racing off to save him, I must tell you about it."

She pressed her hand to his chest, feeling the rough hair and warmth of his skin, and the slide of muscle beneath as he propped himself up with one arm. "I stopped racing off anywhere without a plan after that incident with Beauregard," she chided him.

"Indeed? Well, then, I won't argue about the finer details."

"What else?"

"His exact words were 'I did it for her . . . for both of them.' "

"Both?"

Max nodded. "I had plenty of time to think on it during my ride here, and I'm certain he spoke of Giulia." His voice roughened at the mention of his sister's name. "It's no secret that the cause of enmity between us began with Giulia, and . . . well . . . continued with you. So when he says 'both of them,' that's what he means."

"But what would trading himself to Lilith have to do with Giulia?"

"I cannot pretend to understand how his mind works, but he did say to ask Wayren about the 'long promise.' Something to do with Rosamunde."

Victoria frowned. "You have no idea what he meant? Does he think he might find something in Lilith's hideaway that might help Giulia? And wanted a chance to look for it?"

Max shrugged, and she couldn't help but notice the smooth movement of his broad, dark shoulders. She swallowed and had to resist the urge to touch him again. There *would* be time for that later. "He must have some reason to go willingly into that place. He's spent a lot of time with Wayren lately, and Wayren . . .

well, you know she is very profound. She's guided me more than once."

"And me. I'm glad she's safe."

He nodded. "But now, as for Sebastian. Victoria, he may not want to be rescued."

She stared at him. "What in the bloody hell are you talking about?"

"My, you've acquired quite a vocabulary for a genteel marchioness."

"I've been around you too much." But the levity faded, and she continued. "I'm going to kill Lilith, so Sebastian will be rescued whether he wants to be or not. Are you coming with me?"

"In very short order." And he slid his hand down between them as he gathered her close for a kiss.

Max approached the hidden entrance to Lilith's lair as confidently as he had in the past. He had no fear of being accosted or injured by anyone but the vampiress, for every one of her minions knew how important he was to her.

A benefit to being the obsession of a vampire queen. The only damn one he could think of.

The sentinels, Guardians of course, loitered just inside the stone overhang that protected them during the hours of sunlight. Since it was just past noon, they didn't have the freedom to move about onto the jutting balcony-like rock formation, which limited their view of the rocky side of the mountain and the grassy slopes below.

Though he couldn't see them, Max knew that Victoria, Brim, and Michalas had secreted themselves nearby, waiting for his signal.

As before, he stepped forward into full view of the vampires. "I'm here for Lilith," he announced, holding a stake out to the side so they could see it. It didn't happen to be one of his favorite silver-inlaid ones; thus it was expendable.

"Couldn't keep away, could you?" said one of the guards.

"Apparently not." Max stepped closer as a second Guardian moved nearby. "Does she still have that fop Vioget with her?"

"He's in there. A bit jealous, are we?"

"Not a bit," said Max. That was all he needed to know, and he lunged toward the vampire, feet lifting from the ground as he slammed into the undead.

The Guardian crashed to the stone floor, and Max pivoted easily to slam his stake into the second sentinel, then whirled back to the one on the ground. Poof.

By the time the ash from the two guards had settled, Victoria, Brim, and Michalas had clambered onto the stony balcony from their hidden locations. Max made a movement toward the entrance, but Victoria grabbed his arm and tugged him away.

"What is it?" he asked, glancing at the others. They'd started to walk inside the cavern as planned and he was ready to go with them.

"I . . ." She looked up at him, her scratched, bruised face so beautiful, and yet fierce, it made his lungs hurt. "I love you."

"I know that. What else?" he asked, tightening his hand on the stake, waiting for her to give him some other instruction.

She just looked at him and blinked. "Oh."

"Anything else?"

"No. Let's get on with it." She smiled, and then, before his eyes, that softness in her face changed and she became the warrior.

Her green-and-gold-flecked eyes sharpened; her mouth, marred by a deep cut into her upper lip, firmed; her chin lifted. Short, curling hair hung crazily around her cheeks and jaw, making her look as though she'd just risen from a long night in bed, and she brandished a stake in one hand.

Despite the power and confidence emanating from her, Max had to acknowledge—and then dispel—the sudden visceral urge to pull her back, force her to let him go first . . . even send her back down the mountain. Not that there was a chance she'd listen.

He drew in a deep breath and followed her into the tall crevice.

She wears two vis bullae.

Yet he felt a wave of fear as she charged along the stone corridor ahead of him, her figure smaller and slighter than any of the others.

But then Max could stew no longer, for a wave of undead poured from the insides of the mountain. Eyes red or pink, some glowing magenta, the vampires swarmed the four Venators in the tall-ceilinged passageway, unleashed by the sentinels to keep the intruders out.

Familiar power surged through him, the flow of movement and the satisfaction of muscles bunching and sliding beneath his skin as he met the onslaught. After months without his powers, of fighting as a Venator without the grace of the *vis bulla*, this altercation was practically a joy.

His speed had returned, along with the powerful strength he was used to and the bare annoyance of discomfort, rather than the breathless slam of pain, over and over.

He wasn't foolish enough to feel cocksure or lazy about the battle, of course. Especially with Victoria in the damn thick of it, and Lilith waiting somewhere deep inside like a skeletal black widow. But the pure pleasure of being *whole* again gave him even more power and capability.

The air was heady with undead ash, and the quiet explosions sounded like soft staccato beats in the confined area. From the corner of his eye, he caught the grace of Victoria's lunge, and the smooth strike with her stake as she easily dispatched a Guardian vampire twice her size. She kicked out, pivoted, and then moved on to a different target. Thus reassured, Max made a low leap in the space and slammed into a cluster of undead, crashing them against the wall like puppets.

He lost himself in the fight. As it always did, everything seemed to slow around him, giving him ample time to thrust and kick, spin and stab before his opponents knew what struck them. His feet left the ground. He felt weightless and free as he dipped and glided low in the confined space.

They made headway, fighting the vampires back into the area of the hideaway where the passages branched off. Max knew that Lilith's chambers were to the right, but he'd never been to the left or down the central passage.

As it turned out, he happened to be on the left side, well matched with an Imperial vampire whose blade thrust and gleamed wickedly. The Imperial flew low, and he and Max circled in the corridor, vacillating up and down and around along the left passage until the rest of the melee was behind them.

All the while Max lunged and whipped and turned, dodging and clashing with the Imperial, he was fully aware that Victoria was out of sight, clogged in the midst of the battle.

She is Illa *Gardella.*

He leapt and smashed his arm against the stone wall, for the passage had narrowed and settled lower. The Imperial laughed and swiped his blade up, scoring along Max's right arm and drawing a long line of blood. The vampire's eyes gleamed, and he lunged again. Max landed on the ground and somersaulted to his feet, surging up beneath the vampire as he came down. His upward motion sent the undead off balance, and Max helped him go, catapulting him into the wall with a ferocious shove.

She wears two vis.

The vampire crumpled to the ground, his sword clanging after him. Max bent forward and shoved the stake home, then whirled just in time to face his next attacker.

And so it went, one after the other, or two, or three, he pummeled and fought and tried not to think beyond the moment, trying to work his way back toward the main passageway.

When he finally dispatched the last undead foolish enough to come after him, Max dusted himself off, breathing heavily, and suddenly became aware of cries and shouts from behind him.

Turning, he saw that he'd been backed into an alcove ended by a heavy wooden door. A small barred window had been cut from the top, and he went to peer through it.

Inside thronged more than a dozen people, crying, wailing, pleading. Mortals. Lilith's private storehouse of food.

"Christ," he said, and began to tear down the door even as the prickling urge to find Victoria nagged at him. "Hold up. I'm here to help," he called, even as he felt the presence of another undead behind him.

He readied his stake and turned.

Twenty-three

In Which Victoria Receives the Most Unpleasant of Surprises

Victoria lost sight of Max as she fought her way deeper into the caverns.

Brim slashed and stabbed nearby, and she caught a glimpse of Michalas's red-blond curls once before she had to turn away and concentrate on her own battle.

The back of her neck burned as though ice slid over it, back and forth, without relief. Her back raged with pain from the claws and scrapes from last night, but as she moved more, it loosened and the discomfort faded to a throb.

She couldn't and wouldn't be distracted from her goal: Lilith.

In fact, as soon as Victoria had the chance, she slipped off to the side of the battle, snaring a handy vampire by the neck and whipping him around and against the stone wall in a natural little alcove. "Where is Lilith?" she demanded, poising the stake to strike.

"There," he said without hesitation, pointing farther

down the passage in which they stood. He had squinty piglike eyes that glowed red.

"And her prisoner? Beauregard's grandson? Where is he?"

"There, too."

"Take me to them and I'll spare you. Trick me and you'll die." He might die anyway, but she'd worry about that later.

He nodded against her hand, and she released him from against the wall. Shoving him ahead of her, stake close at his back, she followed him down the passage.

Her instincts told her that he was interested in saving his own neck—slight though that possibility might be—and as they moved farther, leaving the altercation behind them, she noticed details that confirmed that suspicion: smoother walls studded occasionally with small torches—which Victoria found interesting, as vampires could see in the dark—their sides rounded into a curved ceiling, a floor clear of dirt and random stones. Turning around a little corner, they came to a large wooden door flanked by two torches. It certainly seemed an appropriate entrance for Lilith's private chambers, although the presence of torches still intrigued Victoria. Perhaps it was more for heat than for light, she thought, remembering that Lilith always seemed to have fires blazing.

She stopped and faced the vampire, slamming him once again up to the stone wall. "Are there guards inside? Is she in there? Speak true or you die here."

"Four guards, always hiding in the corners of the room. She was inside last I know of."

"Will she have heard the fight in the front?" Victoria asked. "Is there another way out of the room?"

He swallowed behind the hand clutching his throat. "I don't know. I don't know about another way out either."

"Call two of the guards out. Now. Give no indication that I'm here." She shoved him toward the door, considering whether she should actually let him go. It went against her grain to do so, but she might be feeling generous if he really had brought her to Lilith.

The vampire knocked on the door as she stood and watched. Even if he betrayed her, she'd have the advantage as the guards came running out the door. And she almost hoped he would so that she wouldn't have to decide whether to kill him.

But he did just as she'd ordered, and when the two Guardians with their blazing pink eyes came out the door, closing it behind them, Victoria went into action. She vaulted herself away from the wall and rammed into the first Guardian. Succeeding in knocking him against the other set both undead off balance, and she used the opportunity to shove the stake into the heart of the nearer one.

When she turned to get the other, however, he was already waiting for her, and he shoved her up against the wooden door so hard it jolted in its place. The dull clunk repeated as he slammed a fist into her face, whipping her head back against the door's metal trappings. Pain burst in the back of her skull, and Victoria felt her knees weaken and her gut tighten. Lights sparkled in her vision, vying with the red-orange flames in the torch next to the door, uncomfortably close to her face.

Fingers closed around her throat, and she gasped a breath, then made herself go limp, holding the stake hidden behind her. The cross she wore around her neck did little but cause the vampire to falter for a moment—he must be very powerful. As he held her, the pendant slipped out from beneath her shirt, and he yanked at the chain. It snapped and the cross fell to the ground.

Her breath still stopped in her throat, she counted, holding her limp position as the vampire squeezed his fingers, willing herself to remain still and not to faint.

At last, when she could bear it no longer—the throbbing of her head, the lack of air, the feel of his undead hands on her flesh—he loosened his grip just a bit. Snatching in a breath, she whaled out with her knee into his gut, then her foot, twisting desperately away.

He released her in surprise, and she crumpled to the floor, gasping for air and trying to steady her vision. The vampire reared over her, then lunged down as she positioned her stake. *Slam.* Up and into his heart as he bent.

He froze, then exploded. Putrid, dry ash burst over her.

By the time she staggered to her feet, Victoria realized that the vampire she'd threatened had disappeared. Not, she hoped, to get more reinforcements.

Her head pounded, and she still felt the remnants of fingers tight around her throat, the feeling of being unable to draw a breath. But she stood up and steadied herself again. That would be nothing compared to what she'd face with Lilith behind that door.

She heard a shout on the other side of the wood and, grabbing one of the torches from its perch, steeled herself. Someone was going to come through.

She was right. Seconds later, the door flew open, and she thrust the torch at the first creature that came out. Flames didn't burn vampires, but the fire served as a distraction as it caught his hair and clothing, giving her time to shove her stake into the undead that came behind him.

Her motions practiced and smooth, she slipped through the open door and slammed it closed behind her, ignoring the shriek of frustration from the burning vampire.

Then she turned.

Her first impression of the room was red. And heat. And heaviness.

But she allowed herself little but a quick scan over the silk-hung walls and rug-covered floor, the flames blazing in two fireplaces, and the variety of furnishings also covered in the color of blood.

And finally, Lilith. Who, for once, appeared to be surprised to see Victoria.

The vampire queen stood, arrested in some movement, and looked at her visitor. Then she straightened and her face smoothed of surprise. "Victoria Gardella."

"Where is Sebastian?" she asked, allowing her eyes to dart about the room again.

"Why, he is there." Lilith gave a careless gesture with her slender hand, and Victoria saw him then. "Come out, my dear."

He'd been obscured by Lilith as she stood, and now Victoria could tell that he sat on a settee of sorts, tucked in a corner. Now, at the vampire queen's bidding, he moved forward. Like Max had been when she came to rescue him in London, Sebastian wore only trousers. Bite marks marred the smooth golden skin of his neck and shoulders. The *vis bulla* glinted proudly at his navel.

"Victoria," he said, "what are you doing here?"

She turned her attention from him, relieved that he seemed to be unharmed except for some bite marks. "I've come for Lilith."

The queen laughed. "And so you have. Where do you plan to take me? And where is my dear Maximilian?"

"It's not where I intend to take you," Victoria replied, fingering her stake. "It's where I want to send you: Hell."

Lilith laughed again, moving her hand languidly

over Sebastian's curling hair. "I regret to inform you that I've already been there. And prefer not to go back."

"Only one of us will leave this room. And it will be me." With that, Victoria launched herself at the tall woman.

Lilith's face metamorphosed into a horrific bansheelike mask, her face growing long and gray, her eyes burning like blinding beacons: red surrounded by glowing blue. Nails shot longer from her hands, curving like ten scythes. She whipped her palms up and stopped Victoria in midleap, sending her crashing to the floor.

Still feeling the imprint of those skeletal fingers and deathly nails raking over her arm and chest, Victoria scrambled to her feet, her ears ringing, careful to keep her eyes averted from the dangerous gaze. Lilith had eased back into her normal visage, and now she looked down at Victoria with scorn and dark wickedness. All trace of humor and benevolence had disappeared.

"Maximilian tried that one time, long ago," Lilith told her with disdain. "If I didn't want him so much, I would have killed him then. I have no such compunction regarding you."

Victoria didn't respond. She stood, gathering her wits and her strength, cataloguing the arsenal of weapons available to her. A quick look around the room confirmed that there was nothing to help her: nothing of wood, no sword. Even Sebastian appeared unable—or unwilling—to move. He merely knelt on the floor next to Lilith's chaise, the same sort of empty expression on his face that Max had had while in the vampiress's presence.

All she had were the stakes on her person, the holy water. Her wits.

And, possibly, the secret Adolphus had told her.

She had only a moment to assess all of this, for Lilith had been angered, and she no longer played the gracious sovereign. No sooner had Victoria steadied herself than the vampire queen flew at her.

Fangs sharp and extended into her bottom lip, and her long coppery hair swirled with the horrible scent of roses. Lilith knocked her to the ground, then reached down and grabbed Victoria by the front of the shirt and slammed her to the wall.

The impact set her head to bobbing and pushed the air from her lungs, but Victoria held the stake and made a swipe at Lilith. It scraped along the vampiress's face, leaving a long gouge and blood dripping from it.

Victoria gasped, twisting from Lilith's superhuman grip. Fumbling in the pocket of her trousers, Victoria found one of the bottles of holy water, and, ducking and rolling away from the vampire, she tried to pry the top off.

Lilith slammed into her, knocking the bottle out of her hand, and swooping toward Victoria with a delighted shriek, fangs ready and wide. Her eyes blazed now, and Victoria felt herself snagged in them, slowed, and the thrall begin to wrap around her.

No.

She shook her head, forced the hold to sever, and twisted along the ground toward the lost bottle, stake still close in her hand. Lilith followed, but Victoria was faster. She bucked back and flipped the vampire over her with a quick kick, lunging for, but missing, the bottle, thankful that the stopper hadn't come loose.

With a shriek and a swirl of hair, Lilith rose as Victoria came to her feet, holy water in hand. As the vampire lunged toward her, nails curving wickedly in the air, Victoria ducked, and as she twisted around the queen, grabbed a handful of that awful snakelike hair.

Though it glowed like copper fire, it felt like wire,

thick and hard, not springy at all. Victoria wrapped it around her wrist quickly and gave a good hard jerk, pulling the vampire off her feet to the sound of a great shriek.

Victoria dashed herself against the vampire queen, her arm still coiled in the hair, and they crashed into a wall, then tumbled to the floor. The bottle of water was just . . . there. She shoved the stake down the front of her trousers and reached for the vial . . . crying out with relief when her fingers closed around it, just as Lilith arced out with a long, powerful leg.

Bringing the bottle of holy water to her face, Victoria used her teeth to pull the stopper out as she kicked and yanked at Lilith, who scratched and clawed viciously back at her. But the crazy, twisting creature beneath her couldn't get free from the trap of her hair, and the two scrambled across the floor, rolling, bucking, twisting.

At last the stopper came free and water splashed out, but Victoria managed to redirect the small flume onto the vampire writhing beneath her.

"Help me!" Lilith cried, then screamed as the water spilled on her face. Her bucking motions grew stronger, the horrible sweet scent of roses climbing up and around Victoria, but she kept her head clear.

Now. Victoria reached for the stake at her waist, closed her fingers around it, pulled it free.

She swiped her arm up and around, toward the writhing, snakelike vampire body linked to her by a length of long hair. She stabbed the stake down, aiming for the bony chest of the undead.

Slam.

Lilith twisted hard just as the stake pierced into skin with the familiar little pop, and Victoria felt strong hands pulling at her. She looked up into Sebastian's face.

And his glowing red eyes.

Twenty-four

In Which the Vampire Queen Invites Her Companion to Dine

"No!" Victoria half screamed, half gasped. *"No."*

Not Sebastian.

But it was. Those red eyes gleamed at her, heavy and alluring, capturing her so unexpectedly, so very quickly. And in the midst of the shock, she realized that Lilith's hair was still wrapped around her arm. Somehow, when she stabbed up and around from under her, the stake had not gone deep enough, or hadn't hit the heart.

The vampire queen lived.

All of this occurred in the barest of seconds, and then suddenly, the weight of Lilith was off her, and Victoria was jerked to her feet.

Still stunned, feeling as though someone had slammed a boulder into her belly, she staggered, trying to catch her breath, to understand how it could have happened. . . . *How? Sebastian?*

Too late.

I'm too late. Just like for Phillip.

Hands grasped and grabbed, shoving her, and she caught herself before falling, kicking out swiftly before she tumbled onto something soft. Like cushions, pillows. Soft and smelling horribly of roses and blood and death.

All of a sudden, the memory . . . the terrible, red-hot memory of Beauregard, assaulted her. Hands, nails, teeth . . . lips . . . on her, something soft beneath her, red eyes glowing with pleasure. No, no . . . those were Sebastian's eyes.

And Lilith. Red eyes . . . not pink ones. Beauregard had pink ones.

Victoria tried to blink, felt the strong rough hands pressing on her and something linking around her wrist. Metal, cold and heavy, and she thought suddenly, clearly, of Max, and how he'd worn manacles when Lilith had had him in her presence. She kicked out blindly, catching something soft, but she couldn't see, for the red eyes had her again.

They had her . . . trapped, lulled, loose, and murky.

Hands on her clothes, pulling them away from her neck, tearing the cotton away from her chest. Her cross was gone, torn off during the fight with the Guardian. She felt the heat of the room on her damp skin, felt the brush of wiry copper hair over her throat and cheek, then the smell of roses stronger.

She couldn't move. Her legs were held by a heavy weight. Hands grasped her head, pinning it still to the cushions beneath. One hand held by a heavy cuff, attached above her head; the other hand left to flail free, to catch at Sebastian's soft curling hair and vainly at the stone wall. . . . *A bit of a tease*, she thought sluggishly, leaving one hand free to try to fight.

Vaguely, she realized this was important. . . . She tucked her hand under herself in an effort to keep it free, to hide the fact that it was loose, make them think it was trapped beneath her.

But then the rose smell, and the intense heat of the room clogged her nose, slowed everything along with those hot red eyes, burning, lusting, in a face that had been dear . . . was so dear.

"Sebastian," she cried. "No."

"Oh come now," whispered a voice near her ear. Not Sebastian, but Lilith. Crooning lovingly into her flesh. "You will enjoy it, Victoria Gardella. I understand you know Sebastian quite well. And he is very hungry. He has refused to feed since he drank from me, the poor darling."

Victoria twisted powerfully, freeing one leg from the weight on it, using the hand beneath her for leverage, and slammed her foot into something living that she couldn't see. It might have been Sebastian, for he was right behind Lilith. His red eyes showed the jolt from the impact of her foot.

He refused to feed.

Thank God. Still a chance.

She bucked and twisted again, and then that heavy weight came on her legs once more, and there were hands smoothing the hair away from her face, scraping it back harshly so that her skin spread taut beneath those skeletal fingers.

And then Lilith moved closer, and Victoria felt the leap of her veins as the fangs came out, came close, and the warm hot breath. She struggled, looking up beyond the coppery hair coming closer, trapped by the red eyes, hot red eyes . . . lustful and needy.

No, no, not Sebastian, please . . .

The fangs slid into her skin, and she jerked at the sudden pain . . . then a rush of horrible pleasure. The blood burst from the wounds as if freed from its confines, and she felt the horrible sensation of one cold, one warm lip suctioning on her flesh. Lilith's warm breath on her skin, the proximity of her body, her hands pushing the hair away, positioning her head, holding it harsh and in place as Victoria strained beneath her.

Victoria smelled the blood, and there beneath the thrall, she saw the craving leap in Sebastian's eyes. She saw them narrow, and his fine nose flare, the beauty of his face still as angelic as before . . . except for those eyes. And the slender fangs that tipped gently into his lower lip.

No.

She felt the warm blood draining from her, and deep inside she pulled all of her energy, gathering it into her belly, imagining it settling below her strength amulets, drawing from them. She had to fight free.

Please, God.

She marshaled all her power, let her free hand shift under her, into the back of her trousers. She might. . . . She gasped, hesitated, as Lilith sucked harder, suddenly, and she felt the awareness begin to drain from her.

No. I am Illa *Gardella.*

Victoria slipped her hand from beneath her, moving as though she were underwater, as quickly as she could but oh so slowly . . . to the duo of *vis bullae* beneath her torn shirt. She touched the holy silver, and felt a jolt of strength blast through her. She breathed deep, pushed away the scent of blood so close to her, the feel of lips on her skin, fought to sever the connection with those hot red eyes burning behind Lilith's head.

That wasn't Sebastian anymore. Not the Sebastian she knew.

Like Phillip.

Anger roared up from beneath the thrall, the sluggish red world, and galvanized her. Giving a great, last, harsh buck and twist, she managed to slip her hand beneath and under her hips, scrabbling for the stake behind there as Lilith forced her back into place. Her only chance . . . Had the demon spoken the truth?

Victoria's fingers closed around the wood of the ash stake, made from a fresh branch on the mountain only a short time ago, and relief surged through her when she slipped it free of her waistband. The bark and point scraped against her skin, already raw from claw marks, as she forced it from beneath her prone, weighted body, sidling it under the edge of her hip.

It seemed to take forever for these little movements, and Victoria felt the strength draining from her as the blood coursed from her veins, straining for relief, for release.

Then Lilith stopped. She gave one last, gentle, sensual suck, then withdrew her fangs. Settling back, she looked down at Victoria, whose chest rose and fell as though she'd been running. She could barely focus. The red eyes lulled. The heat pressed down on her. . . . She felt warmth trickling from her neck, leaking down, iron-scented, into the crease of her shoulder and seeping into the fabric beneath.

"There, now," Lilith said in a husky voice, looking back at Sebastian. "See how I've prepared her for you. The fight is gone from her. . . . Perhaps now you'll not be so reluctant to feed."

He didn't speak, but through the fog, Victoria saw the need . . . the deep lust and craving in his eyes. His nostrils flared wide, as though drawing in the scent of blood like a man draws in oxygen, and he was breathing just as harshly as she was. His lips, as full and sensual as they'd been when he wooed and coaxed her, parted.

No.

Sending up a last prayer, she drew in a deep breath and tore her eyes fully from Sebastian's enthralling red ones. It was a physical break; she felt the ties loosen, but not completely disappear, as she pulled away. The incessant tug eased. . . . The stake in her hand rose, flying up as if of its own volition. She saw it as if from underwater, from a distance: slow and foggy . . . the point slamming into the white skin in front of her.

Lilith jerked aside in time, and the stake pierced, not her heart . . . but the soft part above her collarbone, slamming in deep. Victoria cried out in frustration as the vampiress froze above her.

Froze, and was, indeed, still. Her eyes wide, shocked, her bloodless lips parted.

The green ash stake protruded from her skin, and Victoria had a last bit of consciousness left to yank it free, then drive it directly into the vampire queen's heart.

Brushing away the last of the vampire ash, Max tucked the stake into his trousers and turned back to the door. Using a knife blade, he wedged it down under the metal to work the lock's hasp free. He shoved and jimmied, and at last the groan of the brass came free. Working as fast as he could, he pulled the lock off and tore the door open.

The people poured out, more than a dozen of them, terrified and blank-eyed.

"This way," Max said, trying not to think about what else was going on deep in the chambers of this mountain. *She wears two, dammit.* "Hurry."

But something pushed at him, nagged. . . . Impatience screamed as he urged the captives out of their prison; many of them stumbled or were too dazed from shock to understand. As they streamed out of the room, a vampire made the mistake of coming around the corner, apparently running from some other threat. The undead found himself skewered on Max's stake before he realized it.

"Is that everyone?" Max asked one of the men who seemed somewhat lucid.

"Yes," the man managed. "But this one can't walk."

Without another word, Max slung a tottering woman with glassy eyes up over his shoulder. "Here," he said, fumbling for the cross around his neck. With a good yank, he broke the heavy chain and handed it to the man. "Hold this in front of you if you see any of them."

He gave another woman a vial of holy water, and yet another vial to a second man. The back of his neck chilled, shifting, portending the approach of more undead. The would-be victims had moved out into the corridor, and he heard shrieks and screams as he came around the corner.

The prison behind him, a deadweight woman on his shoulder, Max found himself back in the melee again.

Stake in hand, he pushed through the terrified mob, which had been stopped by three large vampires blocking the corridor. *Damn and blast.*

"Throw the water!" he shouted as the crowd surged back, away from the vampires. He pushed forward, they stampeded back, and he felt the woman over his shoulder begin to awaken and fight his hold. The vampires lunged toward the group, fangs out, eyes burning, and the prisoners fell back, into Max, and he nearly lost his balance.

Bloody damn hell. Idiots.

"Let me through," he bellowed, but no one heard him over the panic.

He couldn't put the woman down, or she'd be trampled in a moment, but she severely limited his movements. And now she was fighting him, like a crazed cat, pummeling his back already sore from claws and talons.

And beneath all of that, also pounding at him, was the need to find Victoria.

He shoved the woman at the nearest man, ordering him fiercely, "Hold her!"

And he pushed his way through the surging crowd, ramming people into one another and the walls to get by, to get it through their thick heads that he was there to help them.

As he reached the trio of vampires in the front, he saw the tall, dark figure of Brim appear from behind them.

"Where is Victoria?" Max shouted, barely looking at the undead he was striking. The poof and subsequent explosion told him his black stake had done its trick as he sought Brim's eyes.

Brim staked another of the undead from behind as his mouth tightened in worry. "Thought she was with you."

Max's world stopped, then released into the fury around him. "Take this," he said, shoving the last vampire toward Brim, who easily dispatched the undead before Max had even passed him.

He calmed himself even as he ran off. She'd be all right. She had to be.

Twenty-five

The Temptation of Sebastian Vioget

The blood.

He breathed the iron scent, felt the driving need for it. A red haze filled the room, clouding his vision, his senses.

Victoria's blood.

He swallowed, the unfamiliar fangs nipping his lips. *Oh God.*

Could he even say that anymore, with a damned soul? Oh God?

Would He hear? Would He care?

No . . . Sebastian drew in a breath that felt like no breath he took when he lived. He wasn't damned yet. Not yet.

It enraptured him . . . the *smell* . . . the sound, the faint whistle, of Lilith's gentle sucking. Each low gulp pounded in his ears, drummed through his body.

He could fairly taste the thick, heavy iron, feel it running down his throat. His heart pounded, its rhythm matching that of his sire, of Lilith . . . but fighting to control Victoria's. His hands closed around her slender ankles, holding her prisoner as she writhed and bucked and twisted.

The little noises she made under Lilith's hands and mouth, the little gasps and heaving breaths, reminded him of other things, other writhing and bucking, and he felt the need pound through him even stronger.

The haze grew heavier. Darker. Burning.

Lilith pulled away from Victoria's neck, leaving Sebastian with a full view of the hot crimson blood, shining in thick trickles down her flushed, damp skin. Her grimy shirt was torn away, by his own hands, and one white breast half bared from the struggle. Black hair plastered to her jaw and neck, a mass of curls on the pillow beneath her, and her lovely red lips parted, gasping and panting.

He swallowed again, felt the trembling of his fingers.

Lilith said something he barely heard, but he knew it was his turn. She wanted him to feed.

He wanted. . . . Oh, he wanted.

He couldn't.

But his mouth watered; his fingers shook. He felt the burn in his eyes grow hotter, stronger. His heart pounded, echoing through him to his fingers, his knees.

He had to. He *must*.

Then a sudden sharp movement from Victoria, her arm winging out from nowhere. Lilith froze, her eyes wide as she looked at him over her shoulder . . . and then, unbelievably, she jerked from some great force . . . and then . . . *poof*.

She was gone.

Unbelievably *gone*.

The control, the power over him waned . . . released.

He breathed on his own. He smelled ash and roses and . . . blood.

Still, the blood.

The craving hadn't eased. No, it pounded just as fiercely.

"Sebastian." Victoria's voice penetrated the haze, just a bit. She twisted and moved, and he saw that she was trying to free her manacled hand while she kept her eyes on him. She had a stake in her hand.

A stake that, he realized, could kill him now.

He didn't remember moving, but then he was on her, his hands holding her delicate shoulder to the pillows stained with her blood, knocking the stake from her hand. His weight pressed her into the softness as he'd done before, and he smelled her. . . . She surrounded him, her blood, her scent, her skin.

She fought against him with one hand; he heard her say his name, urgent . . . pleading. Victoria, pleading.

But he didn't care. He couldn't stop himself. . . . The red haze blazed through him as he covered her mouth, tasting her, smelling the blood that would soon ease his craving. He crushed her lips, his hands sliding over her skin even as she arched and twisted, her stake just out of reach, his weight and vampire strength . . . and the manacle . . . holding her in place.

Overcome by unbounded craving, he needed to taste, to kiss, to fuck, to possess, to *control*. . . .

"Sebastian." Her voice was sharp, a bit thready, in his ear as she yanked her face away.

The blood was there, beneath her ear, there in front of him. He lost everything else, everything but that beckoning red streak.

It was there . . . teasing, taunting . . . he shouldn't. There was a reason. . . . He shouldn't, he couldn't . . . but saliva pooled in his mouth, and the blood coursed from the wounds in her neck, the distended vein that swelled, teasing him, even as he watched, as she writhed beneath him.

"Giulia," she gasped. "Sebastian, remember Giulia."

She moved sharply, knocking him askew, and he felt her hand moving toward that stake.

No.

He grabbed her wrist, but she twisted and yanked, forcing him to release her grip. He moved forward, into her throat. His lips brushed against her hot, salty skin, and the blood. . . . He touched it, warm and sleek, with his mouth.

Pleasure, lust, craving blasted through him at the faint iron sense on his lips. More. *More.*

He opened his mouth, his fangs, still so odd, slipping out, sliding against her skin.

And then he felt something in his back. Sharp.

"Sebastian." Her voice, low, gasping, pleading. "You cannot."

He scraped his fang over her skin, sliding over the saltiness, a bit of that luscious blood slipping with it. The stake pushed harder—how had she gotten it?—but she said, "I'll do it. I don't want to, but . . . I'll do it."

He *needed* this. . . . He couldn't see, think, conceive of anything but this. . . . The blood on his lips touched his tongue. Pleasure burst inside him, and he nearly shoved his fangs in right then. Nearly.

"Sebastian, think of *Giulia.* You can't. Please. Don't. You're stronger than this." Her breasts moved against him as she drew in the breaths to plead. "You wear the *vis bulla.*"

The *vis bulla* that burned every time he touched it now; it annoyed the skin at his belly when it touched, a constant burn. But he wore it. . . .

Wayren. Her face popped into his confused, red, blazing mind. The heavy silver ring on his left hand.

His head felt heavy, but . . . *Giulia.*

He didn't care. He cared about nothing, nothing but the blood. The need, the driving pull.

It called to him. That siren song lulled and teased and pulled, and with one movement, it would be over. Pleasure coursing through him. The need sated—the need he'd fought.

Victoria heaved suddenly, powerfully beneath him, shoving him off balance. He slipped to one side, and she slammed him with a knee, in the side of the face, then followed with her other foot.

He tumbled onto the floor, and she scrambled on the bed, frantically working on the manacle. It fell away with a clink, and the stake was in her hand by the time he gained his footing.

Breathing hard, he looked at her: the face he would never forget, the woman he loved, the eyes, sharp but pleading.

"You're strong, Sebastian. Don't."

She sat there, unafraid, free now, waiting. Stake in her hand. A breath away.

He swallowed. Reached for her.

His fingers closed around her arm, her warm arm.

"I'll kill you before I let you feed. I won't let you damn yourself. But I want to know why." She beckoned, gave him a look that burned through him.

The desire bumped again, and he thought he might move, lunge toward her. Get one taste before . . .

His hand fell automatically to the *vis bulla* at his belly. He touched it, winced at the pain, but felt . . . something—power? relief?—mixed with the pain.

The need ebbed that little bit.

"Why did you do this? Let me help."

He could breathe now. Words floated through his mind, filtering through the haze.

The long promise. The new world. A savior.

Rosamunde's words came back to him.

*And in the new world shall be a savior who carries
the deepest taint. A long promise shall the savior make
and in the end those for whom he lives will be saved.*

A long promise . . . and in the end those for whom
he lives will be saved.

In the end. Was this the end?

The door burst open, and the next thing Sebastian
knew, he was jerked from Victoria, thrown against the
wall. Whipped, like a sack of flour. And Max Pesaro
had him pinned there by the throat.

Twenty-six

Two Farewells, and a Shocking Instance in Which Victoria and Max Agree

"Max," Victoria said, stepping toward them. He had Sebastian by the throat, his stake ready. "Release him."

Not only did she not need his help, but the imminent danger was past.

She'd seen Sebastian's eyes fade from the burning, needy red into their normal amber color, and knew that his moment of weakness was past. Whether he would face that temptation again in the future remained to be seen, but for now, he controlled it.

And before she sent him to his rest, she wanted to learn why he'd done this, taken on this burden.

Max ignored her command, holding an unmoving Sebastian pinned. Instead, he asked, "Did he feed on you?" His words came out tight and more clipped than usual. "Or . . . anything else?"

"No." She took a moment—just a moment, now that the danger was past—to admire Max in all his dark fierceness. She was, after all, a woman. And she was completely besotted with the man.

Max adjusted his stake as though reluctant to put it away unused; then he dropped his hand and turned from Sebastian. He looked around the room, his gaze skipping over Victoria as if afraid to land there. The same as it had after he succeeded at the Trial, but this time she thought she understood why. "Lilith?"

"She's dead," Sebastian replied. True to form, he'd merely stepped away from the wall and adjusted his clothing, as though nothing more traumatic had occurred than an askew neck cloth.

"Dead?" Max's voice held rare surprise. "Truly?"

"Dead by Victoria's hand, of course. Did you ever doubt the woman could do what she set out to?" If it hadn't been for the terrible situation moments earlier, Victoria wouldn't have known Sebastian was changed, for he replied in the same offhand fashion he might have if this conversation had happened two months ago.

His blank-eyed look had disappeared, likely because Lilith no longer existed to hold thrall over him, and he seemed more conscious of his surroundings.

With that revelation, Max seemed to have the courage to look at her, and when he did, his brutal expression became darker. "Christ, Victoria, cover yourself."

She looked down and realized that her tattered shirt exposed half of her chest, including one breast—with the other fairly ready to pop out of its sagging bindings if she were to raise a stake. She was amazed at the amount of blood streaking her skin and shirt, and as she gathered the pieces together as well as she could, she glanced up at Sebastian.

His eyes had narrowed, and she saw the beginning of a glow starting there. His breathing quickened just a bit, his lips parted.

"Sebastian," she said sharply.

Her former lover looked at her, and she felt the faintest tug there in his eyes. More than a simple tease.

"He needs to drink," came a familiar—but wholly unexpected—voice.

Victoria turned to look and saw Wayren standing there. She didn't bother to express her surprise or delight at the woman's presence. There was no point in doing so.

"He needs blood," said Wayren, moving into the center of the room. She looked around as though curious about the lair that had belonged to the demonic Lilith. Victoria supposed that wasn't terribly surprising for a scholarly angel.

"I am feeling a bit . . . deprived," Sebastian said. "I think I must feed, and soon. A revolting but wholly necessary aspect of my new . . . shall we say . . . life?" His lips twisted unpleasantly, then smoothed into a self-deprecating smile. "I do apologize for the previous . . . scene, Victoria. My base emotions got away from me."

Though he spoke lightly, she saw a combination of hunger and disappointment in his face. Victoria gave a little shiver. Sebastian had a difficult path ahead of him, if he chose to remain as he was. Had he truly chosen this?

Wouldn't it be best to put him out of his misery before he gave in to his urges? Save his soul, as she'd done for Phillip? She hefted the stake in her hand, ready to put it to use.

At that moment, Michalas charged into the chamber, stake drawn. Brim came at his heels. When they saw the tableau, both stopped and gave little bows to the ageless blond woman.

And then Michalas asked what Victoria had declined to: "Wayren, how did you come to be here?"

The angel gave him a beatific smile. "I knew it was time. Sebastian needed me."

Max stifled a snort, and Victoria could imagine what he was thinking. *A vampire in need of an angel's guidance. A bloody understatement.*

Wayren shot Max a glance that did what Victoria had been unable to do: wipe the arrogance from his expression. Then her pale face smoothed, and she said to the newcomers, "If you haven't recognized it from the chill at the back of your necks, Sebastian has allowed himself to be turned. He needs blood, or Victoria will continue to need to defend herself from him. Michalas?"

If Michalas thought that an odd request for a Venator, he didn't show it. And in fact, as he disappeared from the chamber—presumably to find something for Sebastian to drink—Wayren turned to the rest of them. "Sebastian accepted this change willingly, unlike you, Victoria, when you were faced with the same. The situation is wholly different from your battle with Beauregard. There is a purpose for it."

Victoria nodded, remembering awakening from the slumber after nearly being turned undead to find Max with a stake, ready to plunge it into her heart. She would do the same for Sebastian—in fact, would have already done so if she hadn't needed to understand why. To make certain he'd completed whatever task he'd set out to.

"He didn't have to be turned," she said, speaking what had been on her mind. "He might have offered himself in Max's place, but come ready to . . . take care of himself."

"To die, rather than be turned," Max said. "As I'd been prepared to do if necessary."

Wayren stepped near Sebastian, who seemed to be made a bit uncomfortable by her proximity. "He chose this path as a sacrifice. By putting himself in Max's place, he gave up his freedom, and then he gave up his soul in exchange for Giulia's. She'll be released from her damnation once his task is finished."

"His task?" Victoria asked. "Can we not just stake him now so that he won't be tempted again?"

"Er," Sebastian interrupted, "I prefer not to have my demise, such as it would be, discussed so casually. But I do have a question, Wayren, if I may. I read Rosamunde's prophecy, and understand that it did—or could—apply to me. But how long is this 'long promise' and when might my task be done?"

Wayren smiled, and the warmth of it seemed to flood the room . . . not in the same sweltering, suffocating way that Lilith's fires and presence had done, but in a soft, pleasing manner. "You'll know when it is time," she told him. "But I suspect the Venators will have need of and welcome your assistance for a century or more. Particularly since my time has now come to leave them and return to my place."

Victoria looked at her. "You'll be leaving us?"

"And Vioget is to take your place as adviser?" Max sounded exactly as if it had been suggested that he, too, might join Sebastian in a state of undeadness.

Wayren shrugged, and her smile continued to warm the rest of the room. She seemed clearly pleased with the turn of events. "He has knowledge of the vampires that even you don't have, Max, and he'll be around long after you and Victoria and your children. I'm certain he'll find some way to be of assistance to the Venators."

"Never fear, Pesaro," drawled Sebastian. "I'll be taking myself off to America in short order. I doubt that I'll be here when the child comes."

Victoria glared at him, knowing that Sebastian had

purposely chosen to drop that piece of information at this moment as a last one-upmanship to Max.

How did he know she hadn't told him yet? Likely because Sebastian knew that if Max were aware she carried a child, he'd have become much more protective of her.

He grinned at her, in his Sebastian way, still making warm flutters in her stomach. And that was when the realization struck her. Really struck her.

Sebastian was gone. For all intents and purposes, he was gone.

He had given his life for her, and for Giulia, and taken on a more dangerous, challenging task than she and Max would ever do. She'd had only a short while of fighting such deep cravings, such instinctual needs, the deep potential for evil that vampire blood had brought.

How could Sebastian think to live years, decades . . . perhaps longer . . . without giving in to those base instincts?

Their eyes met, and he allowed only a flare of glow to color his, as if to remind her of what they'd shared . . . and what they could still share, if she were willing. One last bit of that devilish side of him.

Victoria made a decision at that moment. "I'll send someone with you, Sebastian. Someone to stay with you, at least . . . at least for a while."

He gave a wry smile. "My own Tutela member?"

She understood his attempt at humor and let it pass. "A Venator protector. You're still a Venator, Sebastian. You wear the *vis.*"

"I do. And will. Though I don't know if it will be enough." Sadness graced his eyes, and Victoria felt her heart pang.

Let him be strong.

"And the ring," Wayren said. "The ring you wear is there to give you strength, as well."

Michalas returned at that moment, and Sebastian looked over at him as though drawn by a string. His nostrils flared as though to scent blood on the air, and even Victoria could smell the faint rust. "Come with me," said Michalas.

Sebastian nodded, murmuring something about preferring venison blood to that of beef, and Victoria was glad that he wouldn't have to feed on whatever animal Michalas had found in front of the rest of them.

Then a thought struck her, and she looked at Michalas, then glanced meaningfully at Wayren. The angel nodded. Yes, he would be a good person to send with Sebastian, as odd as that might seem for a Venatorial task.

Sebastian left the room, and a silence fell over the chamber. Victoria felt the sharp sting of a tear and, annoyed with herself, dashed it away. She looked up to find Brim easing out of the room, and Wayren following him in a smooth glide.

When she glanced at Max, she saw why.

His face was thunderous.

"Are we going to fight now?" she asked impudently.

"Tell me . . . just tell me that you didn't know."

"Max," she said patiently, "I am not going to sit back for nine—rather, eight . . . perhaps seven—months and do nothing."

She heard the grinding of his teeth from where she stood, several feet away. She narrowed her eyes in delight. Max speechless?

"This is going to be an ongoing argument, isn't it?" he said at last.

"Max, really. I'm not like other women."

He snorted. "Is that so?" Then he was across the

room, pulling her into his arms. "I am delighted. But there's one thing you'll need to understand."

She looked up at him. "I'm sure you're going to tell me."

"The child will have Gardella blood. But it will also have my name. Do you understand?"

For once, she was in complete agreement.

Epilogue

Wherein We Are Assured That Though Nothing Will Change, All Will Be Well

Lady Winnie and Lady Nilly gushed over Victoria, smoothing her hair—which had grown nearly to her shoulders—and fussing with her skirts.

"You couldn't look lovelier, my dear," Lady Winnie said, backing away to look fondly at Victoria. There might have been the gleam of a tear in her eye, or it may simply have been the fact that she spied the new tray of biscuits that Verbena had carried in. Chocolate iced pumpkin. One of her favorites.

"Indeed," sniffled Nilly, under no pretense whatsoever. Her handkerchief was damp, and her narrow shoulders shuddered a bit as she tried to hold back the tears from pink-rimmed eyes. "I just adore weddings." She burst into renewed tears as Winnie patted her back while continuing to eye the biscuits. "And babies."

Victoria, for her part, felt like an ungainly sort of cow. The size of her belly, fortunately hidden beneath the yards and yards of sea green fabric, couldn't possibly grow any larger . . . but she had been assured that she had several more months to expand. The very thought was inconceivable.

It was a very good thing that the vampires seemed to have remained out of London since Lilith's death. Victoria couldn't imagine trying to wield a stake, or kick, or even run in this sort of condition. In fact, the last time she'd tried to train with Kritanu in the *kalari*, Max had walked in, taken one look at her front-heavy figure and uncomfortable pose with a *kadhara* blade, and immediately backed out.

She thought she might have heard the rare sound of his laughter, but decided it was in both of their best interests to decline to investigate. After all, she still did wear two *vis bullae*, and she might hurt him.

"And here is the bride!" squealed Nilly, her tears momentarily forgotten.

Victoria looked up as the door to her mother's dressing room opened and Lady Melly stepped into the small adjoining parlor.

She beamed and glowed like any bride would—particularly one who'd managed to snare one of the most eligible bachelors in all of London. For a moment, Victoria felt a bit envious of her mother's slender figure . . . but not the least bit put out by the fact that Lady Melly would be taking over the title of Marchioness of Rockley, and her daughter would merely remain the dowager.

This was an odd happenstance that had been remarked on over and over in the *on dit* section of the papers, but other than feeling a bit sorry for the poor rejected Lord Jellington, Victoria felt nothing but happiness about her mother's new match.

She might have felt a pang of remorse for the delight in knowing that Lady Melly's maternal attentions would now be divided among three daughters—two of whom had come with the widowed Rockley when he returned to claim his title—but that was to be forgiven.

"Why, Mama," Victoria said, eyeing her parent's intricate hairstyle as she bent to hug Winnie. "Your coiffure . . . it is most unusual."

"Do you not like it?" Melly said, her face shining with joy. "I particularly asked your maid—Violet, is it? No, Verbena—if she would do it. I have always loved the way she arranged those little sticks in your hair."

That was another thing about Melly's newfound love match. Her memory of certain instances seemed to have softened or even completely altered. And Victoria was so delighted for her mother that she wasn't about to remind her of her previous criticisms of the feathered or decorated stakes that Verbena had secreted in her own curls on more than one occasion.

Instead, she merely admired the pearly white ones that gleamed amid Melly's similar dark curls, complete with flimsy feathers and diamonds.

"It looks lovely," she said, catching Verbena's eye as the maid came in to admire her handiwork.

Verbena, who'd always been a lusciously stout woman, had become a bit more stout in the last few months herself. Since she and Oliver, the groom-cum-footman, had gone to Vauxhall Gardens on the evening Victoria had come to think of as the Night of the Frothy Pink Night Rail, they had been inseparable. By the time Victoria and Max had returned from Romania, Verbena and Oliver had needed a wedding themselves.

Speaking of Max . . . Victoria turned to the twittering ladies and excused herself under the pretense of not wanting to ruin the bride's entrance by slogging awkwardly down the stairs in front of her.

Nilly and Winnie patted her stomach several more times, and allowed Victoria to escape as they fussed and pecked and picked at their friend's hair and skirts and jewels.

"I hate weddings," Max murmured when Victoria found him skulking at the back of the chapel at St. Heath's Row, the Rockley estate. A garden wedding had been out of the question in January, and despite the fact that it was out of Season, Melly and her fiancé had been so besotted, they didn't care about the timing of the nuptials. "They could simply have eloped and put an end to this."

"My mother was traumatized enough by our elopement," Victoria reminded him. "It was only the fact that she had her own wedding to plan, and the promise of two more in her new stepdaughters', that we remained unscathed."

"I would have remained unscathed regardless," Max reminded her. "I do believe your mother is still a bit intimidated by me."

Victoria smiled. "A bit? The way you looked at her when she suggested naming the baby Ermintrude? I was surprised she didn't faint dead away right then."

"A ridiculous name. And I'm—we're—perfectly capable of naming our own child." He shifted, leaning back against the stone wall of the chapel and eased her so that she rested her weight against his hip. "When is this bloody thing going to start?"

"Soon, I expect."

"Not soon enough," he grumbled. "The last time I was at a wedding was yours, and it started late as well, as I recall."

She looked up at him. "I'd forgotten about that. You were just as annoyed as you are now."

"You'd invited me to stand guard for vampires," he reminded her. "I didn't want to be there in the first place, and then you had the effrontery to ask me to watch for undead while you married yourself off to—someone else."

Her eyes narrowed in delight. "So you were jealous."

"No. Of course not." He looked at her as if she'd grown two heads. Perhaps three.

"Of course. Just as you didn't peek while I was changing in the carriage. Come now, Max, admit it. You watched me change. You couldn't resist."

"Absolutely not," he said, but he was smiling now, little crinkles showing at the corners of his eyes. "I would never have done something so crude."

The music began, wheezing from a small organ at the front of the chapel, and Victoria saw that the groom had taken his place at the altar. "I do believe I shall find a seat. It wouldn't do for the daughter of the bride to be hovering in the back. Are you coming with me?"

"Anywhere, and everywhere," he said, holding her gaze. And then he ruined it by adding, "Someone has to keep a bloody eye on you."

Read on for a sneak peek of

BOUND BY HONOR

Available from Signet Eclipse Trade in May 2009

"Well, now," said a surprised voice. "This must be the famous Lady Marian come to greet Robin of the Hood and his merry men." His arms tightened around her. "You are well come to our Sherwood, my lady," he added.

In the midst of the furor, Marian heard the rumble of laughter from the surrounding men, and she turned to look at who had the effrontery to hold her in his arms as though she belonged there. Her angry words died in her throat as she met familiar blue eyes, sparkling with mischief and jest. Despite the beard and mustache that covered half of his face, she recognized him.

"Robin—!" she began, but before she could speak his complete name, he covered her mouth with an impudent kiss.

After not seeing him for so many years, she couldn't have been more surprised by the kiss. Although she'd always been attracted to him, his charming personality, and handsome appearance, he'd done little more than tease her into a fury. He certainly had never tried to kiss her.

By the time Marian had caught her breath and freed herself from the man she'd known as Robin of Locksley—not Robin of the Hood—he had swept her up and run into the woods with her. A moment later, he thrust her up onto the saddle of a horse, and Robin vaulted up behind her before she could untangle her legs from her skirts and slip back to the ground.

The outraged roars from Bruse and the responding threats from the band of thieves faded as Robin kicked his horse into a gallop, crashing through the brush with his captive. Branches slashed across her face and caught at her veil, pulling it half off, as they dashed through the forest.

"Robin! What are you doing? Are you mad? It is you, isn't it?" Marian hardly knew what to think. The last she had heard from the young man who'd fostered at her childhood home, Mead's Vale, was that he'd gone on Crusade with the newly coronated King Richard.

"Aye, indeed, Lady Marian," he said, stressing her title a bit. "I thought it would be a fitting welcome to you as you journeyed to that blackhearted cocklicker's court."

"Robin," she gasped, all the air jolted from her lungs as they galloped through the woods. "What are you talking about?"

Suddenly, he wheeled the horse into a small clearing and slid down from the saddle. Looking up at her, he gave her the slow, easy grin she remembered from their youth, and rested his hands at her hips as though to help her down. But he didn't; instead, he curled his fingers firmly into her flesh and then slid all along the sides, from thigh to knee. Little bumps rose on her skin, tingling at his intimate touch.

"And little Marian is all grown up now, into a beautiful, rich lady. I am honored that you should remember me after all these years." His eyes sparkled with naughtiness, and the next thing she knew, he pulled her down from the saddle, sliding her body all along his. *All along* his, so that she felt every bump and crease of the mail hauberk he wore. And something that most certainly felt like the beginning lift of a cock. "You've grown quite beautiful."

"Robin," she said, truly happy to see him. She'd always favored him, always found him irresistible. With his easy personality, bright eyes, and handsome face, it would have been difficult to feel otherwise. "What are you about?" she asked again, aware of his thighs pressed against hers, her slippers captured between his heavy boots. And, most definitely, the growing bulge of his cock. Her hand didn't have anywhere to go but flat against his chest. "Are you truly an outlaw?"

"An outlaw of great repute," he said, his lips curling. "Have you not heard of Robin Hood and his band of men who make merry with the king's coin? I thought for certain tales of our waywardness had reached the court's ears by now. Alas, mayhap I shall try harder, take more risks . . . be more daring!"

His face swooped toward hers, covering her mouth with his for the second time in a matter of minutes. Before she could react, his tongue slid into her mouth, licking in and around and tangling with her own.

Marian allowed the sleek kiss this time, even kissed him back for a moment, surprised at how much she enjoyed it. As much as she might have admired him as a young boy, she never imagined that actually kissing him would be this exciting. Kisses and coupling with her husband had been little more than duty, and, thankfully, of short duration—not only in each time he'd come to her bed, but also in the number of years in which they'd occurred. She'd been married for only three summers before Harold died of a fall during a boar hunt.

Robin's arms tightened around her waist and his tongue thrust deep as she came flush against his body. His lips were soft, but there were other areas of his body that were hard and insistent, drawing another unfamiliar response from Marian. She felt a heightened awareness, and a low, twisting sort of tickle deep in her belly.

After a moment, he pulled back a bit, kissing her and smiling into her mouth as she opened her eyes. "Not so bad, was it, now, Lady Marian?" he said lightly. "Your veil is slipping too, sweetling," he added, giving it a good tug off the back of her head.

"Robin," she said, pulling the veil back up to cover her braided hair and trying to act as though she kissed men in the forest all the time, "tell me what has come of you. Why are you here, in the woods, instead of at Locksley Keep?"

Now the humor slid from his face to be replaced by an irritable expression. "'Twas all a mistake, and now here I am, running for my life. I never made it to the Holy Lands with the king," he confessed. "We were set upon by bandits when we put ashore in Greece, and I took an arrow to the thigh. Fever set in and I could not travel, though it was not deadly. The king wanted to make haste, and continued on. And I had no choice but to return to England. And to Locksley . . . I thought."

"You thought?"

He shrugged, stepping back, and she saw that though he stood only a hand or so taller than she, his shoulders had broadened quite a bit from the last time she'd seen him. He'd been fourteen, and she had been only twelve. His hair had darkened with maturity to brown-streaked honey, and he wore it cut short across his forehead and long over his ears. "When I returned, it was to find Locksley having been entailed to the king—through the prince, of course—on the claim of treason."

"Treason!"

"It's a lie, of course, Marian. Just another way for John Lackland to seize as much control as he can whilst his brother is fighting the infidels in Jerusalem. He has raised taxes and raised them more, and he skims more than his share off the top."

Marian had heard about Prince John's propensity for sly coin . . . among other things. After the overthrow of the unpopular William Longchamp, King Richard had allowed his brother John to act as regent of England while he was out of the country.

Eleanor had also left England to go on Crusade with Richard, but word had reached her that John was conspiring with King Philip Augustus of France. John had been old King Henry's favorite son, but that hadn't stopped him from plotting against his father. Eleanor did not doubt for a minute that he was now conspiring against his older brother, Richard. Even at the cost of the family lands in Normandy—what Philip would certainly require as payment for his complicity—it would be worth it to John to get permanent control of England. Yet the queen must first attend to business in her native Aquitaine. The delay would enable Marian to act as her own secret eyes and ears, and to report back to her about any possibility that John was communicating with Philip.

"But it is the king who raises the taxes, to pay for his war," she reminded Robin, trying to keep the bitterness from her voice. She had no liking for the Crusade. It had taken many of the young men away from England, including her own brother, Walter. He hadn't returned from the Holy Land, for he'd been buried there.

"And then John raises them that much higher, so as to line his own pockets."

"But how did you come to be an outlaw? How could they take Locksley from you while you were away fighting at the king's side?"

Robin looked distinctly uncomfortable. "As I said, 'twas a mistake. I returned to find Locksley closed to me, and then I went hunting in the woods—*my* woods—for a meal. Then I was arrested for poaching from the king's forest."

Poaching from the king was indeed a serious offense—punishable by hanging, gouging of the eyes, or cutting off of the hands. "But surely once the mistake was found, you were released. Even the cruel Sheriff of Nottinghamshire could not keep an innocent man of the king's in prison."

Robin laughed. "Released? Nay, Marian, I made my own escape from the sheriff."

At that moment, a deep voice interrupted their conversation. "Did you indeed?"

Marian whirled to see a powerful black horse standing at the edge of the clearing. Atop it sat an equally powerful-looking man, dressed in equally dark clothing, holding a sword at his side. She stepped back automatically, but he inclined his head regally to her.

"Lady Marian." He urged his horse into the grassy clearing.

Robin released her, fairly shoving her away so that she stumbled with the force as he moved quickly away from her, gathering up his reins. "Ah, so to speak of the devil himself," he said, launching into his saddle. "Sheriff." He nodded. "I trust you'll see my lady to the keep."

These last words floated back behind him as he bolted off into the wood, leaving Marian standing in the center of the grass, suddenly alone, and feeling more than a bit disheveled.

Marian turned to look up at the man, who remained astride his mount, edging his horse toward her, but not, thankfully, chasing after Robin. She was grateful for his restraint, for he would have had to fairly run over her to go after the bandit.

The sheriff sheathed his sword, but still held the reins in one gloved hand. The hooves on the majestic animal were larger than the trencher plates at a court dinner, and he was pure coal black from hoof to mane to wild, flaring nose.

The man himself had dark hair that fell in thick curls onto his forehead and brushed the sides of his neck, and he was clean-shaven but for the shadow that comes late in the day after a morning's shave. His mouth might have been considered sensual if it weren't settled and thin—and the same could be said for his face, dark with tan as well as obvious annoyance. As she gazed upon the Sheriff of Nottinghamshire, Marian was overcome by the sense of expectancy, and indeed, when she looked up into those shaded eyes, she felt set off balance again, as if she were mistaken about something.

"I trust you are unharmed, Lady Marian," he said at last. "I apologize for the delay in coming to your aid, but we had heard your caravan was held up and thought to provide an escort at Revelstown."

"Delayed for a broken wheel, aye, but 'twas fixed readily," she replied, realizing with a start that he would indeed think she'd been in need of rescue. And, truth be told, if it had been anyone but Robin of Locksley, he would have had the right of it. But Marian had no fear of her childhood friend Robin, outlaw or no. In fact, she'd already decided that she must find a way to enlist the queen to help rid him of the charge of treason.

"Have I changed so much, then?" the sheriff said,

sliding abruptly from the saddle. He landed on two steady feet next to her, and the destrier shimmied and snorted at the loss of his master's steady weight. "Marian."

She looked up at him again, closely this time, and recognition washed over her. "Will?" Perhaps it was the way he'd said her name, or that he now stood on the ground next to her—still much taller, but at least not towering so from the saddle.

Aye, indeed it was William de Wendeval before her now. The boy who'd grown up with her and Robin of Locksley on her father's estate.

But a boy Will was no longer. Just as Robin had grown broader and taller than she remembered from the summer she'd seen them last, ten years ago, so had Will.

Taller, aye, and broad of shoulder . . . but he had not lost the sharp edges of his cheeks and jaw, and the reserved chill of his gaze. A handsome man he might be if the tension and reserve left his face and stance. But that had always been his way. While Robin had the lighter hair and dancing sapphire eyes, and personality to match, Will had been the quieter, more thoughtful, and, at times, gloomier of the pair.

And as their personalities tended to clash like oil and water, so had the two young men. Competitive and intense, they'd been rivals serving the same master, with their differences buried beneath civility and honor.

And now here they both were, on opposite sides of the law, here in the forest of Sherwood.

Don't Miss the Other Books in Colleen Gleason's Gardella Vampire Chronicles

THE REST FALLS AWAY

Vampires have always lived among them, quietly attacking unsuspecting debutantes and dandified lords as well as hackney drivers and Bond Street milliners. If not for the vampire slayers of the Gardella family, these immortal creatures would have long ago taken over the world.

In every generation, a Gardella is called to accept the family legacy, and this time, Victoria Gardella Grantworth is chosen, on the eve of her debut, to carry the stake. But as she moves between the crush of ballrooms and dangerous moonlit streets, Victoria's heart is torn between London's most eligible bachelor, the Marquess of Rockley, and her duty. And when she comes face-to-face with the most powerful vampire in history, Victoria must ultimately make a choice between obligation and love. . . .

"With its vampire lore and Regency graces, this book grabs you and holds you tight to the very last page."
—*New York Times* bestselling author J. R. Ward

"A paranormal for smart girls who like historicals. Buffy in a bonnet takes on the forces of darkness in Regency-era London."
—Janet Mullany, award-winning author of *Dedication*

RISES THE NIGHT

Lady Victoria Gardella Grantworth de Lacy has been a vampire slayer for just over a year, balancing her life as a peer of Society with the dangerous role that takes her out on moonlit streets, stake in hand. She has learned brutal and heartbreaking lessons about the sacrifices that must be made in order to save humanity from the evil that secretly preys upon it, but she has not wavered in her vow to fight on.

Now, in Italy, a powerful vampire is amassing the power to control the souls of the dead. As Victoria races across Europe to stop what could be the most deadly army the Gardellas have ever faced, her unlikely companion is Sebastian Vioget, a man as tempting as he is untrustworthy. But when Victoria discovers that she has been betrayed by one of her most trusted allies, the truth will challenge all her powers as a Venator—and as a woman. . . .

"Sophisticated, sexy, surprising!"
>—*New York Times* bestselling author J. R. Ward

"With its wonderfully witty writing, action-infused plot, and sharply defined characters, *Rises the Night*, the second in Colleen Gleason's irresistible Regency historical paranormal series, is deliciously dark and delightfully entertaining."
>—*Chicago Tribune*

THE BLEEDING DUSK

As Rome prepares for its Carnival, the new leader of the city's vampire hunters—Lady Victoria Gardella Grantworth de Lacy—must prove herself as never before. For, in order to gain access to the secrets of a legendary alchemist, Rome's vampires have allied themselves with creatures as evil and bloodthirsty as they are.

Reluctantly, Victoria must turn to the enigmatic Sebastian Vioget for help, just as Maximilian Pesaro arrives to help his fellow slayers—no matter what the sacrifice. Desire puts her at the mercy of Sebastian, while loyalty binds her to Max, but can she trust either man? Especially when a seductive vampire begins luring her into the shadows. . . .

"Action, intrigue, sensuality, and a kick-butt heroine add up to one unforgettable read."
—Kathryn Smith, author of *Night of the Huntress*

"The undead rise to great heights through Gleason's phenomenal storytelling. She creates a chilling world with the perfect atmosphere of fear and sexual tension. The sophistication and intelligence of her storytelling is evident on each page of the Gardella Vampire Chronicles."
—Kathe Robin, *Romantic Times*

WHEN TWILIGHT BURNS

Ruining Victoria's homecoming, a vampire stalks the streets of London—during the daylight. Not only is Victoria unable to detect the vampire with her heightened senses, but she's being framed as the prime suspect behind the killings.

Meanwhile, her heart is still divided between the enigmatic Sebastian Vioget and her fellow slayer Max Pesaro. The battle is made even more difficult by the legacy of a vampire's touch—a vampire who left in Victoria's veins boiling blood that forces her to fight evil on two fronts: against the new breed of undead threatening London and against the darkness within herself.

"Buffy the Vampire Slayer meets Jane Austen."
—The Book Standard

"A series that is unique, sexy, and definitely very intense."
—Romance Readers at Heart

ALSO LOOK FOR EROTICA TITLES BY COLETTE GALE. . . .

UNMASQUED: AN EROTIC NOVEL OF THE PHANTOM OF THE OPERA

"Lush and sensual from beginning to end, erotic and romantic in the extreme, *Unmasqued* is sure to please fans of historical fiction as well as erotica."
— Erotic Romance Writers

Christine Daaé has heard the rumors of the hideous Phantom said to haunt the great Opera House, but she alone knows the truth of the man she calls her Angel of Music. For, as he tutors her to become a brilliant singer, he also teaches her about hidden passions. He comes to her only in the darkness, awakening her with the velvet timbre of his sensual voice and arousing her with his touch. He is real. Her inspiration. Her *Ange de Musique*.

But beautiful Christine has attracted the attention of Opera House patrons Raoul, Vicomte de Chagny, and his lascivious brother, the Comte, who has his own reason for hating the mysterious Phantom.

Soon Christine will find herself torn between the luxurious life of the handsome Vicomte and the only man who understands her music and her deepest desires. She will have to make the choice between living a life in the light of nineteenth-century Paris society—or spending the rest of her days revealing her love to the Phantom in the shadows of the Opera's catacombs.

MASTER:
AN EROTIC NOVEL OF THE
COUNT OF MONTE CRISTO

"Inventive and steamy and clever all at once—this is Gale at her best."

—M. J. Rose, author of *The Resurrectionist*

Edmond Dantès spent years imprisoned for a crime he did not commit. Once free, he returns to Paris in the guise of the powerful Count of Monte Cristo, seeking vengeance on those who sent him to jail. But his plan also includes a different kind of revenge—on the woman he has never forgotten, the lover he has made it his mission to possess.

Mercédès Herrera Mondego was devastated when the man she loved disappeared. Now she is trapped in a loveless marriage, but her passions are reignited by Edmond's return. And though she alone sees through his disguise, this harsh, angry man sends chills down her spine even as his very touch reminds her of the desire they once shared. She realizes soon enough that his plan to avenge himself on the men who incarcerated him also includes another sort of revenge—on her.

From the seaside town of Marseille to the exotic caves of Monte Cristo Isle, an erotic battle of wills unfolds in the most electrifying game of love ever played between man and woman, between master and slave.

BOUND BY HONOR: AN EROTIC NOVEL OF MAID MARIAN

Trapped by Duty . . .

Maid Marian, now Lady of Morlaix, is sent to the court of Prince John—not to take part in the debauchery of his Court of Pleasure, but to spy on him for his mother. Little does she know that her secret mission will thrust her into a whirlwind of intrigue, terror, and carnal temptations.

Bound by Honor . . .

At court, Marian finds herself torn between her duty to the queen and her desire for two men: one, the mysterious highwayman the peasants call Robin Hood, and the other, the dark, cold Sheriff of Nottingham. When she is given an impossible choice, she must submit to the carnality of Prince John's court in order to fulfill her duty and maintain her honor.

In the end, there is only one man for whom she will risk her life and give her heart, so they can both be redeemed by love.